THE BATTLE FOR TRIMERA

BOOK 1 OF THE RULING PRIESTESS

TANYA S.M. KENNEDY

Tanya S.M. Kennedy

Printed in the United States of America
Edited by Kristen Corrects, Inc.
Cover art design by Winter Bayne

First edition published 2019
10 9 8 7 6 5 4 3 2 1

Kennedy, Tanya
The Terarch rebellion / Tanya Kennedy
p. cm.
ISBN-13: **978-1-7340896-1-5**

By Tanya SM Kennedy

Terarchs:

The Terarch Rebellion
The Terarch Raivien

Assassins:

An Assassin's Redemption

The Ruling Priestess:

The Battle for Trimera

Tanya S.M. Kennedy

To Baby Ezra who, even as I type this, is drawing his first breaths.

PROLOGUE

The cave walls flickered with torchlight. The air was damp and glistened on every surface. This was the night, he could feel it. All the work, all the years of research, all the failures—but tonight he would taste success.

How many times had he heard the snickering? How many times had he been chastised for talking about what he was about to attempt? Too many to count, that was for sure. His mind echoed with the words of his teachers and mentors. "You will never get anywhere if you do not clear your mind of these fantasies." "Good boys do not think of such nasty things!" Anger boiled up at the memories, but he suppressed it. They couldn't understand what he was trying to accomplish. A new world, full of new possibilities.

For years, priests and priestesses dealt with an unspoken power struggle: Those with more strength had the power. He was smart enough to know that this didn't always mean the right people ended up in charge. He had the answer, he was sure of it, but none of them would listen. They were just intimidated. They didn't want a priest of middling strength to be responsible for the solution they were all too scared to risk themselves. That's why they had punished him, rejected him. He would show them. He would show them that he wasn't someone they could just ignore. He would show them he was better, better than their foolish Council. He would make them pay for not recognizing his potential.

An altar faced the cave wall covered with a smattering of crystals arranged in a circle. They lent the cave a pale-yellow haze that pulsed like a heartbeat. In the center of the circle sat a starling egg and a lump of clay roughly shaped into a man. He stood at the altar, his naked body catching the light with a sheen of sweat. Shadows cloaked the edges of the cave, but every now and then, one moved behind him.

He glanced behind him at the movement. It had taken him days to catch, always took him days to catch each one by himself. The shadow shuffled into the light, pressing against the crude bars of the cage. Long gray limbs ended in sharp black claws. It stood on its hind legs, like a man, and wore tattered armor that was stained and rusted. Yellow eyes watched him with a curiosity that bordered on intelligence. There was some semblance of recognition as it watched him. Thin, pointed ears twitched toward him. Its head tipped back till its sharp nose brushed the ceiling and it sniffed the air. It could smell the magic.

Grinlo were truly fascinating creatures. They were drawn to magic, could absorb it by consuming the bodies of those who possessed it. It made them a wealth of untapped power. Creatures of low intelligence but with incredible strength, it was foolish of the Lorien not to utilize them. But he would change all that. Future generations would exalt his name.

He turned back to the altar and drew a fingertip along his palm, trailing a cut through the skin. He tipped his hand and held it over the starling egg. With a few squeezes of his fingers, crimson drops splattered across the shell. He cupped his hands around the egg, heedless of the still-bleeding wound, and focused his inner strength down through his arms. It was a trick the Lorien had frowned upon. They hadn't understood it, hadn't understood *him*, but they would see.

A glow burned from his palms, bathing the small egg in an unearthly glow. The shell pulsed with its own glow as the crimson stain absorbed into it. It flashed as it hovered above the altar cupped in his palms. He moved his hands until the egg was suspended over the clay man that lay on the table. The light intensified as it lowered toward the lumpy clay.

The egg sank into the clay body and the world disappeared in a roar of white.

When the cave around him returned, he smiled down at the infant screaming from the altar. The child was cold to his touch as he lifted it in his arms, a perfect tiny replica. It stared up at him with his own bright blue eyes.

Child cradled to his chest, he turned and crossed to the caged creature. A knife sat in a crevice along the wall and he snatched it up as he passed. Light caught along the blade as he stopped before the cell.

The creature within watched him intently. "Ank out."

He inspected the creature before him as the infant in his arms shook with newfound vigor. The screams pierced his ears as he lifted the knife and plunged it into the newborn's chest. The body of the child glowed a warm white as its echoing scream was cut short.

A wave of strength swelled in his chest. He let the worthless corpse tumble to the floor. Lightning arced down his arms and jumped across the expanse between him and the monster.

The creature roared as the sparks danced along its skin. It threw its head back as its wail rattled the cave walls around them. The creature fell to its knees. "No more!" it cried.

The power flowing down his arms pulled deep on his strength. His heart raced in his chest, sweat poured from his skin. Blood spouted from both nostrils and still the magic flowed. The cave floor collided with his knees as he lost his footing and collapsed. The cave spun around them, a swirl of flickering light.

The hard surface beneath his cheek was wet and cold when the world returned. His chin and neck were tacky and every inch of his body ached. Something scratched against the floor as he struggled to bring his thoughts to the surface.

Dry grit coated his eyes as they cracked open. The torch had blown out at some point, and the crystals' magic had faded, leaving him in an inky black. The air screamed into his chest and filled his lungs with fire. His fingers creaked open and he called a crystal to his palm. With the last of his strength, he pulsed magic into the rock, igniting it with light.

It took a blink or two for his eyes to adjust. The first thing to come into focus was a claw a mere handbreadth from his nose straining to reach him. Its scratching against the cave floor was the origin of the scratching that gnawed at his mind.

Fear leapt in his chest, overwhelming all thought. The monster had its shoulder jammed against the bars in its frantic attempt to reach him. If he'd have fallen one breath to the right he would be in its grasp.

With a heave, he rolled onto his side and scrabbled away from the cage. Blood rushed in his ears as he collapsed against the floor. His chest heaved and his head pounded. The pounding slowed and faded as he let the distance relax him. The roar in his ears calmed enough for him to make out a high-pitched plea coming from the cell.

"Master?"

His heart leapt back to a gallop. "What did you say?"

"Master hurt?" it asked.

His body trembled as the crystal's light caught and flashed in his sharp blue eyes. Could it have worked? Could he have finally succeeded after all these years of failure? He struggled to his feet. "Master is not hurt." His lips pinched between his teeth, he waved at the locking mechanism on the cell. The cave echoed with a loud crack as the locks released and the door swung open.

The creature pulled its arm back into the cell and crawled toward him. His stomach quivered with the creature's every step. Sweat beaded across his forehead and upper lip as its claws rent into the cave floor and it dragged itself closer. It crouched against the floor, hesitant but compelled to move closer. One long, razor-sharp claw snagged the toe of his shoe and a sweep of adrenaline rushed through him as the ingrained fear refused to let him go. His mind screamed to run, that at any moment the claw would slash and tear and kill.

But it never did.

He glanced down at the grinlo that cowered at his feet. Something deep within him clicked into place. A fire flickered to life in the base of his gut. It ached to be released, to be used. It was new and enticing and everything he had ever wanted, more than he had ever had himself.

Triumph crashed over him. This was it, he had done it! He had moved forward from the cringing meek failure he had been. He was becoming something new, something more than anyone had ever given him credit for. He had tapped the greatest well of magical strength known to man. He had become legend, entered himself in the lists of other dreamers, other brilliant men who had dared to not let the fears of others hold them back. He was a new man, a new being, and one day all of Reia would tremble at his name. One day soon—but for now on he couldn't be associated with his old name. He couldn't have the world seeing him as the loser he had been branded in his youth. From now on he would call himself Neram.

And the man who called himself Neram had just succeeded in taking control of a grinlo.

A DEEP WOUND

Prince Inan opened his lips to command his guard to retreat but a flood of thick crimson muffled any words. He coughed his lungs free and forced a gurgled breath into his chest. He was gone, beyond the help of any soldier.

From his vantage on the hard-packed road he could see his beautiful wife Isala, her eyes already clouded in death. *I am coming for you, Isala,* he thought even as his heart broke. Soldiers fought to the left and right, would fight to the death. It was the honor of the royal guard, to fight to the death to protect their prince. As he lay in the spreading pool of his blood, he knew he was their prince no longer. The title would fall to his son, a lad of fourteen. He had no worries about Janu—his son was smart if stubborn, and had High Priestess Lana as his advisor. The woman had overseen his father's rule before him and would watch over his son in his absence.

His true worry was Pria, his daughter. She was so young; would she understand why they never came home? That problem was beyond him now, as were all troubles. He wasn't getting up from this road.

An arc of blood sprayed into his vision from his right and a soldier fell, blocking his view of Isala. The man's panicked eyes met Inan's and the prince wished he could tell the soldier he had done all that could be expected of him.

The encounter repeated itself in his head. Commander Viro had sent scouts ahead to find a suitable camp for the night. They were still a good day from Amber Keep and well within the patrolled borders of Trimera. It had been years since any grinlo raids had made it that far south. The sun hung low but there had still been plenty of light to see. He had ridden up to talk to Isala as she rode in the wagon. She deserved a carriage but such luxury would never survive the trip to Amber Keep. She was a vision, and for what seemed like the millionth time he wondered how he had gotten so lucky in an arranged marriage to be paired with such an angel.

The attack had come from the south, grinlo pouring from the trees in waves that crashed over them. He couldn't remember drawing his sword but it was there in his hand as a gray monster slashed at his mount. He took the beast down with a chop to its throat and called for Isala to abandon the overran wagon. She latched on to his hand and landed astride his horse as he lifted her up behind him. Despite her proper upbringing and courtly training, Isala was the most skilled rider he had ever seen. She jerked a short-sword from his saddle and slipped her free arm around his waist. Together, the three of them danced as one deadly creature, cutting down the grinlo that came for them. His guards and soldiers rallied to him, brave and valiant in the face of their attackers.

But the attack never ceased.

Line after line, the horde poured from the trees as if driven by some madness. Every creature felled by their blades was replaced by a dozen more. They were hopelessly outnumbered, and he watched as man after man fell to the overwhelming odds. He felt the killing blow to Isala as if the blade had pierced his own chest, which, of course, it had. Right into his heart. He had died long before any blade had landed a killing blow on him. The instant she fell, he knew he would follow her. There was no life without her smile.

The soldier before him was fuzzy now, hard to focus on, the details blurred and faded. The breaths came harder now, unable to fill his chest. Darkness settled down on him and he faded into its embrace.

The pain in Pria's stomach gnawed as she clutched at the hand clamped around hers. The mad dash through the Seat's passageways, being jerked this way and that to avoid notice, was more than her young body was willing to put up with this morning. The colorful tapestries and sparkling wall sconces that would normally draw her five-year-old attention rushed by before she could even notice them.

The Seat was her home, the fortress from which her father Inan ruled Trimera and protected Reia. Trimera was the last defense of Reia against the beasts that lived to the north, in the Frontier. It was her family's legacy, had been drilled into her from the moment she could understand the words. Her mother and father had often put her to bed with valiant stories of her family and battles against the monsters. Her brother, as heir, would follow in the footsteps of those ruling princes before him to protect the border from the horde.

She, however, had a different destiny. On the day she was born, her father's advisor had declared that Pria was born a high priestess. She had no idea what that meant other than that she was hovered over and protected by everyone around her. High Priestess Lana, her father's advisor, talked to her often about being sent to study at the Lorien, the base of priestesses in Reia and a school for future generations. And she wanted nothing to do with it. What could the Lorien teach her that she couldn't learn here from Lana and her family?

For as long as she could remember, she had been given private lessons by Lana. Her brother and Mian had classes with her too, where they discussed history and art, politics and decorum. Lana poured knowledge into her like a pitcher into a basin. It grew boring at times, but she enjoyed her time with Lana. On a rare occasion, Lana would even guide her in using her power. It was never anything too exciting: moving objects around the room or fanning the flames in the hearth, but it was exhilarating nonetheless. So, who needed the Lorien?

Her arm twanged as she was jerked around another corner and into an alcove when a maid rushed by down another hallway. Her eyes drifted after the woman but she had no time to wonder what was going on. She blinked up at the older boy at the end of her arm. His name was Mian, and he was entirely hers—from the shock of red locks to the ends of his toes, every fiber a slave to her whims. The best friend of her older brother and nearly ten years her senior, Mian was her world. Well, he and her brother Janu. And her parents, of course, but none of them were Mian. The son of a noble, Mian and her older brother Janu had been inseparable from the second they had laid eyes on each other. In her young eyes, neither of them could do wrong.

The boy himself ghosted across the floors in soft leather boots that whispered along the hallways' decorative runners. Mian had dragged her from her bed before the sun was risen. All he would say, as he threw a blanket around her shoulders, was that he was taking her to Janu. His simple brown coat was cinched with a leather belt. The coat did not match the décor around them but it was his common outdoor attire. It was what he wore to blend in.

They crouched in the shadows left by the lit candelabras set at intervals down the hallway. The Seat always had those familiar pools of darkness where the candlelight never reached. Mian had taught her how to use the stretches of midnight to avoid notice; she was a quick study.

The stone was hard beneath her soft slippers as they stood waiting, silent. The hall around them was polished gray and echoed with voices. They had to avoid others; she didn't know why, but Mian said they needed to, and that was enough for her. She looked down at her favorite dress. Not that she didn't love her breeches too, but this was her favorite dress. Blue satin bodice, velvet blue overskirt and cream-colored underskirt, all of which just brushed the floor. Just like her mother's.

But her mother wasn't here.

Her parents had left the Seat to visit Amber Keep, Trimera's northernmost fortification. It was a common run but still held its danger. She wasn't worried, though; her father was the best warrior in the kingdom, and that meant he was the best warrior in all of Reia. Nothing could stop him.

The voices faded away as whoever it was moved on. Her body wracked with uncontrollable shakes when he took off again, darting from alcove to alcove, avoiding the eyes of the house staff as they rushed through the fortress in a mad frenzy. The entire castle was abuzz with anxiety, liveried servants darting about in every direction. Something was going on; she just wished she knew what. Her eyes burned as Mian pressed her against the wall behind them.

"Mian, where is Janu?" she asked, her voice an echoless whisper.

"He'll be there, I promise." He smiled down at her, beautiful green eyes bright with pain. His red hair was a tousled mess atop his head, curling down around his forehead and cheeks. "Just a little farther."

She ran to keep up with him, his long legs forcing her to work hard. She glanced up at the unfamiliar area. Gone was the gilt and glitter she was used to, replaced by bare walls and coarse rugs. "Are we even allowed here?"

Mian glanced around the corridors as he stopped beside a door. They slipped inside a dusty room with a high ceiling supported by columns. Something was stacked along the walls covered in dusty drapes. Mian slipped the door shut behind them and their feet echoed frantic slaps across the room to the far wall and an unadorned window. Kneeling, he looked her in the eyes.

"Pripri, I need you to trust me, can you do that? Just trust that I love you and would never hurt you, okay?"

She nodded and he smiled, cupping her cheek.

"This next part is going to be scary, but you're not going to worry, right? You won't worry because no matter what happens, I will always have you."

She wrapped her arms around his neck and giggled as his red curls tickled her nose. "You're taking me on an adventure!"

He rubbed her back. "Yes Pri, an adventure."

Fists planted on her hips, she shot him a challenge. "I can handle anything you can dish out!"

He snatched at her nose and she swatted his hand away. "I'll remember you said that. I'm going to put you on my back now, okay? You'll need to hold on to me."

She nodded in excitement as he turned and she wrapped her arms around his neck, laughing as her feet dangled when he stood. He smiled over his shoulder. "Hold on tight now." She wrapped her legs around his waist, her mind racing as he moved to the window. He pulled a rope from behind one of the tarp-covered piles and secured it to one of the columns. He pushed aside the fabric covering the window and tossed the loose end of the rope over the sash.

"Ready?"

"Always!" She tightened her grip as her eyes scanned the forest beyond the window. Blue-tinted leaves swayed in the breeze atop the thick trunks that grew almost to the Seat's walls.

Mian climbed up on the sill, gripping the rope as he crept out onto the side of the building. Pria glanced around as he picked his way down the wall. Her dress whipped like a flag behind her, carried by the wind that smelled of the forest's damp earthiness. A bird chittered at their intrusion as Mian's slow descent led them past her nest. His soft boots made little noise on the leaves as he dropped to the ground.

Letting Pria off his shoulders, he pivoted and smiled. "Having fun yet?"

Her eyes sparkled with a brilliant glee. "What now?"

He took her hand and darted off, pulling her along behind him. At this end of the castle the forest grew close to the walls, and he led her into its darkness. The sun was brightening the sky to the east, but the trees jealously held their shadows.

When they entered a small glen, he trotted to a gray mare, pulling the reins loose before snagging Pria up and tossing her onto the horse's bare back. He leapt onto the mount behind her and hugged her to his chest. She clapped as the horse shot off, charging through the trees with Mian, who diligently guided it around the shrouded trunks.

The forest canopy above blotted out most of the sky, only revealing blue through wind-shifted leaves. Pria leaned her head against Mian's chest, eyes bright with excitement. Her gaze was beautiful, sharp, blue, and alight with intelligence someone her age shouldn't possess. She was a precious jewel and he would die to protect her, had known it since the second he laid eyes on her. *Precocious* they had called her, *destined for greatness.* Every citizen of the Seat felt great pride and affection for their princess. He tightened his grip on her protectively. Headstrong and fearless despite her small size, she would follow him and her brother into a den of monsters if that's where they led.

Everyone watched over her protectively, their precious special gift. He had heard her parents talking with his. She would grow up to be a priestess—and not just a priestess, but a high priestess: a person of great magical talent born to rule. He didn't know much about high priestesses or how they differed from just an everyday priestess, just that it made her rare and special. The only other living high priestess ruled over Trimera currently. High Priestess Lana was the picture of prim propriety…and she hated Mian with every fiber of her soul, although he wasn't sure why. Something about deviants corrupting her prodigy. The priestesses were protectors, ambassadors, and advisors for the rulers of Reia and one day Pria would be among them. But for now, she was just his Pria chasing around the castle after him and her brother Janu.

Pria's bright laughter was nonstop when he slowed the horse, letting it amble along a slow river. The stream babbled its way over the water-smoothed rocks. The trail along its bank was nearly indistinguishable but he knew it well. The horse picked its way along and Pria's excitement cooled to a constant jabbering as she scanned the forest and river around her. By the time the sun had grayed the shadows around them, he had just caught sight of another horse tethered to a tree in front of them.

Pria jerked forward. "Does that mean we are close to Janu?"

He laughed. "We're almost there, are you going to make it?"

He dropped from the horse's back and reached to lift her down. When she touched the ground, he watched her run down to the river, where she waited impatiently while he tied the horse beside Janu's. She bounced as he approached, taking his hand in hers. "Mian, what is going on?"

"What do you mean?" he asked.

"I'm not stupid." She stared up at him with a flat glare.

He tucked her to his chest. "I know, Pri. Janu will tell you when we get where we're going, okay?"

She took a deep breath. "Will I like it?"

"No Pria, you won't." His face twisted in sympathy.

She studied him, her young eyes searching his. "Then let's go. I don't want Janu to worry."

"We're going to have to climb a bit from here."

"I'm ready," she said.

He led her down the river, helping her up over rocks and ledges as they went. He was worried about her being able to keep up, but as usual her stubbornness and ferocity kept her going. She was advanced for her few years, with a sharp mind and willful attitude. She took his offered hand, confident that he knew what he was doing. He had been with Janu when she was born, second child to the ruling prince. Not a day went by that they had not seen each other. He was closer to Pria and Janu than most of their family.

Ahead of them was a tall waterfall that crashed down over slick rocks into the river far below them. She stared up at it. "How are we going to get over that?"

"We're not."

A trail wound its way along the side of the water, narrow and uneven. Trees leaned down over them as they made their way. Mian lifted her over a large gap in the rocks and smiled at her confidence. Not much ever fazed her, but it wouldn't last, not today.

The mist from the waterfall created tiny rainbows, beckoning them toward it. He kept her hand tight in his as the rocks became wet and slick. Water roaring over his left shoulder, he crept around behind the falls, keeping Pria far from the cliff edge. After a few feet on the shelf, they walked into a decent-size cave lit by a fire near the back.

Pria broke from his grip and ran to the young man waiting beside the blaze. He pulled her into his arms, and Mian could see he was fighting the tears that still glistened in his eyes.

Mian turned back the way he came. The siblings would need time alone.

Pria slid to the ground, wiping at her brother's cheek with a tender hand. "Janu, what is going on?"

He collapsed to the floor of the cave and patted the smooth rock beside him. "Sit down, Pria."

Her eyes watched him as she folded her legs under her. Janu, in the middle of his teenage years, had a shock of black hair and gentle blue eyes. He wore browns and blacks, which camouflaged him as did Mian's attire. His normally handsome visage was pained.

"There was a raid on Mom and Dad's convoy."

"Are they coming home then?" Pria asked.

He dropped his face and stared into the fire in front of him. "No Pri, no they're not."

"I don't understand."

He sighed, pulling her into his arms. "Pria, they didn't make it."

She shook in his arms, his fear feeding hers, confusing her mind. "But—"

"There weren't any survivors. They are dead, Pria."

The world beneath her cracked open and crumbled away. She clutched to the only solid form available to her, Janu. He was, after all, her only family left. Her stomach cramped and the pain only raged higher as Janu's arms tightened around her and his own chest began to shake. The only thing that held her together was his warm embrace: he needed her now more than ever, and she him. They were alone in this abyss, this darkness.

She pulled back from him and ran a tiny hand beneath her eyes to dry the tears. "Why are we out here?"

For a moment, emotions struggled across his face. Ever thinking of others, she forced a smile and cupped a hand to his cheek. Their mother had always done that when they were upset. More tears slipped from her eyes as she realized she would never feel that again. He blinked at her, his moist eyes sparkling in the firelight.

"They want to take you away from me, Pri. Lana says they won't have time to teach you properly with Father dead. They want to send you to the Silver City, to the Lorien."

Her eyes grew wide as the thought of being torn away from Janu ripped the chasm in her heart even wider. A thought of standing alone in this agony flashed through her mind and her eyes were haunted with the image of it. "But I don't want to go. You can't leave me!"

"You won't go. No one is taking you anywhere," her brother said, his sadness taken over by a look of determination. "It's just you and me now, and no one is going to take you from me."

She curled against his chest, her tiny body shaking as she began to cry again.

"No one is taking you anywhere."

High Priestess Lana glared out the window into the forest that marched up to the very walls. She had argued for years to get Prince Inan to cut them back, but he insisted the trees were sacred. She pressed her eyes closed as a wave of agony washed through her. She had presided over the man's birth, watched him grow into the crown. Inan's death was a keen pain, but nothing compared to the possibility of losing his daughter Pria. Like Lana herself, young Pria would grow to be a high priestess, the first since Lana's own birth. The Lorien was full of priestesses, but only a few grew strong enough to be deemed a high priestess. No one knew what caused the difference, but the level of power could be as much as tenfold between priestess and high priestess. That something was in the girl, something hidden, although Lana could feel it. Only five years old, the girl was destined to become one of the most powerful priestesses to ever live…providing Lana could find her again.

Neither the girl nor her brother Janu, the new ruling prince in the wake of Inan's death, had been seen since the messenger had arrived with the news of the attack. There was no doubt in her mind that Janu had Pria with him. She saw her error now. In her efforts to prepare Pria for her destiny, she had neglected to foster a connection with the boy. She had expected years to work on her relationship with Janu once she had Pria safely tucked away in the Lorien, but life was never easy. She was sure the boy saw her as some villain in a children's story, some monster waiting in the shadows to snatch the only family he had left. The flaw was hers for assuming she would have time to bond with Janu, but it was nothing she couldn't fix. And she *had* to fix it. Somehow.

With Trimera's ruling prince a boy barely in his teens, her time would need to be devoted to the throne. She would be unable to spare any time for Pria's training and the loss would ache at her soul. The girl was truly remarkable, devouring everything she threw at her with an intense hunger. Even at five years old, her powers were already extraordinary. Lana had a hard time keeping the girl to small duties; without constant supervision she would soon be attempting tasks beyond her control and possibly hurt herself, or others.

No, there was nothing for it but for Pria to go to the Lorien. Only in the Lorien would she have the proper attention, teaching, and guidance to grow into the powerful priestess she was born to be. As much as it twanged Lana's heart, Pria had to go to the Lorien now before she was hurt by her curiosity.

Lana stood in a swirl of fabric, her robes brushing the floor in a flood of lavender silk. She was an older woman with silver-laced hair pulled into a tight bun. A slight spiderwebbing of lines marred the skin around her eyes but did little to flaw her handsome face. Wrinkles were a sign of strength, a mark of distinction that symbolized years of wisdom—and she wore them with pride.

The room was her study, neat and tidy. This had been her office for three rulers of Trimera—first when she served young Janu's grandfather, then his father, and now under Janu himself, but only if she could breach the gap that had opened between them. The boy was bright enough and she was sure he would make an incredible ruler.

She glided past the ordered shelves of books and well-tended plants set upon the windowsill. History had been her favorite class at the Lorien, and the subject dominated her shelves even now. The Seat, despite its decoration and comforts, was a fortress—the political center of Trimera, the northernmost kingdom in the land of Reia. She had fought for her position there, a kingdom steeped in history and integral to the protection of Reia. The post had been a coveted one, but as a high priestess there were few who could challenge her claim to it. It didn't take much to convince all involved that, as the strongest living priestess, her place was providing a barrier to the Frontier. The fact that it afforded her an excellent opportunity to study the Frontier had no small effect on her decision.

The Frontier formed the northern border of Trimera, an expanse of dark forest populated with monsters that preyed on magic. For generations the ruling princes who sat on the throne of Trimera stood as a barrier, a buffer between the lands to the south and the wilderness to the north. It was the ruling prince's charge to keep the monsters that lived in the wilderness at bay, the most dangerous and troublesome of which were the grinlo. Few outside the Lorien knew about more than the grinlo. Aggressive, primitive creatures, the grinlo attacked in a horde and wanted nothing more than to plunder. In Lana's expansive collection of books, there were even known instances of them training and using other creatures from the Frontier to hunt, though those were thankfully few. The grinlo themselves were dangerous, and smart enough to use weapons and armor. In large numbers they could easily overpower even the best trained and seasoned soldiers. And she had the perfect seat from which to observe them.

And observation was needed.

Books filled with instances of skirmishes with grinlo, of advances and retreats in the Frontier, sat on her shelves. Trimera had actually been formed from a line of watchtowers that dotted the northern border of Reia, built in response to a string of grinlo raids that led to the loss of hundreds of lives and acres of farmland. The line of watchtowers soon bonded together and formed larger settlements and stronger fortresses until they became their own region and bloomed into Trimera. Though the grinlo still occasionally raided farms on the fringe—decimating crops, killing farmers, and stealing livestock—Trimera kept the threat of a large-scale influx of grinlo to a minimum.

The grinlo themselves were not overly complex creatures, not possessed of great intelligence. They were hunters, aggressive, but they normally kept to the Frontier. Only the males ventured past the barrier to increase their hunting grounds and prey on humans. Humans provided a larger amount of meat than their normal prey, and on the off chance that they found some magic, allowed them to absorb it to increase their strength. To the best of the Lorien's knowledge, no one had ever seen a female grinlo.

In her reign as high priestess of Trimera, Lana had seen several farms raided by grinlo with no creature left alive. Supplies scattered, houses burned…there was never anything resembling food or weapons left behind. Amber Keep and the Seat were well protected, surrounded by walls to keep out any raiding parties and protect the citizens, but not all cities in Trimera were secure. Farther south into Reia, none of the cities had defenses. They instead relied on the buffer Trimera's soldiers provided them. Amber Keep, the Seat, and Austeria were the last line of defense between destruction to the rest of Reia at the hands of the horde.

If the protective buffer were to be stripped away, thousands of lives, acres of farmland, and untold numbers of livestock and structures would be lost to the monsters. Land lost to the Frontier in the past took thousands of deaths to recover and years to restore. The Seat alone had been rebuilt and restored over seven times in fifteen generations—some due to battles, others to the retreat of Trimera's soldiers. Visions from her memory still haunted her dreams: children gutted and left in the dirt because they were too small for the grinlo's purpose, however nefarious. Bodies had been recovered afterward—some with teeth marks as if they had been consumed, some with obvious signs of magical residue discernable only to priestesses, and others had no marks on them at all. Anyone's best guess was that the grinlo took people for food—but that didn't explain the residue or the bodies that were untouched. It was a point of contention in the Lorien as to which the bigger mystery was: the untouched bodies or the ones with residue. These very questions were what brought her to Trimera, but she was no closer to discovering answers today than she had been when she was first stationed here.

The attack on Inan's caravan had her worried, though. This move was bold for the grinlo; the caravan had been heavily guarded and traveled well within the border of Trimera. The entire situation smacked of something more, but she couldn't wheedle out what. The thing that irritated her most was that she had no firsthand accounts, no witnesses to question. She had, of course, visited the battle scene, but it wasn't the same. The patrol that had found and returned the bodies had escorted her there, so she could at least see the scene with her own eyes. The site was still littered with the bodies of grinlo, the dirt churned with prints. With that and her examination of the bodies, she had drawn a decent picture of what had transpired.

The ambush had come from the south, which probably explained why it had been so successful. The party had been on a well-traveled road well within Trimera's borders; they would have had no reason to worry about an attack. The creatures would have had to evade the patrols and travel alongside the road in order to get so far behind the party. The grinlo dead outnumbered the royal guards, and the tracks leaving the scene indicated nearly as many again had survived. Why would the grinlo have come so far south with such a large number? It was not a hunting party; no prey they would have found would have sustained such a number.

It almost looked like they knew Prince Inan was among the party, but that was silly. Grinlo were not smart enough for that.

Still, the attack naggled at her mind. If only a single man had survived that attack, to tell the truth of what had transpired… But there was no use hoping. She had what she had, and she would have to make it do.

Her slippered feet whispered across the decorative carpet, a silver-trimmed pattern of flowers and vines sent from the Silver City. The door swung open on silent hinges to the hallway beyond and the runners that trailed along the passage.

It was a habit of hers to wander the halls of the Seat when she had a puzzle to worry out. She found herself at it more and more of late. The grinlo always tested the boundaries of Trimera, seeking to expand their hunting grounds. Terrible creatures, the grinlo. They destroyed anything they touched, but lately their attacks were verging on ordered. It was a disturbing pattern that had lost them Prince Inan. Hopefully with Pria safely tucked away in the Lorien at her studies, Lana would be able to focus her time on the increasing trouble with the grinlo. Janu would need her counsel in the years to come.

The windows in the hallway opened out toward the forest, from a different direction than her study window. As she passed, movement caught her eye and she stopped to glance out. Through the trunks of trees, darting from shadow to shadow, she could just make out a dark shape. The silhouette caught an errant shaft of light filtered through the leaves and her lips curled at the flash of red.

Mian.

She should have known.

Of course, the addition of Mian complicated and simplified things. On the one hand, she had no doubt he knew where Janu and Pria were; on the other, the boy could be bullheaded beyond reason even if handled carefully. She would need help with him.

She turned from the window and continued down the hall. A tapestry dangled askew at the end of the hallway and she paused to regard it. Her hand stretched out to straighten the hanging and an unexpected pang pierced her heart. Years spent at the side of Prince Inan came rushing to the surface, ripping and tearing as it went. She closed her eyes and stood frozen as she wrestled those feelings back down inside.

After several breaths, she was confident she had her emotions under control and opened her eyes to the hallway. She couldn't grieve yet, not with Pria and Janu still missing. Not with Mian to face. She had no idea how she was going to outsmart the boy, but the very future of Trimera depended on it.

The Silver City was beautiful at night. Sconces and oil lamps lined the streets, tended by an army of men whose sole duty was to keep them lit. Every street, no matter how small, was bright with dancing flames. The light kept the crime rate low; it was hard to conduct dark business with no shadows to hide in. Most criminals were cowards and wouldn't brave the light of day—or the light of fire, it would seem. No garbage littered the streets, no homeless camped in the corners. The Lorien had an army for that too. They swept the streets for anyone unfortunate enough to find themselves without a roof to stay under. They were given shelter, food, and found work if they needed it. The Lorien took care of the Silver City, protected it, always had.

The Lorien had long been the base of strength for the priestesses. Currently its halls were swollen with men and women, girls and boys, all hoping to become priestesses. Some would, some wouldn't. It was the way of things. Those who were strong enough, and who had the spark of magic within them, would be taught in magic and diplomacy, decorum and history, politics and biology—all the subjects that a priestess may need in the world.

Priestess San strode along the market district, hoping to relieve the tension in her mind before she had to return to the Lorien. Today was her day to sort new applicants. Every day a priestess was given sorting duty—the process of filtering through the applicants who sought entry into the ranks of the priestesses, and to root out those who may show promise. It was tedious and tiresome, but a great break from the stress of her everyday work. She spent her days juggling the intricacies of the leaders of Reia. Kachi had a blood feud with Aundrien, Naturin wanted ancestral land returned from Oadren, and none could be allowed to come to blows. Truly the only kingdom that didn't give her constant trouble was Trimera and that was only because no other kingdom dared to distract them from their sacred duty. No one would risk the threat of weakening their protection from the Frontier and the grinlo, but they would go out of their way to bicker among themselves.

Hawkers cried out for her attention as she walked; they knew the robes of a priestess and hoped to wheedle some money out of her. In her youth she had become quite known in this market for her extravagant spending, to the point that the Council had pulled her aside and had a word with her. She was not that headstrong girl anymore but her eyes were still drawn to the finery that littered the marketplace. A cluster of stalls to her right displayed silks and fine fabrics all dyed in exotic colors. The Silver City was known for its fabric. To the north, secluded on an island in the center of the Heart River, lived the Monks of the Lightbringers. The monks were renowned for their talents of crafting, but most especially for their fabric. Several bolts dotted the market, all of it kept well behind the tables, out of the reach of any who may want to acquire it without paying.

She wasn't here for fabric, though.

Beyond the fabric marched tables of shoes. Tall boots, delicate slippers, the strange strap sandals the locals seemed to prefer—all were laid out for sale. The next cluster of stalls hit her like a wall. The raucous mixture of spices assaulted her as she approached. The cloud of scent mixed and swirled until no single scent could be picked out from the whole. Her nose protested as she braved further into the cloud, was enveloped in it. This was what she had come for.

She had a contact, a purveyor of rare and expensive herbs. His stall was located deep in the cluster of spice-laden tables. The aroma within the cluster was beyond description, an overwhelming blanket of relentless sensation. She stopped here and there, bought a bag of cardamom, ginger, a handful of spices for the kitchens. They could be used but were not necessarily needed; the point was to disguise why she was really there.

A small, unassuming table littered with dried plants and flowers stood at the end of the grouping of spice merchants. The merchant, Anders, had a shock of thick black hair and skin the warmed brown of toast, and a thick accent it had taken her years to decipher. Now it fit in her ears like her own mother's voice.

"Anders, how good to see you again," she said with a warm smile.

Anders offered her his own smile as he took her hands across the table. "Priestess San, always a pleasure."

"Do you have something for me?"

Anders winked as he turned to dig into sacks stacked behind him. He delved into the bags up to his elbows, then further up to his shoulders. When he emerged, he held two satchels of waxed linen tied with a strip of ribbon. He stacked one on top of the other and handed them across the table to her. "I am sorry to have taken so long, Priestess," he said, "but I had to travel into the forest south of Ndalla."

She pressed a satchel to her nose and inhaled, struggling to catch the scent of its contents. Mired among the aggressive spices and aromatics, she could just sense the acrid smell of the herb encased in the satchel. "You have done well, Anders."

She slipped the satchels deep into her robes and pulled out a purse full of coin, pre-counted just for the occasion. No need to draw attention to their transaction by flashing coinage. They had already agreed on the price, and she had included extra for his trouble. Their long relationship gave him the courage to slip the purse into his clothes without even peeking inside.

"As always, Priestess, a pleasure."

She left the spice stalls behind, allowing the relatively clear air beyond to clean out her nostrils. She ran a few other errands: bulk orders of grain for the kitchens, bolts of fabric for charges and the servants and workers the priestesses employed, before turning back toward the Lorien.

She caught her reflection in a shop window. She was not young anymore, by any means. Gray peppered her dark hair and creases lined her eyes. Despite that, she still presented a stately appearance, neatly trimmed and well-turned. She looked every minutia what she was, an ambassador.

It was a warm day and San could feel her skin slicking with sweat as she padded along the streets. The moisture plastered the inner layer of her silk suit to her skin unpleasantly. Silk was not meant for this heat. It was going to take her quite a while to get back to the Lorien, well into the night, but the heat rarely released its grip on the city this far into the season. It would be another restless night tossing in the still air.

She was hoping the day's post would have brought her news from Lana. Of an age with San, Lana and she had shared many classes growing up in the Lorien, but while San could never hope to equal Lana's strength, they had formed a fast and strong friendship. All eyes were locked on Trimera, Lana's station. She had written the very day of the prince's second born's birth. She knew even then that the child had the gift to become a priestess, but it had taken closer study to realize she would be a high priestess. The news had rocked the Lorien. No one had been born with the strength to be a high priestess since Lana's own birth, more years ago than were polite to mention. Lana had mentioned entering the girl in the lists several times already but something always stopped her. Lana was headstrong and stubborn, but her heart was as soft as goose down, especially when it came to the royal family of Trimera. Not that San could blame her—the woman had presided over two generations of rulers already and had started on a third.

Her letter passing on the news of Inan's death had been so heartbreaking that San had opted not to enter it into the official archives. No one else needed to know her heartbreak. Much of the Lorien worried what the death of Inan could mean. Some of them saw the loss as a portent to a greater tide of sorrow to come. San wasn't sure how such nonsense wasn't knocked out of them long before this point, but it wasn't her place to root out superstition among the priestesses. She had her hands full juggling thrones.

What it all boiled down to was that the Lorien would have to wait to get their claws into their new high priestess. San wouldn't admit it to anyone else, but she was thoroughly ecstatic at the prospect. It didn't help any that she was fed on a constant diet of updates from Lana on the girl's progress. She seemed to be a prodigy; not even Lana had developed so quickly. Then again, Lana had not had the benefit of a high priestess teaching her either.

The front steps to the Lorien were black veined marble lined with statues. Each statue depicted an influential priestess from the history of the Lorien, marching up to the walls like sentinels. Seven of the statues were high priestesses, some of the strongest men and women of their order. What San liked most was that the statues weren't only the strongest of the strong. To make the line of statues, a priestess had to make a great contribution to the land of Reia. San had always been unremarkable when it came to strength, always the middle of any group she was in, but she was diligent. Where she excelled wasn't in her strength in magic but in her mind. San had excelled in history, politics, and international relations. She had personally been able to avert three civil wars, countless squabbles, and a multitude of territorial disputes, and arranged alliances between previously warring countries. She had heard it said several times that she was fast becoming one of the most influential negotiators the Lorien had ever seen. Her jaw set in determination. The stone faces staring down at her had always been her inspiration.

But San didn't turn up the marble steps.

She often walked past the front doors but she rarely used the entrance. It was too public—led straight to the front lobby that was full of visitors, petitioners, and staff—and the crowds and noise were more than she wanted to deal with. She continued on around the corner and took an alley toward the river. She could hear the water from here, crashing over the rocks as it raced along past the city. Along the side alley was a small servants' entrance and that was her preferred way into the Lorien.

Even this entrance was guarded, with a large muscled soldier on each side of the door. They wore the colors of the Lorien, the livery of the priestesses, black and gold. As she approached, one of the soldiers stepped forward and held the door open for her to slip inside. The interior of the Lorien was cool and damp thanks to the river and it felt delicious against her hot skin.

The corridor beyond was deserted and dim, a hazy veil of grays and blacks. Her soft slippers shushed along the floor as she glided past the tapestries and sconces. It was peaceful, calming after the bustle of the market. She turned right onto the stairs and climbed to the third floor where her room was located. Her room opened up onto the river, providing her with a breathtaking view of the churning water. Every night it soothed her to sleep. The rooms at the Lorien were not lavish, but neither were they small. Each priestess was allotted their own room for any time they were in the Silver City, even Lana who had not left Trimera in decades.

Lana's rooms were next to her own, sharing a view of the river. Before Lana had left for Trimera, she and San would often stand at the windows and chatted long into the night with the river rushing below them. They were some of the fondest memories she had.

The simple fact of the matter was that she missed her friend.

She had never made another friend like Lana, and at her age there was little chance she ever would. She didn't mind too much; she had her work and it kept her plenty busy, so it wasn't like she needed friends to fill her time. Simply, she wished she had someone to share her worries with. She remembered keenly the relief of sharing worries with a trusted confidant.

She shook herself as she pushed the door to her room open. There was no sense in worrying over what you didn't have. The door swung shut and the whisper of the river enveloped her. She had enough work without wasting time and energy wanting.

Mian paused at the doorway, ear pressed to the thick wood. The hallway outside was quiet as he slipped from Janu's room, shouldering a satchel of clothes. The entire castle was still in a frenzy as they searched for Janu and Pria—even more so after a week with no sign of them—but they wouldn't find them, not where he had them hidden.

Slipping along the halls, he tried to look as innocent as possible as he made his way toward the kitchens. No amount of acting kept the suspicious glares from shooting his way—he had a bit of a reputation for mischief around the castle. With a bright smile, he hopped up on a stool as the tall cook came over to greet him. She was plump and pretty, despite her age. Gray touched her temples but her warm beauty shone past the fine lines of her face. A pristine apron protected her red livery and a towel draped across her shoulder. Her chestnut hair was knotted at the base of her neck. She returned his bright smile with one of her own.

"Young Master Mian, what sorts of trouble are we up to this morning?"

He batted his large eyes at her. "I would never cause trouble, Eeda. Can you pack me up some food? Father is planning a little ride today and he asked me to get us provisions."

Eeda gave him a warm smile as she ruffled his red curls. "Anything for my Mian."

He leaned on the table before him and watched as Eeda moved around the kitchens, spouting orders and collecting a bag full of dried meats, cheeses, and fruits. The kitchen was a maze of working tables, heavy cook stoves, pots, and kettles with its own army of cooks, pages, and assistants. The air was warm and pleasant and full of the luscious savory scents of meats roasting on spits and the soft airy scent of breads baking in the stone oven.

Eeda returned to his side and handed him the bag, planting a warm kiss on his brow. "You and your father be careful; the horde gets bolder by the day."

"We will, Eeda."

He darted from the kitchens and deftly dodged the castle staff and soldiers as they continued to sweep the halls for any sign of the missing Janu and Pria. A couple of the soldiers eyed him, but he evaded them with ease. He had snuck food and clothes from the castle all week while avoiding his parents' suspicious questions. He was lucky so far, but it was only a matter of time before their eyes turned his way. Everyone knew he was Janu's closest friend; when they failed to find any trace of them, suspicion would turn to him.

Paused in an alcove, he waited for a group of soldiers to pass by before slipping toward the door. With a smile, he pivoted, hiked the satchel higher on his shoulder…and stopped dead, facing his parents and High Priestess Lana.

Lana loomed over him, an imposing woman. Her eyes bored into him like a fox eyeing a sleeping hen. She had on her full ceremonial silk suits today; she was ready for a fight. Behind her, his parents waited like a thunderhead. His father, tall and dark, glared down with gray eyes, his mother smoldering beside him in a halo of red curls.

He plastered on a well-practiced charming smile. "High Priestess, to what do I owe the honor?"

"Where are they?" She glared down at him.

He shrugged. "Who are you looking for?"

His father stepped forward, jerking the satchel from his shoulder. "Young man, I think you and your friend have worried this house enough for two lifetimes. Where are Janu and Pria?"

"What makes you think I would know?"

His mother stepped forward to grip his shoulders. "Mian, you have to tell us where they are. I know they are scared, but they cannot hide forever. We just want to help them."

Mian glanced up at Lana, his jaw stubborn. "They won't come back. Not while she's trying to send Pria away."

His mother's face twisted in sympathy. "Mian, Pria will have to leave eventually. Soon she will have to go to the Lorien to be taught to control her power; there is nothing anyone can do about that. It doesn't mean she will leave today. Now you go and tell Janu that it is time to come back to the Seat."

"Or are we going to have to go after them?" His father's brow hitched in a threat and Mian felt his determination falter. Falter, but not dissipate.

"You'd never find them," Mian said as he glared up at the taller man. "Unless you can convince me, you'll never see them."

Lana cocked an eyebrow. "You think you are smart, don't you? The second you leave this castle I will follow you. How will they get food, or clothes? You will never escape me. Eventually they are going to get hungry. You don't want them to grow hungry, do you?"

"Priestess, please," he said, his voice lilting with mirth, "I have been sneaking out of this castle for nearly a week now and no one has caught me yet."

"*Mian*!" His mother's voice rose in scandal.

Lana bent over him, snagging his coat between her fingertips. His eyes grew wide as her hand glowed. The light bled into the fabric and settled a chill along his skin. "You have been evading soldiers and servants, boy. You will *not* evade me."

He stared down at the corner of the coat and shrugged. "I have other coats."

Her smile was predatory. "Do you now?"

His father snatched his vest, jerking him forward. "Enough of this! I don't know what you think you're playing at, but it is over here and now. You will take us to Janu and Pria and you will do it this instant!"

Mian sighed, his shoulders slumping in defeat. "I can't just take you; I gave my word."

"You gave your word that you would not take anyone to them, but they will listen to you," his father said, his voice softening into sympathy. "Now you go to them and tell them that if they come back I can personally guarantee that Pria will not be sent to the Lorien until she is ready."

Mian stared at him, searching his face. "I'll try, but they are very upset. I don't know if they will listen."

The man laid a hand on his son's head. "You'll do your best. I know you can do this."

Mian dropped his gaze, staring at his feet for a moment before glancing back up at Lana. "Only if she promises not to track me with her magic."

His mother crossed her arms. "I would love to know where you got this attitude from."

"I promise to not track you unless you fail to bring them back," Lana conceded. "Mian, you succeed in this and I will never punish you for the insolence you so wantonly flaunt."

He cocked an eyebrow at her, a crooked smile crossing his young face. "Now that is a compromise I can live with."

Janu watched Pria as she charged the horse around the open glen. The animal was sweaty with exertion as her gentle urgings sent him dancing and gliding over the mossy ground. Her bright laughter rang off the surrounding trees. She spent much of her time riding; it was the only thing that kept her mind from dwelling on the loss of their parents. Her eyes were red from crying and her voice cracked, but she was strong, she would be okay.

He didn't turn at the steps behind him; only Mian knew where they were. "I was beginning to wonder if you had forgotten about us."

Mian dropped to the ground next to him with a heavy sigh. "Yeah, hit a bit of a snag. Ran into Lana, and my parents."

"And?"

The other boy hesitated. "I promised to talk to you about coming back."

"And if we don't?" Janu asked.

"You'll have to find someone else to bring you supplies. Lana put some kind of spell on my clothes so she can follow me." He plucked the neck of his coat for emphasis.

"Can she do that?"

Mian's shoulders hitched. "Your guess is as good as mine, but by agreeing to talk to you I now have free rein to speak to Lana however I feel, so not all bad."

Janu stared at him openly. "She really said that?"

He tipped his head side to side. "Not in so many words. Really she just said she wouldn't punish me for insolence. Not sure if that's the same thing, but I'm going to take it like it is."

"You have a wish for death, don't you?"

"I have heard that before," he said.

"*Mian*!"

He laughed as Pria crashed into him, toppling them both over. "It is good to see you too Pria." He cradled her to his chest as he sat up and looked over at Janu. "So, are you going to come back?"

"I thought we weren't going back." Pria giggled as Mian leaned his chin on her head.

"What about Pria?"

"Father promised he would not let her go to the Lorien until she is ready," Mian said.

"And Lana?"

"If she plans to fight with Father, she will regret ever having the idea. Stubborn is a family pastime."

Pria giggled as she fiddled with Mian's shirt. "Poor High Priestess Lana!"

Janu stared at the panting horse in front of them, its head hanging pathetically. "I want to talk to them myself. I want to hear from Lana's own mouth that she won't take Pria. Will you stay here?"

Mian ruffled Pria's hair. "We'll see how much mischief we can get into without you."

"Where is your horse?" Janu asked. "I dare say Pria has overly abused this poor creature."

Pria stuck her tongue out at him as Mian smiled. "He's just down the path," he said.

"You're not leaving me?" Pria's face paled.

Janu rubbed her head. "Not for long. Mian is going to stay with you."

"We don't need your silly brother, do we?" Mian said, bouncing her on his lap.

She snuggled into his chest. "No."

Janu glared at her. "I'm glad you are so attached to me." He stood, glancing at the ground. Despite his words, meeting with Lana was the last thing he wanted. Oh, she had never outright done anything he could deem even slightly nefarious, but still, she made him nervous. Father and Mother had always spoken so highly of her, but all he could see were her plans to take his baby sister off to the Lorien. What did Pria need to study with the priestesses for? Surely there was nothing she could learn there that she couldn't here. Thoughts of the Lorien always sent chills down his spine despite the stories that their mother had told Pria.

"Stay close to her; I'll be back as soon as I can."

Lana set her book aside and came to her feet as she faced the boy who had appeared behind her. He was a handsome youth, though it would take him a few more years to grow into the looks his father had passed on to him. His dark hair was neat, trimmed recently by his mother. His eyes were the same sharp blue as his sister's.

"You did not trust us enough to bring your sister?"

"She is safe," he said. "I would know your mind before I let her return."

"Pria was born to be a high priestess," Lana said. "There is nothing you can do to change that." She caught the tightening of his eyes but he held his ground as she continued. "Eventually she will need to go to the Lorien to learn her power."

His young visage twisted with the force of his words. "Can you not understand? She is all I have, and I am all she has. And you want to tear her from her home, her family. She would be alone there!"

Lana's eyes dropped to the floor. How to explain to this headstrong young man his sister's destiny? "I am not heartless, Janu; I can understand your worries, but you cannot hold Pria forever. Sooner or later she will have to leave, and you will not be able to stop it. I cannot teach her everything she must know to become a priestess; she will need the tutors at the Lorien for that."

"But not until she is ready."

"Lord Aanor and I will discuss her readiness and decide when she will go. Janu, even you must know that the time she can remain untrained in her talents grows short. The crack in the North Tower should be evidence enough of that." The crack was a result of a nightmare, brought a little too real to life by an untrained hand in magic. Lana had been in constant contact with the Lorien since Pria's birth. At five, Pria would be the youngest initiate by several years, but neither Lana nor her contacts were in doubt that she would benefit from starting her training.

"She is not ready. Not now." His voice was strong but wavered.

"No," she breathed, "not now. Lord Aanor has offered to take you in, both of you. If you return, you will be kept together in his house until you are old enough to rule on your own."

He lowered his gaze. "Lord Aanor is a good man."

"It will give you both family," she said, "and Trimera a bit of experience behind its young prince."

His eyes met hers, cautious but optimistic. "It won't be like we are with strangers."

"No, it won't, and you will have your friend that you are both so attached to. Most importantly, you will have a home with people who care about you." She watched him as his mind worked out the situation. It was clear he still didn't trust her. "Why did you run away, Janu?" Her eyes narrowed as she folded her hands before her.

His gaze locked with hers, burning with rekindled passion. "My entire world was caving in. I had just lost my parents and the only thing I had left you were trying to take from me."

She smiled kindly. "Even when Pria goes to the Lorien, you will never lose her. She will always have a connection with you—nothing will change that." She took a step forward. "So, will you come back?"

He glanced up at her. "Did you really tell Mian you wouldn't punish him when he talks back to you?"

She nodded. "A small price to pay to get my future prince and high priestess back."

"So you say now; I don't think you quite understand what you have gotten yourself into there."

She smiled down at him. "I think I can handle a few barbs from a boy."

His own smile was incredulous. "You don't know Mian." He chewed on his lip in thought. "We'll come back."

"I'm glad to hear that."

Janu watched Lady Mesha as she guided her horse along, her red curls glinting in the sunlight. He wasn't sure how far she was going to make it in her long flowing dress and delicate court slippers, but she had insisted on coming—some fear that they would corrupt Pria if left alone with her much longer. More likely, Lana was afraid they wouldn't return and the three had decided Mesha would raise the fewest objections.

He jumped as she patted his hand. "There is no more need for worry, Janu." She glanced down and met his gaze. "You're safe with us."

He had always liked Mian's mother. She'd been kind to him, warm. She would be a good guardian, and a far better option than Lana herself. But she wasn't his mother. She wasn't Pria's mother. The thought brought a sting deep in his chest, alongside the smiling face of the most beautiful woman in the world. Piercing blue eyes, lovely sunny hair, his mother. His dead mother, and he would never again see her face, feel her touch. Days had passed and the pain was just as keen as that first.

He urged his horse forward, letting the narrowness of the path push her back. He spoke over his shoulder. "You're going to have to hang back soon. There's going to be some rough patches coming up."

She watched him for a moment, not dropping his gaze. "I can make anything you can."

He stared at her skeptically before he turned back. His horse picked the path as he eased it to a quicker pace. The small pen he had built for the steeds was just ahead and the tall gelding nickered amiably as he caught sight of them.

Janu jumped as a high-pitched scream shattered the solitude around them. His eyes snapped wide as he leapt from the horse and took off flying through the trees. "Pria!"

Mesha was at his side in an instant, skirts hiked over her knees.

His heart was pounding when they finally reached a pond, sliding to a halt at its edge. The lake sat at the base of a wooded valley with pines growing down to the water's edge on three sides.

Standing thigh-deep in the water stood Pria and Mian, both coated in sticky mud. Pria's eyes sparkled with excitement as she held out her cupped hands. "I caught one!"

Mian plastered on an innocent grin as his mother's face twisted in horror. "Mother, Janu… I didn't think you'd get back so quickly."

Mesha glowered at him as she knelt beside Pria. "Caught what, dear?"

Pria opened her hands and Mesha screamed, falling backward as a large spotted frog exploded from the child's muddy grip. Pria stomped. "Ah, I lost it!"

The girl pivoted to trudge back out into the water but Mesha grabbed her arm and hastily pulled her up on shore. Mian was still sporting his foolish grin as the tall woman rounded on him.

"Young man, your father and I are going to have a serious talk about you when we get home."

Mian grumbled under his breath. "What else is new."

She shot him an angry glare as she pulled a kerchief from her sleeve and wiped at the thick goop covering Pria's face. "You are beyond filthy, child."

Pria rolled her eyes. "Of course! Frogs are very crafty; you have to have camouflage!"

Mesha sighed as she glanced at Mian, who had returned his innocent smile, but Janu couldn't help but see her as the wicked stepmother. She stood, keeping a firm grip on Pria.

"Mian, clean yourself up this instant. Janu, I want you to go fetch anything you two have brought out here and meet us back by the horses, and I do *not* want to have to come find you."

Pria rode behind Lady Mesha, as "young ladies do not charge around on horses." She tried to hold her irritation down but it was hard especially with Mian and Janu riding along to each side of them.

The walls of the Seat towered over them as they rode toward the gates. Never before had the fortress walls risen so ominously before her. Burning tears welled up behind her eyes but she fought it back. She couldn't cry in front of Lady Mesha. She felt a hand clasp hers and looked over to see Janu stretched toward her from his horse. His eyes were locked onto the sweep of stone that loomed before them. Devoid of her parents, the Seat looked like exactly what it was designed to be: a fortress. It was no longer her home, no longer inviting.

Guards swarmed around them as they passed through the gates and into the courtyard. A guard lifted her from the horse and set her down on the cobblestones. Her eyes traveled the length of the courtyard to finally settle on the group standing in the open gates. Her knees trembled as Lana stepped toward them. Pria could feel herself being pulled from her home. She heard Mian and Janu move to her side, building her confidence as Lana stopped before her. At her back stood Lord Aanor, an older mountainous version of her Mian.

Hands landed on her shoulders, one from each of the boys at her sides. Lana towered over her, a storm of irritation. "Prince Janu, Princess Pria. I am glad you have decided to return."

Janu's grasp tightened on her shoulder. "Priestess." His voice quivered with hostility.

Lady Mesha scooped Pria into her arms and placed a hand on Janu's back. "High Priestess, it has been a long day for everyone. Aanor, let's get these two settled back in."

Mesha stepped around Lana, guiding Janu along ahead of her. Pria's eyes remained locked. Janu had said that Lana had agreed to not send her to the Lorien yet, but the high priestess was not known for her compromise. Her view of the woman was cut off as Lord Aanor fell in step behind them, Mian meek at his back.

The corridors of the Seat looked to be lined with every citizen, soldier, and staff as they passed. All eyes sought them, sliding from her to her brother. Every gaze held a mixture of relief and sympathy and invaded their grief. Who were these people that they forced themselves into their pain? Fire welled up and evaporated the sadness like morning mist. They had no right! Her clothes were too tight, too hot.

She buried her face in Lady Mesha's hair as if the wave of curls could block out their eyes. Mesha's skin was warm and smelled of wildflowers, but it wasn't the smell she wanted. It wasn't her mother's smell, and it never would be. Just like the man ghosting along in her wake would never be her father. The thought raged through her mind, crashing around inside her skull like a rabid fox. She fought against the arms around her—against what they meant, against the eyes prying into her misery.

Mesha cried out as Pria jerked from her grip and dropped to the ground. The pressure in her chest leapt forth, burning deep as she glared her anger at the crowd still watching, still prying, still intruding. Her tiny fists knotted in her hair as she struggled to contain her anger. The scream that tore from her lips shocked even her as it shook the walls around them.

All around her was chaos, fear, but she couldn't stop the scream. Her skin burned, from the top of her head to the tips of her toes, like she was doused in hot oil. Too hot, too much to hold on to. Her hands curled into claws as she fought to hold the torrent.

But she couldn't.

Her arms flung out to her sides, her head dropped back. The pressure in her body rushed forth in a flood. The stones below her quaked, the walls rumbled. Her lungs screamed for breath but she could draw none. Her vision blurred and her eyes stung but the flow of energy was endless. She couldn't stop any more than she could disappear.

Janu ducked and dodged the citizens and servants who fled the magic storm before them. He had never seen anything like it. Dust rained down around Pria's tiny form as fire and light stormed out from her. Lord Aanor struggled with Lady Mesha as she screamed Pria's name. Mian stood stunned as people rushed past him.

Janu jumped as a brick of stone broke loose and crashed to the floor. He had to do something. He pulled his legs under him as he moved to stand but a hand pressed him back to the floor. He glanced up into Lana's serene face.

"Stay back, Prince Janu. You cannot help her now."

Janu felt an urge to resist her but one glance to Pria burned it to ash. Lana guided Mian aside then whispered into Lady Mesha's ear, stilling her protests.

Then she turned her attention to Pria.

The girl herself stood in a swirling cloud of flame and crushed stone. The halo had hollowed-out ruts in every surface it touched. Her dress whipped about her in tatters, caught up in the current. And still she screamed. A scream so filled with heartache it stabbed directly into his chest.

Lana raised her hand as if brushing away dust and the storm parted before her. She slipped into the eddy and stepped up to Pria's back. Everywhere Lana's hand moved, the storm fled as if it feared her touch, but Janu knew better. Pria's shoulders dropped a hair as the flood of fire faltered. Lana leaned down to her ear and whispered. Pria's body began to shake; the storm around her stuttered and flashed. The scream wavered and coughed then faded into echoes. The flames guttered as her arms dropped to her sides.

Lana's hand cupped to the back of Pria's neck. The girl crumbled into Lana's arms. Stone dust swirled up around them as Lana cradled Pria to her chest. Pria's fists knotted in Lana's robes and tears washed her face. Lana rocked her as she rubbed her back. The image shook Janu. He'd never seen his baby sister look so young.

It took him several heartbeats to realize the soothing music he was hearing was Lana. Her sweet voice crept into the raw hole in his chest. He'd never heard Lana utter a note. But as Lana leaned her cheek on the crown of Pria's head, he knew he had heard the song before.

His feet were moving before the thought formed in his head and he soon found himself kneeling at her side. Her right hand left Pria's back and came to rest on his shoulder. The tears came out of nowhere, catching him off guard with their force and suddenly he understood Pria's pain. Not just the loss of their beloved parents but also the loss of their home. The Seat would never again be the safe haven it had always been.

Lana's song faded into silence but the calm it had instilled remained. Pria had fallen asleep in her arms.

"That song," he said, uncomfortable in the silence, "I know it."

She seemed to sense his shift in mood and let her hand fall from his shoulder. "I sang it over your crib. As I did for your father before you."

He tried to hide his shock. He'd been told, of course, that Lana had presided over his birth as she had over Pria's, but that was a lullaby. That song was an overture of love, raw emotion he had never before encountered from the priestess.

He couldn't hold her gaze and returned his attention to Pria asleep in her arms. That was little better. How could this be the same cold woman who was trying to send Pria away?

"Is she all right?" Janu leapt at Lady Mesha's trembling voice.

The interruption drew his attention to the hallway around them. All the servants, all the lords and ladies of the Seat, had fled from the magical storm. They stood alone in the hall with Mian and his family. The hallway itself was in shambles. Dust from disintegrated stones formed drifts and piles along the walls and in the corners. Large chunks of the walls, floor, and ceiling were gone as if the architects and masons had not finished the structure.

Lady Mesha and Lord Aanor knelt with their arms around Mian, protecting their only child. Their eyes, however, were locked on Janu, Pria, and Lana. Fear filled those eyes, but not the fear that had filled the eyes of the other witnesses to Pria's rage. Their fear was for Pria, not of Pria.

Mesha rushed forward at Lana's nod and lifted the girl from her arms. Lord Aanor helped Lana to her feet as his wife fawned over Pria. The girl's eyes never flittered as the small group made their somber trip to Pria's chambers.

Lord Aanor stopped Janu and Mian at the door as Lana and Lady Mesha continued into the room beyond.

Lana would regret her decision in the morning. She was not a young girl anymore, but there was nothing more for it. She couldn't chance leaving Pria alone so soon after her blow up. She would need to be watched for a while to make sure she didn't hurt herself or anyone else. It was the first time Pria had initiated magic on her own, and the first time was always followed by more. With such an intense first manifestation, any subsequent conjuring would always be intense.

So, here she was, propped up in an overstuffed chair. The girl herself nestled deep in her piles of blankets. With the amount of energy she had burned, it was unlikely she would wake during the night, but Lana wasn't willing to risk it. If something did happen, it would be fast and she would need to be close to react.

Lady Mesha had argued to stay as well but Lana had finally persuaded her to her own bed. One of them had to be rested for the morning. The next few days would try them all, if she had any guess. Janu would be hard enough, but with Pria throwing magical tantrums as well, the best they could hope for was interesting.

She resituated herself on the chair to ease an ache in her tired back. She held her breath as her ears caught voices out in the hall. It would be Janu with Mian in tow, no doubt. And in fact, not two breaths later, the chamber door creaked open and two heads poked in.

"If you intended to catch me asleep," she said, "you are out of luck."

The boys hesitated for a moment before entering. Mian gave her a wary eye, but Janu's attention was fixed on Pria. "I had to see her."

"To confirm that I had not secreted her away?" she challenged.

The boy did not rise to the bait. "To see that I wasn't alone." Janu folded his legs and sat on the carpets, attention still on the bed.

Mian gave her another glance before joining him.

"Tomorrow will be a long day. We must begin plans for the coronation, the state funeral."

"I'll be ready," he said.

Lana leaned her head back; it wouldn't only be a long day for the boy. She and Lord Aanor would be acting as regents until Janu was old enough to rule.

"What was that?"

Lana jerked at the sound of his voice. She had just started to drift off. "In the hallway?"

He nodded.

She sighed as she fought her way back from exhaustion. "That was Pria's first manifestation of magic."

Both boys' eyes moved to her, but Mian seemed content to be an observer. Janu, however, was full of questions. "First manifestation? But she's done magic with you loads of times."

"That was a magical guiding," she replied, "not the same thing. This was Pria's first magical conjuring she did herself."

Janu dropped his gaze, his mind working out the implications. "That's significant, isn't it?"

"It is the first step every priestess must achieve. The first manifestation is always followed by waves of reoccurrences. Until she can learn to control it herself, she will be at the mercy of the magic."

"She didn't hurt anyone," he snapped, voice defiant. It was not her he was trying to convince.

"Not this time, no." She tried to be gentle. He was still hurting but she needed him to face reality. "But it will not stop just because you'd like it to."

"I am not a child, Lana." No respect, no deference. He would make her earn it. She had a lot of work to do with him.

"No one is saying you are," Lana replied, "but she is. She may not act it, but she is a child who is dealing with emotions and abilities that could tear her apart."

Mian laughed, his first response since he entered the room. "You can't truly consider Pria a child? Any other kid her age, but not my…" He stopped himself short, but she knew what he had been about to say: Not *his* Pria.

And that was the true center of the argument. To them Pria was not a future priestess, a princess, or even just a little sister to protect. Everything Prince Inan had said to them they had taken to heart. Pria was their treasure, he'd said, a gift. He'd stood over her cradle and filled their young minds with stories of gallantry. They didn't understand that that could never be her story.

Mian eyed her openly now. It was obvious he didn't like that he'd given something away to her, no matter how small. He would see it as a loss in the little game they had started, and it was a game to him. She returned his cocky smirk with a smile of her own. She would let him play; she had gotten what she needed.

"I understand she is precocious, but she is still five."

Mian held her gaze, confident and bold. Despite their antagonism she had to admit respect if not the beginnings of affection for the boy. She could already see he would grow to be a good man—intolerable maybe, but good—and she had to respect his loyalty and bravery. There were few grown men let alone fifteen-year-old boys who would willingly stand down a priestess for any reason even for a friend. And though it had galled her, Mian had earned her respect.

"Get some sleep, boys."

Pria pulled the door shut behind her, careful to make no noise. It had taken all her stealth to avoid waking the three people who littered her bedchambers like snare traps.

Minutes ago, she had been pulled from her slumber by a bone-chilling frost. She had expected to see the panes iced over, her breath a cloud of mist, but neither greeted her in the hazy dark cast by the dying fire. Nothing to explain the cold she felt. The cold nestled deep in her chest and swirled around in a vortex, despite the warm room and her pile of numerous blankets. Whatever the cause, she couldn't return to sleep despite the lead weight in every muscle.

Her bare feet slapped against the stones of the hallway as she padded down the hall. Her body protested every move. Once she had fallen from a tree trying to follow Janu and Mian. She'd thought that ache had been the worst pain she could feel. But the jolts and twinges that shot through her entire body upon waking paled the memory to fog.

She passed Janu's chamber door, across the hallway from hers. The next door led to her parents' chambers. Her feet froze to the stone floor. Her throat dried up and a weightlessness made her head swim. She reached, and the tips of her fingers brushed against the wood.

She pushed the door open. A wave of scent enveloped her in memory. Her mother's soft floral aroma, her father's rugged manly musk. Home. Comfort. Love. Eyes closed, she let the world close in around her, to spiral down to nothing more than that scent. She pulled it deep into her chest. Could she pull enough of the scent into her to tuck the memory away to last the rest of her life?

She opened her eyes and cast about the room before her. Had anyone been in this room since the attack? There was no way to tell.

It took her a moment to gather enough courage to step inside. This room whispered from every corner. Her mother's armoire stood to her left. She chose this first.

The hinges were silent as she pulled open the doors. Draped on pegs and hooks were gowns, cloaks, coats, undergarments, and other clothes. She crawled into the chamber amid the folds and creases. She took each garment into her hands, pressing it to her face, rubbing it against her cheeks.

She pulled down a cloak and wrapped it around her as she leapt from the armoire to the floor. The cloak flared out behind her as she crossed the room. From her father's she chose a loose white blouse. She slipped the shirt on below the cloak. It hung well below her knees and flowed around her like a tent. Despite both wrapping her in a fluffing formless mass, a chill still clamped around her chest.

The weight of the cloak pulled her shoulders back as it dragged behind her across the floor. She struggled toward her mother's vanity and climbed onto the stool. The vanity was strewn with her mother's personal possessions. Creams and powders, she only wore them for state occasions. A set of delicate silver combs sat waiting to adorn her mother's golden hair.

Pria's hand trembled as she ran a finger along the closest comb. It was cold and smooth against her palm as she picked it up. The morning light danced across the tines.

"Would you like it in your hair?"

She didn't jump at the voice, didn't think she was capable of that much reaction. Not with the cold. She glanced back over her shoulder to see Lady Mesha in the doorway. Should she be ashamed to be caught here? She wasn't sure.

She turned back to the vanity. "It's too nice for me."

Mesha crossed the room in silence and took the comb from her fingers. "Don't be silly, my dear," she said. "You are a princess."

Mesha lifted a gilded brush from the vanity. With her free hand, she gathered Pria's hair and pulled it behind her shoulders. The brush whispered across her scalp, tugging against her brow. Pria had done this before, sat in this stool getting her hair brushed. Her mother loved to brush her hair.

The cold settled deeper. It was a strange sensation. Ice burrowed deeper into the pit of her stomach. She grabbed the brush from Mesha's hand and set it back on the vanity.

Mesha didn't comment, didn't protest, just held her hand out to Pria. "Come on, dear. Let's get you back to bed."

Pria slid from the stool and followed, enveloped in her billowing memory. Her small hand was encased in Mesha's, lost in its warmth. The grip was strong and comforting but soft and gentle at the same time. A mother's touch.

In the hallway waited Lord Aanor. He didn't speak as he fell in behind them, taking care not to step on her trailing cloak.

She stopped as Mesha reached for the latch on her door. "Do I have to call you mom now?"

A glimpse of emotion moved across the older woman's face, but it was Lord Aanor who responded. "You may call us whatever you wish." She turned to face him as he knelt at her side. "We do not wish to replace your parents. No one can do that." He brushed a hair from her forehead. "We only wish to protect you."

Pain lanced up through her eyes but she forced it back. She pulled the cloak tighter around herself as she held his gaze. He had Mian's eyes, green and deep, and though they were somber today, she had seen them sparkle with amusement. He was strict but kind.

With a nod she turned back to her room. She pushed past Lady Mesha and pulled the door shut behind her. Janu and Mian were slumped where she had left them. She nestled in the space on the carpet between them, bundling the cloak into a bed before curling into it. The floor was definitely not her stuffed mattress, but the layers of cloak atop the rug were comfortable enough.

For a brief moment she worried the cold would keep her awake, but as she let the tension ease from her muscles, she found an ease in the chill as well. A core of ice remained deep within her but the edges of the glacier warmed and melted. That chunk of ice would take years to thaw, but she wasn't alone. Not with Janu and Mian.

Janu wiped the sweat from his eyes then tucked the kerchief into his belt. Summer in the Seat could get stifling and the dead air in the central courtyard didn't help matters much. Not so much as a gentle breeze wafted through the stale air. Towers surrounded them, walls rose high above them and blocked any hope of a refreshing wind. Even the grass in the courtyard stood parched and browning, crunching with his every step.

He pushed the heat away and refocused his attention to the far end of the yard and the targets set up there. Mian smirked beside him, gloating at the precise patch of arrows blooming in a cluster at the center of his target. Janu's splattered haphazardly across the target. He couldn't focus.

Behind them paced Lord Aanor, a constant watchful shadow. Almost a year he and Pria had lived in his household, and the man had proven to be both understanding and fair. Not if you talked to Mian, of course, but Mian put effort into mischief. Though Lord Aanor had warmly accepted Janu and the boy could find nothing to complain about, it was nothing compared to his attachment to Pria. The man doted over her. She already had a closet full of more dresses than she could ever wear. When he had learned of her love of horses, he'd filled their family stables so she'd have her choice whenever the mood struck her. It had gotten so bad that Janu had taken her aside and told her to stop mentioning when she liked something. He was worried she was going to disappear in a pile of gifts. Aanor had a simple joy in spoiling his adopted daughter.

Janu, however, was to be molded into a ruler. He could be loved and cared for but he also had to have constant instruction. Every morning began with a breakdown and study of any reports of horde activity. They would discuss the behavior of the grinlo, the reaction of any defenses against them, and what could be done to improve. Lord Aanor also liked to periodically discuss fortifications for the Seat, Amber Keep, and even Austeria when the mood struck him. This usually occurred following a reported encounter. Though an unusually quiet period followed the attack on his parents' caravan, encounters soon returned to more normal numbers. That very morning, they had sat in one of the smaller studies and discussed a raid on one of the northern farms. Mian often was victim to these discussions, as—according to Lord Aanor—no son of his was going to be ignorant of his duty.

But it wasn't Lord Aanor's looming presence that had his mind ensnared today. Today, like every day for the last month, his mind, his worry, and even his dreams were filled with the Lorien. Every lesson with Lana somehow ended up there. He knew what she was doing, he wasn't a fool. She was gauging his reaction, seeing how open he was to letting her ship his baby sister off to some far-off place for darkness knows how long. He wasn't falling for it. Pria was fine, right where she was. Sure, there had been a couple of mishaps, but nothing Lana couldn't handle.

Breath rushing from his lips, he raised the bow back to shoulder height and laid the arrow along his finger. His jaw tightened as he drew the fletching back to his ear. Focus, breathe, and…

His body rocked with a scream that rang across the courtyard. The two boys spun as one toward the Inner Tower and the cries of alarm as guards rushed toward the enclosed gallery where Lana sequestered Pria away for her daily lessons. Janu's feet were racing before his mind told his hands to drop the bow and it clattered beneath his feet, nearly tripping him. He could hear footsteps behind and knew that Mian and Aanor followed.

Guards leapt back as he crashed through the door to the gallery, his eyes immediately seeking Pria but instead finding Lana crouched on the floor. He couldn't tear the scowl from his face as he stormed toward her, every muscle rigid. Sitting on the ground, quivering under Lana's hand, was Pria.

"What happened." It came out a growl but he couldn't soften it. Losing your temper with a priestess was a fool's venture, but he was far beyond reason.

Lana glanced back at him, her face insufferably cold and calm. "Just an accident, nothing to worry about."

Something white-hot raged up inside him. "An accident?"

"Everything is fine, Janu." Pria's broken whisper drifted up to him. She was curled with her hands in her lap, her head down. "I'll be okay."

"Tell me what happened!"

The room around him froze as his words echoed back at him. Lana stood, the picture of grace and patience, and faced him with frosty confidence. "I am not a tutor, young man. Accidents will happen."

Mian pushed past him and helped Pria to her feet. Her hands were curled into claws and colored the red of raw flesh. Lana never dropped his gaze as she laid her hand on Mian's shoulder. "Take her to her room and see that she is comfortable. I will follow shortly."

A childhood fear of the high priestess crept into his chest but he forced it away. He needed everything he had to fight her and he couldn't give her that advantage. "That looks like more than an accident."

"Magic is a dangerous pastime."

Janu's eyes trailed Mian as he led Pria from the room before returning to the high priestess, who stood composed before him. "I demand a better answer than that!"

He heard Lord Aanor step to his shoulder, a large mountain of a man though Janu had never seen him stand up to Lana before. "High Priestess, Prince Janu asks for nothing more than the reassurance that you are guiding our beloved Pria in the safest way possible. I do not think that it is too much to ask."

Janu felt a warmth spread through his chest, grateful. Lord Aanor and his wife had welcomed Janu and Pria with kindness and compassion upon their return to the Seat. Despite the crushing pain in his chest from the loss of his parents, his time with Lord Aanor and Lady Mesha had been pleasant. They had put every effort into making Pria and Janu feel loved. Lady Mesha made them their favorite sweets and Lord Aanor took him hunting and Pria riding. They weren't his parents, and they never could be, but they were kind and he couldn't help but like them. Now, standing as a wall against the impenetrable Lana, Janu realized he loved the man.

Lana studied them both for such a long time he was sure she was going to refuse them; it was within her right. Priestesses were called counselors and advisors, but it was all just for show. Lana was under no obligation to follow his commands. That was something his father had imparted to him before his death: A priestess chose whether she wanted to obey or not. At the time he hadn't believed him but now, staring into eyes of stone, he knew them to be true.

The blink was slow and deliberate. "Prince Janu, I have told you before, magic is not something one makes a hobby of. It takes focus and discipline that a child of Pria's age does not come by naturally. We were trying a simple technique that backfired because I didn't notice that she became distracted. I have told you before: She will soon outgrow my abilities to protect her in this. She *needs* the Lorien."

He felt that old fear leap up in his chest, the monster of loneliness tear into his heart. He could see the acknowledgment of that fear in her face, in the softening of her jaw.

"Until then, we must all anticipate accidents."

She turned and left them staring after her.

Mian winced as he submerged Pria's angry red hands into the basin of water. Her face was tight and, if he hadn't known her, he might be convinced that she was fine. But the very tightness that would suggest she was fine told him her level of pain. Her face was usually a map of emotion. She was mimicking Lana's cool exterior and it bothered him more than it should.

"Lana should be here soon," he said just to fill the awkward silence. He hated that too; there never used to be awkwardness between them. He could feel her confiding more in Lana, pulling away from him. It was subtle now, but it would only get worse. He couldn't expect her to always look to him, but the thought of that loss ate at his heart.

"I'm not worried." Her small fingers straightened and curled in the water, tinging it pink. "It hurts but Lana will know what to do."

"What happened?"

She hitched a shoulder. "I didn't listen well enough," she said.

"A pertinent lesson for next time." Lana glided into the door and secured it behind her. "Thank you, Mian, for staying with her."

He watched as she approached and felt as if he were the mouse to her cat. "I will always be there for Pria."

"That is good to know," Lana said as she perched on the bed beside them in a fluff of silk.

Pria shot him a warm smile but the moment faded as Lana pulled her scalded hands from the basin. Her head gave a curt dip. "As I suspected. You said *inderel* not *anderel*."

Pria deflated as Lana lowered her hand back into the basin. "I am sorry, High Priestess. I will try harder."

Lana waved her off as she dug into a satchel she had brought with her. "I should have made you repeat it before trying it. No harm came of it." She handed Mian a vial from the pack. "Rub it into her hands."

"No harm?" He could feel the heat of his words but he didn't rein them in; Lana had been good to her word of not punishing him. "I'd hate to see what you would call harm. And isn't the entire point of you tutoring her to keep her safe?"

Lana tapped the vail in his hand, cool in the face of his anger. She held the quiet until he began to work the salve into Pria's hand. "I tutor her so she can learn control. Her strength grows every day, and soon, nothing short of constant supervision will be needed to keep her safe."

Pria kept her eyes on his hands, not as confident in her mentor as she seemed. That small rebellion warmed his heart, showed him she wasn't lost to him yet.

"I am sorry I failed, High Priestess," Pria whispered.

"You only fail when you stop trying." Lana stood from the bed and straightened her robes. "All seems under control here, I must go and tend to the throne."

And just like that she was gone.

Gone leaving his Pria hurting.

She flexed the hand he was working on. The skin was pink from rubbing but the flesh had healed. He moved to the other hand with a new dab of salve.

"It's getting worse." She dropped the statement between them like a stone sending waves out toward shore.

He pulled her hands back to him, sure he had missed something. "Do they still hurt? I can run for Lana."

She slipped her hands from his grip and stared down at her cupped palms. "They don't hurt." A weight settled over her and he watched the age tick away in her face. "Things keep happening, Mian, things I can't control. This time it was me, but next time…"

"There won't be a next time because you'll have it figured out by then."

And he believed it. There was nothing she couldn't do. Confidence bloomed in her face, her shoulders, and she beamed up at him, convinced in his belief.

Pria's tongue sat trapped between her teeth as she stared at the stubborn candle stuck to the table with melted wax before her. She could do this, it was child's play. She'd done much more impressive feats with Lana's guidance; surely she could handle one candle! Five years of tutoring and she was still nothing more than a child chiseling away at a mountain. Never mind that she was a child; she was a ten-year-old on the road to becoming one of the greatest powers in all of Reia.

And she could do this.

She ignored the pain as her teeth bit harder into her tongue and her eyes dried as she stared at the wick jutting out of the wax.

It. Would. Burn.

A tingling started at the very tips of her fingers, but she ignored it. Breath eased out through her nostrils as she coupled the force of inner strength with an inciting note. The tingling intensified into a mild ache but her eyes remained focused on the wick and the almost imperceptible finger of smoke trailing up from it. She jerked her hands back as the fire leapt into being and she reveled in her creation. The flame was tiny, barely sustaining itself in the breeze of her own breath, but it was hers.

A quick glance at her fingers revealed reddened skin, nothing she hadn't experienced before, and her body inflated with accomplishment. She had done it by herself, with no aid from Lana. The woman was mad thinking she needed to go to the Lorien when she was obviously needed here. But this tiny flame, so proud and fragile, was her proof that she didn't need the Lorien and she couldn't wait to shove it in Lana's face.

She jerked as an acrid stench singed her nostrils. Where was that coming from?

Her eyes popped wide and her jaw dropped open as she turned to the room behind her. Or what was left of it.

Behind her was a shamble. Furniture smoldered, edges still being consumed by flames invisible to the naked eye. A stuffed chair was reduced to a black skeleton of ash beside the window, the bed a heap of glowing debris. The air was thick with smoke and soot darkened everything.

Her chest protested the fouled air and she hacked as she rushed to the window and threw up the casement. Sweet, cold air rushed in to dilute the smoke, but it wasn't enough. She had to clear the room. She gulped a lungful of air and ran for the balcony doors, swinging them wide. The cross breeze pulled the cloud from the room. That was better, but what to do about the mess?

She stood in the center of the room as the smoke swirled past her. Her bed was destroyed, the chair was a loss. Her shoulders slumped; there was no way to hide this.

Even as the thought settled on her, a knock rang through the room and she froze. Panic seized her in a vice. How could she explain this?

The knock came again. "Pria? Are you in there?"

She was doomed. "Yes, Lady Mesha." She slumped to the door and pulled it open, eyes inspecting her shoes.

Mesha's gasp sent a quake through her body. "What happened here? Are you okay?" She rushed into the room and cast around for any active flames but only ash and embers remained. She spun back to face Pria. "Pria? Are you all right?"

Pria shrugged, not daring to lift her eyes. "I…had an accident."

"An accident!" Mesha shouted. Mesha never shouted; she was a quiet woman unless Mian and Janu got her riled up. She sputtered for a moment. "The room is in shambles! It's destroyed!"

Pria's chest constricted as words fled her tongue. Traitorous tears burned behind her eyes and along her nose as she stared up at this woman who wasn't her mother. Mesha had no obligation to keep her at the Seat. If Mesha decided the magical little sister of the prince was too much to handle, Pria would find herself on the first transport to the Lorien before she could say boo. Her hands trembled against her thighs as she stared up into her irate guardian's eyes.

Only, she didn't look that irate. After a moment of standing in silence, Mesha's face softened. She held a hand out to Pria. "Come, let's get you cleaned up and we'll find someone to clean this mess."

"And tell Lana," Pria said.

Mesha paused. "We shall see."

Mian scratched at his neck as he surveyed the groomed forest around him. It could hardly hold the title, though; the fenced-in patch of trees was more like an overgrown garden than a forest. It was Lord Huran's private hunting grounds at the edge of Austeria, a town to the west and up into the mountains. He stocked the garden himself to provide sport and feed his city's needy. A rash of attacks spanning from Amber Keep to nearly the Seat itself had them huddled down in this poor excuse for wilderness. Being out in a real forest beyond defensive walls was out of the question.

Nestled among the foothills of the Guardians, Austeria was well protected from any grinlo threat. Despite that, he was surrounded by a contingent of twenty soldiers in full armor. They were here for one reason: to protect Pria during her training. Though what she was doing was beyond him. The girl in question stood an arm's length away, eyes closed, hands spread before her. Today was her eleventh birthday, and unlike any normal child of a royal line, she was spending it training.

They had been in Austeria for almost a week, attending banquettes in honor of Janu and Pria and discussing trade and defenses. Pria and Lord Huran's young daughter Narita had sparked a fast friendship. The two had terrorized the castle every moment since. Mian had actually spent hours looking for them before they could come to the forest. He'd found the girls sequestered in the stables, conspiring and slipping treats to the horses. After several minutes of playful ribbing, Pria finally allowed herself to be pulled from her new friend's company.

Mian glanced up at the sun over his shoulder, just visible as a bright patch through the foliage. "Are we going to stand here until the forest dies around us?"

One blue eye cracked open to shoot a hostile glare toward him. "You are breaking my concentration."

He nodded. "Right." He glanced back up at the sun. "It's just that we've been out here for hours and all I've seen you do is stand there with your hands out."

She spun on him full this time, fists balled on her hips. He did love to see her angry, his tiny little tempest. "Standing here with my hands out? *Standing here with my hands out!*" She screamed up at him, anger boiling out of her frustration, hands clawed before her. "Do you have any idea how hard it is to track a magical trace? Hmm, do you? Well it's not easy, I'll tell you that!" She spun back toward the trees, grumbling under her breath. "It was hard enough in the castle, but there is so much out here, so much wanting my attention."

With a shrug, Mian pulled an apple from his pack and crunched into it. Silly girl could stand out here all day and starve if she wanted to, but he'd be a fool if he would. He took a second bite and Pria's scream snapped across the forest like a whip.

"Are you serious? Could you chew any louder?"

They stared at each other as the silence stretched around them. Mian leaned over her and crunched another bite directly in her face. "Guess I can."

Her eyes narrowed and darkened as she stood her ground. She wouldn't flinch, would never back down.

Janu crossed his arms as Lana chose a comfortable place on a soft patch of moss. She dropped to the ground and took a moment to arrange her silks. "There is something you wish to say?"

He turned his back to her and stared off into the trees. All of the soldiers with them today were guarding Pria. He was the only guard with Lana and he had the strong and unsettling feeling that she had some plan for him. It would be just like her to pull him out here to corner him on some issue. She was always looking for some way to face him, usually on the subject of sending Pria to the Lorien. Every accident, every important meeting, every chance she got she reminded him that Pria was destined for the Lorien.

"I don't have anything to say," he said.

He glanced over his shoulder at her but she wasn't looking at him. Was that a ploy? Was she trying to draw him out? He straightened. He wouldn't give in to her.

"I am not your enemy."

His shoulders spasmed. "I never said you were." He didn't turn back to her, wouldn't give in to her.

"But you act like I am," she said.

He let his anger bore into the tree trunk before him. "I am quite aware of your importance to my kingdom."

The breath hissed from her lungs. "Your kingdom, but not you."

He turned back to her, his anger only fanned by her calmness. "I don't know what you want from me, Lana."

She studied his face for so long he wasn't sure she was going to answer him. Then, as he watched, her shoulders slumped and her calm face melted into a resigned exhaustion. She patted the ground beside her. "Come sit, Janu."

Still shocked by the revelation of her inner emotion, Janu stood frozen.

"Please."

The mossy ground was more comfortable than he expected, but did little to lessen his discomfort. Lana had never shown any cracks in her façade to him before and it was jarring. After a moment, she began. "Janu, I am sorry that I took for granted that we would have more time to bond together before you took the throne. It was a mistake on my part. Your sister takes so much of my time, always has, that I neglected to focus on our relationship, and it is a relationship that is vital."

He risked a glance at her face, expecting the icy priestess demeanor, but was caught in a rush of raw emotion. In a blink, his mouth went dry. He had no idea how to react to this. "I…" He had to swallow before he could continue. "I mean, you are my advisor, right? I have to trust you, don't I?" He felt trapped, locked in the force of her concern.

"But you do not," she said. "I presided over your birth, Janu, just as I presided over your father's. To heal the wound of his death, we must be as one. We must work as one."

He felt something crack within him: his view of the old antiquated vision of the high priestess. He had seen her without the mask now. He had been given a rare glimpse into the inner workings of one of the most powerful women in all of Reia. And that glimpse had shown him an enormous burden and a fear of not being able to bear it.

White-hot rage consumed Pria's mind as she stared up at the irritating green-eyed man before her. Why couldn't he understand the level of scrutiny she was under? If she didn't start showing marked improvement, she would be shipped off to the Lorien, locked up there for years in training. Away from her home, while her family protected the border without her. Years where she could lose the only family she had left. And what was he doing but distracting and irritating her! Distracting her from what could be the most important—

The anger evaporated like mist as her senses caught on something. Mian had noticed the change. "What's wrong?"

Her face lit up with wonder. "I know where they are."

She spun and left him slack-jawed as she headed off into the trees straight toward Janu and Lana. If someone would have asked her what it was she was following, she would not have been able to answer them. She couldn't even form some type of impression in her own mind of what she was following, there was just something pulling her along. Lana had talked to her about where this task was leading, to her attempting to sneak up on the more experienced woman, but with a halo of clanking, armor-clad soldiers tromping through the underbrush and Mian at their head, she couldn't sneak up on a corpse.

She didn't see why she needed so many guards; they were in a fenced-in park inside of walled-in Austeria. The chances of anything more than a sprained ankle happening to her here was about as likely as her sprouting wings and flying to the Lorien. But none of those facts lessened the number of armed soldiers around her or freed her from Mian, who was sitting on her like an old mother hen. She was quite capable of taking care of herself.

But for now, she put all that from her mind. Let them hover. She had more important things to worry about.

In a hazy image at the back of her mind she could see Lana sitting in the underbrush, or what passed for underbrush in this groomed forest. Beside her, sitting in a patch of moss looking stubborn and cornered, sat Janu. A strange way for him to look, but Janu was strange around Lana. She'd tried to talk to him about it but he hadn't shared his worries about Lana to her in some time now. It had taken her a while to determine the difference, to realize that there was now something between them that remained unspoken. She wasn't sure why but all things to do with priestesses and magic were now off limits between them. It didn't make any sense, but the topic of it *not* being a topic was also off limits. Foolish, but true.

There were no cumbersome skirts for her today, not in the forest—and she was too young and inexperienced for the robes of the priestesses—so instead she wore a boy's breeches. Her brother's breeches, to be quite accurate, from when he was younger, and tailored to fit her. She was small even for her age, her legs little more than sticks. She didn't appear anything like the ladies of the court, like her mother had looked. They were all tall and beautiful with curves and swells that made their expensive dresses draw the eye of men. Beautiful dresses she had, and ladies in waiting to weave her hair into intricate patterns, but she was still slim and shapeless. It never used to bother her, not when she was younger and chasing around after her brother and Mian when she was incredibly sheltered from just about everyone else. What had really pulled her attention to the situation was seeing her brother and Mian notice other girls in the Seat. Pria had never had to fight for their attention before, and she hadn't appreciated the change. They were hers and everyone should have known that!

She had tried broaching the subject with both Lana and Lady Mesha but neither had been very helpful. Lana had told her that as a priestess, such concerns wouldn't matter to her and Lady Mesha had laughed and patted her on the head saying she would understand one day. But she didn't want to understand one day, the problem was here today. She glanced at one of the offenders as he hovered behind her now, unassuming and irritating. Who did he think he was not being at her beck and call? He caught her gaze and she screwed her face up in a glare as he shot her his characteristic grin. Like he was blameless in the whole situation.

It had even led to bickering. It felt like a wedge was working its way between them and she couldn't figure out how to broach it. Sometimes she thought that it was just how things went, that people grew apart as they grew older. The thought haunted her. There was nothing without Mian and Janu. They were her world.

She returned her attention to the task at hand. She would have to figure out the solution herself if no one would help her. She had always been told she was gifted; surely she would figure something out, just like she'd figured out how to find Lana hiding in this forest. Eventually it would just come to her, like so many other solutions. Not even Lana was sure how she did it. It was just a talent she had.

Janu could feel the force of Lana at his side. Despite the silence that had fallen between them, he knew that she was not finished—not until she got what she wanted. There was nothing he could think of that she hadn't gotten; it was just a matter of time.

He struggled to keep his eyes from her, his thoughts. He was just here to protect her, not to become her friend, not to cave in on his last holdout. He hadn't changed his mind; he still didn't see a reason for Pria to have to go to the Lorien. He could see her progression every day. Her talents grew, her knowledge expanded. Sure, there had been some accidents, but even Lana admitted there were accidents at the Lorien. Pria was destined to be a high priestess. Why would she go to the Lorien when the only living high priestess was right here in Trimera? It only made sense that she stay here, in Trimera, with Lana. With her family.

The problem was that he could see Pria's mind changing. He could argue with Lana, Mesha, even Aanor, but Pria was another matter. She had their father's temper, quick and sharp, but what was more dangerous was the pull she had over him. She had that pull over just about everyone she met. Maybe it was because she was a princess, maybe it was because she was destined to be a high priestess, he wasn't sure, but it was impossible to deny. Even Lana had succumbed to Pria from time to time, but not on the Lorien. Not on sending her away.

He glanced back at Lana as she sat looking innocent. "You've broken her, haven't you?"

She drew a deep breath. "If you mean I have convinced her of the need to enlist herself at the Lorien, yes, I have worked very hard to convince her of that fact."

He felt himself crumble inside. "That's it then, isn't it? I've lost."

"You haven't lost anything," she pressed. "This isn't some game to lose or win. I must focus my attention on the throne, on helping you. Pria needs constant attention, constant tutoring. Do you truly wish for me to turn my attention from Trimera to focus on Pria's training?"

He didn't have a response to that. It made him feel just as it should, like a child throwing a tantrum. Of course, he couldn't expect her to pull her attention from Trimera. His people had only them; Pria could have the entire Lorien to watch out for her. All he had to do was let go.

He was saved from having to respond as a sound caught their attention. In a handful of breaths, Pria herself crashed through the underbrush and burst into the clearing. She beamed with pride as her eyes landed on Lana sitting behind him.

"Ha!" she shouted, one fist pumped into the air.

Mian stumbled through the underbrush after her. "Good, we found them. Can we get out of this park now?"

Lana stood, composed. She dusted debris from her robes. "That was excellent, Pria." She turned her attention to Mian and the soldiers behind him. "We can indeed get out of this park now, young man."

Lana led Pria off through the trees trailed by the soldiers assigned to watch the princess. Mian held back with Janu as the soldiers disappeared among the trees.

"She's going, you know," Janu said as they watched the line of soldiers fade. "She's going to leave us."

Mian clapped a hand to Janu's shoulder. "Even if she does," he said, "she will come back. You know that. This is where she belongs, where her heart is."

A stream ran past the Seat. The stream's headwaters were at the base of Amber Keep, and from there, it ran through the countryside gathering small streams and brooks, dotted with villages and farms. Though the stream wasn't large—from the age of ten Janu had been able to leap its breadth—it managed to water the fields of the Seat. It wasn't truly large enough to have a name but that didn't stop some former ruling prince to name it the Jewel. Janu and Pria had spent many an afternoon in their childhood splashing among the rocks of the Jewel. Today wasn't for fun, though.

Seated on a rock at the stream's edge, his twelve-year-old sister dipped her toes in the water. She was a child, in truth, too young for the knowledge and expectations on her shoulders. They weren't alone—they were never alone—but they were in as much solitude as he could offer them. A group of soldiers ringed them led by Lord Aanor. The man himself was the closest of them and the only one within earshot.

Still, Janu hesitated.

He didn't want to start this conversation. There was no possibility that it would go his way and he didn't like starting out at a loss. He stood now staring off into the trees.

He leapt with a shout as water splashed into his back and soaked into his shirt. Pria's laughter sparked in the warm afternoon air as he turned back to face her accusingly.

"Are we going to sit out here all day or are you going to get to what you want to say?" she challenged, her eyes alight with amusement.

"You are a brat, you realize."

To this she promptly stuck her tongue out at him. She was like that, though. She didn't like to dance around anything. If it was worth worrying about, it was worth facing straight on. He shoved his hands in the pockets of his trousers. "You've sided with her, haven't you?"

There was no need to specify what he was talking about. "You know the answer to that," she said.

"I have to hear you say it," he pressed. "I have to know you have joined this insanity."

She pulled her feet from the water and slipped her satin shoes back on. "It isn't insanity, brother, and you know that." She stood and moved toward him. "We cannot be selfish in this. You need Lana's full attention; I need a full-time tutor. We cannot have both here."

"How can sending you away from the only other high priestess in existence help you learn?"

He watched as her body deflated. Her shoulders slumped and her head dropped. "Janu, I have learned so much from Lana," she said. "There is a great deal more that I can learn from her—neither of us will argue that. I will not, however, risk my home, my family… And I don't think if you really stop and think about it, that you want that either."

The statement hurt, as she knew it would. He knew it wasn't her intention to hurt him, just to shock him into seeing the truth. It left a pressure against his chest. Would he risk his kingdom, his citizens, all those lives just to hold on to the last vestige of his family? There was some selfish, childish part of him that wanted to say yes, that wanted to turn his back on his duty, on his responsibilities. He hadn't asked for this role in life. He hadn't chosen to be a ruling prince. Why should he be forced to sacrifice everything for these people? It wasn't fair, it wasn't right!

Righteous anger raged through his veins as he rounded to face Pria, but he stopped short. She watched him in silence, blue eyes so like their mother's. He saw her own worries plain across her face. All he was doing was losing his baby sister. In that moment he saw what *she* was facing, what *she* was losing. She was willing to walk away from the only things she had ever know, face the possibility of never coming home ever again. And he was the one afraid to let go.

He couldn't look into her eyes and tell her he wouldn't accept her sacrifice. All of his arguments froze in his throat and his worst fear was acknowledged. She had made the decision and there was nothing he could do to change it.

Pria held her breath as she stared at the parchment before her. She'd known it was coming, had been trying to prepare herself for the day it would arrive. But here she was, the letter to her destiny in hand, and it felt like the end of the world. She knew she had to go—there was no way around it—but now that the day was here all of her resolve drowned in a sea of terror. She wasn't ready for this. She was leaving her home and she would be alone.

It had been seven years since her parents' death and she was now a slim awkward twelve. Her years had been filled with training and classes and diplomats. Years to grow, though she remained petite. Mian and Janu loved to use her small size to pick on her, but she didn't mind—too much. Some destiny she had. Twelve years of having everyone dote over her like she was some kind of priceless treasure, endless lessons under the watchful eye of her mentor Lana…and none of it could make her ready for ten years being locked in the Lorien to become a priestess. How could it? The Silver City where the Lorien resided lay leagues to the south, much too far for any casual visits. With that and Lana's description of the workload she would be expected to maintain, she was sure not to see her family or friends much in the span.

The worst part, the thing she tried hard not to think about, was what would happen to her after her training at the Lorien. Everyone kept saying once she finished her training she would return like some conquering hero, but that wasn't how it worked. Lana had spent many of her classes ensuring she understood how unique and precious she was. It was meant to instill a sense of pride in her, warm her to the thought of becoming a high priestess, but she understood at a deeper level. Precious and rare meant she wouldn't be allowed to choose her future. She would be put where she was needed most, and Lana here meant this was where she was needed least. She wasn't foolish enough to believe they would assign two high priestesses to Trimera, no matter how important the station. Every step ahead of her would lead her further and further from her family.

Her eyes surveyed the room around her, situated on the top floor of the North Wing in the Seat. Her room. The stone walls were polished to gleam a light blue. The walls had been imported from a mine far to the north; there was nothing else like them in the entire kingdom. Her bed was draped with imported colorful gauzy cloth. A carved heavy vanity sat to the left wall with bottles of perfume, brushes, combs, and various other trinkets and bobs. All gifts, most untouched although she cherished them anyway. They were tokens of affection from her people; she wouldn't part with them even if she had no intention of using them. Her windows stood open to allow a fragrant breeze waft in from the East Garden. She sank into a thick, feather-stuffed mattress piled with colorful handmade quilts.

She had known for as long as she could remember that she was to be a high priestess, the strongest of their kind, of *her* kind. She stared down at her hands as they lay open on her lap. Somewhere in those veins flowed unimaginable power. The priestesses were tasked with studying to hone their power to guide and protect the citizens of the land. One day, she would be assigned to counsel a ruler and offer her magical protection to their lands and people. One day.

She threw her legs over the edge of the mattress and made her way to the vanity. On its corner sat a porcelain pitcher and basin. Her hands shook as she stretched toward the handle. A jolt rocketed out through her arm and leapt from her fingertips. She had a split second to gasp—and the entire pitcher exploded in a shower of sparks and splinters, dispersed among a cascade of water. She stood unmoving until the last of the pieces had clattered to the floor.

She pulled her hands back toward her with her eyes closed and spread her fingers wide, palms up, before she looked at them. She worked a porcelain shard from her palm and stared at the crimson that dripped from it. The rest of the basin spread around her in an arc—some pieces embedded in the wall, others scattered around the floor. Luckily only the one piece had found flesh.

The door flew open as a young lady came crashing in. "Pria, where have you been? You missed our archery lesson."

The daughter of the lord of Austeria and Pria's best friend, Narita was tall and beautiful, with long, sleek limbs muscled from weapons classes. The two had met years ago and wrote to each other constantly when they weren't together. With her hair braided down her back, Narita wore a green dress, narrow skirts divided for riding, though she wouldn't likely sit astride a horse today. Narita preferred the freedom of movement. It was a miracle she wasn't in breeches.

The girl saw the shattered pitcher, spun to face her. The color drained from her visage. "What happened?"

Pria waved at the shards around her. "Nothing. Just *another* accident." She glanced down at the stain of blood and shrugged. "Like every other day anymore."

Narita waved her off. "Lana said those would go away once your training is more structured." She offered Pria a hand as she picked her way out of the field of broken porcelain. "So why weren't you at practice?"

Pria lifted the parchment from a side table before dropping back onto the bed behind Narita. "My training is about to get very structured and I don't think I will be attending any more lessons."

"What are you talking about? You'll need all the practice you can get to keep yourself safe from the grinlo, *and* the boys."

"I got my summons from the Lorien." She held up the missive between them. "I have two weeks before I have to sign in." Pria's head rolled toward her, eyes searching the familiar expression of one of her dearest friends.

The blood rushed from Narita's countenance. "Oh." Narita broke her gaze and turned instead to the window. "I mean, I guess it had to happen sooner or later, didn't it?" She dropped into silence and the room around them grew heavy. She barked a laugh. "I'd like to say it would be better if we had more time, but I don't think time is the true issue, is it?"

Pria spread her arms. "I've had my entire life to get ready for it and it's not helping me right now."

Narita's head bobbed in a nod. "Has Janu heard?"

Pria shook her head before standing and crossing the room. "I just found out today. He's not going to take it well."

Narita sat forward, her expression serious and impassioned. "Surely he understands." She swept a hand toward the shattered crockery. "I don't think you need to be any expert in magic to realize you need more training than you are getting." She laughed. "Fool man acts like he'll never see you again!"

Pria felt a twinge of guilt as she let her friend believe the lie. There was no reason to make her departure any more painful than it already was. She would bear this one burden herself. "He still thinks I will overcome the 'mishaps' as he calls them, but I can't keep living like this. Without the Lorien I might well grow to become a bigger danger in the Seat than all the horde combined!"

"Are you saying you want to go?"

Pria traced the slice in her palm. "What I want doesn't matter, I have to go. Besides, it is what Mother and Father wanted for me. How can I turn down what the Lorien can give me?"

Narita's eyes blinked wide. "Well, then, I guess—"

The door flew open again, spilling a wave of noise and commotion as Janu and Mian burst in. The two boys—now young men—had both grown tall and lanky and were even more inseparable now that they were practically brothers. Atop Janu's temples sat a golden crown, a tasteful piece. She hadn't seen him without one for a few years now. "Where is my baby sister?"

Pria crossed her arms as he rounded on her. "Now what are you two up to?"

Mian smiled devilishly. "When are we ever up to anything?"

She tried to fight the smile that bloomed across her face but failed as she always did. "When you are breathing."

They laughed as they joined Narita on the bed. "So, what is the agenda for the day?"

"Packing and goodbyes." All four jumped as Lana suddenly appeared in the doorway and shut the door behind her.

Pria closed her eyes. "I have two weeks," she pleaded.

"You will need those two weeks to travel and get settled. I will be accompanying you."

Janu was on his feet. "Accompanying her where?"

Lana was unfazed in the face of his anger. "Pria has been entered in the lists; it is time for her to begin her training."

"Training? But…already?" His voice lost all strength and returned to a slight boyish plea.

"You knew that this day would come," Lana said. "Her training starts in two weeks; to make in on time, we'll be leaving before the day is out."

Mian rushed to Pria's side. "You said you wouldn't take her, not until she was ready! You promised."

Lana drew a deep calming breath. "I did promise, and she is ready. She has had time to mature, and if we let her continue for much longer without training, she will become a danger. Her future lies at the Lorien. I suggest you take this time to say your goodbyes," Lana said and turned to leave, likely to begin her own packing and preparations.

Pria let Mian's presence ease her worries, as it always did. She let her mind fill with the knowledge that he would face down the world for her. Let her heart be comforted with the confidence that were she to ask, he would stand down Lana. Janu and he would guard her like one of the knights from Lady Mesha's fairytales and she could stay here forever. She would live safe and protected just like those princesses, dressed up like some doll. Well, at least until she pulled the fortress down around them. She'd never understood the princesses in those stories anyway; she'd always wanted to be the knight—they got to have all the fun. But none of that was her tale. She was no ordinary princess, and this was no fairytale world.

He tightened his grip on her. "I don't care what she thinks; you are not going anywhere."

Janu nodded emphatically. "That's right. Lana is just my high priestess, she has no right to command me. How much danger can you really be?"

With a heavy sigh, Pria broke from Mian's embrace and smoothed her visage. "Lana is right. The Lorien is the only place where I can learn to control my power."

Janu waved a hand around him. "You can control it now!" he yelled, his voice cracking with his irrational conviction in the face of contradiction. This was not a ruling prince arguing a point, this was a brother desperate to stop the inevitable.

She gave him a flat glare. "You call this control? Last week I flung a server out a window. That isn't control, Janu." Drawing a slow breath, she said, "I have to do this before I really hurt someone. This is the road before me, and I must take it."

Janu's eyes were wide with pain. "I don't want you to go."

"Your place is here, Janu. You must honor Father and reign as prince."

"While you go off on your own?"

"I'll manage," she said.

Mian stared at her. "And just who is going to look out for you at this Lorien?"

Pria met his pain with open amusement. For all his mischief, Mian was fiercely protective of her. "I won't need looking out for; there won't be any fiendish boys to lead me into trouble at the Lorien."

His brow furrowed. "Where is the fun in that?"

Narita was on her feet in a blink, arms tight around her friend. "Pri, I miss you already!" She reached into her pocket and pulled out a tiny bag, pressing it into Pria's palm. "I got this this morning for your birthday, but as you won't be here for it…"

Pria returned her friend's warm embrace. "Thank you, Narita. I will cherish it always."

Narita rushed from the room, hands to her face to hide her tears.

Janu snatched a vase and lobbed it across the room into the fireplace. "This isn't right! They can't do this!" She could see the rage pouring through him, fueling every jerk and movement. Her brother hated being in a helpless situation, and this was one he could feel evaporating through his fingers. There was nothing rational in his face.

Pria stared at the shattered pottery as it scattered about the floor and mixed with the pieces from her basin. "Janu, Mother bought that vase in Schtadd; it was over a thousand years old."

He glared at her. "I don't care about any stupid vase! How can you be so calm about this?"

"Because I know this is what must happen," she said, "and so do you. I've always known I would have to leave—Mother and Lana have been grooming me for this since my birth."

Mian jerked her back into his arms. Stubbornly fighting the tears in his eyes, he kissed her ear. His grip loosened as he slid his hands up to her cheeks and pressed his forehead to hers. "Come back to me."

She smiled up at him. "Always."

He forced a laugh. "You always did have more courage than sense."

"Like you're one to talk."

Mian glanced behind him at Janu and shot her one last brilliant grin before leaving them alone.

Janu rubbed his mouth. "I can't believe you are just going along with this."

She spread her arms wide. "What would you have me do, Janu? Squander my abilities so I can stay home? Deny Mother and Father's hopes and wishes for me because they are inconvenient? This has always been the path before me; I have known it for as long as I can remember. I am no longer a child, Janu. I cannot ignore the increasing danger I pose to those around me."

"And we are just supposed to go on without you?"

"You have always been strong, Janu, you will find a way."

Janu's body slumped as his jaws corded with tension. "I hate her for doing this."

Pria sat on the bed staring up at him. "Don't do that. Lana does what she does because that is what must happen. It is her duty, always has been. Sometimes it is unpleasant or unpopular, but she must have the strength and the knowledge to do what is right and what must be done…and so must I. So must we all. As the children of royalty, we have been born with more burden than most will ever know, and we must be strong for it."

He coughed a laugh. "*Burden*? I thought we were born to privilege," he said, voice dripping sarcasm.

"Privilege comes with a price, my brother, and this is the price of mine."

"Lana told me once that we would never be lost to each other, that our connection would never be cut no matter the distance." His eyes were filled with the emotion that heated his words.

"Of course it won't. You will always be my brother, Janu." She hugged him tight, her heart aching with anticipation. "But for now, we have to be apart. I will always be there for you." She pulled from his arms and turned her back to him. "I need to pack."

He stood; she didn't need to tell him she would prefer to be alone. "I'll see you off. Please don't leave before I can do so."

"I will wait for you."

The bitter wind was cold as Pria sat atop her tall mount. It whipped the trees that lined the Kylian Road as it ran south toward Kyneira. Snow-topped mountains circled all around her like sentinels. Clouds ringed the sky, but not dark enough to promise any precipitation. The sun warmed her shoulders as soldiers milled around her. Behind her loomed the Seat itself, her family's fortress stronghold, the military and ruling center of Trimera. Stone spires reached for the sky topped with her family's crest. Guards lined the parapets and bridges, all polished in their ceremonial uniforms. All the high lords and ladies in their finest lined the courtyard, a rainbow of colors in the latest fashion.

Her honor guard buzzed around her, each atop a fiery charger with lances streaming gold and black. Pria's own mount was a leggy mare with a fine arched neck and slim fetlocks. Though she wore dusty traveling clothes, her best dresses were packed in a chest chained to a wagon in the procession behind them. Lana was in a linen priestess suit, her own pristine silks on the cart as well. The soldiers lined the courtyard awaiting Lana's command, heavily armed.

Pria glanced behind her and met her family's eyes: Janu, Narita, Mian, each face determined not to show fear or pain as they stood at the head of the stairs that led to the portcullis. They were being strong for her. She straightened her back and worked a smile across her visage as Lana patted her hand. "It is time, Pria."

Her heart leapt into her throat and fluttered there like a suffocating fish. In her entire life she had never been out of Trimera, never even past Kyneira. Now she was going all the way to the Silver City, in the heart of Krenalyn. She worked free the lump in her throat and swallowed. She was sure her eyes were the size of saucers in her face, not exactly the cool calmness that Lana was so good at exuding.

Pria closed her eyes and drew a deep breath as she faced the road ahead of her. There was nothing else for it. Her fingers drifted to the trinket around her neck, the contents of the package from Narita. It pulsed a warmth across her body, the feel of love. A heartstone was thought to absorb the strength of affection one feels so that the power of that emotion could be transferred to its object. Lana must have ordered it for her from the Lorien.

"I'm ready."

THE SPACE BETWEEN

At the southern edge of the Frontier, at Trimera's northernmost point, sat Amber Keep. The Keep itself was named after the largest pass in the Guardian Mountains that separated Trimera from the Frontier. There were a handful of other passes spanning the length of the Frontier, but the only passage big enough for more than a handful of bodies was Amber Pass.

Amber Keep itself was a fortress with no pretense. No runners graced the hallways, no decorations drew the eye. There was no room for frivolity here. The man walking its halls couldn't have matched it better; Lord Renor was a warrior with no pretense. Other than the family crest adorning his breastplate and the knot of rank on his shoulder, his armor was plain. The gray of his beard proclaimed his age proudly. Old age was an achievement in Amber Keep, one not granted to the weak or careless. Raids were common this far north and everyone partook in defense. All citizens from toddler to crone were prepared to take up arms. Amber Keep would give every last life in her defense. The border would be protected.

The horde had broken her defenses before but they had always pushed them back. There was not a soul alive in Amber Keep that didn't know someone taken by the beasts. He had been ten when a raid had breached the city walls. As the oldest child not already serving as a soldier, he had been put in charge of protecting the other children. He had worked with blade and bow and staff for as long as he could remember.

The children had been gathered together into one of the cellar chambers with a large bolted door. It was dank, dark, and the sound of running water could be heard over the children's hushed and muffled breathing. Despite being so sequestered, the grinlo had stumbled onto them. It wasn't till later in his life, following a visit by High Priestess Lana, that it was revealed one of the children sequestered in that room was destined to become a priestess. It was the scent of that one magical child that had revealed the room's location and prompted the attack.

His knuckles were white on the hilt of the overly large dagger that served as his sword. A handful of children around him stood ready with whatever weapons were available. None stood without fear, but all would stand. Duty had been drilled into them with every meal, every lesson, every sunrise. They would stand and protect those weaker than them. Feet spread in a sturdy stance, they held their line as the door rocked and splintered.

He had killed his first grinlo that day. He and the other children had held until the soldiers had arrived to push the horde back. It had felt like years in that room, his arms burning from exertion, the children behind their line crying. The sight of his dead friends haunted his nightmares for years. That hadn't been the last invasion to breach the walls at Amber Keep, but they had always pushed them back.

His path took him past arrow slits and portcullises, murder holes in the ceiling and reinforced doors to strongholds. The temperature increased—but never to be considered warm—as he climbed floor upon floor toward the battlements on the roof. The rooms in the Keep were each outfitted with oversized fireplaces but they barely warmed the spaces. Life at Amber Keep was not for the soft.

He had to put all his weight into opening the door to the rooftop. The hinges in Amber Keep were only greased to the point of function, and the door groaned as it opened. A little inconvenience allowed for enough edge to warn of any passing.

Eyes turned toward him as he made it through the door. The soldiers turned back to the parapets as the door swung shut behind him, ever vigilant for danger. He joined his men at the parapets as they scanned the land below them.

A frigid wind snapped his cloak as it howled past through the turrets and parapets. Below him stretched the uninterrupted span of the entire estate around the Keep. Groomed and cleared, much of the land was cultivated for crops and livestock to support the fortress. Livestock spread across the rolling countryside. In the event of attack, the livestock were moved within the walls to stables that lined the outer city. Animals that couldn't get collected in time were left to run free.

Among the livestock, soldiers patrolled with the celebrated Amber hounds, massive beasts with heavy coats used for everything from guarding livestock to taking down grinlo. They had been bred by his ancestors for generations and were used as an early warning system.

Renor turned from the battlement, intent to continue his rounds, when a chorus of deep-throated barks broke across the roof. He leapt back to the waist-high wall and leaned out to catch sight of the commotion. He couldn't see any reason for the uproar, but even as he caught sight of the braying dogs, more took up the war cry. An older officer rushed to his side to take his command.

"Orotid, sound the watch," Renor said.

He kept his eyes to the forest while Orotid rushed to sound the watch. The alarm system had multiple levels: all clear, warning, watch, attack, and retreat. The air around them cracked with three sharp, short blasts from a brass horn. Around them, guards and officers took up the call, and the air reverberated with the echoing trumpets and chorus of dogs. In the fields, the shepherds gathered their flocks, ready to head to the gate at the slightest call. The warning call faded into the surrounding land and left a pregnant silence.

The battlement had changed from constant vigilance to intense scrutiny. Renor scanned the empty span between the fortress and the forest. Despite an ever-increasing line of snarling hounds, no sign of a threat appeared.

A full seven-second blast sounded out from the north parapet. The call was picked up on the battlement.

Renor raced toward the northern face of the Keep, his armor clanking. He slid into the guard wall beside the soldiers there. Below, hundreds of grinlo poured from the treeline. He gasped at the sight. Just a hundred yards away from the grinlo, the soldiers and shepherds rushed the livestock toward the gates.

Renor snatched up a spare bow and a handful of arrows then returned to the battlements. "Open fire! Give our citizens time to reach safety!" He drew the arrow to his jaw and let it fly toward the advancing army. A series of *thwacks* marked the flight of arrows around him. Breaths passed as a second barrage took flight and a third before bodies fell in the advancing army.

He smacked a palm onto the top of the guard wall in triumph. These men knew their job, so he must do his. He was running, passing citizens rushing for shelter or preparing defenses, when he realized someone was on his heels. He glanced back, but he knew who would be there. Orotid would not leave his side until the danger passed. He was a good man, sharp and experienced.

When they made the ground floor, the last of the livestock were filtering in with the soldiers close behind. Soldiers rushed forward to secure the gates. The gates clanked closed and the roar of the moving mass was increased with clanks and rattle as soldiers worked to affix the locks and braces.

The courtyard drained as the livestock were moved on toward the pens. Lord Renor shared a glance with Orotid at his side. Now they waited.

Pria couldn't help but feel like a giant target as all eyes fixed on her. Her first day of transmuting and everyone was watching her. Transmuting had its dangers and Pria was young to start learning the discipline. The tutor at the head of the class studied her with cautious excitement. Her fellow students watched with the abject hope to see her fail. She didn't blame them for it; classes were competitive and placement depended on performance. It didn't help that she was the youngest in the class at fifteen, a full four seasons younger than any other pupil.

When she had first arrived at the Lorien, she'd been told her training should have started at a younger age. Many of the other girls and a couple of the occasional boys that graced the halls picked on her for it. But as the weeks passed and she tested out of class after class, the rude comments and teasing words faded away. Not that they had bothered her; she wasn't here to impress the rabble. She was here to learn.

This class was a guided tutorial. The tutor walked the room, assisting each girl as she came to her. Pria had yet to learn the tutor's name but she had seen her around. The tutor was not a full priestess, just a higher-ranking student, but no tutors were allowed to teach transmutation without being close to graduation. The woman before her was nearly thirty, with black hair tied in a neat tail and sharp eyes that weighed Pria to the ounce.

"Pria, are you ready?" The woman stood directly before her.

All eyes swiveled to her.

"Yes, tutor."

Pria didn't need instruction; she'd studied the process in theory for a month before being allowed to join the class. Every student was required to.

On the desk before her sat a polished stone. Unremarkable and downright boring, it was what the stone represented that made her heart race. Transmutation was the first truly complex magic a student was allowed to attempt.

And she was ready.

The room grew silent as she picked the stone from the desk and tucked it into her palm. It was cool and slick within her hand.

"Now don't be discouraged if you don't get it the first time. I don't know that any student in the last twenty years has!" The tutor's words were meant to be encouraging but Pria could hear the snickering around her. She blocked it out, it did nothing for her.

The tutor cupped her hands around Pria's fist and magic sparked along her skin. It was a led demonstration. The tutor held the spell, Pria had to copy the magic, add the tutor's to hers, and then act it upon the stone. Lana had done similar in the Seat before she left for the Lorien.

The transmutation spell was an intricate weave, but that didn't worry her. She felt the spell against her skin and began the exercise to mimic it. Tones whispered past her ears, pulling at her mind, her heart, her soul. She drew the tones from the air using her own resonance, a note that only her heart knew. She started with the highest note, snagging it from the twisting mass the tutor had generated. She sank the notes into the stone, setting it vibrating in her palm. Next she drew a note near the middle, letting it tangle with the first note. She continued like this one tone at a time until all were pulsing within the stone in her palm.

She cupped her free hand over her fist. A pulse deep in her belly crashed up toward the stone through her arm. The stone grew warm in her hand, then hot as more power poured into it. Her face twisted from the pain as her hand flew open.

The stone was gone.

Her eyes turned toward the desk at the front of the room, where the stone sat, plain and boring, still pulsing with the glow of magic. Pride and accomplishment warred across her face as whispers bounced around the room.

Pria's eyes lifted to the tutor, who stared openmouthed at her empty palm. She blinked a few times as if trying to clear her vision. "You did it."

The buzz in the room increased as everyone turned to stare incredulously at the stone. The fire of accomplishment burst from her chest as she met the tutor's stunned gaze.

"Let me try again, I can do it faster," she said.

Renor felt the strain in his back as the crossbeam finally lifted above the braces of the door. No one would call him a young man by any stretch of the imagination and the constant strain of battle wouldn't let him forget it. The crossbeam slammed into place and the handful of soldiers that had been helping him lift it collapsed against the barricade in relief.

They had already lost the courtyard and inner wall. Every inch the grinlo gained the soldiers of Amber Keep made them pay for in blood. He had never seen such a push before. Their numbers seemed endless. What could they possibly gain that could balance such an effort? The grinlo didn't live in buildings. What would they want with the Keep?

The men around him jumped back as a loud crash announced the advance of the horde to the latest stronghold. Renor did a mental tally of the lives lost, the strength of the doors remaining between the horde and the citizens of the Keep. He didn't like what they pointed to. He scanned the soldiers around him, boys mostly. Good soldiers, strong, to be sure, but few with any true leadership skills. Then his gaze landed on Orotid. Gray with years, the man had more experience than any soldier the Keep had to offer. Renor wasn't quite ready to command a retreat; for now all were safer within the fortress than attempting to flee across the countryside, but he was desperate enough to send up the warning.

"Orotid!" he barked.

The man was at his side in a blink. "My Lord?"

Renor had to steel himself for what would come next. It wasn't retreat, but he couldn't lie to himself that it wasn't the last step before. "I need you to take word to Prince Janu at the Seat."

The muscles in Orotid's face contorted. He knew the implications of such an order. "Sir?"

"Take what you have seen here. Travel as fast as your body can take you." Lord Renor swallowed a lump that had mysteriously appeared in his throat. "We will not be far behind."

The cloud of knowledge darkened both their faces. "I will bring aid."

"You will provide your prince with whatever knowledge he needs and you will heed whatever commands he gives," Renor said.

He watched the conflict play across the older man's face. In better times Orotid would have argued, railed against being sent on an errand when swords were needed to protect his home. Finally, his face settled on resolve. "I will provide what data I can."

"Gather whatever supplies you need and leave before nightfall. The dark will cover your passage." Orotid's shoulders slumped as Renor continued, "We'll hold as long as we can, give the evacuation time to gain ground." A tremor worked its way along his spine and settled like a stone in the pit of his stomach. The words were out now, there was no denying it. He could see the blow on Orotid's face.

"I will not let you down, sir."

Orotid was gone in a blink and Renor had the terrible fear that he had made an awful mistake. How could he allow a seasoned sword to leave in the midst of a siege? It was too late to change his mind now. Now, he had an evacuation to organize.

Orotid crouched as he crested the low rise. The gelding stood ground tied a few yards away, hidden among the trees. He had slipped from the Keep at dusk, one lone man and his gelding sneaking off into the dark along a path meant for women and children. There was nothing brave about it, but then bravery was for foolish boys, not seasoned soldiers. He did as he was told. It had taken a full day to make his way along the canyon path, slowly, to mask any noise and avoid drawing the attention of the creatures besieging his home. It had given him plenty of time in his own mind. Coming to terms with the real reason he was chosen. Lord Renor couldn't afford to lose a younger soldier, but the message had to be sent. When he had made the first path to get out of the canyon, Orotid had turned the gelding toward a small town in the direction of the road. He could see the vultures circling for miles over the rolling hills of northern Trimera.

The first bird hadn't raised his ire much; vultures were pretty common and from far away they were hard to distinguish from hawks. As he rode closer, their numbers grew and after several hours he could no longer fool himself in thinking they were anything but vultures. As he crouched now with the small village of Ler spread out below him, the ominous cloud of carrion eaters grew his anxiety to a raging inferno.

A stomach-churning mixture of burnt meat and rot clawed at the air even from this distance. His gut and its precarious grasp on his noon meal begged him to go no further, but his conscience couldn't let him just walk away. He had to be sure. If even one person was left alive, he was duty bound to help them and warn them to evacuate.

He pulled a rag from his coat and cast around him among the plants and grasses. In a few moment he had a tiny packet of sweet-smelling wild flowers and crushed mint. He knotted the rag into a pouch and pressed it to his nose. A test inhale filled his head with the soft gentle scent overlaid with the pungent mint. It would have to do. Crouched low, he crept toward the outermost building, a curing shed.

The slope was gentle but he took it carefully, each foot well secured before adding weight to it. It did good to keep him from falling and made his passage as quiet as possible. The grass shushed against his breeches and filled the air with a gentle rustling. The blood pounded in his ears as his throat was coated with the acrid tinge of ash. The eerie silence was broken only by the screech of the vultures. No sounds of voices, no sound of work rang across the fields or houses, not even livestock.

Eternity passed with his heart in a frantic race before he made the curing shed. Breath staggered into his chest as he allowed himself a moment to rest against the rough wooden planks. No sound came from within the building. Courage gathered, he crept along the wall until he reached the corner. He peeked around the edge of the building and swept the inner city beyond for any signs of movement, but the village remained frozen.

A sturdy if rudimentary wall surrounded the houses at the center of the village. The outer buildings were workshops, stores, storage. Basic necessities like livestock could be moved within the wall in the event of a raid. The paths between the buildings were cleared and lined with harvested riverstone. His soled boots were loud against the stones, louder than he would have liked. He increased his effort to soften his steps as he progressed.

A handful of vultures watched him from the guard wall, wings spread in a warning. He came up short as a wall of putrid stench slapped into him with the wind change. He struggled to keep his knees from buckling. His nerves were frayed and his energy spent. The eyes of the vultures followed him as he gave up stealth and trotted along the wall.

The gate, such as it was, stood ajar, splintered and broken. A large log sat discarded beside the gate, obviously used to smash it in during a raid. He stood frozen, staring at it for a moment. A lead weight settled in his gut, freezing him to the spot. Nothing good would be beyond that gate, but he had to be sure. He pressed the sack of plant clippings to his face and breathed in the scent. The walkway crunched under his boots as he stepped into the gateway.

Beyond the fence lay a nightmare.

The walkways were painted with blood, clotted and darkened with time. For a heartbeat all he could see was the red. He choked down the lump from his throat and forced himself to look beyond. Orotid was no stranger to battle and had seen his share of carnage, but the sight before him was beyond any battle he had ever participated in. Not even grinlo reveled in this level of carnage. The first house was rubble, a pile of splinters and debris coated in gore. Black flies coated everything, filling the air with a skin-crawling buzz.

Bile rushed up his throat, threatening to overwhelm him but he wrestled it back. "Hello!"

His voice bounced around the houses, ringing back at him and fading away. The only response was the angry squawk of the vultures affronted by the intrusion.

He took a hesitant step forward. "Is anyone there?" He was stalling.

Eyes closed, he pulled a deep breath through his mouth. Even that left a foul film on his tongue. He opened his eyes and inspected the town before him. Not the damage or the gore or the carrion birds, but the town. All northern towns in Trimera had a stronghold for when the walls failed. Sure enough, a roof rose above the others. That was where he would find survivors.

Set on his plan, he entered the nightmare.

The buildings creaked in the wind as they settled and the vultures called out his position as he passed. To his right stood a pen for livestock. Where it should have deafened him with bleats and calls only mounds lay, alive with nothing more than the death watch of flies and buzzards. Such a waste. He turned from the sight and continued on. The gore around him could be explained by the animals. The citizens could still be alive.

He rounded a corner and startled a large red-headed vulture crouched over the body of an Amber Hound, his duty now paid. The bird hissed, wings spread over its meal. The animals concerned him. Grinlo were vicious, aggressive, but they were rarely wasteful. With so much meat about, why waste the energy to force their way deeper into the village? And why leave the meat to rot? It made no sense.

He picked up his pace and trotted the last few steps to the large building. It was far from ornate but still managed a steeple that could be seen from the fields beyond, a landmark for emergencies. It was surrounded by a garden once filled with vegetables now trampled and defiled. The stench was stronger here as well, putrid sweet mingled with excrement. The horde had wanted to send a message.

The entrance would face north—the watchers were always vigilant. He took the last steps at a dead run, eager to be free of the horror around him. The door stood ajar. With any luck, the citizens had fled after the battle to safety. One last stretch of carnage and he glanced inside.

And fell to his knees.

If outside was a nightmare, inside was the Master of Dreams himself. Lining the wall, shoulder to shoulder, secured with spikes through their chests, were the citizens of the village. Closer to the door were the men, killed defending their families then nailed up like some macabre festival wreath. Beside them were the women, smaller and weaker but fierce and stubborn; they would have stood between danger and the children. Toward the back wall, not as neatly secured, the children hanged pinned against the wall. The youngest, in swaddling, was the most disturbing. The spike formed a gaping hole in its chest.

He lost what tenuous grasp he had on his stomach and doubled over, retching onto the stoop.

Lord Renor snapped the arrow shaft a hand's width from where it protruded from his shoulder. Blood trailed along his chest and glistened in the torchlight. His bow was gone, his sword too. The axe in his hand was a tool, not a weapon, but it cut flesh when the need arose. The wood of the door at his back tugged at the fabric of his clothes where they were exposed beneath his armor. The dank scent of musk and sweat assaulted his nostrils.

At his feet lay two soldiers. Good men, though neither would see the sun rise tomorrow. All of his men were gone, lost one by one as they fought the invading army. His ears longed for a reprieve from the constant barrage of fighting. It felt like a lifetime since he had experienced silence. He pushed off from the door, his limbs leaden and sluggish. Each crash against the barricade behind him sent a quiver through the wood. He needed to make the next barrier.

He pushed himself along the coarse stone of the hallway, and he found that each step required extra effort. There was nothing he could do for the trail of crimson behind him. All he could do was keep moving. Stairs loomed above him at the end of the hallway. Steep and impossible, they were worn nearly smooth from generations of boots. His body dropped him to the steps but he kept moving, crawling on his hands and knees. He couldn't give up. The noise behind him became louder as the grinlo hacked through the door. They would be on him soon.

There was no end to them. No end to the horror.

His hands left wet red prints on the stairs and in his slow progress he reached the landing. All he had to do was get past the door. Knees quaking, he pulled himself to his feet and struggled against his racing heart. Would it burst from his chest? It would have to soon.

He pushed against the door, but it didn't budge. He stepped back and threw himself against it to no avail. His body crumbled to the floor. Snapping wood and roars announced the grinlo as they smashed through the lower door. He planted the axe head and wrenched himself up to standing. He would die on his feet.

Sweat lathered the horse's neck as Orotid urged it faster. The beast heaved as it consumed the path beneath it. It couldn't sustain the pace much longer, he knew, but a sense of urgency possessed him like a fever. He had to get to Prince Janu and the high priestess. Whatever was going on was far beyond his means.

He eased the horse back and let it stutter to a halt. Sides heaving, it hung its head. It needed rest and so did he. He slipped his boots free of the stirrups and slid from the saddle. He snatched up a handful of grass from beside the glorified game trail that passed for a road here. His nostrils filled with the sweet scent of horse sweat as he rubbed the handful of grass along the horse's body. The destroyed village of Ler had changed his plans; now, he was on the shortest route to the Seat. The path he was on was much too narrow for anything more than a mounted man. It was rarely used since it didn't offer the respite of villages and inns along its length.

Brush rustled against his breeches as he led the horse toward a large guardian pine. The cone-dotted branches dropped down to provide decent shelter from the elements. Beneath its canopy, he switched the horse's bridle for a halter and secured it to one of the branches. The sticky bark pinched and scratched at his back as he wrapped his cloak around his shoulders. His eyes darted toward the trail but fatigue battled his anxiety. It wasn't long before he was dozing against the tree, the shadows settling around him.

Pale moonlight met his eyes as they shot open in the dark. How long had he slept? Hours? Nothing seemed out of place: The horse stamped in its sleep just over his shoulder, the insects buzzed and whirred in the dark, a smattering of night birds trilled across the valley.

But something had drawn him awake.

Rustling drew his attention to his left—a rat, maybe, or a chipmunk. With no discernable threat, the pounding in his chest slowed and his eyelids grew heavy again.

Then he caught it. Not so much to draw attention, but enough to notice. Footsteps. Someone or something was creeping around in the dark.

Pressed against the trunk, he let his head fall back. He needed whatever was out there to think he was asleep. Eyes cracked, he searched the shadows along the deer path. Was something moving against the wind? Another footstep sounded behind him. Too quiet for boots, too quiet for men.

His eyes cast around although he kept his head still. *There*—a shadow along the path separated from the others. As large as a man, but it didn't move quite like a man. There was an animalistic quality that he couldn't pinpoint.

The shadow stretched up and he knew it was testing the air. Did it know he was there? His eyes remained locked on the shifting dark. His grip inched forward until it secured on the hilt of a dagger tucked behind his belt. His hand itched for the sword at his back but the movement would draw attention. It was the dagger or nothing.

Lord Renor's shoulders screamed as his weight hung from them. Each arm was grasped by a massive grinlo as they dragged him along the halls of Amber Keep. He had taken down two before they swarmed him. His boots made an awful screech along the stones but his limbs would no longer respond to him. His head swung from his neck, a dead weight with a tenuous grasp on consciousness.

The grips on his arms vanished and his face smashed into dirt. Pain flared as grit tore at his eyes and face, choked his lungs. Boots crunched all around him but for lack of energy, his head refused to lift from the dirt.

A shadow fell over his body. "Well now, what do we have here?"

A sharp pain lanced through his side but instead of a breath for a scream, his mouth filled with a cloud of dirt that sent a wrack of coughs through his body. Clawed hands grabbed his shoulders, slicing into his skin as they lifted him up from the ground. His blurred vision picked out someone standing before him, and his abused mind formed the shadow into a man—but that couldn't be possible, could it? But the voice…

"Who…" he ground out.

They bent before him, close to his face. He could feel the warmth of breath against his cheeks. "Don't you worry about who I am," the shadow said. "You won't be alive long enough for it to matter."

The words filtered up through the haze of his mind. He tried to work moisture into his mouth but the dirt refused to release his tongue. "Whaa?"

"Shhh." A finger pressed to his lips. "I told you it wasn't important. Now, you are going to give me some information. If you are forthcoming, I will not draw out your pain for longer than is necessary. I want you to think very hard about what could happen to you in this situation and how futile said situation is. Fighting will get you nothing."

"Won't…won't…" he stuttered. Every breath was an effort.

"Oh, you will talk. It's just a matter of how much pain you will endure before you give me what I want."

Orotid's breath stuttered as he lost sight of the shadow among the trees. Perhaps his mind was just running away with him? A branch snapped behind him, sending a tremor down his spine though he fought to maintain stillness. The horse startled awake at his side with a nervous whicker, then stamped as it caught the scent of the creature stalking them. He prayed the horse wouldn't bolt; if he lost the horse he would never make the Seat in time to send help.

He closed his eyes and let the night fill his senses. At first all he could hear was the anxious breathing of the gelding as it danced at the end of its tether. He settled deeper and felt the night around him expand into a symphony of sound. Insects, birds, rodents, and frogs, all the normal sounds of night—and four sets of footsteps circling in on him.

He swallowed the lump in his throat. He was a decent hand at the sword, but four to one was chancy for any man, especially in the dark. If it were four grinlo in the dark, he would be lucky to see the light of morning.

He focused in on the closest noise just to his right, toward the horse. Whatever was out there was smart enough to go for the horse. Whatever was out there didn't want him to get away. He could move quietly for his age, but the grinlo had superb hearing; he would need speed as well, something a little harder to procure.

Now.

His palm leapt from his dagger to his sword as he jumped to his feet. The move put him closer to the horse and masked his movements with the larger animal's shuffling. It also, however, masked the sounds of the creatures around him.

Each footstep screamed in his ears as he struggled to hone in on the first attacker. The stench of sweat and filth accosted his nostrils—the stench of grinlo. His blood chilled with the realization. They had followed him, found him… He had to survive, or now Amber Keep was doomed.

The night erupted as he drew his sword and leapt toward the first creature. The horse screamed against the tumult as blade and claw struggled for flesh. His swing resisted as it contacted flesh, though he couldn't tell what in the dark. With his back to the horse, he swung away with his sword, hoping to put a swift end to the skirmish before either he or his steed could be injured.

The man who called himself Neram stepped back from the spreading pool of bright red at his feet. This was the third person he'd questioned and the third he could not make talk. He had heard of the stubbornness of the citizens of Trimera, but what he'd seen so far extended past loyalty. Everyone had a limit, of course, but he had not been able to find that limit before they expired. It could be coincidence—perhaps their injuries from the battles were too much to survive further torture.

Whatever the reason, it didn't matter. Information would have been nice but it was far from necessary. At least he had some firsthand insight into the people of Trimera. Knowledge was vital when one was trying to overtake a kingdom. Trimera would be quite the feather in his cap, the perfect way to announce to all of Reia his true power. Let the other kingdoms tremble in fear as he gathered power.

He turned from the carnage and made his way toward the open doors that led into the heart of Amber Keep. Every door he passed stood open, every room tossed and searched. Not a living citizen of the Keep remained alive, or at least none that they had found so far. The grinlo would feast well tonight. He only wished they had found a creature of magic—the boost to their magic always gave him a jolt—but no such luck.

He glanced in each room as he passed. Storage closets, meeting rooms, barracks for soldiers, small rooms for servants…nothing that would suit his means. He needed space. He came to a set of stairs and trotted to the next floor. The rooms here were larger but he kept going until he came across a massive room with high windows facing the north.

He lifted a finger to the ceiling and gave a gentle mental tug on the network of power that flowed through him. He stood in anticipation until he heard the approach of one of his creatures. This was one of his favorite aspects given to him when he gained control of the horde. The spell he had cast created a connection between himself and the creatures under his control. All he had to do was summon, and one of his thrall came running.

A massive gray creature shuffled to his side and groveled up at him.

"Bring them here," he said. "There is much work to do."

Crashes and snaps marked the progress of the other creatures as they groped blindly toward him. His blade sank into soft flesh and he threw his weight against it. The shadow circling him cried out as a loud pop freed the blade and let it continue on its arc. He was already spinning when he heard it thump to the ground; wounded or dead didn't matter, as there were more pressing threats.

Orotid pressed himself back against the horse, letting his presence soothe the beast while he tried to pinpoint the next attack. The horse pressed back against him, eager for a point of reference. How long before dawn? The darkness was just as much a disadvantage to them as to him.

Something bumped into his elbow and he slashed out with his sword, finding only air. Claws scribbled around him, drawing his attention this way and that. Too much noise for it not to be intentional.

Almost like…they were distracting him.

His breath raced as he tried to filter through the shuffling. What were they doing? A branch snapped to his left and a heavy weight barreled into him from the right.

The sword flew from his hand.

He crashed to the ground, a weight pinning him down but not moving. The dead weight pushed the air out of his lungs as he struggled to gain purchase on his belt knife. Anything sharp.

Blood rushed through his ears as he twisted to gain another inch closer to the blade in his knife. Relief rushed through him as the handle of the blade slipped into his palm. A guttural grunt made known one of the creatures to his right. If he didn't know better, he'd have sworn the creature had spoken, but that was just silly. Grinlo couldn't talk.

The horse grew more frantic behind him. He was running out of time.

He wrestled against the weight above him. Razor sharp claws sliced into his calf, and he cried out. Orotid slammed the belt knife across the clawed fist latched to his leg and jerked back as his forehead crashed into a solid lump he assumed was the grinlo. The stabbed creature skittered away in a crash through the underbrush, but another replaced it almost instantly.

The horse whinnied as it danced at the end of its lead in an attempt to escape.

He froze as a massive wet thump landed above him and the shape curled into itself. The weight rolled away and he skittered backward, away from the horse's crushing stomps.

Now, his back against the trunk, he froze to listen. The forest was alive around him: whimpers and cries and breaking branches. His skin burned from cuts and scrapes.

Dagger clutched to his chest, he stared up at the sky praying for a flicker of daylight, but nothing but darkness greeted him.

In the next breath the night around him stilled, leaving nothing but the wind and the panicked horse.

He held his breath and prayed his elderly hearing would suffice. What were they doing? He caught a snippet of the almost-speak again. He let his breath ease out of his nose. Every fiber of his being was alert but shaking with exhaustion. They would come soon; he was sure of it. The night stretched out around him in silence.

Orotid's eyes flew open in sudden fear. He had fallen asleep against the tree trunk in the dark. Before him, the small stream and pine tree he had sheltered beneath now lay exposed to the harsh dawn light. The horse stood beside him, muzzle drooped near to the ground. Dirt was churned in a circle around the area, every inch the horse could reach while tied to his tether. Nothing out of the ordinary stirred in the grass around Orotid. Blood splattered the dirt around him but no bodies marred the ground.

He couldn't afford to wonder where they'd gone; he needed to leave—immediately. He jerked the horse's lead loose and started the creature awake. Even its exhaustion couldn't mask the nervous roll of its eyes. The only remnant of the desperate night was an angry red line that trailed along one of its hind limbs.

The Seat was chilly, as it was so many mornings. It was designed for defense, not comfort. Ten years Janu had officially been sitting prince for Trimera, granted under the close observation of not only High Priestess Lana but also a plethora of Trimera's most prominent lords and ladies. Lana's support was crucial. Having been raised to the throne at the age of fourteen meant that most in the kingdom didn't have much faith in his abilities to rule. Alas, being fourteen basically meant he didn't have *any* ability to rule. He would have never admitted it at the time, but Lana's guidance was the only thing that kept contention for the throne at bay. He had heard the word *child* tossed around beneath many a breath in the courts, but none had the spine to stand against a sitting priestess, especially when that priestess happened to be Lana.

On his twentieth birthday, Lana had suggested that he move into his parents' apartments. She would never demand he do anything; a priestess did not demand things from her prince. A priestess could, however, strongly suggest. And a smart ruler listened when his priestess suggested, so into his parents' chambers he moved. There was many a night he would lie awake, positive his parents had just walked across the floor. The drapes still held their smell. Perhaps someday it would be his room, but for now he was an intruder. An untested ruler standing on the backs of stronger men and women before him.

But he had no time for any of that to dwell too long in his mind. Every second of every day was laid out for him. It was still dark as he slipped from the overstuffed mattress. The floor was covered with imported rugs from most of the countries of Reia and even a couple from the mysterious island of Lyshia; still, the cold seeped through. His feet were bare and complained whenever he stepped off of the decorative runners.

His wardrobe stood across the frigid room, blessedly close to the fireplace. A servant slipped into his chambers at night to keep the fire stoked, for what little good it did; even a roaring fire only produced a halo of warmth that extended, at most, twenty feet from the mantel. That halo of warmth was why he had asked the steward to move the wardrobe. There was nothing worse than slipping into freezing clothes.

The wardrobe doors squeaked as he pulled them open, releasing a wave of fragrance. Lessel was fond of leaving satchels of dried herbs and flowers in the shoes. Lessel was an amazing steward.

Janu rushed to dress before Lessel came to assist him. It was a game he played with the older man. He dressed himself in somber clothes, mute in decoration and dark in color. But Lessel would insist on gilt and embroidery, frills and pomp. That was all right on days where ceremony was involved, but frivolous and garish for every day in the dreary old castle.

He dropped on the edge of the mattress and barked a laugh as Lessel flung the door wide. Janu stomped a foot into a tall worn black boot as he looked up at his steward. "What took you so long?"

Janu's eyes danced with amusement at himself as the steward pushed the door closed behind him. The man would never break his composure. "Shall I choose your crown this morning, my prince?"

Other boot stomped onto his foot, Janu leapt to his feet. When he had turned eighteen, Lana and Lessel had conspired to convince him that being seen in a crown was important. It reminded all that despite his young age, they still had a prince. He felt foolish but had acquiesced to their suggestions. At the time all arguments against it just seemed foolish, so he allowed himself to be pranced around fluffed up like some peacock. And they were right; the citizens of the Seat responded to the crown with cheers and renewed vigor that hadn't been seen since his parents' deaths.

So, he wasn't seen without one of the court crowns if only nothing more than a simple coronet of gold. Crowds cheered their young prince.

"What would you recommend?"

Lessel's deft fingers opened the tabletop cabinet that housed the array of court crowns and studied the headdresses with a dark seriousness most men could never achieve. "The sapphire, I think, today."

Janu slumped. Of course, the sapphire. It was the most ostentatious headpiece in the collection: two fighting stags, antlers intertwined with sapphire eyes and a large magnificent gem secured among their tines. "The sapphire, really?"

Lessel merely cocked an eyebrow as he waited. It was Janu's punishment for dressing himself. Lessel never chose the monstrous thing unless he was denied a right he saw as his. Janu sighed as he dropped into a ladder-back chair and let the steward balance the contraption atop his temples. Lessel fussed for a moment with Janu's hair before stepping back satisfied.

Janu gave a rueful grin as he stared at himself in the looking glass. "Thank you Lessel." The steward nodded and faded back to begin his normal perusal of Janu's rooms. He would report anything he didn't like to the cleaning staff and the room would be spotless when Janu returned.

Outside his chambers stood his guard, ten of the best soldiers Trimera could produce. Leaned against the wall, as always, was Mian, well-cut coat unlaced and askew. The young men shared a mischievous glance before falling in step as if of one mind.

That was the thing he loved about Mian, it was like they shared thoughts. Lady Mesha always said they were more like twins than friends.

Even now in their majority it was hard-pressed to find one without the other, a fact that irritated Lana to no end. She would constantly complain that they were only civil alone and barely then.

The woman in question swept around the corner toward them, moving faster than he could ever remember. One glance at her blank expression sent a jolt of ice into his gut. She brushed past the guards and blocked his path with the presence of a majestic owl deciding which mouse was to serve as her dinner.

"Prince Janu, there is urgent news, I need you to come with me."

Mian's usual flippant attitude toward Lana appeared to catch in his throat as Janu stared at her dumbly for what felt like an eternity. "Of course, High Priestess; lead the way."

There was nothing worse than Lana in her icy calm. He had learned quick that the cooler Lana appeared, the hotter her emotions burned. What could possibly have her feeling so agitated? His mind immediately jumped to the worst possible scenarios: Pria had been injured in her training—or worse, killed; someone was challenging him for the crown; the coffers were empty and the citizens were going to starve. He shook the mesh of racing thoughts from his mind and focused on the flowing waves of fabric in Lana's wake. Whenever he became overwhelmed he would calm himself with the repetitive swirls of silks. He was so concentrated on the fabric he nearly walked straight into her back when she stopped in front of him.

He looked up and frowned at the small conference room as she commanded his guard to set up around the door. The room was far from the court traffic in the castle, and so, seldom used. What were they doing here?

Her eyes narrowed at Mian as she turned to face them. "Young man, I do not have the time to argue you away." She swung the door wide and ushered them inside before securing it behind her. She had shut all of his guards outside.

"Lana, what is it?"

She drew a calming breath and he allowed himself to see her as she actually was. Her hair gathered into a neat bun at the back of her head was more silver and white than the pale brown it had been in her youth. A web of fine lines surrounded her eyes and mouth. More than anything, she looked tired. She gestured behind them.

Mian and Janu turned as one to a desk behind them at which sat an older soldier. The man was covered in dust from travel and looked exhausted.

Lana stepped to Janu's side as the older man worked to his feet. "Your Highness, this is Orotid. He traveled here from Amber Keep. Orotid, could you please repeat what you told me to Prince Janu and Lord Mian?"

Janu waved to the seat and took one for himself. "What of Amber Keep?"

Stillness settled on the room as they sat expectant, apprehensive. Orotid took a moment to gather his thoughts; it was obvious the man could barely keep his eyes open. "Lord Renor sent me with word, ahead of the evacuation."

Any expression on Janu or Mian's face fell like lead weight to the floor. "Evacuation?"

Orotid nodded. "Aye, your majesty. Our defenses were failing. The raids from the horde went from periodic to nearly constant almost overnight. He intends to stand until the citizens are evacuated."

The room around him faded into gauzy silence. This was madness. Amber Keep couldn't have fallen. This man must be confused. Janu had visited the Keep as a child with his father, had visited since his father's passing as prince. It was impenetrable—anyone who caught sight of the defensive walls and battlements would know that. No mere grinlo raid could take the Keep, not and hold it. What would they want with the Keep anyway? Grinlo couldn't understand the significance of its location. Without the Keep, there was nothing to guard the largest pass from the Frontier into Reia.

He wouldn't lose the Keep, he couldn't. His father entrusted Trimera to him, and he was not going to tarnish his memory by failing that trust. He couldn't leave Trimera open to an endless flow of grinlo from the north.

Janu lurched to his feet. "Mian, find my commanders."

Orotid gaped at him as Mian rushed from the room. Lana shot him a cool glare. "What do you intend to do?"

Janu's gaze returned to the soldier across the desk. "We ride for Amber Keep. If we cannot hold the fortress, we will at least guard her citizens while they retreat."

The world around Pria faded away as her focus narrowed down to the stone in her palm. It was not a special stone, just a pebble collected from one of the gardens.

Alone atop the student barracks at the Lorien, she had a view of the Silver City in its entirety. From the docks along the Heart River, the river that bisected Reia, to the northern border that nestled up against the foothills of the Overlook Mountains, the city was a gateway between northern and southern Reia. The city itself was a marvel, filled with more cultures than could be kept track of, at least for a girl of fifteen. Each playhouse was capped with a glorious golden dome, or at least one painted gold if the real thing couldn't be afforded. There were exactly eighteen within the limits of Silver City, one within the grounds of the Lorien, and three in the sprawl that seeped out into the countryside around them. She had managed to visit three.

Spires and steeples speared the sky. She hadn't found a commonality among the spires yet; they seemed to depend on taste, but the steeples always signified a holy gathering place. The Silver City had enough religions within its borders to confuse even the most pious man. There were the strenuous monks of the Lightbringers, whose steeples were unadorned but stood among the tallest in all of Reia. The very secretive Order of the White Stag held the northernmost temple in a valley surrounded by orchards. Silver City even had a faction of the extremely rare Orxn Brothers, but no one knew enough about the practice to know if they were authentic or just trying to fleece money out of unsuspecting people. The ones that drew her attention the most had to be the Ladies of her Majestic Heart. They cared for the spirit of the Heart River. Their temple sported the shortest steeple, though its adornment of moonstone glinted any celestial light into almost a beacon. She had managed to see their mysterious ceremonies a handful of times, a difficult task, as they happened in the dead of night beneath the moon. In pristine white silks, the Ladies would gather at the riverside and call on the power of the moon and river.

Of course, the most interesting thing about the Silver City, what drew more people into the city than anything else, were the shops. Shops of all kinds lined the streets. There was an old saying: *If you can't find it in the Silver City, it doesn't exist.* It wasn't true, of course, but it was close enough to not make much difference. Cakes and sweets, exotic fabrics, the finest porcelain, and blades imported from lands she'd never heard of before—all could be found within the limits of the Silver City.

But she couldn't let any of that distract her now.

She had to keep her focus on the stone. It had sat against her skin long enough to take up the heat of her body but refused to ignite into the heat of true magic, and much to her frustration, wouldn't flash away from her palm. Her teachers were quite clear that the art of transmutation took a full year to master, but that was for average students. But as the priestesses were so fond of reminding her, she was a high priestess. Lana was recorded as mastering transmutation in four months. Pria's eyes flared wide as the stone took up a spark of heat. She would do it faster.

She jerked with a gasp and the stone dropped to the roof, steam rising around the tile where it had landed. She cupped her hand to her chest and risked a glance at the skin. The sight of the angry red welt jolted agony up her arm. Well, she was going to have a hard time explaining that away.

Lips pursed, she blew on the welt as she pulled a book closer. The book was *A Priestess's Introduction to Magic* and she had been studying out of it all year. It was actually a seventh-year book, reserved for older priestess trainees, but with the extent she was already venturing into magic, the priestesses thought it safer to build her control. Control was all they ever preached, but she was ready for so much more. If only she could show them.

She scanned the neat, stilted writing on the page. All books in the Lorien were hand copied by the Sisters of the Golden Flame, a fraternity devoted to the preservation of knowledge. Each had a lovely sketch in the inside cover of a stylized woman enveloped in flame, the symbol of their order. Pria had always found the picture intriguing. With a wave of her hand she sent the pages in the book flapping. Her jaw set in determination, she snatched the still-warm stone from its smoking spot on the roof. One more time, the stone would move.

Smoke drifted in lazy tendrils from the open gates of Amber Keep and settled in the dips and hollows of the surrounding land. The threat of rain kept the smoke from rising as the contingent of soldiers waited atop a rise some four hundred yards from the city walls. The fires had all burned out, gutting the stone fortress of any flammable material. A heavy stench filled the air and burned the nostrils: human hair and flesh. Janu had never smelled it before and it churned his stomach.

No one spoke. Not even a whisper broke the solace of the Keep in the hazy evening light. Janu lowered his head, unable to look at the vacant walls anymore. The grinlo had left no one alive, not woman nor child, in the Keep. Bodies had littered the street when the small group had broken free from the larger party and ridden in, hoping to sweep the enemy from their lands. They couldn't remain within the walls—the decay and stench were too much, too dangerous. The city belonged to the ghosts now. It would take months to clean the death and contagion.

"Janu." It was quiet, insistent, at his right shoulder. Mian's voice evoked a chill that he didn't think possible in his numb body.

Janu lifted his gaze and felt the sky crash down around him. From the darkened trees marched a line of grinlo, mismatched armor ill cared for and dented.

They had come to claim the Keep.

The soldiers at his back shifted in discomfort as the line of monstrous forms marched for the open gates. Janu gathered his reins and heard the men around him form up, ready to follow his lead. The tension sent a jolt through his body.

Light fingers landed on his wrist. Lana stared up at him from her own sturdy mare. She didn't have to speak for him to know what she was thinking.

"We can't let them have the Keep."

She nodded toward the advancing army. "Stop and think, Janu. We will not make the Keep before them. We will be facing superior numbers in a highly defensible position. It would take months for us to make the Keep habitable again in order to hold it, and we would never be able to do so while fighting an invasion. The Keep's defenses have already been breached; it would take more resources than we have to make repairs like that. We have already swept the city for survivors, all we would be fighting for are walls."

His chest tightened as her words fell like a hammer. He swallowed. "But…we can't abandon the Keep. It would leave us vulnerable, give the enemy control of Amber Pass. There would be no way to stop the influx."

Mian deflated beside him. "They are at least twice our number, if not more. If we engage them now, we will not live to see the morning. We need time and numbers, and we have neither here." He eased his horse closer to Janu's. "There is no battle here today, only death. We will guard Reia from the Seat, build our numbers, prepare a true assault. Nothing will come of us dying here today."

A twinge jolted through him. They were both right; there was no way they could save the Keep—not with the number they had, not without a large loss of life. But still his heart held out hope. Some miracle could still befall them. The advancing army could turn and leave, could decide to chase them instead, allow them to circle back and reach the Keep that offered no safety and promised disease.

The world fell away as the first mass of grinlo reached the city gates. The creatures poured through the broken defenses, filling the Keep with filth and despair. They had the numbers to outweigh the broken defenses, and every dead body was food. It was over.

Janu had lost Amber Keep.

He jammed a fist to his mouth to subdue to rising gorge. He stiffened his face to hide the horror he felt. He couldn't let them see how shaken he really was.

Generations of his ancestors had protected Trimera from the invasion of grinlo. Generations holding the borders and protecting Reia. He felt the world crush down on his shoulders. His fist cupped around the coronet on his temples. He pulled the gold from his head and stared down at it. It was a symbol of duty and he had fallen short, disgraced his family and bloodline. Every citizen in Amber Keep had trusted him to protect them and he had failed them. Failed everyone.

Right there, in the hills around Amber Keep, he made a vow to himself. He would never again wear the crown of Trimera. Not until he avenged every citizen of Amber Keep and earned back the respect of his family.

The man who called himself Neram watched the small group of men from his hidden vantage point, safe among his thrall of grinlo. Even if an observer was able to pick him out among the mass, they would more likely attribute it to a trick of the mind rather than the truth their eyes told them. So few would believe a man would be able to survive among grinlo that he could use their disbelief as a weapon.

The grinlo around him murmured as they sniffed the air. "Magic."

He scanned the group harder. Indeed, he saw the smaller, graceful shape of a woman. It could only be Lana, Trimera's high priestess. Perfect. Let her watch. Let her see the fall of Amber Keep. Let her report the army before her to the Lorien so they could fret and worry the implications. With control of Amber Keep, he could freely move his horde from the Frontier into Reia. From Amber Keep, he would build his numbers and prepare his next move.

He had allowed them to see the Keep for themselves, to see the decimation his creatures had caused. Let their fear build. They would despair the loss of life. They would lament the detriment of losing such a vital tactical position. And all the while he would be preparing, growing.

With the acquisition of Amber Keep he could begin the true expansion of his power. When Reia looked back on his glorious rise to power, this would be the point they would look to as a turn. Safely hidden among their number was the key to his success and the Keep would be its base. His influence would spread like plague, and soon all would whisper his name in fear.

This was a truly great day.

The wind tugged at Pria's cloak as she perched atop the guard rail that lined Heart Road. Her feet dangled out over the water of the Heart River that not only bordered the road but also gave it its name. The water was brown, clogged with silt from the recent rains, but it wasn't always like that. Usually, it was clean, white, churning beauty across rounded boulders.

The sweet roll in her fist was warm and sticky and half gone. The hood of the cloak shaded her face from most casual observers, though she could tell the baker had known her. She'd visited him often enough and he'd never turned her in yet. She'd been sneaking out of the Lorien long enough to know who to trust.

Foot traffic passed along behind her, oblivious to the princess perched on the edge of the river. This was one of her favorite places in the Silver City. Above all the beautiful bridges, the lush gardens, shops, and temples. When the sun rose over the Heart River the water became a column of gold. But it wasn't morning and there was no glistening gold. Just the crashing roar of the water as it rushed past the city.

She popped the last bite of sticky bread in her mouth then sucked the syrup from her fingers. With a swing of her legs, she swiveled around and dropped to the street. She would have to hurry to make her first class but the distraction was worth it. She had been sitting in exams all morning testing out of basic history, language, and economics classes. They weren't the first classes she'd tested out of and she was glad to be skipping them. Nothing was worse than repeating history and politics. She wasn't worried about how she'd done on the exams; they weren't nearly as tough as Lana had been.

She broke into a trot, darting among the other traffic on the streets. The cloak billowed around her in a windblown dance. It had started raining again before she reached the back gates of the Lorien. She would have to find somewhere to ditch the damp cloak. Any other girl could show up to class late in a wet cloak and get away with a reasonable explanation, but Pria already had a reputation for mischief. The priestesses had long since given up punishing her for sneaking out. It had quickly proven inefficient and since they could never prevent her escapes, they settled on only punishing her when her trips interfered with her classes.

She darted between two well-bred ladies and turned into an alley. The alley was wide and clean and served the staff of the Lorien for supplies. The laundress' entry at the far end was seldom closed and never locked. Today it stood open, billowing steam into the morning air.

Hot, damp air enveloped her as she trotted through the open door. Inside the laundry, clouds of white mist drifted about, obscuring the staff as they stoked the firepits, stirred the laundry vats, and draped the clean items across lines strung below the ceiling.

Women called out to her as she danced through and around them. With one hand, she unclasped her cloak and sent it soaring into a pile of dirty laundry. It would be returned to her eventually.

The laundry led to the servants' quarters, packed with the staff that were the true heart of the Lorien. Those who truly understood their own power knew that without the servants, no house, palace, or stronghold would survive. Here again many called her name. Unlike most of the students at the Lorien, Pria knew that no priestess was better than any who served beneath her. So, while the other students ignored or even disrespected those who cleaned their linens and prepared their meals, Pria knew most by name.

But she had no time for any of that today.

The servants' stairs were opposite of the laundry to prevent the moist air from spreading into the Lorien. She took the stairs at a run and burst from the stairwell on the third floor. The hallway beyond bustled with initiates all on their way to their classes. She breathed relief and let herself slow and meld into the flow.

A tall girl several years older than she fell in at her side. She was thin and awkward with a mass of red curls that haloed her pale face and crashed down her back. Inala was one of Pria's few close friends.

"Running late again I see," she said. "Where did we go this morning?"

"Just out for breakfast." Inala enjoyed Pria's tales of mischief, though she never broke even the smallest rule herself. All the tutors loved Inala. She ranked top in her class.

"I still don't know how you get away with such flaunting of the strictures."

Pria flashed the older girl a wicked grin. Inala was a true treasure, one of very few older girls who did not consider Pria as a threat to their status. Inala, like Pria herself, knew her worth and wasn't intimidated by anyone else's talent. When Pria had first arrived at the Lorien, she had been handed over to a mentor, an older student who could show her the ropes. Her mentor had been Inala.

"It is because my talents at rule-breaking far exceed their abilities at rule enforcing!" Pria said, a hint of pride tinging her voice.

Inala rolled her eyes as she veered off toward her own class. Pria's room was at the end of the hall. It was a new class she had just tested into, Advanced Diplomacy, and she expected it to be a breeze. The hallway behind her still bustled with students as she stepped into the classroom.

A small, wild-haired priestess stood behind a meticulous desk absorbed in a stack of paperwork. Priestess Ludra had been the tutor who'd first suggested Pria be tested out of some of the lower classes. Students still milled about the room, filling the air with squeals and chatter. Pria took note of a couple of students she'd had trouble with in the past. That would be what she would need to look out for.

She had a polite smile ready as she approached the desk, the perfect eager young student. "Good day, Priestess Ludra."

The woman glanced up at her. "Pria of Trimera," Priestess Ludra said. "Report to Priestess San immediately."

Pria's heart leapt to a gallop in her chest. "But…I was on time."

Priestess Ludra pointed a long finger at the doorway in silent command.

Irritation welled up as her shoulders schlumped. The hallway was deserted when she made her way back out. Her steps echoed along the corridor with no students to block it. San occupied an office just above the top floor reserved for classrooms. It wasn't her real office, just a room she used when dealing with students, though Pria had never seen her counsel any other student.

Every step was slower than the last until her feet dragged across the tile floor. The door to San's office stood open with the woman in question seated behind a plain wooden desk. San's eyes found her among the shadows of the hallway.

"Pria, please join me."

The soft, soothing voice jolted against her nerves. Anger she could handle, disappointment, but the gentle tone awoke instant fear. It was the tone of someone with bad news. She came to a full stop, her eyes wide. As long and she didn't step across that threshold, she wouldn't have to hear whatever made San's voice sound like that. All she had to do was avoid entering that office and everything would be fine.

"Do I have to?" she asked.

San stood and crossed from behind the desk. "I am afraid so."

San's hand was warm as Pria's fingers slipped into her grasp and she crossed the threshold. The door closed behind her and she jumped with the sudden noise. San guided her to a chair and motioned her to sit. The office was comfortable though it felt a little bare, but a chill settled along her bones nonetheless.

"Can I offer you something?"

"Please, tell me what this is about," Pria pleaded. "I'm really getting anxious."

San sank into her chair behind the desk, hands folded before her, eyes downcast. "I'm sorry it has to be me to bear this news, Pria," she began. "I'm sorry it can't be someone closer. Pria, the horde has overrun Amber Keep."

Pria knew San continued talking but she wasn't listening anymore. The Keep was gone. Trimera's northernmost outpost in the hands of the grinlo. How could that be? Grinlo weren't smart or organized, how were they able to overthrow the defenses at Amber Keep?

It took her several breaths before she realized that San was still talking, continuing with her report on the fall. Pria lifted one hand, palm toward Priestess San. "Survivors?"

San dropped her gaze. "Only one," she said.

Pria's hand flew to her mouth as tears burst from her eyes. San sat forward. "They fought well. Held for quite some time. They were planning to evacuate the citizens while the soldiers held the fort but something went wrong."

It had been generations since the Frontier had advanced to any human strongholds. To have Amber Keep fall…it was unprecedented. "The Keep…"

"The attempt to retake the Keep was deemed impossible. It must await the building of an army."

Her body crumbled down into itself.

Mian watched the older soldier in awe. The first time he'd seen Orotid, the man had been on the verge of collapse. In the two years following as he watched the officer fight and work, he now wondered what he had gone through to get him in that condition.

Oh, he complained enough. Orotid had a comment on everything and how his age affected it. Mian had come to expect them. Orotid repeated himself often. As Mian watched him now gathering firewood, he knew exactly what the older man would say.

Mian ducked his head to hide his amusement as Orotid approached their campfire. "All this bending is going to wreak havoc on my back in the morning."

Mian's shoulders shook with laughter as Orotid piled firewood on the ground. In the two years following the loss of Amber Keep, Orotid had become a dear friend and proven himself quite the accomplished soldier. Mian felt rather lucky any time the man found himself among one of his commands. His command was a small group today, only a handful of soldiers. Their circuit would take in several villages around the Seat. They were to assist in fortifications and gather together any stragglers. Solitary farms were particularly at risk this far north; with no defenses or support, isolation made them an easy target.

Orotid set to building a small fire while Mian prepared their evening meal. Nothing special: salted and dried meat and a handful of wrinkled root vegetables boiled into what would only pass for stew to a soldier. None of them would complain though, they were good men.

It was an odd feeling, all these seasoned soldiers following him. Despite his station, he was a new commander, untested. He appreciated every man in his unit leaning on their knowledge. It was less nerve-wracking to give orders that could mean lives with the support and guidance of men with years of experience.

The men settled down around him for the night, each bundled in their own bedroll. He took first watch, as he always did. He felt it polite to let them rest first. At the end of a long day of riding, he was fine with missing a little more sleep. He'd had to argue for the privilege, but in the end, he was still their commander.

As the sun crept toward the horizon, Mian wondered where his scouts were. The scouts took off every morning to range ahead of the main army, sweeping the day's path for locations of farmers. This was the first day of their excursion that the scouts had not returned for the night camp. A search in the dark would be worse than pointless. They would have to fend for themselves till morning.

Mian's struggle to keep his worry private proved futile to the grizzled men of his patrol. They all knew the scouts were late, and they all knew what it could mean. Tracking had never been a talent of his, but the same could not be said of the men of his patrol. Long before the sun crested its zenith, they were tight on the tail of his missing scouts. The trail had led them north, as expected, through a series of abandoned farms and country houses. Near about midday, however, the tracks turned south.

Back toward the Seat.

All of it was enough to build a knot of anxiety in Mian's gut, but what they stared at now chilled his blood. A swath of land nearly ten spans wide stretched from the horizon to the tree line. This wasn't a hunting party hoping to run across easy prey; this was an army.

And it was headed toward the Seat.

He let the knowledge settle for a moment, tried to anticipate every angle. He needed to warn the Seat and he needed to find this army.

He straightened in his saddle and turned his horse to face his men. "I need two men to leave now for the Seat. Orotid, choose out your second, gather your supplies and get to Janu as fast as you can. The rest of us are going to track this army."

He felt a slight relief when the men set to their tasks with no discussion. Respect or agreement were both welcome reasons. Orotid was the only choice to carry the news to Janu; the older man's experience and knowledge made the decision for him. Sending two men allowed for rest and an increased the likelihood that at least one would reach Janu. Thinking through his decisions helped his confidence, helped him believe he had made the correct choice. Despite that, he still felt that the world weighed down on his shoulders as Orotid rode off trailed by the youngest man in Mian's outfit save himself. It was a smart choice; he had expected nothing less. Though still ten years Mian's senior, Laughlet was young enough to have the energy to support Orotid's age.

The remainder of the men watched him. "We all know what this means. We are going to track this army, see where they are going, the numbers we are talking about. Everything we learn will help our people."

The men around him shared a glance before his most senior officer, a man by the name of Meaghen, nodded. "We're with you, Commander Mian. Lead the way."

He kicked his horse into a trot, skirting the edge of the trees in an attempt to make them less visible. The swath of churned dirt and vegetation blazed like a beacon, impossible to miss. He didn't even want to contemplate the numbers needed to make such a scar across the land.

The bigger question was why the horde would waste the energy on such a move. Grinlo had been known to consume humans, even take them to do whatever awful things they did, but he had never heard of anything like this. The grinlo were simple, primitive creatures—they didn't have armies. Not for the first time he wished he was smarter. Not that he was stupid, but he knew enough to know there was a lot he didn't know. He just never thought he lacked knowledge on the grinlo.

They spent the day alternating between leading the horses and trotting but never caught sight of the army they pursued. How far behind were they? As the sun raced them across the sky, his anxiety grew from a spring storm to a violent torrent.

Mian slumped over in a vain effort to slow his panting as they took a brief respite at the base of a small rise. A hand to his back brought him straight up. Adain crouched at the crest of the rise, his gray hair cropped short. One of the younger soldiers in his company, Adain had a sharp mind and a sharper wit, though no amusement showed on his face today. He held one hand aloft back toward them, one finger jabbed toward the ground.

Something was approaching them.

Mian and his men ghosted into the trees, pushing their horses ahead of them. Mian eased his sword from its scabbard as his eyes remained locked on Adain. The man turned, following the progress of the approaching figure hidden behind the rise. It felt like a lifetime passed as he watched before something came into view.

A lone rider used the cover of the army's tracks to mask his passage. He was formless, wrapped in a heavy cloak. Adain crept around behind the mounted man as Mian and the rest of his men prepared their ambush.

Mian raised his hand as the rider approached but the signal never fell. The horse wandered side to side as it walked, as if it had no greater purpose. The rider slouched and swayed in its saddle, barely maintaining his seat. As Mian watched, the wind caught the cloak and revealed the uniform beneath.

"Hold!" he bellowed as he crashed through the underbrush. Adain beat him to the rider but still wasn't able to catch the soldier as he crumbled from the saddle.

Dirt and grass sprayed up around Mian as he slid up beside Adain and the soldier on the ground. A lump choked him as he met the gaze of the rider. "Bastian," he gasped—one of his missing scouts.

The man sprawled on the ground before him glowed pale with shock. His lips trembled with the effort of his breath but his eyes were dull. The tattered armor and clothes beneath the cloak spoke of his struggles in the time he'd been missing. Blood crusted along a tear running across his ribcage and at a dozen others across his chest and abdomen.

A shadow passed over them as the men from the trees joined them. Adain had already set to evaluating Bastian's injuries.

"Get a fire started," Mian said to no one in particular, "let's get him warm." The command wasn't necessary, but his soldiers allowed him the right before setting to what needed to be done. Mian turned his attention to Adain. "What are we looking at?"

"He's lost some blood. The injuries are numerous but nothing is life-threatening. His state is from exposure. He's been riding straight. There's no food or water on him. That, coupled with his injuries, is what you see before you." Straight facts, no gild.

Bastian's lips worked but no sound escaped. Mian gripped the man's hand. Several men returned and they cradled Bastian in the cloak and used it to carry him to the fire they had stoked. A pot of water nestled among the flames with a handful of dried meat formed a weak broth. Mian used his own cloak to cradle the man's head.

As afternoon passed to dusk, the men took turns standing guard, resting, and caring for their comrade. When the sun had set, Bastian had recovered enough to sit up on his own and sip at the broth.

Resigned to the night at their makeshift camp, Mian let Bastian recover at his own pace. As he drained his latest bowl of broth and the color budded in his cheeks, Mian felt comfortable prying.

"You saw them, didn't you?" he asked.

Bastian dodged his glance. "That we did, sir." He set the bowl aside before he continued. "We heard them before we saw them. I've never seen grinlo in such numbers."

"They are heading for the Seat." It wasn't a question, and Bastian did not treat it as such.

"What are our orders, sir?"

"How far behind are we?" Mian asked.

"We encountered them early on our scout day. Heard them, as I said. We had ranged wide, hoping to catch some of the shepherds. We tried, sir, to get a number for you, but we were spotted." Bastian paused to take a drink from a skin. "We barely got away. Elrik is wounded, sir, couldn't ride. I secured him inside a cave. I told him I would bring help."

Mian clapped a hand to the other man's shoulder. "You did well, Bastian. You rest up tonight and we'll find Elrik in the morning. Then we'll find this army. No grinlo are besting us."

Janu forced himself not to falter as Lord Huran shook his hand. The older man was tall, handsome, and one of the most trustworthy men he'd ever known. A trail of citizens filed from the gates of the Seat. Wagons of supplies, tethers of livestock, groups of children. Every non-military member of the Seat was on their way to Austeria or Kyneira. He had given them a day to pack. One precious day to decide what was worth burdening themselves on the long trip.

He could almost feel the army rushing toward the castle walls. The rest of the castle belonged to his soldiers now. Armed men with fargazers lined the parapets and walls. His mind had refused to absorb the news Orotid had brought: an army of grinlo descending on the Seat. It was more than he could handle.

But it wasn't just him.

He had a kingdom to look out for.

So, he'd pulled himself up and called an evacuation of all non-military residents. There were a handful of arguments—some didn't want to abandon their family's homes, some thought they could help out when the battle came—but most set about their tasks and trusted his judgment. Now he just had to prove their trust right.

At his back stood Lana. She hadn't left his side since the news came. He had to admit her presence was a comfort. She wouldn't allow him to make a foolish decision, and the safety net was very welcome. He needed all the knowledge he could get.

His less-constant shadows were an ever-changing contingent of commanders. They flowed and ebbed as their duties allowed but he was never left with less than ten at any one time. A wealth of knowledge at his disposal. Even Orotid made sure to find himself available should the need arise.

The caravan of evacuating citizens stretched across the landscape toward the horizon.

"What if this is a trap?" he asked, anxiety heavy in his gut. "What if their plan all along was to trigger an evacuation and attack our people as they flee?"

He could picture the look on Lana's face even as he remained staring after his people. "The grinlo are not intelligent enough for such a tactic, as you are well aware," she said, no hint of the reprimand he deserved for voicing such a worry. In private they could discuss such possibilities and the implications, but it would be disastrous conjecture to be carried out where other ears could hear it. They couldn't afford for such a rumor to spread among the people. That's how panic spreads. "And if they come across the caravan, the guards will hold them until we can come to their aid."

He glanced back to meet her gaze but she was watching the caravan. He returned his attention to the train of people. "Thank you, High Priestess."

"We should get going, my prince," she said. "There is much to be done."

He felt like he was leading a parade as his entourage fell in behind. He avoided the main gates, their wide iron reinforced doors standing open to accommodate the flow of people and items out of the Seat. He reentered the fortress through an unassuming side entrance. The door was less than two and a half feet wide. All non-main entrances were only wide enough for a man to slip through. During a siege, the smaller doors were easy to secure.

Inside the Seat, the empty hallways screamed with silence. No servants bustled about their chores, no lords or ladies lounged in the sitting rooms. The heart of the Seat was gone, ripped from its chest and bleeding south toward Austeria and Kyneira. Even his own chambers were bare of most amenities. All dress clothes and personal items had been packed up and now resided in a cart heading toward Austeria.

The stables were filled with the best mounts all ready for battle. Only military stable hands remained. A handful of livestock remained to feed and sustain the soldiers, but most were gone. Multiple groups searched the fortress and surrounding structures for any stragglers; Janu wanted no distractions if it came to a battle. Separate groups gathered and worked on weapons. He had set up multiple weapons caches around the fortress. He didn't want to be cut off from arms during battle.

As they trekked around the Seat, they stopped at each cache to check their progress. Messages flowed to and from the commanders at his back but most never reached his attention. He really wasn't needed for much and felt rather useless most of the time. Just a kid too young to rule, but old enough to think he could. And all he could do was sit and watch, as he was only truly given free rein decisions that were paltry at most. Oh, they made a show of him making decisions but there was always a strong suggestion from someone, usually Lana.

At least he could be comforted in knowing his decisions couldn't be foolish or ignorant.

That fact was what comforted him at times like this when he felt worthless. That no matter how bad it felt, at least it was a buffer that protected innocent lives. But what it felt like was one more reminder that he wasn't and never would be his father.

His father wouldn't have lost Amber Keep. His father wouldn't have had to evacuate the Seat. His father wouldn't allow himself to be led around like some puppet.

There were times where he thought about pushing back, asserting his control, taking back his kingdom. But the truth was, he didn't really want to assert control. If he was truly honest with himself, Lana overseeing his decisions was the best possible thing for Trimera, and he had no intention of changing it. He wasn't about to risk his people just for his own pride.

San slid the book in her hand back onto the shelf where it belonged. She hated when things were out of order, and there was nothing more out of order than the petulant seventeen-year-old girl seated before her desk. The book could have waited but patience was a lesson the girl needed.

She had always been trying, but Pria was too smart and too confident for most tactics to work. She had never really had a fear of what she could do. It had all made her difficult to work with but ever since the fall of Amber Keep the girl had become impossible. Every lesson became a race to learn faster, do more, push herself harder. The knowledge that her home was under attack seemed to make her desperate, rash. Where before she pushed herself because she knew she had the ability, now she pushed in a mad attempt to learn faster. The result had ended her in accident after accident, if one could call wantonly risking injury an accident. She was on a downward spiral that would at some point end in her death.

And it was that attitude that had landed her in the condition she was in now. Bandages stretched from the tips of her fingers to well above her elbows. It was nothing too severe, but enough to cause pain and concern. Princess Pria of Trimera, however, didn't have the sense to look chastised, pained, or even embarrassed. Her beautiful young face showed nothing but petulance. Arms crossed despite the bandages, she fumed her irritation.

The bandages covered swaths of angry red welts and cuts, some revealing the meat beneath her pink skin. In the heart-wrenching time it had taken to get the blood to stop gushing, San was sure she had aged a lifetime. She'd carted the girl off to the infirmary once she had stabilized and turned on the pale priestess that had been leading the class. Through her expression, San had eked out what had happened.

Now the offending child sat behind her. San held no illusions that this was going to be pleasant for her. She turned from the shelf of books and met the petulant gaze of the girl. Had she not known Pria, not felt the force of her gaze, San would have thought her dropped face indicated shame or even chastisement. As it were, fire and determination boiled from the girl.

San let Pria stew as she crossed to the desk and settled herself in the stuffed chair. Hands folded before her on her blotter, she prepared where to start.

But, of course, Pria would not allow that.

"I already know the lecture."

"Then perhaps you could let it sink it at some point," San countered.

Pria broke eye contact and showed her petulant teenage attitude. It didn't surface often; she was an even-tempered girl. Impatience was her biggest vice. "If it was that bad, you would have put more effort into healing the wounds."

San pulled back the sigh that struggled to rush from her lips. "You are not a stupid girl, Pria," she began, "and I am tired of wasting my breath telling you about the risks. You know the risks; they have not fazed you. The decision was made to let you live with the consequences of your actions." Sullenness sparked in Pria's eyes. "You will also be suspended from lessons until such time as I deem you are well enough to return to them."

"You can't do that!"

"It is already done." San met the girl's rage with cool serenity. She was sure there was no other way to get through to her. Her tutors returned with stories of classes disrupted, students endangered, and rules flaunted. Pria spent more time recovering in the infirmary than any other initiate. It was only a matter of time before someone got seriously injured. A little pain might just make her think.

San watched her words settle on Pria like a prison sentence. Rules didn't faze her, injury didn't faze her, but time frightened her.

As she sat locked in her battle of wits with a girl a quarter of her age, a light flashed to her right. In a fluff, a folded parchment floated down to land on her desk. She couldn't let her eyes drift to that letter, couldn't afford to distract Pria from the argument at hand.

But of course, nothing with Pria was ever that easy.

Pria felt satisfaction throb through the pain and anger. Neither of them would break to look at that letter. San was Lana's closest friend. Pria couldn't see the seal or the handwriting, but the likelihood of that missive being from Trimera was high.

A smug smile curled her lips. "You have a letter, Priestess San."

Ire sparked in San's eyes at Pria's sass. "I noticed."

"You're not going to read it?" she pushed.

"It can wait."

Irritation boiled up from her toes but she stamped it back down. "Could be important."

San nabbed the corner of the letter and set it on the desk between them. Pria knew her face screamed her interest. She hated giving San that much power, but the truth of it was with that letter in her hands, San could call any shot she wanted.

San laid her fingers atop the letter, a possessive move. She knew what that piece of parchment meant, what power it gave her.

"I don't know if I can consciously disclose sensitive information with someone I am unable to trust."

Pria felt the breath rush out of her lungs. Blackmail. Is that what they had come to? "What were you thinking?"

San's eyebrow hiked toward her hairline. A smug look of satisfaction poured from the older woman as she nudged the letter this way and that. San had a reputation even among the students of being a fierce negotiator, and her little tactic hit home. Every tap of her fingertip sent a bolt of energy through Pria that had to be visible to the other woman, though she made no outward indication of it.

After what had to have been days of fiddling with the letter, San finally said, "If I were to have some reasonable assurance of trust from someone who then provided evidence that they were worthy of my trust and capable of patience and obedience to the rules of the academy…" She paused and pretended to regard the parchment before her. "Perhaps I would feel confident to share such information with them."

San had her. What was worse, was that she knew it. Pria's shoulders dropped to her knees. "Priestess San, I pledge to you on my honor to obey by the strictures of the academy and the priestesses assigned to my guidance." Her voice was small, defeated.

San shook her head. "I have heard such pledges from you before, young lady, to no demonstrable end."

When Pria lifted her gaze, the priestess pierced her with the full force of her station. She wasn't seeing San the grandmotherly woman struggling to protect her student, she saw Priestess San tired of dealing with an unruly supplicant. It was to be crow then. She could bend. For her family, she could bend.

Pria stood and dipped into the perfect curtsy. A tad overdone, perhaps, but she wanted the impact. "Priestess San, I give you my word as the princess of Trimera, on the throne of my father where my brother now rules, that you will find no reason to censure my behavior in exchange for information you receive regarding Trimera." She straightened to gauge her impact and saw a small smile of satisfaction on San's face.

She swept her sinewy hand at the chair behind Pria. "Have a seat, Pria. Let us see how Trimera fares."

Victory.

Glorious victory after years of struggle. San felt like dancing a jig about the room! Felt like grabbing one of the more handsome laborers and showing him what maturity could do for a kiss, but such flamboyant displays were for women with far fewer concerns than San. So she settled for a smug smile she knew was burning a hole through the girl's pride even as she sighed in relief.

The seal on the envelope, of course, was Lana's. They had both known that the second it flashed to her desk. No one else would have sent a letter directly to her office even if they had the ability. It was an intimate gesture from a dear friend.

She broke the red dob of wax pressed with the fierce owl of the priestesses, a large horned owl to symbolize their strength and protectiveness. Wings spread wide, taloned feet open to grab, it cracked along the edge of the parchment and split wide.

San spread the letter out before her. Lana's writing was neat, practical, and efficient. Impatience flowed from the girl across from her as she lifted the letter and read aloud:

My Dearest San,

I bear tidings of grave news. An army marches on the Seat. The citizens have been evacuated and I and Prince Janu stand with the army ready to defend the city.

The air in the room maintained its warmth but a chill rushed along her bones. The Seat was under attack.

"Well?" Pria's hand slapped down on the desk, snapping San back to the room. "Go on!"

San swallowed. "There is nothing else," she said. "Pria, return to your room. Now."

San stood from her desk and left the girl behind. She would have to fend for herself. San needed to inform the Council and there wasn't a moment to lose.

The room around Pria rang in silence. Her home. Her family. Everything she loved was in danger.

She was running down the hall without any thought of where she was going or what she was going to do. It wasn't until she found herself staring up at her gray horse in his stall that the realization that she was running away came forward in her mind.

She tried to calm herself as a groom approached. Just a student, wanting to take a ride. She composed her face as she turned to face the groom.

"I would like to go for a ride, could you saddle my horse please?" She kept her voice sweet, just a helpless girl.

The groom was a young man with the soft brown eyes of a hound and an unkempt shock of dusty hair. He couldn't be more than two years her senior. He smiled and dropped his gaze as a blush rushed up his cheeks. "Of course, my lady." He bobbed a clutzy bow and scurried away.

She grasped her wrist behind her back as she listened to the groom in the tack room. Every tinkle of buckle, every thump of leather and wood against the stall wall, was time slipping away from her. She needed to be gone; she needed to be on her way to Trimera, before—

"Going somewhere, Princess Pria?"

She froze mid-sway at the soft voice behind her. She shrugged a shoulder to her chin as she turned. "Just going for a ride, Priestess."

San towered behind her, though the woman was not truly tall. She never lost her cool demeanor though she had to know precisely why Pria was standing in the stables. "Glad to see you have free time. I am in need of assistance for some errands."

Pria's soul shriveled and died within her chest. "Of course, Priestess."

San hadn't missed the defeat in her voice. "You cannot help them untrained, dear."

"Am I supposed to hide here in the Lorien while my home is under attack?"

A heavy hand landed on her shoulder and she surrendered to the comfort as San pulled her against her side. "Is that what you think you are doing here, hiding?" San said with a soft tease. "If that is true then I must have a word with your tutors about your workload."

"You know what I mean!"

"I do," San said, "and I will remind you of your very first lesson here. Do you remember it?"

Remember it she did. A priestess' first lesson was designed so she would never forget it. "A priestess is from all nations and none."

"Very good. And what does that mean?"

Pria wanted to balk as San led her from the stable back toward her office. Wanted to, but didn't. "It means that a priestess cannot allow her personal views to influence her station or duty."

"And as a student in the Lorien, what is your sole duty?" San pressed.

"To learn all that I may need in my future vocation as a priestess." She did balk now, pulling the other woman to a stop beside her. "So I will never be allowed to protect my family."

"Of course not. You have every right to protect those you love. Just not when it comes at the expense of others."

Petulance raged forth and she stomped her foot to the floor. "Then why can I not go to them now? It wouldn't be hurting anyone!"

San's finger rose in a silent command for stillness. Around them the breeze blew in from the river, dense and heavy. Life went on around them as they stood staring at each other, one finger to the sky above. "It would in fact, Pria, hurt you," San said into the void between them. "It would disrupt and delay your training and impact every life you would have changed upon instatement to full priestess status." Her hand lowered and life rushed back in. "It is no secret that I above all others favor you. My affection is for more than just the girl you are but for the force you will become, and I do not intend to let you cheat this world of that force."

Pria's face burned as her vision blurred. "Will I ever go home?" Tears poured down her face and dripped from her chin. The emptiness in her gut gaped wide as it threatened to engulf her.

San pulled a kerchief from inside her robes and dabbed at her damp cheeks. "You will see Trimera again, my dear," she said. "High Priestess Lana will protect your dear brother and all your friends."

Pria knew the truth of her words but it did little to assuage the guilt and fear in her stomach. She could tell the well of pain was visible by the sympathy painting San's face. "Come, Pria. Work will help distract you from such thoughts."

Mian crouched among the underbrush. Bastian had led them along the scar of churned earth for a full day before turning off from the main path and heading into the foothills to the south. Here at the edge of the trail, Mian could distinguish individual tracks of the outside stragglers. Bastian's path was littered with loose rocks that had been knocked free from the slopes above. Bastian took a sharp left and began to climb one of the slopes.

When Bastian and Elrik had run across the grinlo scouting party, they lost one of the horses in their struggle to escape. Mian could pick out the tracks that indicated the passage of the two men but only because he knew to look for them. Had he been tracking them without knowing where they had gone, he could have easily missed the signs.

Near the crest of the knoll, a dark crevasse marred the ground and Bastian headed straight for it. Mian could already smell the faint whiff of smoke and the remnants of food. Mian and Bastian left their horses with the other men and slipped into the crack of a cave. Light filtered down into the crevasse, illuminating the cave's mouth. The light faded several feet inside the cave, and deep inside he was able to see the amber glow of coals.

The smoke was thicker here but still well ventilated as the wind whipping across the top of the knolls pulled the air out through the opening.

Behind the coals, illuminated in an orange haze, lay his lost scout Elrik. Skin pale and eyes closed, Elrik had a crust of blood dried across his forehead and a second patch darkening across his abdomen. Mian rushed to the man's side. His skin was clammy and his pulse weak.

Bastian knelt beside him. "He doesn't look good, sir."

"We'll stabilize him here," Mian said, peeling back the bandages to see the extent of the damage. "Let's get him able to travel and get him to the Seat. Lana will know what to do."

Bastian flinched at the familiar reference to their high priestess, but Mian had gotten so used to it that he had to actually stop and think to add the honorific. He ignored Bastian and set to securing better bandages around Elrik's wounds. "Bastian, we need a litter." The man left without a word.

Mian sat back on his heels. Elrik would be lucky to see the Seat again. If he could only get him to Lana, she could help him, but he wasn't deluded enough to believe the man had much of a chance of getting that far. He wouldn't give up on him, though. Not with an army rushing toward the Seat.

Elrik's wounds had clotted over long before they had found him. The bandages were sealed to the wounds, impossible to remove without reopening them. He was as stable as he could be made. Mian forced some water into his mouth, waited for him to swallow, and repeated the process. By the time he was finished, the men clamored in carrying a litter fashioned from samplings and a blanket. As his men bundled Elrik onto the litter, Mian stomped out the coals of the dying fire. They slung the litter between two horses and began the slow and painful progress toward the Seat.

Wind cut across the parapets of the Seat to a chorus of snapping cloaks and pennants. It was the only movement on the roof. Soldiers armed with bows lined the guard wall. They could already hear the army's approach through the trees. Lana stood in a void, a calculated ring of safety. Battling with magic was not for spectators. Spell fallout could be dangerous and she wanted no casualties from her side.

She and Mian had argued Janu to direct the battle from on the roof with her, in the relative safety of the battlements. Mian awaited his orders below as he led the soldiers lining the city walls and streets. He had returned with one soldier on the verge of death. The soldier was sequestered below, well away from any chance of the battle. She had little hope for the man; she wasn't a healer. She had tried to be honest with Mian, as she hated giving people false hope, but he had stared at her with such desperation. She had never seen that look of open faith on his face before, not for her. After everything between them, she liked the boy. She couldn't deny her wish to fulfill that trust. So, despite the obvious, she didn't have the heart to tell him the man was dying. She let him believe his comforting lie as she eased the soldier's pain. It was all she could do.

But here atop the Seat, facing the oncoming horror, she couldn't dwell on that comforting lie. There were people here she could save, people she could make a difference for. That was where her focus needed to be.

The army before her occupied her mind now. She had seen many things in her life, but an organized army of grinlo wasn't thought to be possible. Never had she dreamed to have the misfortune to face one. Atop the Seat, awaiting their arrival, she had much too long to contemplate the reason behind such a drastic shift in behavior. She didn't like any of them. But how to determine what was behind it?

It could be a fluke, just some random act of nature that brought several packs of grinlo together to hunt, and the Seat was the closest concentration of human prey. It was farfetched, but possible. There could be an increase in the population, which could precipitate a larger party seeking out a concentration of prey. It was unlikely, but still possible.

It could be an evolution. Perhaps the grinlo had developed to a point where communal living benefited them. They could be increasing their intelligence, learning from watching the soldiers of Trimera. It had happened before—the grinlo had learned to use armor and weapons by observing soldiers; this could be an extension of the same type of learning. She had never heard of any congregation before this to indicate any movement toward such an end, but it was possible.

There was, of course, another possibility, one too horrific to contemplate. But she had to contemplate it, even if only to herself. She needed Trimera focused, not panicked, so she would keep that worry to herself for now, until she had proof as to what was actually behind this strange behavior. She alone would suffer that fear.

If the behavior was an evolution, it was extremely fast. Scouts reported that the grinlo had set up a stronghold at Amber Keep. Grinlo never had a use for fortresses previously. The grinlo lived in small groups but they inhabited caves, not buildings. They were not organized enough to form communities larger than a handful of family units.

It could still be mimicry. Honor and family, let it be mimicry.

Every fiber of her being was numb. She could feel the defeat in her shoulders, the weight of her head, the weakness in her body. In her breast pocket was a report detailing the losses of Amber Keep. Could such a human tragedy truly be translated into mere numbers? It didn't seem possible, yet there it was. A tally of the lives taken in cold digits.

And more were to come here at the Seat.

Her spine straightened as she separated the pain of loss in her mind, compartmentalized it until there was no trace of sadness left in her consciousness. The suffering wouldn't help her.

She turned her attention to the second parchment nestled inside her breast pocket. It was a letter from her dear childhood friend San. They had met during their training at the Lorien. San had stayed on to foster and build peace in Reia while Lana had been stationed in Trimera. Now, San sent her news from the Lorien and, for the past few years, updates on a certain precocious young lady.

A comfort bloomed in her chest and spread throughout her body, bubbling tranquility into her tormented mind. All the pain was worth it for that one bright light. The child would grow to be one of the strongest high priestesses in the history of the Lorien. With any luck Pria would unite all of Reia like no priestess before her. Lana had always had that dream herself but her true passion for research got in the way. But her dream lived on in Pria.

It was a comfort even as she faced the wreckage of Trimera. The Frontier had stood for generations without a significant advance, and here she stood on the parapets of the Seat preparing to face down an army. She was failing her station. She had to figure out what was going on here, find the reason behind this push, not only to protect Trimera and Reia, but also to expand the knowledge of the Lorien. Every tidbit of knowledge could mean lives saved or lost.

Mian glanced behind him at the parapets. He could just make out Janu with his guard at the edge of the void around Lana. Janu had argued to lead from the walls, but the combined force of Lana and himself had forced him to the roof. Mian himself would lead the defense—under the orders of Janu, of course. The people of Trimera needed their ruling prince, and Mian was going to ensure they kept him, no matter the cost.

Mian stood atop the defensive wall, the first line of defense for the city. The wall had few gates: the main gates at the roads, service gates, and a handful of defensive gates to allow for the movement of soldiers. All were closed, secured, and guarded; he'd seen to it himself and had Lana second check him. They couldn't afford any mistakes if they planned to hold the Seat.

He couldn't let Janu down. He'd met his prince's eyes, his brother's eyes, and promised to hold the city. So, he'd gathered the soldiers and ensured any men lacking experience were surrounded and led by senior officers. The wall around him was lined with soldiers, standing guard, delivering weapons, and distributing arrows and other supplies. The Seat was at war, but she had been before. Sending the citizens away had been a precaution. It was how he had to think of it, otherwise it was too overwhelming.

A horn sounded close to him, forlorn in the light of day, sending a wave of tension through his body. The first grinlo had broken the tree line.

The army of grinlo had arrived.

The men on the walls and parapets shifted their shoulders, eased muscles stiff from standing, preparing for the battle as the enemy raged toward them. The men in the courtyard below checked their swords, axes, shields, whatever they carried. There was one man among the soldiers who carried a wicked spiked hammer. Trimera fought with what got the job done.

Mian's eyes searched the tree line for movement, for any sign of the approaching army, but with his naked eye all he could see were moving shadows. The men on lookout had fargazers to enhance their eyesight. He had to trust them in this.

Two horn-blasts cracked across his anxiety. The men around him moved to stringing their bows and he followed suit. Bows lost their strength if strung constantly. If the battle lasted too long, they would need every second they could get. Pages ran by, making sure each man had the supplies they needed.

He always found the calm before battle to be the strangest part of war. Men stood around waiting for death to descend upon them. No epic speeches of heroism rang through the air, no pleas for mercy. The entire affair seemed rather banal, seeing as they were all waiting to stare into the gape of eternity.

In his fantasies of heroism as a child, there was never this gap of boredom. He and his men would charge valiantly toward the enemy, screaming like banshees with swords drawn. But such foolish heroics were just that, foolish. Rushing the enemy wasted energy and lost lives. True battle was a lot of waiting. It gave a man plenty of time to think about what was coming. Even now as the grinlo massed together preparing their attack on the wall, he wondered what the defenders of Amber Keep thought as the grinlo bore down on the city. None of them could have known that they would never leave that place.

Mian pulled an arrow from a quiver at his hip. Once the hand-to-hand battle started, he would toss the quiver aside to free his movement. The bow in his hands was yew, golden and wrapped in suede with leather lacings. His father had made it for him, carved and curved it with his own hands. It stood a good two inches above the crown of his head and pulled like an old mule. It would punch through the primitive armor the grinlo wore, even from the wall.

His eyes returned to the trees and the shadow that spread from them. They were coming.

The air filled with a roar as ranks of grinlo marched across the open span toward the walls of the Seat. They were dug into the fortress; for better or worse, they had to make their stand. Horns sounded the approach and even the naked eye could make out definition now. The creatures didn't rush at the walls but rather formed up in the rough semblance of military formation. Creatures continued to pour from the trees as the advancing line approached.

Every soldier on the wall now held an arrow at the ready, arms still down to conserve energy. None would draw until the line came within range; they needed to conserve their energy while they could. The horns called out codes to signal the distances of the approaching army and every man counted each beat. Mian shuffled his weight from foot to foot as the horn blew again. Almost now.

The next sounding of the horn was met with a well-practiced dance. Mian lifted his bow in a strange synchrony with all the men around him. The arrow sang away from him in a flock of its mates soaring toward the approaching line. Cries announced the arrows finding their marks below. His heart filled his chest; the boredom of waiting was over.

Janu cringed with each crash as the small mass of grinlo worked to bring down the gates in the outer wall. Few arrows sang through the air.

Other than the small tactical groups working on breaking down the gates, the main mass of grinlo waited well out of range of the archers atop the parapets and wall. He didn't let himself think about what that might mean—he'd had enough worry lately thinking about the increasing intelligence of the grinlo. He wasn't positive if this life-preserving maneuver was more intelligent than they should be capable of but he was going to chalk it up to good old common sense. A man had to sleep at night, didn't he? He was sure he'd hear enough about it from Lana soon enough.

Mian had moved from the wall to join the soldiers in the courtyard. How Janu longed to join him. Years of military training had been built up in his muscles and body but when the fighting started, he was always sequestered somewhere safe. He knew the arguments, even agreed with them, but that didn't make it any less palatable watching his friends and others risking their lives while he sat safe behind the lines. He just had to keep reminding himself that Trimera couldn't afford to be broken and go through an unsecured succession.

So here he sat.

He rushed to the parapet as a chorus of yells rang out from the courtyard. Grinlo had managed to break off a massive chunk of the gate and reached through. Soldiers rushed forward to fight back the intrusion. His pulse raged in his ears. It was only a matter of time before they would be able to break through completely.

Then the real loss of life would start.

His father had led battles in his reign, had led men against the influx of grinlo at Amber Pass. Had he also felt the overwhelm of nausea over his orders sending men to their death? How many sons and daughters of Trimera had stained the grounds of Amber Keep with their blood before

Lord Renor realized the fight was futile and that evacuation was the only hope? Too long, at any rate.

Or maybe that had been the plan all along. To push the Keep to evacuation and kill everyone as they escaped.

That was a dangerous line of thought. He wouldn't let his mind fill in that nightmare. There was enough horror for anyone right in front of him at the moment.

Another loud crack announced the failure of one of the smaller side gates. An influx of grinlo poured in east of the courtyard. Soldiers filed toward the influx, weapons slashing and spraying arcs of red through the air. Grinlo rushed forward across the open space toward the wall.

"Archers!" Janu screamed over the din of battle and was answered by the twang of loosed arrows. Here and there among the rush, creatures fell but were replaced by others almost before a gap could be noticed.

The push at the gate became a landslide of grinlo. The main gate failed again, forcing soldiers back on that side as well. The soldiers rallied against the influx but they stood no chance against the incoming wave.

Janu snagged the breastplate of a runner as he rushed by for an armload of arrows to pass around. "Find Mian and tell him to fall back," he said. "We'll hold against the inner gates."

He released the boy without ever looking at his face. It would be harder to send him into what could mean his death if he made eye contact. Protect as many lives as possible and try not to think about the ones you have to sacrifice. It was all he could do.

Even from atop the Seat he could still see men fall down below. Every life was a spike through his chest, his heart. Even one was too many, but the Seat was a vital line of defense for Trimera. If they lost the Seat there would only be one fortress left to fight from. He couldn't afford to lose it.

But neither could he afford to throw away the lives of his men in vain. There seemed no way to balance the two. He needed his soldiers to defeat the grinlo, he needed the Seat to protect his soldiers, he needed his soldiers to protect the Seat. It would never even out. No matter the cost, he couldn't put the Seat above his men. He knew there would be a time where he would have to relinquish the Seat. Somehow, he would have to decide when the lives lost were enough. Or was it too many? As the archers around him turned their aim to the courtyard below, he knew it was already too many.

The crash of swords engulfed him as he lifted his own bow to aid in protecting his men. For now, he could still defend his home. For now, he could still hold the Seat's defenses.

Mian rushed forward with the line of men. He had set up a rotating front line to help counteract the endless wave of fresh grinlo that continued to rush toward them. Men rotated forward to fight, then rotated back to rest. They couldn't beat the numbers but he would do what he could.

His arm screamed as his blade crashed against the battered armor of one of the creatures. His head rang as claws scraped along the metal of his breastplate. With a foot to its chest, he forced the grinlo back and sliced a line deep across its body. The creatures crawled across their own dead and wounded, uncaring about anything but pushing farther into the Seat's defenses. A wiser man might wonder what they could possibly want with the Seat, but wiser men also didn't have the horde screaming for their blood, so Mian left the wondering to them. His job was just to stop their influx.

Whenever one of their own soldiers fell, they tried to pull them back behind the line, wounded or dead. Any body left for the creatures was just food for them, and the last thing they needed was to give strength to the enemy.

Gore dripped from his sword as he resisted the urge to push forward. They held the line close to the Seat's inner gates. They couldn't afford to be cut off. They needed the protection behind them. The courtyard funneled the grinlo and lessened the number they could send at them at once; the Seat's walls behind them protected them from routing, gave them something to push against.

Chaos reigned around him. Creatures slashed at the soldiers, claws against weapons and armor. Screeching grated against the air as claw met sword, shield, stone. His muscles screamed as his sword flashed among the enemy. His ears rang with the abuse, his body begged for reprieve but he couldn't respond to either.

Mian sat at a desk behind the line of fighting, weight pressed down on his shoulders. It was a strange little void in the madness. He picked at a plate of food—he didn't allow himself to waste a morsel; holed up in the Seat surrounded by grinlo, they had no way to get supplies into the city—but his main focus was on the documents before him. Maps and schematics, numbers and supplies, all jumbled together into a pile of knowledge he had to decipher. Janu had a copy of the same information. One of them had to come up with a miracle to save the Seat, to protect the people left here.

He slapped his hand against his forehead. There had to be something. He couldn't fail. Cries of the fallen assaulted him from every side. Mingled with the screams were the roars of the horde, their calls for blood. Something fueled their attack. Nothing else could explain why they pressed even after the substantial loss of life on their side.

A fire raged at the edge of the courtyard, filling the air with rancid smoke and the smell of roasting meat. The piles of rotting grinlo had created a hazard and they had started to burn the bodies to rid the space of the filth. It wasn't perfect, but it was all he could do.

He tallied the remaining numbers of their army and sighed in defeat. He gathered up his papers and stashed them into a travel desk. His plate was clean.

He stood from the table and picked up his sword. He was needed back at the line. He would hold the Seat, it was all he could do for Janu. All he could do for Pria.

Orotid could feel the worry creeping into the back of his mind. He couldn't waste the time drawing comparisons between the siege here at the Seat and his memory of Amber Keep, not with the battle raging just outside. What good would it do? His mind still danced with the bodies strewn about the ground, bodies from the Seat, bodies from Amber Keep. The images rarely left his head.

The same fate would soon come to the Seat, he knew. He couldn't be the only one to see what was coming, but it wasn't his place to point it out. He would follow orders and do as he was told. He had to—there was work to be done. He checked the edge of his sword against his thumb. The blade was scarred and pitted from battle but the edge was keen. He slammed it in his scabbard and turned from his bed.

It was a communal room lined with bedrolls along the floor. This was their second communal room and his third room in the Seat. The invasion had moved them all from their own or semi-own rooms, depending on their rank, to reduce communication times. One room was easier to rouse than many.

They had been pulled back as the grinlo broke through the wall, which had taken a week. The army beyond set up camps and sent a steady rotating onslaught of grinlo at them. The soldiers had shorn up the gates several times, but there was no end to the advance.

And that was the problem. Trimera's soldiers were strong, dedicated, but there were only so many of them. The horde seemed to flow eternal. How long before supplies ran low? Before the loss of life outweighed the loss of the Seat? How long before he was forced to abandon another stronghold?

The Seat was in a constant state of chaos. The footsteps of soldiers never died from the hallways. Men rotated from the defensive positions to meals, repair, or rest if they were lucky enough to avoid the infirmary. There were plenty men there. Far more littered the courtyards beyond.

He'd already seen the struggle in young Janu's eyes. He knew the prince was close to calling it, to leaving his home to the beasts. Orotid understood his struggle, had already seen the aftermath of such decisions. Lana as well bore the ghost of knowledge, though it was harder to see on her. They would be moving soon, of that much he was sure.

He joined with a mass of soldiers all heading to the front. They had lost the wall but after four weeks of fighting they still held part of the courtyard. A mass of soldiers was always dedicated to the doors. If retreat was ordered, they secured the entrance once everyone was inside. The current crew stood to the sides to allow passage but still craned toward the fighting. Door watch was important work and they would not shirk, but the draw of battle gave no respite.

Beyond the door, the world bombarded him with blinding light and the cacophony of battle. He caught sight of Mian, fresh blood on his clothes. The strain showed on his young face. The boy needed a break.

Orotid broke from his line and joined him. "Commander."

Mian waved a dismissive hand in reply. Yet another bandage adorned his hand, turning pink with blood. A network of red haloed his green eyes. "You rested up?" he asked.

"As good as I can get, given the situation." He shot Mian a wary eye. "How about you?"

"I'll hold."

He rushed down the mass of men barking encouragement and filtering fresh soldiers toward a bulge in the line. Orotid ghosted behind him. "We need you more than holding, sir."

Mian rounded on him, fire in his eyes, his face twisted in rage. "You think you can do better, soldier?"

Orotid held Mian's gaze and waited patiently as the fire fizzled to embers. "I'm sorry," he whispered, his voice defeated.

"No need for that, sir."

Mian's hand raked through his already disheveled locks. His gaze scanned the battle around them, the courtyard littered with bodies. "You will hold the line for me?"

"To my last breath, sir."

"I will go rest," he said, defeat heavy in his words.

Orotid clapped him on the shoulder. "You have done well, sir. I will send for you when my shift is over."

Something brushed against his leg in the dark. Impenetrable dark, the type that eats at your soul. He tried to jerk away but his movements were sluggish, as if the very air held him back. All around him he could hear shuffling. There was no way to tell where he was.

"You cannot save them," a voice said from the dark.

He froze, heart pounding.

"I will take them all, you realize?" It came from all around him, from every side at once. "I will save the girl for last, your little princess. She will be mine and you are powerless to stop it."

Teeth flashed at his face, bolting Mian upright in his bed.

His bed in his room—well, the room he occupied. Moonlight played across the bedsheets, glistened on the sheen of sweat coating his skin. A nightmare, just a nightmare. Or was it?

A shape darker than the shadows hovered near the door. His heart erupted as it turned to face him.

"Easy!" Janu called out from the dark. Janu perched on the edge of his bed, a formless shape of black. "I didn't mean to frighten you."

Mian worked the tension from his body but his voice was still breathless when he spoke. "Not you," he panted. "Nightmare."

The prince nodded. "Had a few of those myself."

Duty and obligation rushed into the void left by his retreating fear. "Am I needed at the front? Did I sleep through my watch?"

Janu pushed him back on his bed. "No Mian," he soothed. "I pulled the men inside the doors. We have ceded the courtyard."

Mian's shoulders slumped. "I'm failing you."

"You could never fail me, Mian. You have accomplished more than any man could have in these circumstances." Janu sighed, his dark shape deflating in the dim light. "I cannot further justify the loss of more men." The moonlight glinted off his eyes as he turned to face Mian. "I think we have to abandon the Seat."

Mian felt the words as a physical blow. Memories rushed through his mind, years of playing, mischief, friendship, family. The Seat was his world, for years almost all he knew. Abandon the Seat? Might as well abandon life, abandon breathing. It was his home. Where he met his friends, Janu, Pria, his parents…how could they abandon all that?

But most of those people were gone now. Pria wasn't here, she was in the Lorien. His parents had escorted the citizens to Austeria. All that remained were memories and bodies, and if they weren't careful, they would join them. So he kept his worries and sorrows inside. He couldn't show any of them. Janu hadn't come here for an argument. He needed to hear he was making the right decision. Janu had the same memories he did, the same attachment, but where Mian's parents awaited them, all Janu had left were his memories. So, despite the pain, despite what it represented, despite the gaping chasm that he knew was widening in both of them, he knew it was the right decision. Too many good men had already joined the memories of the Seat, never to emerge again.

Mian forced his back straight and gathered confidence he didn't feel. "I will get started on the preparations. Do we head for Austeria?"

Mian could see Janu straighten in response. "Yes," he said. "It has the strongest defenses. From there we can lick our wounds, gather our strength, and decide our next steps."

Mian's hand clapped to the table beside the bed and the tinderbox that sat there. A few seconds of fumbling in the dark and he had a candle lit. He had slept in everything but his armor, prepared to return to battle at a moment's notice. The flickering light revealed Janu's pallid face.

"Let's get to it then."

Wind whipped across the rooftop, snapping Pria's hair around her head like a tempest, but she didn't care. The sun glared down on her, burning any exposed skin, but it was a warmth she craved.

Below her stretched out the Silver City. A gem of beauty worth the attention of scholars and kings alike, but she barely noticed it. She'd seen it all before. Years in the Lorien had given her ample time to absorb every masterpiece of architecture. Now, all she longed to see were the harsh stone defenses of her home. It seemed such a simple wish, yet unattainable to her. She rubbed at the tension of her forehead and felt the sunburn's angry sting. She would be red as a beet. She'd been up here all morning, since the word had arrived that the Seat had fallen to the horde.

How could this have happened? How many generations had Trimera stood, unchanged, to now fall victim to the largest invasion of grinlo anyone alive had ever seen?

Lana's note had been accompanied by notes from both Janu and Mian this time. Both had been almost the same: apologies for not being strong enough to hold the Seat, for the loss of their childhood home. But they didn't understand. It was not they who were weak. If she didn't have this ability, if she was a normal girl, she would have been there with them, fighting at their side. It was a foolish thought, childish, to think that her one blade would have made any difference, but that realization did not take away the impulse. Or the guilt.

Training for priestesses was not definite. Each woman's progress was determined by her strength, her abilities, and her own absorption of the curricula. Some women never graduated to full priestesshood. There was no way to be sure how much longer her own training would last. She knew she neared the end, but the Council had been saying that to her for years. She wondered if time became skewed with age.

Over the din of the city below, she could just hear soft slippers on the roof behind her. She wasn't worried, though. It would be San. No one else would approach her so soon.

"When we first found you up here, I assured everyone that the behavior would fade with time," San said, though not harshly. San pushed her hard but there was always a fondness behind it. "Yet here I am, at my age, still climbing up here to check on you."

Pria chuckled. "You have many years left ahead of you, Priestess."

"Not if I keep having to climb up here I don't!"

Pria smiled over at the older woman and saw San flinch. "That bad, huh?"

"Were you a tomato, I would pluck you for my dinner," she said. "As it were, I think it is far beyond time you came down."

The skin on her face and arms pulled as she moved. She would be sore for a few days. San waited patiently, hand outstretched for Pria to gather herself. For all her talk of years, San was still strong and Pria was again reminded of the strange view time seemed to gain with age.

She was sure her eyes were veined red from crying. The loss of the Seat was like losing a member of her family. She would mourn for quite a while.

The rooftops were flat this far south. There was no need for slope to keep the snow from accumulating. The Lorien was built for size, to maximize the space available for the priestesses' many works. She had learned so much about the Lorien in her time here, but there always seemed more to know. Every inch of land owned by the priestesses that wasn't devoted to buildings was cultivated. Medicinal plants, magical plants, rare and exotic beauties—there was a garden for just about everything. In her classes she had learned about them all. The priestesses coveted knowledge above all things.

Along the edge of the Heart were pools filled with fish and aquatic plants. One even contained saltwater with fish brought back from the great Antillian Ocean. She would love one day to see the ocean. Water so vast you couldn't see the other side, she couldn't even imagine.

San led her toward the stairs that were the only access to the roof. Well, unless you liked to scale walls. She wouldn't mention how she had actually gotten up there. A girl had to have some fun. The shade of the stairs felt cool, despite how warm she knew it still was. Just the relief from the sun was a blessing, but as soon as it was gone, she could feel the cold again. It seeped into her core and spread out along her bones. She had felt this cold before, remembered it keenly from her parents' death. Back then the Seat felt empty without them. A shell of walls with no heart. Now the cold was from its loss. Strange the change one sees given a few years' time.

She stayed deep in her thoughts and let her feet follow San through the corridors and along stairs. She didn't need to focus for this. She preferred to let herself travel the roads of her memory. She raced along the corridors of the Seat, seeking Janu and Mian. They were always into something interesting. She sat in her mother's lap as the older woman prepared herself for one court meeting or another. Pria had always been allowed to play with her mother's crowns, each more beautiful than the last. Her favorite was made of silver. It was twisted and carved into a forest of trees with a smattering of red garnet flowers among the branches. Every time she looked at it, she discovered something new. Hidden among the branches, the sculptor had hidden rabbits and deer and birds. It was a work of art more than a crown. She hoped Janu thought to save them.

Her mind jolted back to the present as her feet crunched on a gravel path. She blinked up around her at the sky. "Where are we going?"

"I thought you might enjoy a ride," San said with a jovial lilt in her voice. "Though we will have to fetch you a hat to shade your face before you blister yourself into sun sickness."

Pria felt a tiny flicker of warmth push back the cold inside. San really did know just how to bring her out.

Narita checked the closures of her breastplate. Her father, Lord Huran, had commissioned it for her once he realized that no amount of reasoning would prevent her from fighting to protect her kingdom. Women as soldiers was not unheard of in Trimera, but that didn't mean her father was happy to have his only child risk her life.

The city of Austeria was in an uproar. Every room was bursting with refugees from the Seat. It was a constant battle finding enough room and food for everyone, but Trimera pulled together in crisis, always had.

She snatched up a cloak and her sword as she swept across the room. She leapt at a knock at her door, her heart racing out of control. With a hand to her chest, she pulled her nerves back. She'd been anxious all morning, ever since she'd heard the news. Her hands shook as she opened the door.

"We're ready to head out," her father said. He stood in his own resplendent armor.

A lump leapt into her throat and she felt her heart race to join it. "I'm coming." Her voice squeaked with effort and she swallowed. "I'm ready."

A team of horses awaited them in the courtyard. Her own black mare nuzzled against her as she approached. Weapons and armor clanged around her. She wasn't sure what the fuss was; they were only riding to meet Janu at the gates, but Father insisted on ceremony. It wasn't every day your home became the seat of power.

Her stomach fluttered as she stepped into her saddle. Feeling her nerves, the horse reached around and shook her foot with its muzzle. She wasn't altogether sure why she was so anxious—these were her friends. That didn't stop the lump forming in her stomach when her father told her that Prince Janu would be basing the ruling seat here in Austeria. She wasn't sure when that had happened either—referring to Janu as prince—but there it was, nonetheless. It had been years since she'd even seen him.

The streets of Austeria rang with welcome. The news of Prince Janu's arrival had spread through the population like a plague. Her nerves eased as she enjoyed the garlands of flowers strung across the streets above their heads. Everyone was decked out in their finest, most with a basket of flowers or petals to toss as if awaiting a parade. Children ran through the streets streaming strands of brightly colored fabric. It was a joyous, festive atmosphere.

It could almost make one forget the reason behind the arrival.

A small girl rushed up to her, offering a garland of yellow lilies. She gave the girl her brightest smile and draped the floral circle about her temples, letting the tail fall down her back. The people needed a reason to rejoice, now more than ever. She would not be the one to let them down. She waved to the crowd as they cheered.

Soldiers lined the streets once they reached the gates, each man polished and pristine. No one wished to be seen as less than elated to welcome their prince. The gates stood open, allowing her to watch the approach of the party. It was more of an army, every surviving soldier from the Seat.

Runners had arrived the day before, asking refuge in the name of their prince. The request was just a formality, a polite gesture. The prince had the right to take over any structure he saw fit, but that wasn't Janu's way. He would see it an intrusion. She couldn't imagine how hard it had been on him to abandon his childhood home, the only connection he had left to his parents, to Pria. A wailing horn had announced their approach to the city earlier today. She could already make out Mian at the head of the procession, his red hair a beacon.

A smile broke across her face as warm memories flooded her mind. Mian, overprotective and maddening, was the big brother she'd never had. Fatigue painted every aspect of his body: shoulders slumped, head lowered, face slack. It was mirrored in every soldier around him. These men were defeated.

She kicked her horse into a trot, leaving her father and the host of guards staring after her. The prince's soldiers' eyes lifted to her face as she approached, back straight, face warm. She threw her hands wide. "Welcome to Austeria, heroes from the Seat. Every citizen of our fair city and the survivors of yours await to hail your safe arrival."

Mian's eyes were devoid of their usual spark of amusement as he blinked at her. Then between one drop of the eyelid and the next she saw understanding spread across his face. He dropped from his horse, his knees buckling more than they should have. His back was straight when he turned to her, his shoulders strong. "And a hero's welcome well deserved, my lady," he said, turning to face the men at his back. "Not a man among them deserves less."

He waved them past, into the city, to the roaring welcome of the crowd. Every man drew himself up, swelled with pride.

Narita slipped from her horse and joined Mian at the edge of the road as he watched the wave of praise wash over his men. Narita laid a supportive hand on Mian's shoulder and had to struggle to maintain her smile. The muscles beneath her hand trembled with effort.

She forced her worry away from her voice and face. "Why don't you join your men, Mian?" she asked. "We have rooms waiting for you."

"Not until Janu is within the gates." Mian's eyes never left the trail of men, and his smile never faltered.

Her stomach gave a slight twinge but her concern for Mian was stronger. "He is safe. You have done your duty. Do not make me force you."

He glared down at her and she met his gaze with steady determination. She could see his stubborn pride holding off the exhaustion.

A soldier rode up along the edge of the line of men, pulling his horse up at her side. The older man saluted his commander before dismounting. Mian's face closed off and he returned his attention to the line of men filtering into the city. The soldier's jaw clenched but he turned his attention to her. "My lady, my name is Orotid."

Narita's smile bloomed. "From Amber Keep. Your story is well known here. I am honored to welcome you to my home. I am the Lady Narita of Austeria."

She couldn't read the strange expression on his face as he said, "My lady, could I get my commander settled? He will be needed fresh for tomorrow. Perhaps you can get reacquainted then?"

Bright hot love burst through her for this strange old man even as Mian growled beside her. "I'll be fine until the men are settled."

"These are not boys, sir," he said. "They don't need you to babysit them."

Mian's eyes flashed as they met Orotid's. "And I don't need you to babysit me."

Narita shot him a reprimand. "What your men don't need is to see their commander collapse in exhaustion." She lightened her tone. "Our men are here if anything happens. I will move them from the walls and guard the entire line if you will just go with your men and rest."

His shoulders trembled for a moment before dropping a stitch. "That would be best, I suppose. Strong, rested men."

She stretched up onto her toes and snagged his collar to pull him down so she could kiss his cheek. "You are a good man, Mian. You deserve rest."

His arms engulfed her, pulling her to his chest where she could feel the full extent of his exhaustion. He jerked away from her and rushed to his horse. Orotid gave her a deep bow before returning to his mount.

Narita smiled in smug satisfaction. "Krylion!"

A soldier broke rank from the gates and rushed to her side.

She kept her voice loud and strong. "Move our soldiers beyond the gates. Surround these men and guard them. They are a commodity we can ill afford to lose."

Janu smiled as his ears caught on the cheering rolling forth from the city, calls of welcome and rejoice. He didn't think he could ever view Austeria as home but it was a beautiful and welcoming sight, nonetheless.

Lines of soldiers spread out from the city to engulf the line of men marching toward their gates, cheering and encouraging. Janu watched as the chants affected the men around him. He could see the relief as animation came back to them. They may not have saved the Seat but they had survived and they could keep fighting.

When was the last time he was here, riding into Austeria? Seemed like a lifetime ago. He'd visited here when he was just a boy with his father. He remembered running these streets with Mian, good clean mischief. He loved Austeria then. It felt a bit more like betrayal now. This wasn't home, coming here was a betrayal to the Seat. He abandoned his home, but there was no choice.

Just before the gates of the city stood a small cluster of people on horseback. They stood apart from the soldiers. They were too far away for him to see them clearly but he had a feeling he knew who would be among them. Lord Huran was a close friend to the crown, and had been since Janu's grandfather ruled. And if one of those riders was Huran, that would make the small rider among them his daughter Narita.

Narita.

His baby sister's best friend, he hadn't seen her for years. Seeing her in the years following Pria's entry into the Lorien had been almost like having Pria back. His arms grew lighter at the thought of it. How old would she be now? How old would Pria be? He still thought of them both as girls.

He gathered his reins and urged his horse to the edge of the mass of men around him. Lana called out to him but he ignored her. They were safe now. His horse was sluggish after the long ride but gave all it could as it trotted along the line. A tightness eased in his chest as he recognized familiar faces. Lord Huran looked just as he always had, rough and handsome and open. But beside him was not a girl. At his side sat a beautiful woman, proud and strong. This *couldn't* be little Narita. Janu couldn't justify the woman before him with the image of his baby sister; there was no way Pria could be this old.

He pulled his horse up at their side. Tears welled in his eyes. A small piece of the world returned to him and he welcomed it gratefully.

The horse shifted aside with an irritated huff as Mian let the oiled canvas flap on the saddle bag drop against its side. The horse was normally solid but today it fed off of his own nerves. His head was a thunderstorm of worry that left no room for focus on anything else. His men waited patiently by their horses, being sure to draw as little attention as possible. His temper had been hard to control of late; nightmares had been keeping him up and he was not pleasant when tired.

Janu had set up his new command in Austeria. It was a fine city, to be sure, but it wasn't home. They had sent out scouts to check how the Seat fared in the hands of the horde, but none had ever been able to reach it. Grinlo patrolled the grounds around it and they could never get closer than the foothills. Janu had led patrols himself at first, insisting a leader that didn't risk his own life along with his men didn't deserve to lead. Lana had always ridden with him. Mian would never admit it to her, but her watch over Janu was a comfort. She'd never let anything happen to Janu. Most patrols ran into grinlo, especially if they happened to wander too close to the Seat, but Janu's *always* did. When Lana mentioned her worries that the grinlo were after Janu, he couldn't believe they would be intelligent enough. Even after Lana set out that they had killed his parents, he still thought it was odd, but Lana would know better than he did. He couldn't imagine the knowledge the Lorien may have squirreled away on grinlo. Maybe they had some way to identify leaders; they obviously had hierarchy among their own.

So, Lana had convinced Janu to remain in Austeria, which suited Mian just fine. What didn't suit him fine was that Lana had now determined she should ride with his men. She didn't demand to go on every patrol, but somehow she always managed to infiltrate herself whenever they ranged north to check on the progress of the grinlo, as they were today. He wouldn't flinch, though. It wasn't his place to tell her what a fool, stubborn woman she was being, though they both knew he would take that extra responsibility on himself anyway. He was always looking for a way to go the extra distance.

A wave of tension through the soldiers told him of Lana's approach before he caught her footsteps. "Is everything prepared, Commander?"

He turned to face her and lost the response on his tongue. Tension hung from her face, forming deep circles beneath her eyes. Mian snapped his jaw shut. "We are ready whenever you are, High Priestess."

Lana nodded and dropped her gaze. The display of worry was beyond anything he'd seen her show to him. Her gaze swept over the men around them. "Let us get to it then."

He followed her to her horse. He tried to ignore the falter in her glide, the slight slump in her shoulders. Despite his enjoyment at thwarting her dignity and position, he knew her value to Trimera and the true strength behind her frosty mask. The cracks in her strength worried him. He would never admit, not even to himself, that despite her cold, despite the fact that she had sent Pria away, despite the fact that she was completely beyond all reason and completely intolerable, he actually did like her. She not only cared for Trimera but she also genuinely cared for Janu as well. And though she could dig in like a badger in a den, he'd seen her acquiesce to more than one request when Janu had pleaded his case. She was also their last connection to Pria and had proven to be generous in sharing whatever information she had garnered from the Lorien.

Lana paused by the light warhorse she had adopted as her mount and fiddled with her robes, trying to free her legs. Mian dropped to a knee and offered his cupped hands for her foot. Her eyes shot to his, wide with momentary shock before she could cover it. "Thank you, Commander."

His heart sank further at how light she was as he boosted her into the seat of the saddle. Could Janu's safety weigh so heavy on her? If they'd have been more private, more secluded, he'd have dared ask her how she was, if she was feeling up to the ride, if she would stay back and rest. But in front of so many eyes he couldn't afford to show his worry. The citizens of Trimera needed her to be a rock. He couldn't dent that image, not now. Not after they had lost Amber Keep and the Seat.

"Lana," he whispered, "do you really think the grinlo are after Janu?"

For an instant he thought he saw the shadow of doubt in her eyes, but that couldn't be. The flash was gone in a blink, leaving him doubtful. "That is what I said."

She gathered her reins in an obvious dismissal. Mian sighed as he turned back to his own horse. Thoughts tumbled through his mind, keeping him silent as the soldiers rode out.

He hooked a finger behind the neck of his armor and tugged at a pinch to settle the metal better against his skin. Armor tended to ride up in the saddle. It didn't have anything to do with the cold stare of the woman riding at his side. He had made his peace with High Priestess Lana. That by no means meant he was comfortable with her. Her light-stepping warhorse graced the very edge of his periphery, a blazing beacon he couldn't ignore.

Lunch was a quick meal of dried meat, cheese, and bread, eaten in the saddle. Lana didn't want to stop. She'd been uncharacteristically quiet all morning as they rode through the foothills of the Guardians. He knew she was concerned about the grinlo's interest in Janu. Her silence did not bode well for the situation.

At the base of the Guardians, the trees thinned into a clearing and Lana's horse danced its way up beside him. "You have been quiet since we left."

He glanced down at her, his face painted with the shock of hearing his thoughts voiced back to him. He shook the strange feeling from his shoulders. "I was wondering what you were thinking about Janu."

A mysterious shadow masked her features before vanishing as if it never was. That was the problem with Lana—even if you watched closely you could still miss what she was thinking. Her gaze drifted across the rolling patch of open grass. "It is concerning," she admitted.

His attention snapped back to his surroundings as his horse's ears perked toward the far trees. Nothing out of the ordinary caught his attention.

Lana leaned toward him to follow his gaze. "Did you see something?"

He ignored her as he continued his perusal. The sun filtered through the trees, mottling the ground and making it impossible to discern any solid shapes. He opened his mouth to respond but the words turned rancid on his tongue. Dread blossomed in the pit of his stomach, some deep primal fear he couldn't explain. The wind caught the branches across the glen, sending the shadows dancing and creating an army in his mind. His eyelids washed across his vision and the shadow army solidified at the edge of the trees. Before his brain could process the situation, the cry went out behind him.

"Grinlo!"

The monsters flowed from the trees toward them, an unending wave of death and violence. His gaze met Lana's and he felt the world crack beneath him. He'd encountered raids; it was common to come across hunting parties. But this was no hunting party. This was a trap set to capture, and there was only one person in their party interesting enough for such numbers.

His sword was in his hand. His men needed no orders as they formed up around him. Lana's horse bumped against his knees as resolution settled across her face. The knowledge hit him hard: The grinlo were after Lana.

And she knew it.

The air erupted in the metallic clash of swords against weapons and armor as the grinlo crashed into them. From the corner of his eye he saw Lana gather her reins.

He swept his sword toward a small rise. "Get to the high ground!"

The men around him shifted toward the rise and he made sure to keep his horse angled close to Lana. The straining mass surged forward through the soldiers. Lana watched them close, her face curious but unconcerned. The men struggled to force the creatures back but their numbers poured forth regardless of loss. Each creature that fell was replaced with another. Still Lana watched.

Mian's sword cut down a grinlo as it climbed over its fallen brethren. "Lana!" he shouted.

The woman twitched. She blinked over at him as if wondering what he was doing there. Even as she stared over at him, her hand curled and a spark shot from her fingertips. Wherever the arc landed, creatures cried and fell.

Lana threw herself into defense but Mian couldn't shake the unease. Lana didn't freeze. She was proving something to herself. She knew, and she knew he knew. The creatures pushed in waves but continued to strain toward Lana.

He glanced around as they topped the rise but there was no shelter to be found, no protection from the overwhelming mass. His mind raced even as his body parried the weapons around him. There had to be a way out. There had to.

Sunlight sliced in through the gaping curtains, savaging his eyes and dragging him up from oblivion. It was possibly the worst outcome. His head thundered inside his skull. Cold stone pressed against his cheek and every movement sent pain lancing along his body. No, he definitely preferred oblivion.

He could feel the warmth of the fire even despite the chill seeping up from the floor. Someone must have stoked it while he was out. His arms were tangled in a blanket, another new addition. How long had he been here? Hours? Days? The last thing he remembered was talking to Janu. They had been discussing something important—what was it? It had been something he had done.

Then memory crashed down around him, obliterating the room beyond. Stabbing pain sliced through his mind and his lungs seized. He doubled over around his stomach and a wordless scream rushed from his lips as the agony gripped him. No man could withstand this, no sanity could survive this. Breath struggled in and out of his chest as unwanted horror assaulted his mind.

He remembered.

His men were surrounded by grinlo, outnumbered and exhausted. Bloody and beaten, numbers nearly halved by the enemy, they stood valiantly. No soldier of Trimera gave up. Lana rode on his mount behind him, her horse having fallen during the battle. The creature had stomped several grinlo before they could subdue it. The extra weight slowed his steed, possibly might impede his command, but he wasn't about to let her out of his reach. Not with the grinlo singling her out. Every scratch on her skin was a mark against his honor. How could he face Janu when he couldn't keep Lana from harm?

Fatigue leadened his arms. This battle seemed to be unending. No matter how many grinlo they cut down, there always seemed to be another taking its place. Not for the first time, Lana addressed him from his shoulder. "Mian, you need your maneuverability. I can fight from the ground."

Anger built in his gut. Anger at the horde for the damage they did. Anger at Janu for not noticing the truth. Anger at Lana for ignoring it. His teeth clenched so tight his jaw ached. "I need you protecting my back," he lied.

He couldn't let her risk her life for them, Janu needed his priestess. Trimera needed its priestess. All he had to do was get her out of this trap.

A clawed hand grabbed his boot and jerked him off balance, and the ground rose up to meet him.

From the ground, he met Lana's apologetic gaze as she reached forward to grab the horn of the saddle. "No," he whispered, "no."

With strength that belied the exhaustion painting her face, she jerked herself into the seat. The horse leapt through the line of grinlo and charged away from the knot of soldiers.

"No!" He lunged after her but she was already gone. He lurched to his feet. "Get me a horse!"

A soldier dropped from his saddle and pushed his mount toward Mian. He leapt on its back as it ran by, urging it into a gallop. The main mass of grinlo had broken off to follow Lana, which he knew had been her intention all along. Only a handful remained to hold off the soldiers, and a couple of them broke off to give chase after Mian. He paid them no mind as he raced after Lana. A tail of nearly fifty monsters strained after his flagging horse as Lana sent spells back toward them. The gap closed as he watched—but it would be all right. She could hold them off until he got there. She had to.

She pulled his horse up short, forcing the creature into a rear. Her gaze returned to his, resolved even through the pain, as a second force of grinlo swept up a rise toward her, blocking her in. The horse screamed as the horde swarmed over it, claws and teeth grabbing and pulling. Lana sank beneath that writhing mass as he plowed the horse into the pack of grinlo. At some point the horse fell but he continued his assault with his blade. Blood drenched his body and armor. He was no longer making any forward progress. His arms grew heavier with each swing until nothing else stood around him.

Not three yards away lay the carcass of his horse, all around him fallen grinlo…but no sign of Lana. He turned in a circle. No grinlo still fought against his men, none were even in his sight. The soldiers appeared just as stunned as he was. He felt the world give way beneath him.

Mian's mind returned to his room. He couldn't face it, the failure. His feet refused to cooperate as he stumbled through the room. He had to outrun the memory, had to drown the acknowledgment.

The hallway beyond him was deserted and it took him a moment to catch his bearings. Austeria was still relatively unknown to him. Lord Hurd had a winery, he and Janu had found it when they were younger. It took him multiple tries to locate it, startling several maids, a lady in waiting, and one very off-put noblewoman.

He staggered into the darkened room, knocking over a bottle that shattered across the floor. He knocked two more bottles aside before his hand latched onto one. He jerked the cork from the neck and tried to swamp the thoughts struggling toward the surface of his memory, but to no avail.

They had searched for days. Tired, beaten men trudging through the woods, trying to stave off the crushing reality. They followed the tracks of the grinlo for days but never found the offending creatures or trace of Lana.

He jerked the bottle from his lips, sloshing wine across his shirt and gasping for breath. No. He couldn't think it. He couldn't acknowledge it, wouldn't.

"Mian?"

His shoulders slumped against the shame. "No."

A hand landed on his shoulder, strong and insistent. "Come on."

"No." He tried to pull away, tried to ignore the voice, the hand, the thought he was struggling so hard to avoid. But even as the haze of alcohol dimmed the world around him, his mind filled with Lana's soulful eyes, resigned and remorseful.

A tremor worked its way up from his toes, reverberated up his spine. The bottle fell from his hand and crashed to the floor. The strength left his legs and dropped him in a heap. His hands knotted in his hair as the tremor erupted from his lips in a rage-soaked scream. Darkness set in.

When reality returned through the haze, he allowed himself to acknowledge the arms around his shoulders. "Janu."

"It's all right, Mian. Everything will be all right."

Mian felt his head shake, felt the tears dripping from his cheek onto Janu's sleeve. "No it won't! Janu, Lana is dead!"

Janu laid the side of his face along the top of Mian's head as he brushed the hair back from his brow. "I know. I know."

Mian struggled to swallow and gasped as a convulsion tore through his abdomen. "I lost her. I tried, Janu, I tried to save her!" He crumbled in Janu's arms as the world crashed in around him.

Janu stared at the wall before him. He wasn't sure how long he had been sitting there staring at the same slightly mismatched brick among the well-fitted pattern. His desk was a landscape of crumpled parchment, discarded in anger or frustration. He would have leaned on Lana for such a thing, but the thought sat heavy in the back of his mind. Emptiness filled him. A quill still rested clutched in his fingers, ink long since dry on its tip. Lana would have yelled at him for that. She always told him he should take care of his things, even something as disposable and replaceable as a quill. She was funny that way.

He could hear people out in the hallways beyond the office. Soldiers, citizens, ladies or lords, maids or stewards, all off about their lives as if the universe wasn't standing still. All he had to do was this one thing and he was utterly incapable. Something so simple, just write a letter explaining how he'd lost one of the Reia's only two high priestesses. A few words to tell the Lorien, to tell his sister, that nothing would ever be the same again.

There was a sea of parchment to his left that had nothing written on them other than the word *Dear.* How could you start something so dire with such a light word? But he couldn't think of any other salutation. He tried, but his worthless mind refused to offer anything else up. *Dear Lorien, I killed Lana.* In frustration, he had written that several times too.

Lessel had checked on him several times and offered to help him, which he'd refused. He had to do this himself. So, he sat here by himself in this empty room and tried to put to words how he'd lost his sister's mentor and his father's most trusted advisor. How he'd lost Trimera's greatest protector. How he'd stripped the magical protection from his people with one stupid decision to let her go out on patrol.

He should have seen it. Should have known the grinlo were not after him. Lana had surely known. Why else go out there? She was trying to draw them out. Protect people by learning why they hunted her. Everything she did was for his kingdom.

And he couldn't do this one thing for her.

His eyes dropped to the parchment before him. Ink had dripped from the tip of his quill and spread a splattered stain across the page. Wasted. Ruined. He dropped the quill into the cleaning jar, crumbled up the parchment, and added it to the mass of others. He had to do this. They had to know.

He grabbed a cloth and worked the wetted ink off the nib of his quill. He would make her proud. No dried ink blobs would mar his missive. He dipped the tip into the ink jar and positioned it above the fresh parchment.

And again, froze over the salutation.

No salutation then, just a name. Just her name.

Pria.

There. He could do this.

Lana is gone. He stared at that for a moment. Let it sink in. *I wish there were a better way to say that, but anything else would be pretty lies. I lost her. The grinlo have been after her for some time and we just refused to see it.* He stopped. There was nothing else really. Nothing he could add to make it better. Nothing to help. "I'm sorry."

He signed, sealed, and folded it aside before he could crumple it up for how inadequate it was. He resumed his stare at the mismatched brick.

Narita knocked on the door to Janu's office. He'd been sequestered most of the day and she was determined to get him out. He'd become more and more evasive since the fall of the Seat. Everyone close to him commented on it; it was only Mian who could draw him from his dark thoughts. Mian and her.

She pounded on the door, irritated that he hadn't responded to her first knock, but still no answer came. She gave up knocking and pushed the door open. He didn't get to ignore her.

"Come on, Prince!" she called. "Time to get out of this dark, gloomy room."

She froze as her eyes fell on him, slumped in his chair staring out the window. "What's wrong?" He didn't respond. "Janu."

All weight faded from her body. Each step deepened the fog that engulfed her until she made it far enough to catch sight of his face. His vacant stare never left the window before him. Narita's hand shook as she reached out to touch him.

"She lied to us."

She pulled her hand back. "Who?"

A slow blink pulled his gaze to her face. Emptiness screamed from his eyes. "They took her," he said, voice barely a whisper. "The grinlo took Lana."

Her hands clapped to her mouth. "What?"

"She let me believe they were after me. Why did I ever listen to her? I should have known."

She knelt beside him, taking his hand in hers. "Janu, I'm sure Lana did what she thought was right."

"What do we do?" he asked.

Her heart split as he collapsed forward onto his legs, his body shaking. She wrapped her arms around him and ran her hands along his back to soothe his pain. "We'll get through this, I promise you that."

The world passed by as he remained limp in her arms. After a while she managed to talk him from the chair to the floor and he now slept with his head cradled in her lap. She ran her fingers along his hair, sending him soothing thoughts as his tortured mind rested. She would protect him while he dealt with the loss of Lana. It was only too easy to placate him with talk of hope and resilience—if only she could bring herself to believe it. Lana gone was a nightmare come true. But no matter her internal worries, she would pull Janu through this.

Pria knelt in the center of the Sanctuary, a massive tiered gallery. Every priestess in residence at the Lorien stood around her. Before her, seated on a plain ladder-back chair, sat the oldest priestess in all of Reia. It was tradition. When she passed, the next oldest would be sent for to return to the Lorien, if she wasn't already there. Ready and waiting for the next priestess to join their ranks.

At twenty-two, today, it was Pria's turn.

She had entered naked, as was custom. Before her was her priestess robes, folded and ready for her to embrace her duties. The priestess before her was Dierdra and she was every day of one hundred seven. Her hands shook as her knobby, arthritic fingers sat folded in her lap. Not a lick of color graced her hair and a roadmap of wrinkles lined her face. She looked like a sweet old grandmother, though Pria had seen her strength before. Despite her old and frail physicality, her mind was still sharp.

They had been the first to arrive. Alone in an empty room, Dierdra had laid out what would happen today. They would wait, silently, as the Sanctuary filled. Once the last priestess had entered, the doors would be sealed. As it turned out, San was the last priestess to enter the Sanctuary and closed the door behind her. Dierdra waited for the other woman to take her seat among the section cordoned off for Pria's teachers, mentors, and witnesses.

Dierdra raised a wizened hand and silenced the buzz of chatter. "One comes before me today," she began, her voice solid despite her age, "who wishes to join the priestesshood." Her gaze shifted to Pria. "Pria of Trimera, your trial begins now."

Pria tried not to let the word trial settle too hard on her. When San had first mentioned it to her, she had nearly choked. It put her on edge, and she supposed that was the point. She was not to speak during the process. Her deeds were to speak for her.

San stood among the witnesses. "Senior Priestess, I would like to sponsor the student for statement among the priestesshood."

Dierdra nodded but before she could speak again, another priestess stood behind San. "Senior Priestess," said Priestess Bala, one of Pria's teachers, "I would like to sponsor the student for statement among the priestesshood."

Whispers broke out around the room, none loud enough to interrupt. This was not expected. Dierdra nodded to this priestess and another of Pria's teachers stood. "Senior Priestess, I would like to sponsor the student for statement among the priestesshood." Pria felt her eyes widen. This was Priestess Yarem. She had been sure the woman hated her.

The spectacle didn't end there. Before they were finished, the entire witness box—including all her teachers and friends who had graduated before her—and even a handful of the priestesses sitting outside of the witness box had pledged her sponsor. It wasn't unheard of for multiple sponsors to stand for a student, but even Dierdra was staring wide-eyed.

"It would seem," she said once the tirade had quieted down, "that you have some fans, Pria of Trimera." Her hand glided toward a table adorned with a tiny carved hammer and a metal dome. She tapped the dome with the hammer and the room rang with a high tinkling note. "Let us hear the evidence of her worth."

San stood and made her way to the floor beside Pria. She did not kneel nor was she naked, but Pria was glad for the company in her scrutinized position.

"Senior Priestess. I would like to begin with the reading of a statement from the late High Priestess Lana." This caused further stir as the room shared a shocked moment. Pria risked a glance up at San and met her gaze, eyes sparkling with tears. San pulled a parchment from her robes and unfolded it. *"To the Council of the Lorien, I am pleased to announce the official announcement of request for enlistment in the Lorien. My charge's daughter, Pria of Trimera, has within her skills unmatched by any priestess alive. I have had the privilege to teach her and was overjoyed by the strength of her mind. E—"* San's voice cracked and she took a moment to compose herself before continuing. *"Even at such a young age, she shows knowledge and understanding beyond her years. She will one day stand among our ranks as not only a pillar of strength but a beacon of hope and unity to all."*

San folded the letter and replaced it in her robes. "That was written when Pria was five, just before the death of Prince Inan. Since then, I have had the opportunity to get to know Pria as a student and, if I may be so bold to assume, as a friend. I stand here today to say you would be foolish to refuse her. As a priestess or not, Pria will mold this world into her own vision. Let it be as one of us that she does."

San rushed back to her seat among the gallery, covering her face. Silence stretched out before Dierdra called for a second witness.

The day progressed as her witnesses continued with her strengths, her weaknesses, stories that showed her virtues and vices. There were enough of the latter to make her blush. By the time the procession was finished, a group of priestesses had conjured light to illuminate the room. They did not break for food or water, and Pria's wasn't the only stomach growling in the room, although she was sure it was the loudest. Cramps screamed from her legs and back for relief. Sweat dripped along her body and her hair stuck to her scalp and back. No air moved in the room and the heat of the day had settled in long before.

Dierdra tapped the dome once more with the tiny hammer and the room rang again with the clang. The relative silence had filled with the breathing of hundreds of hot priestesses. "The testimony is over," Dierdra panted. "Would any like to oppose the installment of Pria of Trimera to the rank of high priestess?"

Heavy sighs filled the room but no voices rose to challenge.

"Then it is my honor, as senior priestess, to bestow the rank of High Priestess on Pria of Trimera. May she reign in peace."

Pria bowed her head as two priestesses helped Dierdra to her feet. The older woman was handed a chalice of water from the Heart and shuffled her stilted steps to where Pria knelt on the floor. The water was by no means cold, having sat in the heat of the Sanctuary all day, but it provided a refreshing cascade of cleanliness as it rushed over her sweaty body.

"Stand, High Priestess Pria, and join your family."

Pria's knuckles shone white as she knotted them beneath the table before her. She felt like she had been cooped up in this room for eternity. Her graduation from the Lorien had brought a sensitive subject to the forefront: Trimera needed a priestess. The posting had been postponed until she was old enough to secure it, but now she had to convince the Council to station her there.

The problem was there was a strong opposition.

Beside her sat Priestess San, her staunchest supporter. Despite the loss of her best friend Lana, San had convinced the Council to suspend the assignment of the post until Pria came of age.

Pria could still remember the letter from Trimera. It had been addressed to her, not San. She should have known something was wrong then. Oh, she'd gotten letters from Janu before, but always sent through Lana to San. Why waste a man to deliver a letter when she could do it so easily?

The words of Lana's death had dropped her. She could only imagine how much Janu had struggled over writing them, fighting to find some way to not say the only thing that was important. She had rushed to San, her friend, her comfort away from her home. San had allowed them to mourn privately, a small luxury for her lost friend, before she had taken the news to the Council. Even with the news, even knowing how dire the situation in Trimera was, San had stood strong. It wasn't till later that San revealed that Lana's wish was for Pria to replace her as Trimera's priestess. San wasn't about to let her friend down. She was the best negotiator the ranks of the priestesses had ever had. There were already talks of adding her to the honored statues on the front steps of the Lorien, something unheard of during the life of the priestess in question.

But not even her talents and abilities could silence the opposition today.

The Council Chamber was small for its significance, barely large enough for the two desks and the long bench that was the focus of the room. A handful of chairs were set up in rows behind the desks.

The Council itself sat behind the long bench. There was not a strand of color among them. The Council was made up of the oldest and wisest among them, each one elected by their peers. Rumor had it that Lana had refused a posting to the Council a record seven times to maintain her post in Trimera. San was also rumored to currently be in consideration as a Council member.

Council numbers were always in flux. Currently seven sat at the Council: five priestesses and two priests. The inclusion of priests was a recent decision. Priests Bran and Luden were both exceptional and their election had been unprecedented.

As Pria faced them, she could discern no expression on any face, no indication of what any of them might be thinking. They listened and only gave a response after they had heard everything.

All pleas before the Council required debate whether they were opposed or not. A delegate was always appointed to research the cons of a proposal. Pria's opposition delegate was Priest Peetare, arguably the prissiest man alive. His expression appeared as if he constantly smelled something rancid.

While many pleas had opposition chosen by the Council, Peetare had not only volunteered but also spearheaded a campaign against her plea to gather support for his opposition. Every seat in the room was filled with more standing along the walls, all there to support Peetare.

All there to keep her from her family.

Peetare strode before them now, his robes snapping with the force of his movements. One bony finger stabbed at her chest. "We cannot risk the loss of another high priestess. It is madness to even contemplate it!" He spun back to the Council, his hands spread wide. "You have heard my argument, heard"—he swept an arm toward the crowd behind him—"the knowledgeable opinions of so many of our esteemed colleges." His hands spread wide. "We have numerous qualified candidates with decades of experience. Pria, I reiterate, has none." He strode back to his desk. "The opposition rests."

The Council shared glances but remained unreadable. There was no true leader among the Council but there was always a spokesperson. Today, it was a silver-haired woman whose frosty hair had nothing on her personality. Sira turned that chill-inducing gaze toward San. San moved to stand but Pria stopped her with an outstretched hand.

Eyes shot to her as she stood. She had agreed to let San speak for her; it had been the smart move. San was the better negotiator; she had the reputation and connection with these people. But San had no connection to Trimera, no connection to her family.

San had taken Pria shopping just for this occasion. Her first formal suit was crystal blue with cream piping in silk. It swayed around her like a soft whisper.

"Honored Council, you do not know me yet but I am High Priestess Pria of Trimera." The introduction, of course, was a formality. They had been discussing nothing but her all day. "I am the first to admit that my esteemed opposition's arguments are valid. I have no experience. I am young. My connection to Trimera and its people is strong." She acknowledged Priest Peetare before returning her attention to the Council.

"But what his arguments neglect to consider are just as important. The posting for Trimera is critical for the priestesses and Reia—there is no arguing that. So important that traditionally only the strongest among us were allowed to hold the post. That is why High Priestess Lana held the post.

"There are plenty of candidates with more experience than I, but there can be no argument against my strength. That alone should earn my posting in Trimera. Beyond that, there is no other priestess in the ranks of the Lorien that has more drive nor reason to protect Trimera. That is, if you decide to station me as protector and counselor."

Pria's heart pounded in her ears and the eyes of the Council burned into her shoulder blades as she returned to her place beside San. San's hand found hers beneath the desk and gave a supportive squeeze. The worst was over, all they could do now was wait for the decision.

The Council shared another glance before Sira spoke. "We have heard the arguments for both sides. You will be called back when we have reached our decision."

HOMECOMING

The icy chill of the evening clung savagely as she pulled her hood down further over her forehead. The world around her seemed to hold its breath as the relentless rain churned the road into thick mud. The road itself was deserted, lined on both sides with leafless trees. Her gray gelding tried in vain to shake the damp from his coat, sending a ripple along her heavy cloak. Each step sent a spray of water arching up from the road, splattering mud on the horse's already filthy legs. A few belongings bulged in bags secured around her deep-seated saddle. The gloom of the day refused to be dispelled by the weak, cold sun.

Five years since she had seen any of her family—ten since she had seen her homeland. A long time, but her training had been intense. Ten years of the best teachers in the land. Hopefully it would be enough. It felt like a lifetime, and perhaps it was. She definitely didn't feel like the same wide-eyed youth who had ridden from the Seat so many years ago. The intervening years had softened her lanky form into adulthood, though it had done little to add height to her frame. Her training in the Lorien had crammed history and politics into her mind until it could hold no more. Every mirror she found screamed her true age of barely twenty-two, but her mind churned and twisted beyond anything youth could imagine. She no longer had any questions as to why Lana had always been so distant—every interaction with others started an avalanche of thoughts, questions, and possibilities that she could scarce silence.

Feeling her growing angst, her horse stepped up his trot, rushing down the road toward uncertainty.

The gelding snorted in irritation as he slid in the mess. She pulled a sphere from her saddle bags and cradled it in her hands. Along its crystalline surface was a mass of lines and color depicting the land around her. A blinking white light crept along one of the dark lines with a steady persistence. It was a tracking sphere, and the flashing light represented her progress. She was pleased to see a town just beyond the next set of hills. She couldn't wait to sink into a bed and suck down something warm to eat. She urged her horse forward with renewed vigor as she tucked the tracking sphere back into her bags.

Everyone was inside when she rode in, mud flying from her horse's hooves. It wasn't the largest town by any means—only a few houses clustered together along the road—but it was just big enough to have a small inn with a weathered sign swinging out front. A small stable nestled up against its side and she ducked low as her horse trotted into its shelter.

The warm glow of a hooded lantern greeted her from a hook on the wall to her left. Sweet hay and horse sweat filled her senses as she shook the water from her cloak. A boy jumped to his feet from his nap near the back and rushed to take her mount.

She kept her hood up as she followed the sounds of revelry into the common room, where the boy directed her. The dim lantern lights flooded her eyes as she allowed her sight to adjust in the doorway. In her heavy cloak and bulky winter traveling clothes she looked more like a messenger boy than anything else. No one to bother. No one to worry about.

The somber room contained a handful of patrons scattered about the small tables, and a low burning fire. The wide innkeeper eyed her as she approached him, shuffling her bags to reach her coin purse.

"I need a room for the night, and a meal."

He cleared his throat and tried to hide his raised eyebrows at her high voice. "The room will be ten coppers and it includes meals."

She tossed him a gold piece. "I'll eat in my room. Could you see that my horse gets some oats and hay."

He nodded as he stared at the coin in his palm. "Of course… If you'll follow me."

She followed him toward the back and a set of narrow stairs. Her room was clean, if small, and a large fireplace sat waiting for a blaze. A small straw-stuffed mattress was shoved against the side wall and a thick flawed window looked out on what was a field fallow of crops. The floor creaked beneath her soft leather boots as they trailed wet prints.

The innkeeper pulled the door shut behind him as he left and she took the opportunity to strip off her wet clothes. Every layer was soaked, but thankfully her canvas bag kept her spares dry. A thick, warm dressing gown was going to have to do for the night.

A small tired teen delivered her meal, his eyes thick with sleep as she was building a fire in the hearth. She tipped him a silver penny before she shooed him from the room. Wet clothes draped around the fire, she stood with her hands out and a warm glow shot from her fingers, flashing the dampness from the fabric. The morning would find her with fresh, warm clothes.

She set to her meal, wiping the bowl clean with the heel of bread and licking her fingers before dropping onto the mattress.

One more day. How long had she been gone? Long enough. There was a time when everyone for miles around knew her face. No disguise could have hidden her then. Now, the shade of a cloak kept her anonymous.

Squiggled down into the mattress, she tucked the blankets up around her chin and let the dry warmth pull her into sleep.

Two parchments mocked him from the desktop. One was faded and old, crumbled from handling; the other was crisp and new, and stubbornly refused to lay flat. Both fanned an ire deep in his gut.

Janu's attention flitted between the two. The older was a note written by Lana—he'd know her neat flowing hand anywhere. He had found it the day she died tucked among some affects in her rooms.

> *The grinlo are after me. I don't know how long I can keep it from Janu.*

The other was longer and much more stilted.

> *Prince Janu,*
> *The post of priestess for Trimera has been filled. Expect your priestess with the new moon.*
> *Yours in peace,*
> *Priestess Ahn.*

"Expect your priestess."

His hand shook. His priestess. The thought of a new priestess created a battle within him. In order to hold his kingdom together he needed the guidance, protection, and the boost to his citizens' confidence that a priestess would bring. The biggest impact from Lana's death had been the plummet of morale in the citizens. Any priestess was better than no priestess at all, to the people anyway. The people who never had to deal with a priestess.

Janu, however, knew better.

He had grown so reliant on Lana that her loss had nearly toppled his entire kingdom, but that in no way meant dealing with her had been easy. She had kept more secrets than the grains of sand in the Alini Desert. Sometimes her very gaze would chill the marrow in his bones. If she was what he could expect of a new priestess, the adjustment would be hard to say the least.

He turned to the room behind him. The suite was Lord Huran's, Narita's father, lord of the manor. When Huran had agreed to let Janu use Austeria as his base, the man had granted Janu permission to change what he wanted. Looking around now, he couldn't find more than a handful of personalized items. The belongings he had salvaged from the Seat were packed away. His attendants had filled the dressing room with his clothes and just about everything else was Lord Huran's. Austeria was a lovely city, comforting and welcoming, but it wasn't home.

In place of honor at the center of a large vanity was a carved box. His steward Lessel had insisted it remain in sight even if he couldn't convince Janu to remove its contents. Janu hadn't opened the box since the day he had lost Amber Keep to the grinlo.

The crushing weight settled back on his shoulders and shook the thoughts from his head. He couldn't focus on the past, not with a new priestess on her way. He needed a boost of confidence. He swept from the room and made his way down the hall. Several doors down was Lord Huran's personal library. A warm fire burned in the fireplace, diffusing welcoming light among the stacks. When Janu had first moved into Austeria he had discovered a line on the mantle that didn't match up. A further inspection had uncovered a small nook inside the chimney. The nook had contained a soft faded piece of parchment.

The rock scalded his fingers as he pulled it loose and dropped it onto the stone hearth. He pulled the parchment from the nook and pressed it to his chest. He didn't need to open it; he also knew this note by heart. In one corner was a tiny sketch of a flower, an Austerian lily, Narita's favorite. He had worked on it for hours, given it painstaking care, until it was as perfect as he could make it. In all honesty, it looked like a child had drawn it. He had written this note to an eighteen-year-old Narita. Following the fall of the Seat, he had poured his heart out to her, this beautiful, fierce, amazing, warrior woman. Years later when he found the note stashed away, it had given him a boost of confidence he had desperately needed. He slipped the note into his breast pocket. He needed as much of a boost as he could get to face a new priestess.

Morning came too soon with another youth bearing a tray of eggs and meat. The gray sky was cloudy but breaking up as she pulled on her dry traveling clothes. The innkeeper waved as she passed through the common room on her way to the stable. Saddle bags piled around her feet, she waited as the stable hand rushed around saddling her horse. The beautiful creature was of her father's prized stock, bred and raised in the mountains around the Seat. They were known the kingdom over for their endurance, intelligence, and spirit. He was one more connection to her family, one more tie that couldn't be severed.

The end of the rain hadn't improved the temperature, she found as she rode out into the morning haze. Thick fog clung everywhere and masked the land around the town, dampening everything it touched. The squelch of mud was her only fanfare as she urged her horse into an ambling trot. The road outside town was lined with gnarled oak trees that sheltered it from wind but also kept out most of the sunlight. Despite the fact that the road was well-traveled, it was early enough that it was deserted.

Lunch was a quick meal of bread and cheese. The road she was on would take her past Kyneira, one of the largest towns in her homeland. As a child she had spent many summers there with friends. The town itself was a functioning art gallery with towers and palaces designed and built by master masons and architects. People traveled from all over to see their majestic sweeps of marble towers and carved statues.

She stroked the pendant hanging against her skin. Despite the cold, its metal form held a heat that spread out across her chest and radiated along her body. It had been a gift from her childhood friend Narita. She remembered Narita fondly—together they had trained in everything from swordplay to archery. Narita's family's country estates were nestled deep among the mountains commonly referred to as the Guardians and she should be able to reach them by nightfall, if the weather held. With a glance to the sky, she wondered how long that would be.

The terrain opened, allowing the sun to dry the mud from the road, but it could do nothing to shake the cold. It wasn't long before she saw patrols of uniformed soldiers, their armor polished and gleaming. They would swarm around her protectively, give her a proper escort home if they knew who she was. She let them pass, though. No reason to point herself out—not yet. A little anonymity was refreshing.

The road curved around a small knoll before forking around a stand of trees. Nearly all the traffic around her went right, on toward Kyneira, but she opted left, veering toward the mountains and climbing through thick pines that clung to the steepening terrain.

The day burned on. The sun raced toward the horizon and was a small sparkling sliver when she caught sight of the first turret.

Home. Or as close as she was going to get, at any rate.

The trees stopped, jutting against a tall perimeter wall that ran along the road studded with manned guard towers. Men peered at her through the slitted windows, following her progress with nocked arrows, but none challenged her.

She slowed her horse as the opposite side of the road dropped off into a steep ledge, then pulled up at a large gate and rapped with a brass knob from her saddle bags. The window popped out to reveal a stern face lined with age. "Who goes there?"

"A traveler. I wish hospitality," she replied.

"We are not accepting travelers tonight."

"You will accept me," she said.

"Oh, and why is that?" the man asked, his voice heavy with skepticism.

She pulled her hood back and smiled, revealing a young beautiful visage and spilling soft waves of honey hair. "Because I am the high priestess of Trimera."

He pulled back in shock. "It cannot be."

She breathed a laugh. "I assure you, it is. Now are you going to open this gate or are you going to let me freeze to death on your stoop, you foolish old codger?"

His smile was genuine before he dropped from her sight and the gate swung inward. The elderly man rushed out, straightening his helmet and uniform. He dropped to a knee and thrust his fist into the dirt at her horse's hooves. "Forgive me, Highness, I did not recognize you!"

"Get out of the dirt, Krylion, and call me Pria. I think all the times you've caught me sneaking out at night and not turned me in have earned you that." She dropped from her saddle and helped the man to his feet, pulling him into her arms.

"It is good to see you, Pria."

"It is good to be seen. Is Narita home?"

He held her face in his gnarled hands. "The Lady Narita is out, but I do believe your brother is in." He pivoted, leading her inside the walls, the gate swinging shut behind them. "He held for a long time after you left. It was a constant battle keeping the horde back. Years they've had to move, and they are building again. Always building."

"Where is Janu?"

Krylion waved a young man over from the wall. "Narute here will show you to Janu's rooms. Narute, you take good care of the lady here."

Narute bowed low before he turned and offered his arm. Pria eyed it then waved him on. He glanced over at her so often that she wondered how he kept from tripping as they wound their way through the smaller houses and shops on the outer skirts of the estate. Narita's family was wealthy, but unlike most gentry, they didn't fancy a solitary retreat. Their estates had long ago grown into a prosperous town complete with inns and businesses. Shops lined the road they traveled, though many were closed at this late hour. Few citizens hurried along the streets, bundled up against the cold.

Narute cleared his throat. "You know the prince?" He glanced back at her. "Not many people get taken directly to him the second they arrive."

"You do not recognize me, do you?" she asked.

He stared at her openly now. "Can't say that I do, ma'am."

"I have been gone too long."

"Sorry?" He bent down toward her in an attempt to catch her soft words.

"Nothing. Do you know Janu?"

He straightened, chest puffing out. "Only by reputation. The prince hardly has time to commune with privates, ma'am."

"Of course not," she said.

"Could I ask…" He cocked his head toward her.

"No one of importance."

He smiled and indicated a large guarded entrance to the main estate. The estate itself shot up above the surrounding buildings, a sheer wall of stone and mortar. Guards nodded to Narute. She pulled her hood back up. The boy eyed her curiously. "Worried someone will recognize you? You seemed shocked that I didn't."

"Some here would know me," she said. "I'm not sure I want it to be generally known that I am here yet."

"Doesn't sound like you are no one of importance."

She ignored his statement. "How much farther is it?"

"Not long now. The prince likes to stay close to an entrance just in case."

"Do attacks come so often?" she asked.

He glanced back at her. "I wasn't aware that many women were interested in military maneuvers."

"Never assume to know what is in the mind of a woman," said a new voice. They turned as one to see a tall handsome man approaching them. "Most especially when that woman happens to be my sister."

The soldier dropped to his knees; beside him, Pria planted her fists on her hips. "Do you know you are the first to recognize me? Honestly, Janu, you would think I have been gone a lifetime!"

His deep masculine laughter rattled the walls around them as he lifted her around the waist, spinning in a circle. He dropped her to the floor, his laughter renewed at her irate huff. "What is the matter, little sister? The high priestess unable to defend against a bit of manhandling?"

She jerked her cloak straight and tossed her hair back as her hood fell away. "I'm afraid no amount of magic could save me from your stupidity, dear brother."

Narute gathered enough bravery to glance up from the floor. "My lady, you must forgive me, I knew not who you were!"

Janu waved him off. "Had she wished her proper treatment, she would have made herself known. Please stand—you have brought me wondrous news! What is your name?"

"Narute, Your Highness."

"I will be sure to inform Captain Neflan of your promotion!"

Narute coughed in disbelief. "Promotion, sir?"

"Yes, yes, now off with you! I have much information to beat out of my baby sister."

She held her tongue as the young soldier saluted and scurried down the hall. "Promotion? For showing me down a hall?"

Janu waved her off impatiently. "What good is being prince if I cannot celebrate when I am happy?" He swung a door open and guided her inside. "It has been a while since I have had occasion to be happy; I figured I better take advantage of it."

She glanced around the sitting room, briefly admiring the functional but well-designed furniture, then returning her focus to her brother. Not even the years could dampen her memory of his handsome face. His black hair was neatly trimmed and combed, his clothes of high quality and well-made but not ostentatious. She expected nothing less from him.

"What is going on? Amber Keep and the Seat both fallen to the Frontier. Could the horde have grown so bold?"

With a long-suffering sigh, he dropped into an overstuffed chair set up before a blazing fire. He indicated the chair beside him and waited for her to sink into it. "Apparently they were a little further along than we thought. The skirmishes began shortly after you left. Just small bands at first, nothing to really worry about. They were testing us, locating our defenses, tracking our patrols. When they started increasing we didn't really think about it much, thought they would give up when it didn't get them through, but they just kept coming." He paused. "Then one day it wasn't a quick skirmish. One day it just didn't stop. They just kept coming, wave after wave until they were in the city. We held as long as we could so the people could evacuate, but the Seat was lost so fast. They harried our men all the way to the mountains. We watch them from here now. Send out patrols to keep track. We've been trying to gather arms, but there are so many."

In the twelve years she had spent growing up in the Seat, she hadn't so much as glimpsed a grinlo. The soldiers and the northern fortress of Amber Keep kept most grinlo from even laying an eye on the Seat's defensive walls, but what she couldn't escape were the stories. Reports of massacred patrols, raided farms, and slaughtered cattle were so common as to barely raise comment. What struck her the most were the injured soldiers that returned—some with missing limbs, some with nasty scars, some with wounds that tore at the soul and left no visible mark. Those would be what stayed with her forever.

She stared into the fire, watching the flames dance along the logs. She had lost herself in her memories when Janu jerked her back. "I feel like I…should apologize." He met her gaze but dropped his eyes back to his lap. "Not so much you, but the Lorien." His breathing was ragged. "I…I lost Lana."

Pressure built in her chest. Janu's letter was still etched in her mind; such crushing news laid out so simply. She had tried to catch herself as she fell to the floor, but it crashed up to meet her nonetheless. Lana had been a rock, the omnipresent force of protection from her childhood. Every year during her studies at the Lorien, a small present would be left on her pillow on the day of her birth, a small gift from Lana. The gift would contain a short note of endearment—never much, just encouragement and a small personal anecdote, but every one brought a smile to her face. Lana had been a true mentor, a connection to her family and home. Pria bit back her shattered emotions.

"Janu, you cannot believe you are responsible for Lana's death."

The shocking blue of his eyes cracked against her hidden emotions. "I let her go with our men. I let her traipse around like she was a common soldier."

"But she wasn't a soldier," Pria said. "Even if you would have wanted to keep her from accompanying your soldiers, she would never have listened to you."

"Stated like a true priestess."

She waved him off. "What can you tell me of what happened?"

His body shook in a laugh. "I thought they were after me. They killed Mom and Dad, right?"

"Grinlo raids along the borders of Trimera have always been for food and tools, weapons," she said. "Mother and Father could have run across any one of them. That doesn't mean that it was an intentional attack."

"But these weren't raids," he whispered. "It was an invasion. It seemed logical when she asked to join Mian's party. It would keep her safe, right? I had no reason to believe the grinlo would be hunting Lana; I had no reason to think she would be misleading me. Not until Mian's men returned without her." He fell silent and she let him have his moment to collect his strength. "Is that what they want? Why they have pushed so far into Trimera? Are they after priestesses?"

"They hunt magic." She weighed each word with care. "It is well known to any who study them."

Animation blinked back into his body. "The citizens will be overjoyed to have a priestess again. The fear and superstition of living without a priestess has weighed heavy on morale. Hopefully it will be the push we need to reach the numbers to take back the Seat."

"How many have you gathered so far?"

"I have generals in the ten largest cities all enlisting. We are gathering at the Straights of Loren. The latest numbers bring us to nearly thirty thousand." He sat up and smiled. "I'm glad you are back, Pria. Having a priestess at my side will bolster the people's faith." Though he tried to hide it, she could still feel the exhaustion behind his words. Without a priestess, the people had no protection, no figurehead to rally behind. The loss of

Lana was more to Janu than just the loss of an advisor. She had a lot to live up to.

She tucked her legs under her. It had been a long time since she could relax and be herself. "How long before we move on the Seat?"

"Soon, hopefully. With the losses from the Seat, we have had to start recruiting in the southern cities. Once they are recruited, they need to be trained." He shook his head as if shaking the thoughts away. "Narita will be ecstatic to see you again. She's been helping me hold everyone together. She's quite the woman."

Pria gave a knowing smile. "I have always thought this." Narita's letters to her had been filled with stories of Janu. It didn't take much reading between the lines to determine that something was growing between her friend and her brother, and Pria couldn't be happier. Janu needed a strong woman to help him lead and there were few stronger than Narita, even if her own opinion of the woman was a bit biased.

There were few places filled with more potential than a crossroads. One could stand still while the world passed by and still see multiple directions at once. To the northeast lay Kyneira, the largest city in Trimera, and almost the geographical center as well. To the north lay the Seat, the symbolic position of power and center of the ruling prince's power. Farther north was Amber Keep, an outpost only truly important as a last defense for invasion from the Frontier. Not that it had done them any good. To the west and up into the mountains lay Austeria. The town itself was not so much of interest to him except that it now held the ruling prince and his governing party.

Arms spread wide at the hips, the man who called himself Neram stood motionless at the fork in the dirt road, his head tilted up to the sky. A throng of travelers ebbed around him, though they couldn't see him—instinct drove them around him, a spell kept him invisible. He paid them no mind; they were inconsequential.

His attention was focused, honed. Everything had stopped in that instant when the scent tickled his nostrils. He reveled in it now, exalted in it. It was sweet on his tongue, like honey. There was no way he had missed it before; this was new.

When his eyes sprang open, the road around him was dark, deserted. He had stood here too long. A cool breeze ruffled his robes and brushed against his skin. The trees lining the road danced as he looked to Austeria. The scent intensified as he turned toward the mountains. He was pulled on by it, enticed.

It was the scent of magic, latent magic to be sure, but magic nonetheless. It would have been more pungent had it been active, had the source been utilizing the magic, but it was powerful—that much he could tell. Much more powerful than anything he had sensed in a long time. He ached to possess it. More than that, he *needed* to possess it. Perhaps this time he would get it right. He had learned from his mistakes, though.

The memory of the first encounter with the knowledge that the horde could be controlled was burned forever in his memory. He had been fourteen, a student in the lists of the Lorien. No one had accused him of being a good student. The most common comment he received from his teachers was *distracted.* He was known for daydreaming and slacking. It wasn't his fault, though: He had been born for greater things than to study history and politics, greater than to just be an advisor for some spoiled monarch. All the power in the universe, and the priestesses spent their time *advising.* It was foolish beyond forgiveness and it was nothing he wanted for himself.

He did, however, excel at his training in using magic. He was the first one to be able to transmute an object, the first to be able to enchant an object. But his destiny had only truly become clear when old Priestess Hoffena gave the doom and gloom lecture on that most taboo of subjects, magical control of the horde. It was considered vile, twisted, a perversion of what they stood for, but in reality, they just didn't understand. He did, though.

His father had been a farmer, grown sheep and vegetables. Eked out a living from the hard soil. His entire family labored for every scrap of food they got, but he wouldn't. His destiny was clear. He would be the strongest priest to ever live, and he could do it too. He was already well on his way. Soon he would have enough strength to move against the priestesses directly, make them pay for doubting him, but first he had to get Trimera out of the way. First, he had to possess the magic that teased and tweaked his senses.

The light of the moon faded as the trees closed over the road. The dark held no power over his eyes and he continued on in his ground-eating pace. A chorus of wolves broke over the dark and he smiled. The night was for predators.

Janu tapped the strange sphere with the nib of his quill. A flash of color rippled out across its surface in a wave. It was beautiful. Reds, blues, greens, yellows, all chasing each other across the curved surface.

"How does it work?" He cradled the sphere to his chest, still mesmerized by the undulating.

The sphere clouded as Pria turned from the balcony. She drew a circle at the apex of the globe them tapped in its center. The colors appeared to sink into the globe as a sheet of green spread. He coughed a laugh as flecks of black erupted from the center of the growing patch of green. The flecks stretched and twisted into roads, trees, rivers, and mountains. In a blink, Trimera stretched around the sphere in his grip.

The tracking sphere threw shadows and flashes of light across the walls around them. "I knew you would like it."

He balanced the globe on a tripod on his desk. He gave the globe another tap and watched the tiny landscape twitch.

"They didn't tell me it would be you." He kept his attention on the sphere as the trees and mountains around Austeria settled and a small pulsing flicker flashed out a code.

"It was barely decided before I left."

Janu's mind caught on her tone; there was something strange in it. He studied her face but couldn't find any trace of it in her expression.

"The Lorien wouldn't want any possibility of being seen as incorrect."

Janu's thoughts skipped a beat. "Wait, are you saying the Lorien almost sent us someone else?"

"The placement of a priestess is never an easy thing. Many factors must be taken into account," she said. He thought he caught a tightening of the muscles of her face but it was gone so fast he couldn't be sure.

"Well, I'm glad it was you. I can't imagine what we would have ended up with otherwise," he said, trying to force mirth into his voice. He didn't like how serious the visit had gotten. "We will have to have rooms set up for you. I'm afraid I have procured most of the castle from Lord Huran but we should be able to find somewhere for you. I'm sure you would like to freshen up a bit and I have a few meetings to attend to before I can retire for the night. Perhaps in the morning we can announce your return publicly."

"We'll see."

He pulled her into his arms as she came to her feet.

"It is good to be home."

She sat on the edge of a cushioned chair before a mirrored vanity table brushing her soft waves of hair. The room she had been given was one she had stayed in when visiting Narita in her youth. It was lavish but comfortable with a warm fire and several couches and chairs for company. She had changed from her baggy travel clothes and now glistened in the silk suits of her profession.

She stared into the mirror, into her eyes. Anyone else who looked into them would see the strong, perfect priestess that she had been drilled to project. But to her eyes… Tightness marred her face. Atop the vanity sat a journal. Within its pages was every scrap of detail the Lorien knew about what was befalling Trimera, and she had been made to memorize every word before she set foot outside the Silver City. She was as prepared as she could be to take over Lana's post, but she felt completely naked. Lana's reports to the Lorien were few and held little in the way of facts. It was the consensus of the priestesses that she was holding back. But why? Why would she hold back information that could hold the key to protecting Trimera?

A letter sat beside her, the ink drying in the chill air. It was a missive to the Lorien, telling them she had arrived. She folded the letter until it fit in her palm. Eyes closed, she concentrated on an image of the Lorien.

When she opened her hands the note was gone, winging its way to the Silver City.

She could still hear the Council as they pronounced their verdict…

Sira pinned Pria with her glacial eyes. "High Priestess Pria, come stand before the Council."

The blood drained from her face as she stood. Her footsteps echoed around the chamber as her slippers flapped against the floor. She stilled her hands at her sides, willed herself not to fidget.

"The motion before the Council is the post of Trimera," Sira began. "The candidate in question is High Priestess Pria of Trimera. On this point, the Council has decided. High Priestess Pria, though it is true that no priestess in our ranks can match strength nor your knowledge of and familiarity with Trimera, the point still remains that you have no experience outside of the Lorien. We also cannot afford the loss of another high priestess."

Pria felt her heart lift and sink with Sira's words. It was the first time she really accepted the possibility of losing the post in Trimera. Everything she worked for, gone, left to watch from afar as her family fought for her home. An emptiness caved in her chest as Sira continued.

"Our decision is this: The post of Trimera must have an experienced priestess to deal with the dangers and complexities of Trimera."

Murmurs of chatter kicked up around the room and Pria heard several comments of approval and a couple of suggestions of priestesses to fill the post.

"However," Sira said, her gaze sweeping the room and vanquishing any voices before she continued, "we feel that High Priestess Pria's strength and knowledge are necessary for the position. High Priestess Pria is hereby assigned to the posting of Trimera. To counteract her inexperience, the posting will be on a probationary status. Prove to this Council that you can overcome your inexperience and attachment to your family and friends and put your duties first and the post will be granted unconditionally." She slammed the round crystal gavel against the bench, and the room resonated with the clang. "The discussion is closed."

Chaos erupted as people struggled to be heard, but it didn't matter. Trimera was hers.

Now she just had to keep it.

She couldn't blame them for their fear. Some of the first lessons at the Lorien revolved around the failures of priestesses over the years in their posts. So many disasters involved the distraction of a priestess when she tried to mix her duties with family that it was a widely accepted theory that being with family was such a distraction that directly led to disasters. The loss of her home was a fear that ate at her very soul.

She didn't know how she was going to live up to this level of scrutiny working with her closest friends and family, but the only other alternative meant she would have to watch the fight for her home from the sidelines. She wasn't about to sit idly by while Trimera struggled against the grinlo. All she could do was try to exude the perfect air of priestess and force the horde back to the Frontier. The citizens of Trimera were all depending on her now—for magical protection, for educated guidance—and so many at the Lorien didn't believe she was up to the task. Trimera was symbolically and literally the most important post in Reia. She was the first and last line of defense against the predatory and aggressive grinlo. If she failed to turn the tide of the invasion, there was nothing but innocents in the sights of the horde. She dropped her forehead into her palm and waited for the anxiety to pass.

With a gesture, her bag slid across the room toward her and she stood to secure a gold linked belt about her waist, its wide, heavy length hanging low around her hips. With a swirl she tossed a cloak across her shoulders and swept from the room, her slippered feet padding silently amid the swish of her pants.

The wide, shocked eyes of others met her progress along the halls, most not even recovering enough to bow to her before she passed, but she didn't care. Her position was of respect and strength; the pomp of courtly ceremony just seemed silly to her. True, she was their princess, but to be their priestess she needed more than bows and deference, and she had no choice but to be a perfect high priestess. There was too much riding on her position here for anything else.

She glided past a hallway, not glancing at the soldier who nearly dropped his sword as his eyes fell on her visage. She heard him rush to catch up to her and pulled away, spinning to face him as he reached for her. Her heart leapt into her throat and she had to root her feet to the ground to keep from leaping into his arms. She hadn't been ready for such a flood of emotion upon seeing him. He was just as she remembered him, tall and handsome, his red hair a casual drape atop his head. She could feel the priestess in her mind shrieking danger. She had no way to determine what might be deemed as inappropriate and get her posting removed, but she knew for a fact that any connection to Mian would be viewed as risky. She knew instantly that he was her biggest worry. "Do you know at whom you are grabbing?"

Large, amused green eyes smiled down at her, the same eyes that filled her memories of home. "Not if the voice hadn't proved it. When did you get back?"

She turned to continue down the hall, waiting for him to fall in beside her. She could feel his presence like a fire warming her skin. "I've only just arrived. Where is Janu?" She kept her voice cool, distant. Of the dangers for losing her focus, this soldier held some of the highest potential. Oh, he was older now, grown into his looks, a man just into his thirties, but she could feel his very essence in her bones. Her fear of failure often involved him more than anyone else.

He hooked a shock of red hair behind his ear, trying to hide his glances as he watched her walk. His uniform was crisp and neat with every inch of metal polished to a sheen. He kept his long stride to her pace. "When we took up here, Janu turned the solarium into a war room. He is there more often than not."

"Thank you, Mian."

"You have a lot to catch up on," he said.

"I'll manage."

His deep laugh wrapped around her, made her heart beat just a little harder. "You always do, don't you? You look nice."

She glared at him without missing a step. "Seriously, Mian, if you stuff anything into my clothes I will beat you to within an inch of your life."

He held out his hands to show his innocence. "I wouldn't dare play such a childish prank on the high priestess." He jumped in front of her and slid a strand of light honey hair through his fingers. "But I will admire the fit of her dress suit."

She rolled her eyes as she shoved him away. Impatience fueled heat in her words. "You are hopeless."

With a shrug he held open the solarium door for her, bowing low. "If I wasn't, no one would recognize me."

A smile spread across her face after she was sure he wouldn't see. No need to encourage his raucous behavior; it would only make it harder on her later. Several eyes turned toward her as she glided in among the waiting generals. She let her gaze take in the room with its walls of glass all designed to capture the morning light. The generals stood gathered around a center table. All eyes locked on her as she walked through the room. Janu had given them no warning that a new priestess had arrived. If any of them recognized her, they hid it well. Mian fell in behind her and became a shadow as she caught sight of Janu and made her way toward him. Janu was fighting a smile as she stopped at his side, facing a table littered with maps and orders.

"Sister, Mian."

Mian bowed over his sword. "Your Majesty."

A gruff older gentleman waved at the mass of maps. "Can we get started? Some of us have duties to see to."

"Easy, General Yan, no one wishes to keep you from patrol," Janu said. "For those of you who haven't heard, we have been assigned a new priestess. High Priestess Pria, we are all grateful to have you here."

Pria nodded to the men around her. "I'm sure I will be able to talk with each of you individually in the coming months. For now, please continue with what you were doing."

Janu returned his eyes to the maps before him. "Have we heard from our scouts to the south yet?"

A stout man with a heavy scar across his cheek stepped toward the table. "Keenan came back this morning with a total of 137, but a flood kept him from several towns. He should be heading out again shortly."

"No one else?" Janu rubbed a hand along the base of his neck.

"Not today, sir."

"With our new priestess, we will need to redouble our efforts. We should have enough men to push for the Seat soon. What are the newest distances?" Janu asked.

"The closest report we've heard today was thirty miles and that was a hunting party. The grinlo seem to have slowed for now." A younger soldier passed a map along the table.

"And our raids?"

"There is no telling if we are making any impact or not," said a tall man to her left, "but it could be possible that the raids are what's keeping the horde at bay for now."

Janu rubbed his chin. "It could be."

Mian leaned an arm on the table as he glanced past Pria to Janu. "Or they could be trying to lull us. Draw our men out into the open."

Pria glanced at him skeptically. "Do you have reason to believe they're doing this?"

"They have led us into traps before." Janu rapped his knuckles on the table, silencing the buzz that had spread around the room. "You have your assignments. Mian, would you stay behind."

Pria clasped her hands together and let her eyes follow the commanders from the room. As the door shut she drew herself up, ensuring that she projected the perfect air of priestess. "Grinlo are not smart enough to set traps."

"I know." Janu leaned against the table behind him.

"Then I take it you have in mind who could be calling the shots," she said.

Mian coughed a laugh. "Not a clue."

"Do they know?" she asked, nodding toward the door and the commanders who had just filed from the room.

Mian considered the door through which the soldiers had left. "Some of them might. They definitely have suspicions." He scratched his chin. "There are a few men who have dealt with the horde before. They have mentioned some fears to me in passing."

She turned her back, afraid Mian and Janu would see her worry. Someone with enough strength to control the horde would be a terrible opponent to face. Many a priestess had died trying to stop individuals who had done just that. Her mind cartwheeled as it trailed the thought down into the depths. Of the rules a priestess was expected to live by, the dark magic that was necessary to gain sway over the grinlo was one of the most harshly punished for discretions. The level a priestess would have to descend to in order to achieve such a task was usually enough to ensure that only the most foolish or twisted would even contemplate it. If such a person was active, there was no telling what nefarious plans they could have in mind. No one with any morals at all would even attempt such as monstrous an act necessary to gain the control needed to preside over the horde. If someone had set themselves over the horde, they would be subject to trial and punishment through the priestesses for their crime. "I need to observe this behavior," Pria said. "I am going to accompany one of your commanders on a raid. If they are truly capable of setting traps, I need firsthand knowledge of it."

"I figured you would. Mian, do you think you can keep my little sister from getting herself into too much trouble for me?"

She raised her eyebrow at Mian's inevitably mischievous grin, but she held her tongue. "It'll be difficult but I think I'm stubborn enough."

"Find her horse, would you?" Janu had to cover his mouth to hide his grin as Mian shot Pria's angry glare a wink before strutting from the room. He closed his eyes as he held out a hand to forestall Pria's tirade. "I know you think Mian is, well, Mian, but he's really proven himself since you have been gone. Enough that the soldiers recommended him to me. He's Battle Leader, and I'm not letting you go with anyone else."

She crossed her arms with a glare. "Fine. I better go change." She spun on her heels and let her stride carry her down the hall. She drew a deep breath as she rounded a corner and saw Mian lounging against her door—a complication if she ever saw one. A priestess must be focused, her only priority guiding Trimera to push the Frontier back. Protecting citizens from the horde was her only thought. "I'm not going to slip off on my own if that's what you are wondering about."

"You've grown so prickly toward me, I could never figure out why," he said.

She planted her fists on her hips. "It is more efficient to be constantly upset with you than to constantly have to figure out what you've done."

He leaned toward her and smiled down at her anger. "You've been gone ten years. You don't think there's a chance I've changed?"

"A rock will weather eventually," she said, "but you are hopeless."

He pressed a hand to his heart, his expression twisting in comic exaggeration. "That hurt, Pria." He pulled a hand from behind him. "One of Narita's breastplates should fit you well enough."

She took the armor from him with care. "Thank you."

With a smile he pushed off from the door and swung it wide. She nodded acknowledgment as she slipped past him, careful to note his hands. She dropped the armor into a chair as she heard the door shut.

"You don't have to be so formal with me." His voice held none of the normal tease.

Her back straightened as she spun to face him. "Why are you in my room?"

He shrugged as he crossed the floor toward her, thumbs tucked behind his belt. "I've been in your room before."

She took a measured step back from him. Gone was the tease replaced by serious Mian, protective Mian, her Mian. Even more dangerous Mian. "Mian, even you should know better."

Inhaling, he leaned a hand on the table behind her, his face just inches from hers. "What possible mischief could I get into?"

She stepped back from him again. "That is why I must be formal with you."

He waved around the empty room. "No one is here to see. You can loosen up a little."

"And you could gain some common sense."

His deep, masculine laughter filled the room. "I have plenty of common sense, but through years of hard work and diligence I have learned to overcome it."

Her visage rippled as she fought laughter before losing and clapping a hand over her mouth. "Would you get out!"

He shoved off from the table then leaned down toward her. "I'm going, but I just want you to remember, I won."

"Out!" She stomped her foot to add weight to her command.

He twisted as he walked, his chest facing her. "I'll be outside whenever you finish getting ready. Do try to hurry, we don't have all day."

"*Mian*!"

He pulled the door shut behind him, mischievous grin plastered across his face. Pria growled angrily. "Stubborn, irritating man!"

The door cracked open and Mian peered around the edge. "Did you call me?"

"Out!" She lobbed a shoe at the door, stomping in disappointment as he ducked out of its way.

Eyes closed, she pulled herself to her full height. She could feel her grip relaxing, loosening. He'd always had that effect on her: soothing, disarming. No, she wouldn't let him get to her. She couldn't risk the horde taking Trimera, killing her family—what little family she had left. She stood there silent as she worked her way through the list of examples from history the Lorien had drilled into her head. The number of dead, the destruction of cities. The last time the Frontier had to be pushed back, the horde had taken all the way to the Silver City. It had taken the full might of the priestesses to correct it. Nothing was worth risking the lives of so many.

When she was sure she could trust herself to maintain control, she opened her eyes.

She shook her head as she made her way over to her trunk, digging through the few clothes she had brought with her until she found her riding breeches. She changed quickly, not wanting to give Mian any reason to check on her again. She slipped into the armor and cinched it tight, turning to inspect the fit in the mirror. It fit a bit loose in the bodice and tight in the hips but it didn't leave any gaps or restrict her movement terribly so it would have to do.

After pulling her hair back from her eyes and securing it with a cord, she flung the door wide, confusion painting her expression as she found the hall empty. She stepped out and caught sight of Mian a few yards away speaking to another soldier. The stranger nodded before pressing a hand to his heart and bowing.

Mian turned to her as the other man left. "Ready then?"

She rolled her eyes at his outstretched arm. "I do not need to be coddled, thank you."

He pulled his arm back as he fell in at her side. "That was not coddling, that was merely a courtesy extended to my priestess."

"Who was that?" she asked, her eyes following the soldier down the hall.

"That was Jeran, my lieutenant. He'll be your dear brother's errand boy while we are off prancing in the woods."

His flippant remark irked her. "A Battle Leader is hardly an errand boy, Mian. I do hope you take your position seriously."

"I take my position as seriously as you do, I just had the stick removed."

With slow, deliberate blinks she pushed back the urge to laugh, to rush into his arms, to let his very presence comfort her. She was her own comfort now. She wiped the expression from her face, showing only stoic contemplation as a gaggle of maids bowed to her before fleeing Mian's reach. Obviously his reputation preceded him.

He glanced after the women then leaned close, whispering in her ear. "I think you intimidate the maids; they are usually very chatty."

She glared up at him but there was no hint of his normal tease. She snapped her jaw shut and tossed her hair back. "As well I should. I am their priestess, not some silly princess."

He sighed as he stepped forward to open a door. With a finger to her chin he waited for her blue eyes to meet his. "Sounds to me that a priestess leads a very lonely existence." He stepped aside as she walked through.

"A priestess is a life of duty and service. People look to me for guidance."

"And that means you can't be human?" His voice was soft and gentle.

"That means I can't be seen to be foolish or ruled by emotion." She hated the heat of her words, how easily he was able to raise her ire.

"So what, you're going to turn into a depressing old prude like the last priestess?" he asked.

"Priestess Lana was a brilliant woman. Filling her shoes will not be easy!"

He shrugged. "Your aim will have to improve. Lana never missed when *she* tried to kick me."

"Well, you did give her plenty of practice."

He smiled in reflection, his green eyes sparkling. "Yes, it was fun." He clapped an arm around her shoulders, jerking her hard to his side. "Don't worry, your aim will improve."

She shoved against him as she laughed. "Get off me, fool!" She screamed as he jerked her off her feet and tucked her easily under his arm. "Mian! Let go of me!"

"Did you say something, Priestess?"

"Mian, you really don't want me to stop you, it won't be pleasant!"

He tossed her into the air, this time with his weaker arm. "You know Pria, for someone so all-fired important, you certainly don't weigh much."

"*Mian*!"

He kicked open the door to the stable and stepped out into the musty dimness. Pria drew a deep breath as she concentrated several balls of air around him, then after centering her own weight, she bombarded him. She lowered herself to her feet as he dropped to the floor and tried to protect himself with his arms.

"I give, I give! I'm sorry!"

She smoothed her hair as she ceased her attack. Bending down beside his ear, she whispered, "I believe I win."

The stablehand's eyes were wide as he clutched reins to his chest. "Uh, Priestess?" He jumped as she turned toward him.

"Oh, yes, my horse. Thank you, young man."

Mian uncurled and stared up at her from the floor. "That was completely unfair."

She pulled her mount's muzzle over her shoulder and leaned her head on its cheek. "No, that was just evening the odds. Adding some weight, as it were. I can play unfair if you like."

He held up his hands in surrender. "No, that won't be necessary."

"Then I suggest you get up off the floor, Commander."

Mian stared after her as she led her horse out into the western courtyard before looking to the stablehand cowering against the wall. "Women are all crazy, my boy, never forget that."

His trembling hand pointed toward the still-open door. "She…she floated! She just…floated!"

Mian jumped to his feet and clapped the younger man on the shoulder. "Floating is the least of my worries."

Mian had often thought about what it would be like to see his Pria again. He had accepted the fact that he may never set eyes on her again, that the Lorien would station her far away—but he had never considered that he could get her back and still have lost her. He could see the priestess hiding in her eyes. He'd never seriously thought that they would end up married like he joked when they were kids, but he'd always thought she would be his same Pria.

He paused in the shade of the overhang and watched the woman in question. He couldn't think about any of that. Right now, his only concern was protecting his prince's new priestess and sister. Not the loss of some fantasy that would never happen.

The men of his patrol all eyed him as he strolled from the stable. Pria sat her leggy mount as she pulled on a pair of tanned riding gloves. Her eyebrow rose in challenge when she noticed him watching her. "Are we quite ready to go, Commander?" Her frigid tone grated along his nerves. He guessed she had to act that way, to be seen as a priestess, but there was no reason to act like that with him, not after all they had been through. Surely even an almighty high priestess could have friends.

He snatched his reins from the older man beside him, grumbling under his breath before vaulting to the animal's back. "Forgive me, Priestess, if I kept you waiting."

The older man glared at him as he took his customary position to Mian's left. The man's visage was creased and sun-worn, grizzled with age and battle but still with a grandfatherly air. His hair was gray and thinner than it used to be but he was strong and sharp minded. Pria kneed her horse to Mian's, settling the cowl of her cloak high over her head as they rode from the Western Gate. The man to his left cleared his throat and rolled his eyes toward Pria. Mian sighed. "Orotid, I don't believe you've had the pleasure of meeting the high priestess."

Orotid beamed at her as she turned in her saddle. "My lady, it is an honor." He bowed from his horse. "To what do we owe such pleasant company for our patrol?"

"Pr—" Her glare jerked to him so fast that for a moment he thought she was going to hit him again. "The *priestess* wishes to observe the horde personally."

Orotid's smile warred between knowledge and pride. "Well, we'll be sure to be extra careful."

"There is no need. I am quite capable of protecting myself."

Mian urged his horse forward, inching it past Pria's gray. "Even so, a priestess, especially a high priestess, should take care to protect herself, so no recklessness for today, Orotid."

The older man's grin grew wider. "I'll try to restrain myself, Commander."

"Commander?"

Mian shifted his glare to Pria. "Yes, Priestess?"

"I would like to know your plans for this patrol."

He leaned toward her, keeping his voice low. "This is really annoying; can't we just talk like normal people?" He growled as she shifted her horse away. "Fine." He sat back up and ran a hand through his hair. "You should be pleased, we'll be meeting up with Narita's patrol. She has been ranging around the Midrow Highlands for a few weeks now. Orotid and my men will relieve her patrol."

"But not us?" she whispered, her voice soft and dangerous.

"The prince made me promise to return with you."

She shot him a reprimanding glare. "And he doesn't trust me to return on my own."

"Maybe he just doesn't want to face your sniping by himself," he breathed.

"I can't understand you when you mumble."

Orotid laughed. "That's probably a good thing."

"Hey, how about we focus on the task at hand? Right?" He faced the group of men behind them. "I want a perimeter around us. Two scouts forward, two back. Let's keep our eyes open, soldiers. I don't want any surprises."

Pria's lips curved as men swarmed around them, rushing to follow Mian's commands. Orotid eased his sword in its sheath and nodded as the men flowed past drawing Pria's attention. "Orotid, I don't believe I remember you," she said. "How long have you served under Prince Janu?"

"You wouldn't remember me. Before you left I was under Lord Renor stationed at Amber Keep." Orotid shifted in his saddle, preening under the attention.

"The Keep was the first to fall," Mian said. "Lord Renor died holding back the horde as his citizens evacuated." Mian's voice dropped as he leaned back toward Pria. "When the attack began, he ordered Orotid to flee the Keep ahead of the evacuation to warn Janu. He was the only survivor."

Orotid's head was down, face turned away when she looked to him. Her expression softened into affection for the older gentleman. "Many times, the hardest thing to do is what needs to be done," she said. "In such cases, it must fall to those who can see the benefit as well as the pain."

"My Lord sent me, as I was among the oldest of his men and likely the least useful in battle."

Mian shook his head. "Now don't start with that again, you old fool. I've seen you fight. I'd bet your sword against most of my seasoned soldiers and not lose a moment's rest over it."

Pria fixed him with her most penetrating gaze, a task she had learned well from her time at the Lorien. "And who would have gone in your place? By sending you he was not only warning his prince of the impending danger and saving lives, but also giving him the asset of firsthand knowledge of the horde. You are truly a great hero, not only to the citizens of Amber Keep but also to every survivor of the Seat."

Orotid shook his head. "My lady is kind to say so, but Prince Janu only keeps me around as a courtesy." Her eyes narrowed angrily at Mian's long-suffering smile. "He just found me somewhere where I wouldn't likely get into trouble until they can put me out to pasture."

Pria's face lost all compassion as her eyes hardened into blue ice. Mian dropped his horse back a couple of steps in the hopes of avoiding any flying shrapnel. "Soldier, I will only ask you once to remember whom you are addressing and whom you are speaking of. Prince Janu is hardly a fool and only a fool would *dispose* of people into the Battle Leader's command. Any man here had to earn his right to be here through blood and sweat. It is a place of honor and obligation that should never be coveted." Spine snapped straight, she kicked her horse forward into the void ahead of them.

Mian flashed him a devilish smile. "I think she likes you."

Orotid's jaw hung open. "Sir, I never meant to imply—"

Mian waved him off. "She knows that. Pria likes to point out how foolish you are being by taking her retorts to the extreme opposite. Rather annoying, if you ask me."

"Yes, I can tell how annoyed you are by the way you keep watching her." The older man nodded. "Probably a lonely existence, a priestess. Such a fiery young woman in a position that would keep most from approaching her."

"Am I going to have to order you to shut up?"

"Just pointing out foolishness." The older man hitched his shoulders. "Were I a handsome young man, I hardly think I would be wasting time making conversation with a grizzled old soldier when there was a beautiful girl riding by herself just a few yards away."

Mian held up a finger. "You are way out of line, Orotid. My personal—" His jaw snapped shut as one of his men broke the line and rode close to Pria. "One pretty face and discipline goes out the window." He jerked his horse to a halt beside them, his angry glare shifting from the winter rose in Pria's hand to the soldier's blanched expression. "Is this where you belong?"

"No sir?" The younger man's startlingly blue eyes widened.

"Then I suggest you get back in formation," Mian growled.

With a hasty salute, the soldier spun his mount and charged back to the circle around them.

"There was no need for that," Pria said. "He was only being thoughtful."

He held his hand out in exasperation. "*That* you'll defend? Had he broke formation to save your life you would have sent him back bleeding!" Orotid trotted past them, whistling as he kept his eyes to the trees around them. Mian shook his head. "I must have been insane to agree to take you with us."

"Stop being so dramatic." She held her hands before her, floating the rose into the air as she made a sphere with her movements.

"What are you doing?"

The petals began to glow. "This is a Rose of the Order. It only grows where a priestess has fallen." The flower flashed bright then vanished from the case of her hands. "I'm sending it back to my room where it will stay preserved until I can perform the proper ceremony."

"Oh." He stared at her hands as they took up her reins. "Can you do that with anything?"

"It takes more energy with larger things, but if I had a full coset of priestesses with which to supplement my own power, we could even send *people.* Why?"

"Could come in handy," he said. He winked at her as they trotted up to Orotid's horse and he raised his voice. "All right men, we have at least three more hours before we get to our first camp. Let's step it up! We don't want our priestess to sleep too rough, do we?"

COUNTRY RIDE

At the corner of Janu's desk in his private study sat a portable writing desk, about as wide as his forearm and as deep as his foot, the wood stained a deep chestnut. It had appeared there the day he took over this room as his own. Every meeting in this room was overseen by that small box. He had come to rely on it, as strange as that was. It had become almost a superstition. Any big decision, any hard choice, he felt better making in the presence of that desk.

It was Lana's travel desk. He remembered it from when she had advised his father. Every trip, every meeting, that desk was with her. As a boy, he had always wondered what she kept in there, what secrets it might hold, and in fact, the day she rode out with Mian on that fateful raid, he had finally built up his courage enough to peek inside. There was nothing, of course. It was a writing desk, not for any type of storage, so the only contents had been blank sheaths of parchment. The guilt of that invasion haunted him still.

Now, as long as he left that desk there, he didn't feel as alone.

He should have done more to protect her, he knew that now. He had never really understood her worth, never knew what she meant to him. He wouldn't make that mistake twice, especially not with Pria. The loss of a second high priestess would be beyond devastating to the kingdom, the loss of Pria... He stumbled and caught himself on the wall as a wave of panic rushed over him. No. He couldn't even think of that. He wouldn't think about that.

At any rate, he had a few days to determine how to win that battle. For now, it was Mian's fight, and a fight it would be. Pria stubborn was a force of nature—High Priestess Pria would be a force of the gods.

"Trouble, my prince?"

Janu's heart leapt to a gallop within his chest at the voice at his shoulder. His pride had him hoping the other man had not noticed his reaction as he turned. Behind him waited Jaren, clean cut and smooth faced. It wasn't so much that Janu minded Mian's second in command—the lad was competent, diligent, and even likable. In fact, Janu's entire issue with the young man had nothing to do with Jeran himself at all. It had to do with the memories Jeran brought to the surface anytime Janu was alone with him.

Following Lana's loss, amid the turmoil and pain, Mian had lost faith in himself. Janu had, of course, given him time off to deal with his grief and doubt. But instead of returning confident and strong, Mian had determined that Jeran's successful stint proved he was the better man for the job.

What followed was nearly worse than losing Lana. Seeing Mian so broken had ripped him apart. It had taken weeks of arguing to get Mian to return to his post. Mian and Janu had grown up together, been raised as siblings from teenagers. When he worked with Mian he didn't have to give commands. The man usually knew what Janu was thinking before he had even formed the thoughts himself. The problem was that no matter how good Jeran was, he would never be able to duplicate that. No matter how good Jeran was, he would never be Mian.

Janu smiled at Jeran. "All is well, Jeran."

He slipped from the office into the hallway. Austeria was a lovely city, almost lavish when compared to the Seat. Gardens and statues, fountains and breezeways, Austeria was built to lessen the severity of hiding up in the mountain pass. It was no hideaway, he could still pick out the hidden fortification: a reinforced wall here, a battlement there. Austeria's true power, though, was her people. Strong and brave, they had welcomed refugees from the Seat with open arms and volunteered enthusiastically for her defense.

It was part of the reason he had moved his base of operations here rather than Kyneira. Oh, there were a multitude of other reasons—the forefront of which was the utter lack of a defensive wall in Kyneira—but he liked to romanticize, if only in his head where no one could contradict him. He had found a necessity for distraction in his rein as prince, and he took advantage of it where he could. It was few enough chances even so.

Jeran ghosted along behind him, inching up his nerves. He needed a plan of attack, a way to ensure his sister's protection without making her angry. For now he just had to trust that Mian was keeping her safe. Sequestered in his apartments, he could already feel the anxiety building. Only a few days. He could make it till her return.

His disguise today was a young lordling. The disguises came easily now.

The comfort of the Seat called to him but he couldn't return, not yet. There was work to do, and though he was a lot of things, lazy was not one of them. Austeria didn't really have anything on the Seat. It had its positive aspects, but it still felt as if something was lacking. The streets of the Seat were wide and open to allow for military maneuvers with strong, thick-walled buildings overlooking the wide thoroughfares in case of an invading army. The streets of Austeria, though not narrow, were designed for traffic and aesthetics. They were wide enough for carriages to pass but were also divided by a garden of trees and flowers down the center. Where the Seat had decorations to soften the severity of the defenses, Austeria seemed almost ostentatious with defenses hidden among the decorative accents.

Of course, it could also be the people that were lacking.

The man who called himself Neram hated the people of Austeria the most. He could forgive Austeria her flamboyant decorations, but he couldn't forgive her people. It had taken him years of sacrifice to gain enough control of the horde to take Amber Keep and the Seat. The Seat was his real prize, the jewel in his growing crown. Soon it would be all of Trimera, but he was proud of what he had accomplished. No one would believe what he had amounted to.

At the Lorien, his teachers had lost patience with him often. Obtaining control of the horde was the biggest taboo in their world. Not because having that much power was dangerous—oh, coveting power was frowned upon, but not illegal. What made gaining control of the horde illegal was the lengths one had to go to gain that control. Some killed innocents, some sacrificed parts of themselves, but all went beyond the credo of the priestess.

That had irked him the most, truly. No matter how many priests were in the ranks of the ruling priestesses, they were never referred to as priests unless given a title directly. Men were rare among the rank of priestesses—so rare that traditionally they were believed to be anomalies. Therefore, just as traditionally, the only collective term for them was priestess. It was so condescending it boiled his blood. When he overthrew the ruling priestesses, he would never allow anyone to refer to him as *priestess* again.

She had been here, might still be here, the source of the magical residue he had come across. He didn't need to search too hard; she would come to him, eventually, just like Lana had. It was only a matter of time. He had heard talk as he wandered the streets, talk of the return of High Priestess Pria. He had seen her before, although it had been years. Even then she had been exquisite.

He didn't have time to wait for her to return; he was needed elsewhere but he would be back.

Pria stretched her bare feet out as she enjoyed the feel of air on her skin. Mian's men spread out around them in rows of campfires and picket lines at the base of a valley nestled among low rolling hills. Camping atop the hills would be too visible, but in the valley they had to rely on the watchfulness of the guards. In the open grasslands they were traveling; there was no perfect alternative.

"Little cold for that, isn't it?"

She glared at Mian as he watched her from across the pile of kindling. She laid her finger on the end of a stick, smiling as flames shot along its length, flashing to life with an audible snap. Mian leapt back. "Are you trying to set me on fire?"

She lay back along her bedroll, satisfied with the laugh that barked from his lips. "It's warm now." He caught her gaze and she was frozen for a moment, lost in the green pull. She could feel herself losing to that pull, losing control. But she couldn't let that happen. Couldn't afford that weakness in the face of the Council's scrutiny. He blinked, breaking the connection and she felt the heat bloom in her cheeks as she looked away.

He brushed the dirt and leaves from his knees then dropped onto his own bedroll. "You are a brat." Despite his words, his voice still quivered with amusement.

With a shrug, she curled up beneath her blanket as Orotid returned from his rounds. "Everyone including present company seems to be settled in, sir."

Mian nodded. "Good. Watch set up?"

Orotid nodded as he lowered himself to the last bedroll around their fire. "And one of the men will be bringing us some dinner. Now if you young pups don't mind, my old body could use some rest."

Mian rolled his eyes as he propped himself against a nearby log. Lips curled in a wicked grin, his gaze shot back to Pria. "Pria?"

She curled tighter beneath her blankets with a soft moan, fighting off her impulse to jump up like they were children again.

"Can I ask you some questions?"

She rolled onto her back and stared up at the darkening sky. "What do you want to know?"

"What was it like? Your training? The Silver City? What all did you do?"

A childish glee bubbled up in her chest as his gaze caught her again. Her lips curled in anticipation. "I'll tell you if you tell me."

He smiled and nodded, and she crawled toward him, propping herself against the log and leaning her head on his shoulder. All of the tension faded from her, just as it always did around Mian. She drew a deep breath. What was the worst that could happen? They were at the edge of a darkened camp. Perhaps she could relax a little.

His body shook with laughter, earning him a glare.

"What?"

He patted her thigh and the racing beat won out, sending her heart ricocheting around in her chest so hard she thought for sure he could feel it.

"It's just been a long time since you've crawled over and leaned on my shoulder," he said. "I missed it." She smiled as he wrapped his arm around her back and let her snuggle in deeper to his chest. She could feel his warm breath on the crown of her head.

"When you guys would let me near you!" she retorted. "You always used to hide from me!"

"How is it our fault that when you finally got old enough to be fun, they sent you away?"

"Whatever," she said.

"Come on, tell me all your adventures." He gave her a shake and she had to clamp down hard on a laugh that felt like it would come out as a giggle.

She huffed. "*Adventures.* They kept us locked in the Lorien. Said we were too young and untrained for the big city."

He shook his head. "They obviously didn't know you!"

"Well, the first night we were there, my roommate blew the wall out trying to make her bed, so all in all, not the worst rule they had. They were pretty strict—took me a week to find the loopholes and sneak out. The city was amazing! Even more spectacular than you can imagine! The bridges are all made of glass, it's like flying! Stores, you've never seen the like! They have a bakeshop with sweets you couldn't even imagine! If we ever get the horde under control, we'll have to go."

"With all these shops you snuck out to, you didn't seem to return with much," he said.

She waved her hand dismissively. "It's being shipped."

"And your classes? Or are you just a firestarter now?"

She rammed a fist into his ribs but didn't even get a grunt. Her head slumped against his chest and she could hear his heart loud and fast against her ear. Was he nervous too? But that was foolish, why would he be nervous? "Classes. Life was classes. Every day, history, politics, diplomacy. If you thought Lana was a taskmistress! She couldn't hold a candle to the teachers at the Lorien. But of course, everyone's favorite classes were the magic classes."

"Where you learned how to beat poor defenseless soldiers?" He laughed.

"We learned to defend ourselves, among some other tricks, like not blowing things up." She smiled up into his eyes and felt a pulse of something foreign. Something that drew heat to her face.

He gave her shoulders a gentle squeeze. "Your parents would be so proud of you both."

She drew back from him, her back stiff. His brow wrinkled but eventually he also caught the footsteps from behind them. The young soldier who had offered Pria the flower stepped into the firelight, carrying a tray. He nodded his salute. "Sir, Orotid ordered some stew for you. I…uh, found some wine…for the lady."

Mian glanced at Pria but she kept her expression stoic to hide her emotions. "Thank you, Raber. I'm sure it will be fine."

Raber bounced on his heels with a sheepish smile, throwing glances at Pria. Mian raised a testy eyebrow. "There something else?"

Raber's jaw dropped, eyes wide as he shook his head. "No, sir."

Mian flashed his teeth. "Thank you, Raber."

Pria rubbed her temples as Raber melted back into the camp. "That was foolish of me. I'm sorry, Commander."

Mian licked juice from his fingers as he looked up from the tray of food. "Sorry for what?"

"I forgot. I let my guard down."

He laughed. "Raber was panting at your heels before he saw you on my shoulder. I hate to burst your little seclusion bubble, but you'll have to be a lot more than distant to keep men from noticing how beautiful you are."

The blood rushed to her face, burning up her neck to her hairline as her stomach dropped. Her eyes shot to him and he dropped his face but she still caught the color in his cheeks.

"Trust me, he didn't bring you wine because you are the high priestess."

She stilled her heart for a few breaths. Foolish, to let her heart leap just because some scoundrel called her beautiful. She cleared her throat. "Are you suggesting that I alter my appearance?"

He coughed a nervous laugh. "I am suggesting that we eat before Orotid wakes up and explains why old age gives him the need for more food than us."

She slid off her feet and crossed her legs in front of her before cradling the offered bowl in her hands. "He's very interesting."

"He thinks so too—very difficult to get him to shut up," Mian growled.

She kept her head down as her lips slid into a smile. "Must never be quiet around here with two of you."

Orotid twitched in his sleep. "Is that dinner?" he mumbled.

"That man could be in a coma and still smell food."

The old man sat up. "Unlike you young kids, this old body needs to be refueled often." He drew a deep breath over his bowl and smiled. "Ah, Masteron is a great mess cook."

Mian's smile slid sideways. "A gift from Janu. He was the palace cook. He said if he was going to ask the best from these men, they deserved the best treatment. Masteron was only too happy to join up, had some dumb idea about glory and heroism. He's seen more than any palace cook was ever meant to see."

"It was his choice, he chose to serve." Pria dabbed at her chin with a napkin. "And Janu was right: Your men do deserve the best…and this is pretty close."

"Your brother wanted you with us for a reason." Mian jabbed his elbow against her arm.

"My brother worries too much," she said.

Orotid shook his head. "I have known Janu for a while now, and I doubt over-worrying is one of his attributes. Protecting an asset is a good quality to have."

Pria's face dropped its emotion. "Great, I'm an asset now."

"You're the one who didn't want to be seen as a person. Congratulations." Mian saluted her with his spoon.

Mian wheeled his horse around as his men passed him. Pria and Orotid fell in at his side as he took up the rear position. The wind was strong this morning, whipping Pria's hair around her face as she tried to chat with Orotid. Mian watched her from the corner of his eye as his men spread out around them. His grin grew wider as she snatched at her feral locks. He dug into a saddlebag and slipped out a length of leather strap. With his knees he guided his horse toward her and, waiting for the wind to subside, tied the strap around her temples, pinning her hair down.

She watched him, her eyes unreadable, as he sat back from her. "Thank you."

He shrugged with a grin. "No problem. You'd better step it up if we plan to meet up with Narita today."

Pria's eyes blinked wide. "Today? I didn't realize the horde would be so close."

Mian chose his words carefully, mindful of the storm he was skirting. "Narita is looping back; the horde is still four days' ride from here."

Mian watched the dark clouds move in as Pria's face stilled. "But I wanted to see the horde for myself. Will we be traveling with them?"

"No."

She inhaled. He watched as she subtly changed from Pria to the high priestess. Every laugh-line on her face smoothed as the muscles in her shoulders tensed. He hated that transition. "Commander," she said, "I did not come on this country ride just to keep you company. If I am to give Janu proper advice then I need to have firsthand experience. Now I am not helpless and I resent being treated so."

Mian stretched his jaw. "Orotid, could you give us a second?" He waited for the older man to fall back before looking at Pria. "Janu does not want you near the grinlo."

Her eyes narrowed. "You as well," she said.

He gave a slight nod. "I would prefer to keep you as far away as possible."

"So I am some pathetic doll to hide away, is that it?"

"Pria, you keep reminding me you are the high priestess," Mian began. "Janu needs you and he needs you alive. I have no intention of letting you anywhere near the grinlo no matter how angry you get."

"Mian, this is ridiculous! People are trusting me to help guide this kingdom and I will have all the knowledge I need to do so, with or without your help!"

He reined his anger as it tried to rage forth to meet hers. He always could feel her emotions acutely. If she felt strong about something, it had always been able to jump up his own emotions. But no matter, he wasn't about to let her risk her life like Lana. "I cannot guarantee your safety if we go to the barrier, and I will not risk you. No matter what you do, neither my men nor I will take you there. It is a done discussion."

"It is not even close to done." Her voice frosted over. "How dare you two make decisions for me! Arrogant man! I am his sister, not his daughter. You have no right to dictate my life to me."

"Calm down, Pria. You just got home; we can't really afford to lose you already. Now I'm not going to spend the next two days arguing with you about it. You can talk to Narita and her men and get a decent firsthand account, and after you are more settled we will talk about seeing the grinlo firsthand."

"Talk?" Her voice was flat as the anger dropped from her face.

He glared at her. "Yes, talk. It's like arguing but at a lower volume."

She tossed her head. "That was almost clever. I can't believe even you would be this irritating."

"And don't even think about trying to get Narita on your side. Even if she agrees with you, her men will agree with me."

She halted her horse. "Why drag me out here? Why bother bringing me along at all? You could easily have just let me stay back."

"Janu wanted you to bond with the soldiers." He met her steely gaze.

"You two set this all up. How?"

"When he realized you were back, he came to me. You haven't changed much in ten years either, little Pria. We have been studying the grinlo for a while now and one thing we have learned is that they seem to prefer magic. What do you think happened to Lana?"

She kneed her horse toward him and held his gaze. "Lana died in service to her people."

"She died because we couldn't keep her safe," he yelled with his hands to the sky. "She left us without a high priestess for years, Pria."

"What happened?"

He let his horse walk off, waiting for her mount to follow before he continued. "She insisted on accompanying Janu whenever he went out. Got so bad she wouldn't let him out of her sight. We always assumed the grinlo were after him—I mean, why would they want Lana, right? Then one day I was going to take a patrol around Haven—nothing big—and she decided she wanted to go." He paused. "We don't even know where they came from. One minute we were riding in the open, the next we were surrounded. She was at my side fighting, and then…" Shrugging, he said, "As soon as she went down, they dragged her off, not even bothering with the rest of us." He dropped his head. "I don't think I could survive seeing you dragged away, Pria. Please don't put me through that."

She stared at him openly now but he couldn't look at her. If he turned toward her, he would lose control of the tears he held back.

"Mian, you can't keep me forever," she whispered.

"Yeah, well, I don't have to watch you die either." He took her hand, squeezed it. "So I'll hold you hard for as long as I can."

She rode in silence for a while, her eyes not leaving the path before them. Finally, she sighed and rolled her gaze up to his face. "They didn't kill her, not right away. I can guarantee you that."

"That's really not very comforting," Mian said. The thought of Lana being held by the horde formed a knot in the pit of his stomach. "What makes you such an expert anyway? I thought you came out here to gain knowledge on the horde."

"I came out here to understand *this* horde. If you are correct, they are behaving very strangely and need to be studied. The Lorien taught many classes on threats to priestesses, including an extensive course on the grinlo and creatures that are associated with them. As the largest, non-human threat to Reia, it is a priestess' sacred duty to learn as much about them as possible in order to protect our charges. They use our magic. Lana would have known this. It is not your fault that she was captured."

He met her gaze. "You're still not going."

"You'd rather someone else take me? Mian, I have an obligation to my people, myself, the Lorien, and my brother and prince to investigate this! How am I to advise Janu if I am not allowed to investigate?"

He jabbed his finger at the ground. "I am telling you right here and now, after what happened to Lana, no soldier in this army will take you to the front lines. It's not going to happen. End of discussion!"

"I'll have to go myself, then. Mounted, alone, the trip shouldn't take more than four days total. I'll need some supplies, Commander." She tugged at her lip, deep in thought as she mentally ticked off lists.

"Sorry, Priestess, but my supplies are already rationed to my men and I'm sure you wouldn't want to deprive them."

"Nonsense. I've seen your supplies; you have weeks' worth stored up. I will need a pack horse."

He grabbed her arm, pulling both horses to a stop. The men around them looked on nervously. "I am asking you as a friend, Pria. For your brother's sake—for mine—*please* don't go to the front."

"Mian, I have to. To ignore this threat would be lunacy."

"I am not asking you to ignore it," he pleaded. "Just wait. At least for a little while. You can't just drop in and out on us like this! Just bide your time interviewing the men before you run off to face monsters alone."

She blinked at the glisten of tears in his eyes and gave a slow nod. The tension drained from his body as he cupped a hand behind her neck and pulled her toward him, kissing her forehead. "Thank you, Priestess." He jerked away, trying to cover his emotions with a playful shove. "Well, look at that: You can compromise."

Pria kicked her horse back into motion. Her brow furrowed as the men settled back into their routine. Orotid eased his horse back toward them, keeping a close eye to her and she sighed in irritation. What was she, some kind of wild animal?

The line of men in front of them divided, allowing a rider atop a spotted mare to slip between them. The soldier spun his horse, falling in beside Mian as he bowed his head to Pria. "Commander, Priestess."

"Narig," said Mian.

"They are not at the rendezvous, sir." The soldier's report was breathy.

"How far did you search?" Mian asked.

"An hour's hard ride in the four directions. No sign of them."

Mian rubbed a hand down his face. "All right. Orotid, I want you to take Pria and head back to Janu; have him send us reinforcements."

Pria grabbed his arm. "I have a better idea."

"You are not going."

Pria felt her ire rise but suppressed it. Narita was what was important now, and she wouldn't walk away while the other woman was in danger. "I have no intention of complacently returning to Austeria. Orotid by himself has no way of holding me. Now, if you think rationally, having me with you is a much better asset than having to worry where I have gotten to." She pulled parchment from a saddlebag, digging for a piece of graphite jammed down near the bottom. "I can send word to Janu without wasting the time of traveling back there."

"Then you can go back after you do so," he said.

"I can also create a map that will allow us to track Narita's movements using her armor that you gave me."

Mian stared at her for a moment. "You can do that?"

She finished scribbling on the parchment. "I can do many things you don't know about, Commander." She glared a challenge at him. "So when do we leave?"

Mian stared at her set jaw, her steady gaze. She made sure to project in her stubborn gaze that many hours of futile fighting would still end in his loss. "I'm not going to win this one, am I?"

"I am willing to compromise," she conceded. "I will be a good high priestess and stay close by my Battle Leader's side."

Orotid cleared his throat in quiet insistence. "Uh, sir, we do need to get moving if we have any hope of finding trace of Lady Narita and her patrol."

Mian growled. "Fine. You're in such a hurry to kill yourself, who am I to stop you?"

"Always so dramatic."

He circled his finger at her. "You just get to the map making, missy. If you're going to stay I want to see some of these things you say I don't know about." Mian eyed her for a moment, his face unsure. He waved a hand. "Do you…"

She nodded. "You have the experience, Commander. I will follow your lead."

Gathering his reins, he grumbled under his breath, "Yeah, you'll follow my lead as long as it suits you." He motioned his men closer. "Let's get to that rendezvous, men, we have soldiers to find!"

Pria's gelding stretched out beside his mount as he kicked his horse into a swift trot. True to her word, she kept to his side. She pulled a folded steel dagger from her belt and sliced off an inch of strap from the armor. She dug into her saddlebag, fishing a velvet satchel from its depths, and dropped the strip into it.

Mian watched her as she handed him the satchel then returned to her saddlebag and dug out a tin. "What are you doing?"

"Finding Narita. Hold that open." She pried the tin open, sprinkling some of its contents into the bag in his hands. She smoothed out a piece of parchment and scribbled in the center before shoving it into the bag and cinching the strings. She cupped the bag in her hands and pulled it to her lips. "*Arino foronte.*"

A glow radiated from her palms, flashing blue then red before fading. She handed the bag back to Mian and he opened it, face painted with anxiety. "This will lead us to Narita?"

"Are you questioning my abilities, Commander? I can have the Lorien ship my credentials if it will make you feel better."

He unfolded the parchment, his forehead wrinkled in confusion. "It's blank." He turned it in his fingers.

"Is it?"

He jumped as the scribble in the center began to writhe and stretch. His smile was brilliant, drawing hers to the surface as well. "That was amazing."

"That"—she waved her hand—"was nothing."

He bowed his head with a coy grin. "I misspoke—*you* are amazing."

Her smile deepened as he held her gaze. A warm bloom of pride filled her at the compliment. It was foolish and childlike and undeniable, all things she could ill afford. "Why don't you tell us where we're going?"

He coughed a laugh and shook his head. "Always so practical."

"She is my friend, Mian."

"I know." He scanned the map. "How do I read this?"

She kneed her horse closer and rested her hand on his arm to steady herself as she leaned toward him. Heat flared beneath her fingertips through the soft fabric, but she pushed it away. It was just Mian.

She pointed to an arrow nestled among some stenciled trees. "That is her." Her finger traced to a pulsing dot. "That is us. How far is it?"

He rubbed his face. "Not far." He kicked his horse into a swift canter, shadowed by the men around him. He glanced at Pria as she caught up to his side, her eyes tight with worry. She jumped as he patted her thigh. "She'll be okay, you know. She's a tough woman."

She nodded. "I know." She gripped his hand and this time welcomed the warmth and comfort it brought. "Thank you…for letting me stay."

His grin stretched with mischievous glee. "Like I had a choice." He squeezed her fingers. "I'm sorry we tricked you. We should have told you the truth—you're not a kid anymore."

She looked away from him, scanning the trees as they rushed past. "I wouldn't have listened. You are right though, we cannot afford to be without a high priestess, not with the horde pressing so hard." She looked at him. "As Battle Leader, I'm afraid it falls to you to convince me when I am being stupid."

"Well, that sounds fun," he said. "Is it too late to refuse the position?"

She looked at the soldiers galloping around them as she struggled against pride and obligation. Her jaw was stiff, making her response tight. "When we find Narita, I will return with you, no arguments."

"Really?" he asked, incredulous.

She nodded, just a slight jerk of her neck.

"Well. That'll be a first." She threw his hand back at him, and he stifled an amused chuckle. "Okay, no more joking. Thank you."

"You're welcome."

His horse stretched out, tossing its head in excitement as he referenced the map. "Narita is just over this next rise. Be ready for anything!"

Pria kept her eyes scanning the horizon. She drew a deep breath and strained but the pounding of horse hooves made anything beyond a few feet indiscernible. The forest spread out beneath them as they crested a rise. She wasn't sure what could be going on but the reaction of the men around her did not bode well for her friend.

Her breath caught as Narita's party came into sight. Large, hairy creatures swarmed the edge of the forest, snarling as they struggled to break through a line of soldiers. Narita's soldiers. Most of the creatures were naked but a few wore mismatched armor and tattered cloaks. These were the monsters that threatened her home, killed her parents, took Lana. Heat flared through her as her anger rose. She would not let them take Narita.

Pria raised her hand, fingers clawed toward the group of grinlo and loosed a wave of raw energy barreling toward them. A loud snap shattered across the horizon, flinging some of the creatures high through the air. None moved from where they landed.

Mian's men charged down the hill, swords drawn, wordless yelling urging them on. Pria drew her shortswords and guided her horse with her knees as they closed on the grinlo. The charge scattered their line as the steeds crashed into them, hooves and bodies knocking many to the ground. She shifted as her horse reared, peppering the grinlo before it with quick sharp jabs. Pria slashed one's throat, then spun to block its arm as it snatched at her leg.

The soldiers from the trees rushed out to join them, forcing the group of grinlo back. The creatures turned to flee, leaving the soldiers panting.

In a blink, Mian was at her side, his sword sticky with blood. "Are you all right?"

She nodded, already searching the men around her as Orotid slid to a halt beside them.

"They're retreating. Looks like we reached them just in time."

"I'll say." A tall, curvy woman dropped from the trees behind them, followed by several other archers. Her long hair had fallen from its tight knot at the back of her head and now framed her beautiful face. She drew an arrow from the quiver at her side, nocking it to her bow. Her eyes never stopped scanning as she walked toward them. "I'm impressed you found us so quickly. We weren't scheduled to meet until today."

Mian laughed. "Well, you can thank our high priestess for your timely rescue; it was her magic that found you."

Narita's expression brightened as her eyes finally focused on the woman at Mian's side. "Pria!" She dropped her bow and launched herself forward, dragging Pria from her saddle into an embrace.

Pria laughed. "It is good to see you too, Narita." She pulled back and searched her face. "Are you all right?"

Narita beamed. "No little pack of grinlo is going to do me in!" The men around her roared their support. "You're not staying with our replacements, are you?"

Pria glanced at Mian quick enough that she hoped Narita missed it. "No, I will be returning with you and your men."

Narita jerked her back into her arms, moaning in glee. "Good! Then I'll have you all to myself on the trip back!"

Mian cleared his throat. "Well, not entirely to yourself."

She eyed him questioningly as Pria rolled her eyes. "My brother is afraid I might have a moment's peace and has set his Battle Leader to be my guard dog."

Narita's musical laughter broke across the ravaged hillside. "You poor thing!" She turned to Mian. "How are your provisions? My men could stand a hot meal."

"I think we can handle that, but let's get to a more defensible position first. Or at least a more pleasant one," Mian said. "This one smells."

One of the men ran up to them, leading two horses. His salute was crisp. "Commander."

Narita took the reins of a leggy black mare and scratched the horse's nose. "Well, let's get moving then. If the gnawing in my stomach is any indication, we're going to need that food soon."

Pria vaulted back onto her horse, falling in beside Narita as she started off up the hill. Mian kept his horse back, being sure to give them some privacy. Narita glanced back at him in amusement. "Takes his job seriously, doesn't he?"

Pria rolled her eyes but couldn't help a glance back at the man shadowing them. She waved off Narita's comment. "What happened?"

Narita gave a heavy sigh. "We were a day out from the rendezvous when we ran into the scavenging party. They were too close to home for comfort so we gave chase. They drew us here, where they met up with a second party, turning on us and forcing us into the forest. We've been holding here for the last few days."

Pria's mind tweaked. "Do you agree with Janu and Mian that the grinlo are setting traps?"

"I do—I've seen it too often," Narita said.

Pria pulled some dried meat from her saddlebag and handed it to Narita. "And it couldn't just be coincidence?"

"No, it's just not possible. Those grinlo knew where they were leading us and what was waiting for us when we got there."

Pria nodded. "I'd say I returned just in time."

Narita held out her hand and Pria took it gratefully. "I'd agree."

Being near Narita had always been a comfort to her. Even as a girl, so many people had treated her differently because she was destined to become a priestess. Not Narita, though. Narita only ever saw her as a friend. She wasn't some precious commodity to protect, not some dangerous situation that needed to be handled. As a woman commander, Narita was one of very few people who could understand the importance of avoiding the appearance of weakness. "So are you going to tell me all of your adventures or are you going to leave me in suspense?"

Narita shrugged. "Not much to tell—just boring maneuvers and dull castle life. You're the one who's been having the adventures! Studying at the Lorien, learning magic! I do hope that coddling didn't make you forget all your weapons training—you're going to need it!"

Pria's face brightened with her smile. "No amount of coddling would make me forget that."

Mian watched Pria and Narita joke and laugh as they rode. Every smile from Pria sent a ripple down his spine; every laugh seemed to tingle deep in his chest. He didn't understand it. He could remember her laughing for him, the open trust, that deep connection they had always shared. Did she remember none of that? Why would she embrace Narita like nothing had changed but be so cold and distant to him? Why did he have to be pushed away? All the years waiting for her to return and it was like she didn't even care, like their past meant nothing to her. Could she have forgotten him so easily? He shook his head, returning his focus to his surroundings. "Can't even keep myself focused anymore. That woman is going to be the death of me."

Bright laughter rang across them and pulled his eyes back to Pria, who pressed a hand to her mouth as Narita waved her arms in exaggeration. His lips twitched as the women slowed their horses, waiting for the two men to catch up. Narita's mischievous grin drew a nervous glare to his eyes. "So, Battle Leader, I hear you are returning with us. Afraid you will mess up that pretty hair?" She reached out to amiably ruffle his locks.

"Your prince asked me to return," he growled through clenched teeth.

"Sure he did."

Pria laughed. "Don't credit Commander Mian with too many brains. Janu seems to be quite devious in his old age."

"I'll be sure to torture him thoroughly when we get back," Narita said.

Pria raised her eyebrow. "Excuse me? Do you have nefarious sights on my brother, your prince?"

Narita batted her eyes. "I would never dream to set eyes on your dear brother, my prince."

Their laughter rang out, drawing attention from the men around them. The sound stabbed deep in his chest, punctuating the loss of his friend. Mian gave a heavy sigh. "How am I supposed to keep control of my men when you keep doing that?"

Pria glared at him. "Doing what?"

He waved his hand. "Laughing like that. How is a man supposed to focus on his job with you laughing like that?"

Pria's brow wrinkled as Narita scoffed. "You never got mad at me when I laughed."

"The men are used to you." Mian waved his arm in dismissal.

"So because I'm new I'm not allowed to laugh?" Pria asked.

"It distracts the soldiers. Do you want to laugh or do you want to be safe?"

Pria sat up, drawing the cloak of the priestess around her. "Commander, forgive me if I have disrupted your patrol. It will not happen again." She kicked her horse into a swift canter and left the small group behind.

Narita focused on Mian. "What was that all about?"

His ire flashed deep in his gut. "Did we not just save you and your patrol from the horde? Surely we should be focusing on ensuring they don't surprise us again."

"Your men are watching the trees so hard I'm surprised their horses haven't tripped."

"Until she draws their attention! What if they are looking at her when the grinlo attack?" Mian demanded.

Narita leaned back from him. "Have you lost your sense? Neither your men nor mine are likely to be distracted for too long—they know what is at stake here."

"That's no reason to drop our guard."

"Who's dropping their guard?" She glanced around at the men encircling them.

He threw his hands up at her. "All I know is that since she's been with us, my men's discipline is slipping."

"Then maybe you should see to them, Commander, and stop being a jerk." Narita cantered up to Pria's side, her back stiff and angry.

Orotid kept his eyes on the treeline. Mian raked his fingers through his hair. "You think I'm wrong too?"

"I didn't say that, sir."

"But you're thinking it," Mian said. "You never hold your tongue around me, why start now?"

Orotid sat up and pulled his eyes from the treeline. "All right. There was no call for you to take out your jealousy on that girl. You know she didn't do anything to deserve that."

Mian rubbed his temples as the guilt dug in. "I know."

Orotid wasn't about to let him off easy now that he had been asked. "She's been gone a long time. How do you think she feels, being dropped back in on her own home as a stranger? Seems to me that she'd need a friend right now."

Mian sighed as his eyes drifted to the women now riding ahead of them in silence. "I just have trouble remembering that she isn't the little girl I knew." He tossed his head with an angry growl. "I am never going to hear the end of this." He kicked his horse forward then let it slow to pace Pria's. Neither woman acknowledged him as he gathered his courage. Why was it so hard to talk to her now? He could never remember a time where he worried about what he said to her. He cleared his throat. "I'm sorry, Pria. I shouldn't have blamed you. If my men are lacking discipline, it is their fault, not yours."

"You were quite right, Commander. I forgot myself." Pria kept her eyes to the land before her, ice dripping from her words. She was every inch the high priestess and none of his Pria.

Leaning forward, he snatched her reins and pulled her horse around to face him. Her eyes were blue fire as she stared up at him, but there was something more that he couldn't pinpoint. Perhaps fear—but that was ludicrous; Pria had never been afraid of anything and surely she had no reason to fear *him* of all things. He softened his expression. "No. You have every right to be mad at me. It is not your fault that my men…that *I* keep getting distracted." He felt the traitorous blush rise up his cheeks.

Pria searched his face. The world shrank down to that icy blue scrutiny. Never had he felt such a need to measure up in his entire life. "Why are you distracted?"

He dropped Pria's reins and pulled his horse away from hers. "The point is, I shouldn't have snapped at you."

Pria gathered her reins though her posture remained stiff. "Thank you, Mian."

Mian shrugged away the unwelcome feeling of inadequacy. He had never before worried what a priestess thought of him, and Pria was Pria. A lifetime of connection lay between them—why would he worry now what she thought of him? He shook himself. "Can't have you mad at me. Everyone else is too scared to fight with you."

Narita coughed. "Yes, why would they fear someone whose power is only preempted by the prince himself?"

Mian glared at her. "I'm just saying *someone* has to help these two. Without me, who knows how big their heads would get."

"You are selfless, Battle Leader. How is a commander to compete?" Narita quipped.

Mian's lips curved in a devilish grin. "You don't seem to have too many issues in that area, if I remember correctly."

Narita's face dropped all emotion. "Some of us just have a way with people." She eyed him with a challenge. "I don't think that is a direction you really want this conversation to go, now is it."

He returned her glare. "You never play fair, Narita."

"How is turnaround not fair?" Narita asked.

Pria's brow wrinkled. "Now what are you two talking about?"

Mian glared Narita down. "Nothing for you to worry about."

Narita's predatory smile became savage. "Don't you worry, we'll talk about it later, when there are fewer people to interrupt."

Mian rubbed his forehead. "Why can't you be like a normal woman?"

Narita batted her eyes. "Normal how?"

"Why Janu would even bother trying to fight to keep you around is beyond me. I told him to let you go."

Pria's eyes flashed wide. "Go? Go where?"

Narita waved a hand. "When Janu took over my family's home they evacuated many of our citizens to our summer retreat. I've been wanting to go visit them for a while now but haven't had a chance to get away."

"Janu's been arguing with her at night trying to keep her from going."

"He doesn't want to lose one of his commanders, especially not now," Narita said.

Pria shared a skeptical glance with Mian, who smiled and said, "Yes, he's always so worried when I leave his side. Your brother has a lot of abandonment issues. I blame you."

Pria rolled her eyes. "So how far are we planning to go before stopping? Are you going to let these men starve to death, Commander?"

He jerked as he pulled his horse around. Orotid stopped next to him. "Yes, Commander?"

"Set up camp and get these men fed. We'll be needing to get them back to Janu soon and you'll be needing to head out."

"Of course, sir," Orotid said.

Orotid held out his hand and helped Pria down to a moss-covered log before returning to the harness that he had been mending. Mian dropped down beside her, glaring as Narita jumped the log and took a seat on Pria's opposite side. She met his gaze defiantly. "

Narita nudged her with her shoulder as Raber approached carrying trays of food. She smiled up at Raber as he handed her a bowl. "Thank you, Raber."

He beamed down at Pria as he held a bowl out to her. "High Priestess."

She nodded acknowledgment. "Thank you, Raber."

His smile stretched wide, brightening his eyes as he faced Mian, whose flat glare did little to dampen the man's foolish grin. He snatched his bowl from the tray and waved him away. The man's eyes returned to Pria, watching her over his shoulder as he walked away.

Narita covered her mouth as she watched Mian's face. "Oh, so *that* was the distraction brought about by Pria's laughter."

"Foolish boy. You'd think he'd never seen a woman before."

"He's just awed by Pria, and who could blame him?" Narita glared a challenge at him. "You aren't jealous, are you?"

"Don't be ridiculous. I just don't want the horde to barrel down on us while he's busy being all googly-eyed at the high priestess."

Pria cleared her throat. "I do not think wanting discipline in his men is something that should be chastised."

Mian glanced over at her but she kept her face buried in her food. Warmth spread through his chest. He tapped her leg with his knee as he sopped up some broth with a heel of bread. Her lips curled but she didn't look up. One brief glimpse of the Pria still inside. He felt a bloom of hope sprout within.

Orotid shook his head. "Looks like the return trip will be even more entertaining than ours. Sorry I will miss it."

Pria smiled over at him. "Don't worry, I'm not going anywhere."

"Well, that is good to know. I find myself liking you, High Priestess Pria."

Pria's smile stretched wide. "I find myself liking you too, Orotid."

"Orotid, is there anything you need before we head back? Are you sure you're going to be ready for this?"

"I think I should be all right," Orotid said. "Not my first day in the field, Commander."

"I just want you to be careful; I've gotten a bit used to you. Plus, I think Jeran enjoys getting a break every now and then."

Orotid waved him off. "You can tell your second that I have no designs on his post. I would never have enough energy to keep your fickle youth satisfied. I leave that job to the young." He stood. "Now, if you'll excuse me, I believe I have a patrol to lead." He bowed over his hands and smiled down at Pria. "It was a pleasure to enjoy your company, High Priestess. I do hope Mian doesn't chase you off before I get another chance to visit."

She took his hand, her face warm and open. "I'm quite used to Mian's boorish ways, have no fear there."

Mian glared at Orotid as the older man moved off. "I'm not boorish."

Pria smiled as she set her bowl aside. "If secondhand is all I'm going to get, I'd like it as fresh as possible."

Narita watched her leave before shifting her eyes back to Mian. "So?"

He glanced up at her testily. "What?"

"What? You act like we're mere acquaintances? I think we've stitched each other up enough times for you to confide in me."

"And what precisely am I supposed to confide?" he asked.

She leaned back, shaking her head. "Pria was just a girl when she left, completely under the spell of her big brother and his friend."

"She was never under my spell."

"Please, she worshiped you and Janu. You were her world, all she knew. But that's not who came back, is it?"

He rubbed his forehead. "She used to listen to me."

"She used to be a child, Mian. You didn't really expect her to follow you blindly her entire life, did you?"

"Narita, I really don't want to talk about this with you," Mian ground out.

"Yeah? Then who would you talk to?" She ruffled his hair. "Maybe you should focus more on the woman she *is* rather than the girl she *was*."

He shook his head. "I really don't think that's going to help."

"I think I'm going to enjoy watching her smack you around," Narita said, her voice quivering with mirth.

He brushed the dirt from his breeches as he stood. "Yes, well, before that starts, I would like to get you both somewhere that you can take a swing at Janu as well. Would you mind preparing your men?"

Narita stood, pulling Mian into an embrace and smiling as he awkwardly patted her back before pushing her away. "You are a thick-headed fool, aren't you?"

"I have heard that before." Glancing around, he caught sight of Pria surrounded by a group of four soldiers gesturing as they vied for her attention. Her eyes drank in their every movement as her face remained a perfect stoic mask. "Why does she do that?"

Narita sighed. "She must walk two worlds, Mian. A woman in power always does. She must always be seen as the priestess if she is to reign as one."

"She doesn't have to do it with me."

"We have the hardest job of all, you, Janu, and me. We must see her both as the priestess and as Pria. She will need our support. It will be hard enough for her to fill Lana's shoes without having to fight us to be seen as a priestess." Walking away, she added, "I'm sure you are up to it."

With a slow inhale, he raised his hands to his hips. "I hope you're right."

Pria nodded to him as the soldiers snapped to attention at his approach. "Commander."

"I do hope these men are answering your questions to your satisfaction, High Priestess."

"That they were, Battle Leader," Pria replied in the cool tones of a priestess.

"We will be leaving shortly, Priestess. If you would come with me." Mian held out his arm for her, the perfect image of Battle Leader.

"Of course, Commander."

She laid her fingers in his offered hand. "Thank you."

"Just supporting my priestess." He kept his face resigned to match her somber appearance but the joy he felt at her normal tone of voice screamed inside him. Fool man, he really was expecting her to chase after him like they were children.

"Those soldiers seem to agree with you, even if they haven't put it all together yet."

"Do you have any thoughts as to who could be doing it?" he asked. "I mean, did the Lorien teach a class on all the potentates of the day or something?"

She glanced up at him incredulous. "Potentates?"

He grimaced. "Yeah, thought I'd try it out. I didn't like it either."

"No, the Lorien didn't teach us any classes on *potentates*." She fought to shove down a giggle.

He shook his head. "So, what do we do now?"

"Now? Now, I research and you two miserable conniving snakes go on conspiring against me, I presume."

"You got to see grinlo!" Mian splayed his fingers at the trees around them.

"I had to blackmail you to do it."

"Just get on the horse, woman!" He shoved her toward Narita, who waited patiently with her and Pria's mounts. Pria took one stumbling step, never dropping her composure before glaring down at him from the back of the animal.

"Coming, Commander?"

Mian grumbled under his breath as he walked away.

Narita kept her face stoic as she hoisted herself onto the horse. "What was that all about?"

"He was breaking through my guard."

Narita waited a moment, hoping she would elaborate. When it became clear that she had no intention to, Narita prodded further. "Meaning…"

"He was pulling off my mask, Narita, and I cannot afford that. Not right now."

Narita glared at her through slitted eyes. "So, you're punishing him because he made you comfortable?"

"It's much more than that," Pria said.

"Well, why don't you explain it to me."

Pria's eyes softened. "He acts as if I never left, like nothing has changed. He wants me to fall right back to where I was before I went to the Lorien."

"I know that's annoying but it's hardly reason to continue snapping at him."

"He makes me want to do it," Pria whispered. Her voice trembled with the confession. "Every time I'm around him, all my training just evaporates. I can't think of what I should do because all I can remember is staying up late with him and Janu, sneaking out to the kitchens for sweets, getting lost in the forests, and being confined to our rooms for weeks at a time. I can't afford to be that headstrong foolish girl anymore." Pria's eyes dropped. "I can't afford the distraction."

Narita held out her hand and Pria grabbed it, trying to wipe the tears from her cheeks without drawing attention. "You and Janu had to grow up quickly. You were so young when you left and I doubt the Lorien offered much in the way of a childhood. Everything you are feeling…it's natural." She gave a squeeze. "The position you've achieved requires a lot of you, but you are lucky enough to be surrounded by people who love you, Janu, Mian, and I. You have to keep this rigid face to the public, but not to us. You don't have to let your heart turn to stone, Pria. How will you be able to protect people if you cannot care?"

"I don't know how else to be a priestess. The Lorien drilled us that we should give up all attachments." She turned her head, blue eyes piercing Narita. "But I can't give up my family."

Narita smiled crookedly. "Like you have a choice—we wouldn't let you!"

Pria's eyes closed and sunlight sparkled in the tears that hung in her eyelashes. "You don't understand. You can't understand." She opened her eyes. "The Lorien doesn't trust that I can hold this post. I almost wasn't allowed to be posted here."

Narita felt her brain catch. For a moment her mouth worked, trying in vain to produce words while her mind struggled to catch up. "But…" She shook her head. "So, what does that mean?"

Pria smoothed the emotion from her face. "It means that I could lose this post. It means that I might end up watching my family and friends fight for their lives and my home from the Silver City. It means that I must conduct myself with the upmost care, as the Lorien and the priestesses are scrutinizing my every move. Above all, it means that I am under some type of probation."

Narita felt her heart sink at the thought of losing her friend again, of Janu losing his sister. She lowered her head as she let Pria's words slice into her very soul. For some time all she could imagine was losing her friend again, of having a stranger as Trimera's priestess. Then her eyes fell on Pria, on the hopeless wound that marred her. Being reassigned was more than just a failure to her. It meant the loss of her home. "Pria, you're the smartest person I know, always have been. There is no reason you can't balance being Pria and high priestess. You can figure it out. I have faith in you."

Pria scoffed. "I don't have much of a choice."

Narita shook the image from her mind, not wanting Pria to see the worry on her face. "And we'll be there for you, when you need some release from the stress of being high priestess. You can be yourself around us."

Pria's eyes grew wide. "You cannot tell anyone about this! How can anyone be expected to trust my advice if they knew I didn't come with the full support of the Lorien?"

Narita sighed. "Pria, we don't care about the endorsement of the Lorien! Without it you are still the same Pria that we have always known and trusted. You can still let yourself go around us."

Pria's chest hitched with a heavy sigh. "Maybe." Then her eyes focused on the men around her. "Just not around Mian."

Narita's smile faltered. "Has such an effect on you, does he?"

Pria's face tensed. "Drop it, Narita."

"I'm just trying to figure out why you are acting so ridiculous. Mian is a good man; you don't have to hide from him."

Pria's back straightened. "I don't hide from him."

"Then what do you call this?" She waved her hand.

"This is protecting my image as high priestess so that I can properly serve my prince."

Narita sighed. "I forgot how stubborn you could be."

"I am not stubborn, I am practical," Pria intoned.

"Practical about what?" Mian jumped as they both spun, eyes narrowed. "Sorry I interrupted."

Pria pivoted haughtily. "I am practical about everything."

Mian focused before him as he arranged his saddlebag. "Would you like to have the men rotate so that you can interview them as we ride, Priestess?"

"That will not be necessary," she said. "I will have Narita take me around when we settle."

"The high priestess will be a bit intimidating to a common soldier," he prodded further. "Would you like me to accompany you?"

"They do seem to respond well to you."

His jaw tightened. "It will be my pleasure."

Narita glanced at her, eyes hard. "Mian has a great rapport with my men. When Janu first made me a commander, the men under me were razed for being led by a woman. It was Mian's idea to send out the companies together. After a couple of regiments saw my men in action, the talking stopped."

Pria's face didn't change but her eyes shifted toward Mian, who was being careful to stay inconspicuous. "His intentions were honorable, but your actions would have spoken for themselves eventually."

Narita rolled her eyes, dropping her horse back to Mian's side. "I for one greatly appreciated the gesture." Leaning in, she kissed Mian on the cheek then sniffed as Pria ignored them.

Mian patted her hand, keeping his voice low. "You don't need to do that, Narita. I think I can survive her barbs."

"You shouldn't have to! She is being ridiculous."

He pulled her hand toward him and kissed her fingers. "I think we've both had our ridiculous moments since she's returned but thank you." His lips spread into a brilliant smile. “I will be proud to serve you when Janu finally gets the sense to marry you.”

Her face flushed a pretty red as she rolled her eyes. “Quiet with that—you know Janu wants to tell her himself.”

Mian waved her off. “Like she can’t tell. You’re her best friend and he’s her brother. She knows something is up.”

She slapped his hand as Pria faced them. “What are you two whispering about back there?”

Narita smiled. “Nothing to interest you.”

Pria dropped beside Mian. “What would interest me would be to know why you two look like you are conspiring. Seems to me that my ‘family’ has done little but work to keep me ignorant since I returned home.”

Narita sighed. “No one is trying to keep you ignorant, Pria, and we are not conspiring.” She turned to watch the men around her. “I’ll go see if I can find someone for you to question.”

Mian and Pria watched Narita ride away. He cleared his throat. “We really aren’t looking to keep you ignorant, Pri.”

“Don’t call me Pri.”

A sharp twinge stabbed into his chest at her flat tone. “So I’m only allowed to call you High Priestess now?”

“It is my title, Commander,” she snipped.

“Fine. High Priestess. We really just want you safe. Intentionally putting you in harm’s way is on no one’s agenda.”

She stared into his eyes, her face hard. “Being what I am gives me the obligation to put myself in harm’s way. Why can’t you see that?”

"Only if it is deemed necessary."

"And what would deem it necessary?" she asked.

He sighed. "Pria, I can't promise that I won't lie to you again. I won't promise that I won't try to keep you safe. I will not and you cannot ask it of me." He sat back casually. "All I can do, or at least, all I am willing to do, is promise to keep in mind that you are a grown woman in a position of power."

She glanced at him. "I guess I can accept that. And I guess I can try to keep in mind that you are a strong, sometimes intelligent man." She tilted her head up. "Sometimes."

He coughed a laugh as he shook his head. "I'm glad you think so highly of me."

She tried to keep her face, especially her wide smile, hidden from the men around her. "You need to stop that; these men need to see me as my station."

"Maybe these men need to see that you are a woman with people who love her. Maybe these men need to see that you are someone to love and protect and follow. How can they believe in you, trust you, if all they know of you is this emotionless statue that you try to project?"

Pria's hidden smile evaporated as Narita rode up followed by an older soldier with battered armor. The soldier bowed as well as he could seated atop a moving horse. "High Priestess, this is Captain Liando."

"Captain, I would like to get your opinions on the horde and perhaps some of your experiences."

Liando bowed his head, cupping his helmet to his chest. "Of course, Highness. I have been a captain in Commander Narita's regiment since it was instated, and before that I served under the lady's father. If it pleases my lady, I must say that when I was a young man the horde was not quite as crafty as they are proving to be lately. I do not claim to be a scholar, High Priestess, but if you ask my opinion there is something strange about these grinlo."

Pria studied him, her bright blue eyes searching. "Can you give me anything specific? Instances that made you think this?"

Liando glanced at Mian and Narita before he wrung his reins. "Well, Priestess, I remember when I was a boy going out to fight the grinlo and they were dangerous, but nothing very exciting. If you kept your head about you and were not outnumbered, you didn't have too much trouble. Even today, when we found the scouting party they didn't pose any threat to us. It was only when they led us to the larger group that we had issues. How would they know to lead us into a trap like that? They never had the smarts to do that before."

Pria nodded. "Have you noticed anyone strange lately? Perhaps someone in Austeria asking questions? Someone you've not seen before?"

His brow wrinkled. "No, Priestess, I can't say that I have. You don't think a person can have power over the grinlo, do you? Like train them?"

Pria laughed. "Of course not, Captain; the horde cannot be domesticated. Thank you for answering my questions, that will be all for now."

Still confused and overwhelmed, the man wandered off back toward the surrounding men. Mian glanced at her. "Do you really think whoever is doing this would travel into our cities?"

"I'm positive they would. They might even be posing as a soldier to get information. We cannot exclude any possibility. Not with all of Trimera and the safety of Reia at risk."

Narita shivered. "How would we know?"

"We wouldn't, until it was too late," Pria said.

Mian moved his horse a little closer to hers. "I don't like the uncertainty of this. How do I protect my prince? How do I protect you?"

She kept her eyes on the road before them. "By letting me do my job. Someone with power over the horde means magical talent, something you can't fight. This is my world, Mian; you're going to have to trust my knowledge."

His eyes swept the men around him. How long had he known them really? Could this spy be among them even now? "Let's just get back to Janu. I don't like him being so far away when I feel so confused. How am I supposed to deal with this?"

Pria rolled her eyes at him. "I told you, you don't. It is mine to worry about, and I will deal with it. If I need any help, the Lorien is always just a message away."

His chest heaved with deep breaths as he held his silence, hands working on his reins. Narita patted his thigh, shaking her head at the tension there. "You don't have to save the world, Mian."

"Protecting the realm is my job, Narita. How would you feel to be told you can't do it?"

Pria stared at him in open shock. "I never said you couldn't protect these people. You are quite vital to keeping our cities and people safe. I cannot possibly handle whoever is controlling the horde if I am worrying about the grinlo themselves. You and your men are vital to keeping them at bay; it will do no good to thwart this person if there is no one left alive. Honestly, what would we do without you?"

Narita kept her eyes on the treeline as Mian risked a glance at the woman riding at his side. "Do you really mean that?"

Pria glared at him. "I do not say things I do not mean, Mian."

"So, you do need me?" He hated the hint of tremble in his voice but couldn't suppress it.

"We all need you," she said. "Janu is counting on you. Mian, you are Battle Leader—we can hardly keep Trimera safe without you."

Mian shifted his shoulders. "I am glad you came back, Pria. I hope I can prove to you that Janu didn't make a mistake appointing me to Battle Leader."

She stared at him in confusion. "I know Janu didn't make a mistake. You are a good leader. I don't want you worried about impressing me. Just do your job."

He dropped his head and let his hair obscure his face as a blush heated his cheeks. "I'm glad you think so."

ENEMIES AND FRIENDS

Janu paced his waiting room. The sleeping chamber with its massive four-poster bed lay open beyond the spacious sitting room where Jeran sat with a pile of paperwork. Every now and then, Janu would rush out onto his balcony before sweeping back into the room. From his vantage, Jeran could see the town of Austeria sweeping down toward the gates.

Janu swept by in a breeze that ruffled the papers around him. Jeran watched him from the corner of his eyes as he perused sheaves of orders and requisitions.

"Keep that up," Jeran quipped. "I'm sure it's harrying them plenty."

Janu snapped back to face the other man, eyes ablaze. "That is an awfully light tone, Lieutenant, for addressing your prince."

Jeran grinned in amusement. His dark hair was trimmed short and neat, visage shaved clean. Every line of his uniform was crisp; he prided himself on neatness. "Forgive me, Your Highness; I know not what I say."

"You don't think she bullied him into taking her to the front, do you?"

"I cannot speak to that, Janu, I know very little of your sister," Jeran said, voice flat.

Janu spun back from his balcony, hands wringing. "She always was impossible to handle. Strong willed, stubborn. If he has taken her to the front I will have him flogged, you mark my words!"

Jeran glanced at him before his gaze returned to his work. "So marked, Majesty."

"Narita wouldn't take her side, do you think? Not in this?"

Jeran laughed. "I have enough trouble anticipating Tara's actions; I am not up to the task of helping you with every woman in the realm."

The prince charged back to the balcony, his fist banging in frustration on the doorframe. "She wouldn't do that, not when she knows how I feel." He glanced back over his shoulder. "She wouldn't, right?"

Jeran set his pile of parchment down, eyes focused on his anxious monarch. "Narita is the high priestess' friend, yes? Narita is a strong woman herself, bursting with love and a protective streak that reminds me of my mother. I seriously doubt she will allow anyone to do anything that would put them in harm's way without a pretty good reason."

Janu pressed his eyes closed as his body shook. "Did you have to add that last part?"

"Yes. Sometimes things happen that change the plan that is set out. It is no one's fault and it cannot be avoided, not even by the prince, no matter how huffy he gets."

"I'm not huffy."

"Whatever you say," Jeran said.

"Don't you have work to do?"

Jeran nodded and looked at the paperwork in his lap. "That I do, Your Majesty, and if you are quite finished asking me to divine the intentions of a woman that I have never met and know very little about, I would like to get back to it before my commander returns and demands to know why it lies unfinished."

Janu crossed his arms in a huff before rushing back out onto his balcony. From his room he could see all the way to the estate walls, but their solid expanse hid the roads beyond. Did he make a mistake letting her go? He had had little choice—she would have argued her way into it eventually—but maybe waiting would have been better. Let her get a better feel of what was going on.

His body stiffened as he heard a warning horn. Someone was approaching the East Gate. He darted from the balcony and out of the room, rushing past Jeran who had already knowingly set aside his work and stood to follow him. Jeran was a good man, never afraid to tell his superiors when he thought they were wrong. A good man to have at your side.

Guards fell in with him as he swept through the halls, his heart thundering in worry. She had to be all right and the approaching men had to be Narita's. That was the only reality he would accept. She was all right and the men were Narita's.

He rushed out into the courtyard, not even glancing at the groom that handed him his reins. One fluid motion from the ground to the saddle and his horse was carrying him toward the East Gate. He would get there and greet Narita and Pria. That is what would happen.

Onlookers crowded the streets and lined their path as they passed, but none barred his way. He doubted he would have noticed them if they had, his mind was a constant torment of agony. Three more streets and he caught sight of the East Gate, standing open to allow uniformed soldiers to pass through. His heart pounded as he recognized Commander Zaran on return from recruitment in the Glades.

Stocky and severe, Zaran saluted from the ground. "Your Majesty, I have our latest numbers for you."

As he took the offered parchment from Zaran, Janu struggled to steady his hand and wipe the disappointment from his face. "Thank you, Commander."

Jeran rode up to his side as the man moved off to settle his soldiers. "This does not mean anything happened."

"I know that." Jeran didn't flinch at his sharp tone, just eyed him sideways and waited. With noticeable effort, Janu softened his anger. "I know that. I have no need to worry until I hear something."

"That is good advice to take, my prince."

Zaran's men filed past, leaving the gate open behind them. Janu moved his horse forward to glance up at the guards. "Do you intend to invite the horde inside for tea?"

The man bowed then pointed into the trees. "More men come, Your Highness."

Janu rushed from the gates standing in his stirrups, eyes to the treeline. Snaking their way toward him was another group of soldiers, weary and battered from battle, and flying over their heads the rearing stallion of Austeria. He spurred his horse into a gallop, ignoring Jeran's warning shout. He could hear his own guards behind him as they rushed to catch up. The outer ring of soldiers parted to let him pass. He could see Mian looming over the two women, who rode at his side in the center of the ring of soldiers. Only then did he allow his horse to slow and his guard to catch up. Jeran glared at him. "Happy now?"

"I'd be happy to punish you for insolence," he growled.

Jeran shrugged. "Then do it."

Pria's eyes narrowed at him as they approached but she quickly smoothed her features. "Prince Janu, afraid we would get lost on the way through town?"

"Just glad to see you returned."

The icy chill that radiated off of her froze him in his steps. "I'm sure you are."

Mian cleared his throat. "Let's get inside. Narita and her men are in need of some rest and I wouldn't mind getting out of this armor." He rode forward and passed close to Janu's side. "She's angry."

Janu spun his horse and fell in beside him. "Isn't she always?"

"Yes, well, next time you get to be the one to tell her and then she can yell at you for a while," Mian said.

Janu winced. "Sorry about that. Did she give you much trouble?"

"Not nearly as much as I intend to give you."

He glanced over at Pria, who rode at his side, her face an emotionless mask. He could feel the anger radiating off of her. "You cannot blame Mian;" Janu said, "it was my decision to keep you from the front."

"I have made my recompense with your Battle Leader." Her eyes never left the street before them as they rode among the houses and shops of the outer city.

"So, I am the one sitting alone in your sights," he said.

"Like a helpless little dove."

His chin lifted in satisfaction. "It is worth it to me to know that you are safe."

"You have no right to make decisions for me behind my back." The heat of her words battled with her stoic expression.

"You are my sister."

"I am your priestess. You will do well to remember that once in a while," she said.

He stabbed a finger at the ground. "I need you here, not traipsing about studying monsters."

"I am not much use here if I do not understand what is going on around me, now am I? I understand you do not want to see me hurt, but the next time you lie to me I will leave you with a spell that will itch you out of your clothes for a week."

He smiled. "I will keep that in mind."

"You better," she said, "and if you try to use your commanders against me again, you will find yourself short a few."

He nodded as his eyes searched the crowds. "Any more threats you would like to level at me?"

"I have plenty more, but I will save them for the next time you do something foolish."

"Of course, Priestess," Janu said with a satisfied smile. Mian met his gaze helplessly as they rode on in silence through the crowds still gathered to watch them. Pria fell back to ride with Narita, their quiet conversation barely audible to him. He allowed the ride to soothe his nerves. She was back and safe—nothing would change that.

Raber's blue eyes sparkled in the moonlight as he sighted along the arrow nocked to his bow. Nothing moved in his sight, not leaf nor blade of grass. His attention traveled along the horizon, to a small spring that trickled around among the swelling rolls.

A drop of rain splashed across the bridge of his nose. With a curse, he released the tension and hooked the bow around his ankle. He slipped the string loose and tucked it into his inside breast pocket. It would keep the string dry for a time as long as the rain wasn't intense.

Soon the sky released and dampness made his skin clammy. Droplets gathered on his eyelashes as he tromped through the knee-high grass. Water seeped up the calves of his breeches and the fabric stuck to his skin.

His toes were frozen and numb by the time he made it back to his mount. It was a leggy creature, handsome really, and well-conformed. He was known for his eye for horse-flesh and he prided himself on it. It was something that was completely his, not something his father had given, not something the other soldiers had taught him. The other soldiers sought his opinion on horses; no one sought his father's or even Commander Mian's.

He checked the horse over from nose to tail. He didn't expect to find anything, he just enjoyed exercising his knowledge, to feel like his own person. When he was assessing a horse he wasn't his father's son, Mian's underling, or even Janu's soldier. He was just Raber.

He saved what he could from his soldier pay, what his father didn't demand from him. He was very frugal with his money. When he had a decent amount he would find a good marriage; he was a good man, strong, he would make a good husband. He would take his savings, and his wife's dowry, of course, and set up an estate and get himself some good mares and a promising stud. He would make them a life, a good life, and his family would worship him for the life he provided.

And he would be his own man.

The gelding pressed his head into Raber's chest. Stock black without a lick of white, the horse was stunning in his tack. Raber let the horse nuzzle his palm with its mouth before he stepped into the saddle. His mount stretched out into a canter as the rain picked up and blanketed the landscape. Soon the horse's hooves began to arch water and the chill settled into his entire body.

He lamented returning to the patrol so soon. He preferred to be on his own. No one could belittle him out here. At least Mian hadn't joined them. Raber knew the commander didn't like him. He was probably threatened. Mian knew Raber could be a good leader if given the chance. He could do more than just follow orders, why could no one see that?

He bet Pria could see his worth. Those eyes, so knowing. He'd heard of her, of course, Prince Janu's sister. Being the younger sibling of the prince, she must have understood what it was like to live in a shadow. She was so shy; she must be afraid for others to see her affection, her connection to him, but he'd felt it. They were alike, Pria and he. They were alone in a sea of people who would never see them for what they truly were or what they were truly capable of. His father would tell him he wasn't good enough. That he'd never draw the attention of someone so important and couldn't hold her if he did. But he hadn't seen their connection.

The patrol loomed up out of the rolling hills, the watch picking him out the second he broke cover. He hated having to return to the life of a lowly soldier; he was meant for so much more. Someday, he would show everyone.

Someday, he would be his own man.

A small bombardment spell and the door to the storage room crashed to the floor. Dust erupted in its wake. Pria waited as the cloud settled, revealing what was beyond. The room did nothing to deserve the name. She could fit into the room and possibly bring one other person comfortably, but by any definition, this was a closet.

"*Herishna*," she hissed as she palmed a crystal.

A flash of light flooded the corridor, leaving her vision bleached until her eyes adjusted. Baskets and satchels filled the closet. It had taken a handful of inquiries to determine its location. She could have easily asked Janu, Mian, or even Narita, but they would likely have wanted to join her. She needed solitude for now.

She set the crystal on the floor to the side where it could illuminate the corridor and the objects piled in the closet. She stood to one side so as to not cast a shadow over the contents as she made a cursory examination. Nothing stood out to her so she grabbed the top bag and started piling what she removed along the hallway. When she had finished, the bags and baskets marched along the corridor all the way back to the stairwell behind her. Dust coated her robes and static haloed her hair about her face, but now she could finally begin her true inspection. She began by the stairs with the last bag she had removed. Hand flattened palm down, she knelt beside the satchel and flipped the flap open. Clothing.

"*Reesa*," she said, and a light flared from her palm, shining down onto the clothes. The spell was a resonance spell. The Lorien instructed all priestesses to mark important items using resonance spells to make it easier to find them. Pria's hope was that Lana had thought ahead and marked things she had been working on.

When nothing responded to the spell, she moved to the next container along the line. When she stood from the last bag and still had found nothing, she sat down on the floor and removed each item, one by one. The bag closest to the closet held trinkets mostly, decorative items collected over a lifetime. She spread the items out for future perusal. She worked back toward the stairs this way, cluttering the floor halfway to the opposite wall.

Three-fourths of the way along the hall, she came across a stack of books. She piled them on the floor beside her, one at a time, running her fingers along the covers. A book on history, one on the grinlo, one on the Frontier. The next book was unmarked. Her fingertips trailed along the binding, and gooseflesh marched up her arms. Her pulse pounded in her ears as she opened to reveal handwritten pages.

She knew that writing. It was Lana's personal journal.

She flipped through the pages to the last entry. She read the words aloud. *"Every patrol makes it more clear. Someone had taken control of the grinlo and I seem to be a target. I have managed to convince Janu that he is the target. I hope this will buy me time."*

Her eyes squinted as she tried to decipher a scribble that followed. As she watched, the scribble stretched across the page toward her thumb that was holding the page open. She pulled her thumb away and the ink bunched up at the edge of the page where it had been. She moved her grip to the bottom of the page and the scribble stretched toward her again. She pulled her hand away again.

She weighed her options. There was a slight chance that someone with magical talent could have gotten to this journal before her, or that Lana herself had placed a trap on the book in case it fell into an enemy's hands. Both of which were unlikely—the journal was well hidden not only behind the walls of Austeria but also within her belongings. Lana would expect someone from the Lorien to search through her things if something happened to her, so it was unlikely she would put a trap on the book.

With a steadying breath, she pressed her thumb down over the scribble.

And the world turned black.

Janu's fist pounded on the door to Pria's room. The noise drew the attention of every soul within earshot but no one came to investigate. His hand latched on to the door handle but he couldn't bring himself to invade her privacy, no matter how much he wanted to. His sister had disappeared without a trace and no one seemed to know where she had vanished to. It would be just like her to slip off and get herself in danger. She never knew the meaning of fear. Or caution. Or sense.

"You are creating quite the racket over here."

Janu didn't turn as Mian stepped up beside him. "Where did she go?"

Mian cupped his hands behind his back. "I spoke to the guards at the gates; she has not left the city."

"Then where is she?" He slammed his fist into the door again, rattling the wood against the jamb.

"I offered before and I will offer again, I can set the men to search for her."

"That will go well," Janu said with a roll of his eyes. "Send soldiers to hunt her down."

"There would be no survivors." They shared a chuckle. Mian took him by the elbow and turned him away from the door. "She will show up; she has that annoying habit."

"Excuse me, my prince?" The tiny voice came from behind them, so soft they almost missed it.

Behind them stood a maid, hands tucked at her waist, eyes downcast. Janu recognized her but couldn't bring a name to his lips. He felt a stab of guilt but it was inevitable, he couldn't know everyone in the castle. "Do you need something?"

The maid dropped into a deep curtsy. "Forgive me, my prince, for my rudeness, but I could not help but overhear," she said, her voice quiet but steady. "Am I to understand that the high priestess is who you are looking for?"

"You understand correctly." Janu stepped toward her, trying not to tower over her.

"I may know where you could find her."

She recognized this place. She hadn't seen it since she was a child, but she knew it. This glen was where her father had first taken her riding. She had practiced there often with Janu and Mian. The ground sloped down from her vantage point and formed a hollow surrounded by trees. The valley had always been well-tended by workers from the Seat but now saplings dotted the grasses at the edge, branches littered the ground. The sun beat down as if the peak of summer.

After a moment, she could just make out the approach of soldiers. The noise of armor and horses came from the south—it was a small group, from the sound of it. Movement caught her eye from the edge of the trees, but it wasn't a soldier. Hidden among the shadows crouched a handful of grinlo.

It was an ambush.

She strained to run down the hill toward the approaching soldiers, but her feet remained glued to the spot. Whatever was unfolding before her, she was not meant to interrupt.

The soldiers appeared to the south, oblivious to the danger.

She waved her arms above her head. "Hey! Run!"

She should have been well within earshot but not even the horses perked an ear in her direction. She watched in helpless desperation as the horde swept down toward the soldiers. The soldiers tightened form and backed toward her, toward the high ground. The glen rang with the clash of weapons as the distance closed. A tingle of magic trailed along her arms, like the hint of a memory.

The soldiers gained the crest, and she recognized some of them. As the commander shuffled toward her among the mounted men, she saw that it was Janu. But not the Janu she knew. He was younger than he was now, by at least a few years. Pria's chest clenched as Lana appeared at his side, spell at the ready. She kept herself at the center of the soldiers even as she lobbed spells into the mass of monsters.

Pria stood entranced as the entangled mass barreled toward her. Her heart jumped; she couldn't move, she'd be crushed. She ducked down, tucking herself as small as she could. Hooves pounded around her but none touched her. She risked a glance over her shoulder and realized that she stood in the only spot that was not being churned by hooves. She found herself nestled between Janu and Lana.

Her pulse roared in her ears as she stood, hand reaching out to steady herself on the rump of Janu's horse but finding only air. She lost her balance but the spell rebounded her back to standing. The reverberation left her mind reeling.

Janu and Lana sat on their horses to either side of her. Several dead grinlo lay scattered about the hill, felled with sword, or axe, or arrow. At first, the attack appeared like any other skirmish—a hunting party happening on a patrol. But the more she watched, the more oddities presented themselves. The patrol had started out vastly outnumbered by the hunting party, but had whittled down the numbers and reversed the advantage. It happened often as long as the men were well organized and not overwhelmed. Grinlo, however, would never maintain battle once the advantage was lost unless they had no other choice.

But these grinlo did not retreat once the advantage turned. With every passing moment they became more desperate. No. With every *magical attack* from Lana they became more desperate. Pria wasn't sure at first, but as the moments passed the pattern became clear.

And she could tell Lana saw it too. She waited for the grinlo to tire before launching a spell. Each time the grinlo would rush back at the line with renewed force. They were hunting Lana, and someone was driving them.

This was what Lana hid from them. Not out of malice or mistrust. She was gathering evidence that someone was leading the grinlo, and she couldn't afford to have Janu know and try to protect her. She kept it from them so she could continue to gather intelligence. She knew Janu would not willingly let her risk her life, so she hid this fact for the next priestess to follow her in case she fell.

The glen jerked away from Pria and she found herself staring into worried green eyes.

Mian kept his grip on Pria's forearms as the haze faded from her vision. The hallway around them was a gauntlet of junk strewn about and discarded. At her feet lay a journal, still open to a page with a scribble jotted across it.

She hadn't responded to his calls, instead had started off down the hall past him. She had been where the maid said she would be; an obscure hallway deep in the bowels of the fortress. Nothing was down here but storage. Storage and his high priestess lost in some trance.

"Pria!"

She seemed to grow as she drew a deep breath and glanced around them at the hallway. "Mian," she said, her voice steady if distant. She patted his hand. "I'm fine."

"Fine?" He scoffed, incredulous.

She pulled one arm free, but he kept his hand on her in case she slipped away again.

She bent and picked up the book at her feet. "Yes, fine."

He followed her along the hall, picking his steps, careful to avoid the floor flooded with stuff. "What was that then?"

He helped her clear a patch on the floor near the stairs before joining her. She leaned her head against the wall and closed her eyes. "A spell." She took a handful of breaths then glanced at him through half-closed eyes. "A spell left by Lana."

Mian glanced back at the hallway behind him. "These were her belongings?"

She nodded, closing her eyes again. "I need to finish searching them."

"What are you looking for?" he asked.

"Magical tags."

A heavy sigh rushed from his nostrils as he looked around the hall. "Not much I can help with there." He tapped his fingertips together. He turned back to her and found her slumped against the wall, her face slack in sleep. He stared around the hallway in resignation. He would have to set a guard down here until she had finished her search. She wouldn't forgive him if he allowed something to go missing before she got to inspect it.

He tucked the journal into a pocket in his jerkin before bundling her into his arms and cupping her to his chest. A man could live very well without all this magic, thank you.

Janu studied the map etched into the table before him. Small clay planchets topped with tiny flags dotted the maps toward the opposite side. A design graced each flag, depicting the crest of the commander they represented. Black planchets with numbered flags signified the location of known grinlo hunting parties. As he watched, a page rushed forward from the correspondence table and adjusted a planchet of grinlo and a commander in response to the latest communications from the field.

That line of black planchets mocked him. They marched deep within Trimera, his land, his home. The most galling part was that nothing he did seemed to matter. He sent men to Amber Keep to push back the line of the monster advance, to no use. He struggled to hold the Seat but failed. He couldn't even maintain his advisor. Nothing he did seemed to make a dent in the invading army. None of it changed the inevitable.

He needed an army but none of the surrounding kingdoms were willing to risk sending him men. No one living had seen Trimera fail in its duty to protect Reia, so none of the rulers wanted to risk their own security on the possibility that it might. His shoulders slumped in exhaustion. No one would take his requests seriously until it was too late. Too late for Trimera and too late for Reia.

He raked his hair out of his face and growled as a page moved another planchet farther into Trimera. His entire life he'd studied battle after battle, campaigns, altercations. None of that knowledge, made any impact now.

He turned his back on the map and stepped out from the solarium. He made his way toward Pria's room. Mian stood guard outside her door, looking more like a proper soldier than he usually did. Mian shot him an abused look as Janu pounded on the door.

"You'll have to knock louder than that," Mina growled. "The high priestess is in a magical coma."

Janu hesitated. "What does that mean?"

Mian hitched his shoulders in a shrug. "Ask her."

Janu pushed the door open and glanced around the antechamber. He froze in the doorway, suddenly awkward. Pria's room was one thing—he had barged into her chambers countless times before. But High Priestess Pria…did he even know her? He shook off the feeling of trespassing. She was still his Pria, and his advisor. He had spent long enough fumbling in the dark without one.

He was glad nothing personal decorated the antechamber, that she hadn't been there long enough to put any personal touches on the room. He already felt like he was intruding on a stranger without the evidence of the new woman she had become. Every step into the domain of his new high priestess was an effort. Less than three strides into the room his chest seized in anxiety and he could go no farther.

"Pria," he called, his voice catching in his throat. He struggled to swallow the knot before trying again. "Pria, are you awake?"

His voice bounced around the room, rebounding off the walls and filling the negative space, intruding. Mocking silence answered him. He paused again at the threshold to her bed chamber. Light streamed across the bed, trailing between the curtains and dressing.

And there nestled beneath the bedclothes was the intimate stranger.

She didn't look all that different. Age had filler her out, softened the bony angles of youth. He could see his mother in that sleeping face. Asleep, he couldn't find the stranger that resided within. It wasn't until the high priestess stared out from those all too familiar eyes, he knew, that she wasn't just Pria anymore.

"Pria?" He forced his voice stronger, louder.

Her breath changed but still she did not stir. He pulled the curtain aside and shook her shoulder. Nothing.

"Well, I guess this is what Mian meant by magical coma." He stared down at the unconscious woman then pulled one of the chairs closer and sat. "I don't know what I'm doing here, Pria. Everything I do fails. I'm losing our home." He leaned over his knees and dropped his head into his hands. "I was a fool to fight Lana as long as I did. I see that now. Maybe, had I listened to her better, trusted her more, she would still be here. I need your knowledge, I need your strength, but I can't get over this fear. Lana was a pillar, and we lost her. I don't want to risk you too."

He glanced up from his fingers at his sleeping sister. "It's only now that I think about the consequences of having you back." He stood from the chair. "I'm sure if you were awake, you would call me a fool."

Mian met his gaze as he shut the door behind him. "Dead to the world?"

"I don't know that she is breathing," Janu said with a smile. "But at least we didn't argue."

The air was chilly this deep within the fortress. Cut into the bedrock, the room had no windows to allow in light. Torches and candles dispelled enough of the gloom for any level of inspection she may need and left the damp air thick with smoke. The walls were hand chiseled out of the stone, rough with grooves and tool marks. A chunk of rock jutted up from the floor to form a workspace. Upon the platform lay three bodies, each draped with a cloak. On the floor at the base of each wall sat a bowl of fragrant herbs and incense. A stream of smoke drifted from each to mingle with the haze near the ceiling and filled the room with a heady mixture of spices and perfumes.

Pria leaned against the door behind her, staring at the three mounds as she tested the air with a thin probe of magic. Soldiers brought the bodies back from a patrol. They didn't often find corpses after grinlo attacks, but when they did, the bodies were returned for a proper burial.

Once she determined that the bodies hid no residual traps, she approached the stone table. She folded down the first cloak, a brown tattered rag that had seen many rounds of mending. The cloak revealed a farmer, not unattractive, possibly in his twenties. The patrol had found his body well beyond the northern most established farm. No one seemed to know where he was from or what his name was. The cadaver showed no marks, the skin unblemished. She folded back the cloak to reveal the upper torso.

The man's clothes sat folded along the back wall beside two other piles. She laid her fingertips along the sun-darkened skin of his shoulders. The time out in the elements left the body chilled but strangely unmarked. There were several states a body left by grinlo could fall into: consumed, marred, marked, and unmarked. It all depended on what the purpose the life had been taken. Only a priestess could discern marked from unmarked, which was what she was down here to do.

None of the bodies showed marks from teeth or weapons; all that was left for cause of death was magic. Nothing tingled up through her fingers as she stood beside the young man's head. She drew breath through her nose and let it hiss out between her teeth. A tentative pulse of magic slipped from her fingers into the body, inching along through the muscle and tissue, seeking, searching. She still stood at the end of the table, her hands still cupped the cold shoulders of the corpse, but her senses dove through the vessels and sinew. She focused her attention along each appendage, each muscle, until she assured herself that no magical trigger was hidden within the remains. She pulled her senses back and removed her touch from the shoulders.

She rubbed her palms together and blew across her thumbs. "*Lemora*," she whispered. A glow emanated from her palms, and she spread her hands over the chest. The lemora would allow any magical residue to reflect back toward her and collect in her palms. Nothing caught her attention on the exposed surface of skin.

The door to the chamber opened as she moved her attention to the head.

"I need silence for this," she said without turning.

"You're the one talking."

She glanced over her shoulder to see Mian lounged against the wall. True to his word, he silently hooked his thumbs behind his belt and settled in to watch her.

She dismissed him and turned her full attention back on the body. No resonance reflected back from the head and she moved toward the arms. Nothing responded to the magic in his arms either. She flipped the cloak back up over the chest and exposed the left leg.

Mian cleared his throat and she felt her calm focus quake. "You have an issue?" she snapped.

"I would never question the judgment of my high priestess."

Her hands trailed along the leg, searching toward the toes before she moved to the other limb. She paused as Mian coughed again. She pushed away the irritation and maintained her focus but he coughed again. "What, Mian?"

"You do realize this was a citizen, right?" he said. "This man was loyal to the throne."

"And you would rather I *not* determine what happened to him?"

"Is there no way to do that that doesn't involve desecrating his body?"

Anger rushed up through her core, threatening to shake her control loose. She let the rage burn around her as she put her full force into maintaining the spell. Once she had swept the cadaver she returned her attention to Mian. "If you have a problem with the process, you are free to leave."

"I don't remember Lana stripping bodies to inspect them."

Pria tugged the cloak back over the body. "Mian, just because Lana did not confide the process to you does not mean that it is not necessary."

Mian gestured to the bodies. "And just what did this necessary process tell you?"

"He is unmarked," she said. "There is no residue of magic and no sign of damage to the body."

"Then how did he die?"

"I don't know." She turned her attention to the second corpse. "It happens more than we would like to admit. It is the hope of the Lorien that one day we will be able to determine a cause."

"So he just went through that degradation for nothing?"

She held up a finger as she unveiled the face of the second man. "I am not finished yet."

The man settled back against the wall, leaving the air thick with his concerns while she started on the next body. She didn't have to touch the corpse to feel the residue of magic radiating off of it. This body was marked. She brushed her hands together as if dusting away a layer of dirt. She could not use the same spells to determine the type used to kill the man before her. She let the magic brush against her skin as she tried to determine its resonance. The spell itched along her arms and burned acrid against her tongue.

She jerked back from the slab, her skin aflame. A flash sparked across the exposed chest. She threw her arm to the side to stop Mian as he pushed off from the wall. Whatever had been done to this man had been excruciating.

"Stay back!"

"What is happening?" His voice thickened with nerves.

"The spell reacted with my searching," she said. "It happens from time to time." Sparks of light danced across the remains.

"What was done to him?"

Pria waved a hand over the body. She snagged a tendril of light and stretched it out before her. The line of magical residue trailed between her hands, firelight dancing along its length. Mian, of course, could see none of this.

"This," she said as she plucked the string and analyzed the note it generated, "was a spell to confuse them." She let the strand snap back. "The grinlo are known to use a handful of distinct spells and numerous combinations." She stirred the twisting mess of spells, the agitation separating out several individual currents. She gestured to a cluster here and there. "Confusion, compulsion, a mix of draining, compulsion, and something I'm having trouble identifying." She stretched out her hand and tapped the offending strand with the top of her finger. Her body rocked as a wave crashed over her and she was flying across the room.

The next thing Pria's mind could grasp was floating—her body suspended feet above the floor, traveling down a hallway. It made no sense. A latent spell could cause levitation, but if it was strong enough to lift her, it should still be strong enough to affect the corpse as well. So why was she moving?

She had to focus to breathe, force the air in and out of her chest. Something in the air tingled her senses. It pulled deep on her memories but she couldn't place it. Wind rushed past her, creating a growl in her ears but something pounded in one of them, a muffled timed beat.

Footsteps echoed around her, running steps.

Her eyes opened to a find fabric pressed against the side of her face. Arms held her tight. Her mind still drowned in a sea of fog as whoever was carrying her began to climb stairs. She could hear their breath now, racing. What was going on?

Embroidery on the jacket emerged from the fog. A snarling wolf. *Mian.*

Her fat tongue blurred her speech as she struggled to call out to him. "Mian… Mian stop." Her tiny voice couldn't catch his attention. She ran her tongue around her mouth, trying to work moisture back behind her lips. "Mian!"

"Hang on, Pria." His arms clamped around her, forcing air from her lungs, but he never broke stride.

"Where are you taking me?" she asked.

"I'm taking you to the surgeons. They'll know what to do."

"What could the surgeons do against a spell?" Her head rocked with the movement of his chest, releasing a wave of fog and hazing her thoughts.

Mian stumbled, missed a step, but didn't slow. "They'll know what to do."

She blinked the confusion back. "They won't, Mian," she said. "It's magic, not malady."

He stumbled to a halt, his chest heaving with exertion. "Then what? The Lorien, of course!" He took off again at a trot, sending her thoughts rattling through her head.

"Mian! Stop!"

"We'll need supplies, horses, a guard," he said, not listening to her. "Not too large, of course. I'd say we'll be there in a week if we switch out mounts as we go."

"Enough, Mian!" Her voice cracked like a whip through the corridor. Her vision started to clear.

He stopped again, his arms sagging with her weight. She could feel the agitation in his muscles. "What?"

"The spell is already fading. Even if it wasn't, any spell would likely have faded or killed me long before you made it to the Lorien." She looked up; a gaggle of maids stared at them from across the hall. "Mian, put me down before you fall."

After a moment he lowered her feet to the floor and she put all of her effort into staying on them. She kept a firm hand on Mian's arm, knowing she wouldn't be able to support herself.

"Mian, I am all right, just caught off guard."

Mian's eyes flashed. "I still think you should see the surgeons."

He didn't resist as she turned him back toward the stairs. "It would be a waste of their time, and mine."

"So, what? We ignore what happened?"

"Probing spells carry an inherent risk," she said, "but it must be done."

The muscles of his arm tensed beneath her hand. "And it has to be done by you."

"Do you see another priestess in this manor?"

His jaw clenched tight, he growled through his teeth, "What did we learn from this risk?"

She held her response as they descended the stairs, struggling not to fall. When they made the landing, she took a deep breath. "There are more spells to decipher, but from what I've seen so far I can make a few inferences."

"Like he was thrown?"

"Not necessarily," she said. "That was a latent spell that interacted with my seeking. It does not mean that was its initial intention."

The door to the storage room stood open and she slipped from his arm to the table. Mian hovered in the doorway. "Does that mean the spell was intentional?"

She paused, hand hovering above the second body as she let the thought take root in her mind. It would be easy for someone trained in magic to set such a trap, but to what end? For the spell she had stumbled upon to be of any use, the body would have to come across a priestess *and* be inspected in the field, where the priestess would be vulnerable. It seemed contrived and overly complicated, but what if she'd only triggered part of it? Was there more waiting? Something subtle she had missed? Something strong she couldn't fight in a weakened state?

Mian had noticed her hesitation and there was nothing she could do about that. The truth of it was that she needed to adjust her thinking. She couldn't continue on as if she were dealing with mere grinlo. She had to start acting as if she were working against a rogue priestess because, like it or not, that was likely what she was dealing with.

She stepped back from the stone slab and made her way toward a tray of supplies. She snatched up a handful of crystals from the tray and arranged them around the bodies on the stone table. She felt Mian's eyes burning into her flesh as she moved around the room.

"What are you doing?"

She set the last crystal at the far corner of the table. "I'm creating a resonance cage that will protect me from any latent spells."

Mian's brow creased. "Why didn't you do this before?"

"It limits the effects of my spells as well, and it forces me to work from a greater distance." She took a step back and held her hands up, palms out. "It will make identifying spells harder." She trailed her palms across the edge of the cage created by the crystals. "*Plentia.*"

Lightning arced between the rocks, forming a lattice over the table. After a moment, the light faded and the crystals returned to normal.

Mian's eyes widened. This spell made a cage visible to even those with no magical talent. She ignored his shock as she returned to her inspection. She could still feel the hum of magic through the barrier, but it was like trying to discern the landscape through fog. She could see the spell that had ensnared her swirling behind the shield. It looked so benign—whoever had set it was talented at masking their intent. The shield wouldn't protect her from all of the effects of spells but would slow their release and lessen their impact. It was all she could do.

Mian had braved a closer vantage. "So?" he asked. "What can you tell?"

"I can tell you are going to pester me until I am finished."

"Took you ten years at the Lorien to learn that?"

Her fingertips sparked along the edge of the cage, drawing spells toward her. She pulled the trap toward her. It was a clever mix of multiple spells wrapped in a coating of harmless ones. She would have been lucky to have seen it before it grabbed her.

Orotid made a note of the farm's location in his command journal. He went over his list in his mind: location, families, livestock, incidents. That was everything.

Children were still scattered around the men and horses, excited for the periodic visit. With the horde so often on the move, small clusters like these didn't often get visitors. There were a handful of these clusters dotted around the land between Austeria and Kyneira. Many had been convinced it would be safer farther south or in the cities but several still had fears about abandoning their farms. Orotid couldn't blame them; no one wanted to leave their homes. But it did mean periodic checks by the army to ensure everyone's safety.

Janu made sure each patrol bartered or bought goods from the farms; he didn't want his people to suffer. Janu was a good prince, a good man to serve under.

The men worked to load the last of the purchased supplies. Most would be consumed on the current run, but whatever was left would be sold in the cities to help keep the chain of commerce running. Kingdoms were a delicate balance of supply and demand that couldn't be allowed to teeter too far one way. Raber and Jothie were sequestered with the cluster's elected leaders. Each cluster elected their own group to coordinate day to day life out here. These groups determined the needs for everyone and gave a list to the soldiers so that supplies could be delivered. Organization was key to keeping the system running smoothly.

He referenced his map stored in a protective tube at his belt. A total of seven clustered farms dotted the map. It had taken a large amount of negotiation to settle on the locations. His patrol had crisscrossed that map, hitting every farm as they went. They had one more stop, the last set of farms between here and Kyneira. They never reported any activity. Being so close to Kyneira, they were designated a safe zone, but they still had to check. Janu wanted everything north of Kyneira patrolled.

Orotid tucked his map back into its case. The village around him was a sprawling mass contained in the makeshift "wall" that the farmers had constructed: a mound of dirt four feet high and topped with sharpened fenceposts. It served its purpose.

No sheep or goats bayed. It quickly became apparent that smaller livestock could not be sustained this far north outside of defended cities. These small patches had turned to cattle and oxen. If they were unable to be collected, they at least stood a fighting chance against the grinlo and other predators. Plus, one animal was enough to feed everyone and then some, so fewer animals were needed.

The last of his men returned from their tasks and they set about to leave. They had a long ride before their next camp.

Pria stared at the missive. She had read it a dozen times at least, and that was *after* spending nearly the full morning in careful craft of its contents. There could be no hint of doubt, no suggestion of indecision, but she couldn't let her suspicions of a master behind the grinlo go unreported, not with the loss of Lana. There was a long history of priestesses being turned by fallen members. They couldn't ignore the possibility that Lana's capture had been an attempt to turn her. The grinlo may have just consumed her magic, but without a body they couldn't rule anything out. With the right mix of spells, the strength gained from the grinlo, and plenty of time, it could be possible to alter a priestess' perception enough to skew her loyalties and turn her to their persuasion. It was unlikely to have succeeded; Mian and Janu would have mentioned any rumors of her still being alive.

Another read through the neat script and she was reasonably convinced it would pass. There was no need to check if the ink was dry, her care in its content had assured each line dried long before the next was crafted.

How long would she need to maintain this level of care? How long before the immediate danger of reassignment would be gone? Not soon enough, at any rate. Of course, there was always the possibility of reassignment, but for most priestesses it would take a serious misstep: bias, greed, corruption, a misjudgment that cost a large loss of life—all would lose a priestess her post, but Pria was all too aware that the scrutiny she was under extended well beyond what any other priestess in the past had received. She was too young, too connected.

She folded and sent the report, flashing it away, but remained seated at her vanity. Her careful steps around priestess propriety consumed not only her time but also her mind. She slumped, tired on the stool. Her own family and she dared not to treat them as such.

She turned at a knock on the door. "Come."

A maid in pristine livery stepped into the door and closed it behind her with a quiet *snick*. The woman moved about the room with efficiency and Pria left her to her work. She had her own work to do. She swept from the room, her robes a soft rustle about her ankles.

The hallways beyond were decorated with paintings and tapestries of battles and hunting to break up the neat stone. Though the hallway bustled with servants and soldiers alike, all moved with such silent intensity that Pria could even pick out the whisper of her slippers. The normal cacophony of castle life had been hushed for her. Out of deference or fear—she didn't know—the entire castle looked at her as if she was a mixture of their first love and a deity. Whatever the reason, she took full advantage of the node of quiet to let her thoughts run.

Somehow, some way, a magical being had gained control of the horde—of this she was almost positive. The question was, how would she find them? She let her feet carry her through the endless hallways, turning randomly, keeping no pattern. A pull of ice settled in her stomach and she let her feet stop and her eyes focus. The hall around her was still silent, servants and soldiers alike surrounded in a polite hush. A gaggle of soldiers milled about at the end of the hallway, one eye toward her while they went about their work.

The runner beneath her feet was an intertwined pattern of leaves, thorns, and flowers. Her lips curled. She knew this runner. She turned to her left and the door she knew would be there. The dark stained door was carved with a massive oak branching up to spread out to the wall beyond the door. Limbs snaked and twisted and wheedled down to twigs from which grew individual leaves. Each leaf was decorated in the name of one of Narita's ancestors. The ancestral tree had guarded the entrance to Austeria's library since it had been built some seven hundred years ago.

Her eyes traveled across the leaves and branches then settled on the knob carved like a gnarled limb. She laid her fingertips along its length and felt a tingle travel up her arm. There was magic here, a residue that called to her. With a nudge, the door swung open to reveal the stacks and rows of endless books that comprised the Austerian collection.

The spark of magic pulled her through the door and into the stacks. Her fingers stretched out to brush along the spines of the books along the shelf to her right. She had always done that since the day she was old enough to read. The possibilities of all the knowledge and stories held within those covers shivered along her spine. She wandered the rows, letting the magic pull along her stomach. It had a familiarity to it, a tinge that spoke to her very soul.

Her fingertip slid onto the spine of a large leather-bound history that was as thick as the palm of her hand and as old as the castle in which it resided. A jolt shot up her arm and froze her in her tracks. Her chest pumped with tension as she pulled the book from its slot and cradled it in her elbow. She ran her palm along the cover, letting the spark of magic speak to her as she carried it to one of the tables set beneath a dome in the ceiling.

The cover was stiff and brittle, cracked at the edges and embossed with fading black letters. *The Frontier and its Creatures.* She had studied excerpts from the volume in classes in the Lorien. Its author Priestess Neiala was widely known as the foremost expert on the Frontier.

A corner of parchment jutted from between the pages. She flipped to the page marked with the paper and found a note in neat writing. She pulled the paper from the book as magic sparked off its corners.

Warmth filled her chest. She knew this neat handwriting by heart: that of Lana. It was a note written to herself, thoughts put to paper. Pria spread the memo flat. If there was one, there were bound to be more. She trailed her fingers along the crinkled paper. "Thank you, Lana."

Mian hesitated at the bookshelf, eyes on Pria as she pored through a tome in her lap. She sat in the middle of the floor, surrounded on all sides by open books that she had pulled from the shelves around her. The library itself rose around them, sweeping bookcases filled with Narita's family collection. Large windows to the east and west let light pour in during the day; large candelabras chased away the shadows at night. Here and there stood a pillar supporting the large domed ceiling high above them. Pria had always loved the library, but her fevered research looked anything but relaxing now. She rushed to fill the gap in her knowledge from her absence; he knew that every second that slipped by angered her.

To one side of the library was censuses and genealogy; the other histories, the likes of which he had never heard of. Scattered among them were ledgers of patrol reports from as many commanders as she could corner on her own with more to follow when her list of runners returned with those she couldn't see to personally. A journal sat to her side, the open pages scrawled with notes in her own hand. What she hoped to learn was beyond him. What could possibly be hidden in this dusty old library? He guessed that was what the Lorien taught women, to see things where there was nothing to be seen.

Girded with a deep breath, he stepped forward and picked his way through the open volumes.

He knelt at her side and was enveloped in a heady mix of old books, soft lavender, and a clean soap scent from her skin. "The guards say you haven't eaten since you came in here this morning."

"The guards should learn not to gossip so much." She didn't glance up from her research.

"It is not gossip when they are ordered to watch you and report."

She glared at him. "I think I know when I need food, Mian."

He slipped the book from her lap, ignoring the venomous tightening of her eyes. "Apparently not."

She snatched another book from her stash. "Mian, honestly I am fine. Why don't you go and hover over Janu?"

"Because he is eating." He snatched the second book from her and grabbed up another as she reached for it. Her eyes sparked as they caught his. "I'm not leaving until you do. You can keep picking up books and I can keep taking them away. Do you really want to waste the time of seeing who is more stubborn here? If you eat regularly I will be sure no one bothers you otherwise without a good reason."

She stuck her lip out haughtily, glancing up at him through thick eyelashes. "Can I take one with me while I eat?"

He shook his head in resignation as he handed the books back to her. "Sure, why not."

She tucked one to her chest as he helped her to her feet. Her small hand fit like a key in his, always had. When he was younger, he had just assumed that girls' hands were supposed to fit like that. It wasn't until he was older that he'd learned that not just any woman's hand would tuck perfectly into his. He had almost forgotten what it felt like.

"I really am fine, though."

Her voice jolted him from his thoughts and he remembered the complication he had on his arm. "I'm sure you are."

"The Lorien taught us many techniques on how to sustain ourselves."

"Good," he said, "that will likely come in handy, but let's save it for a time when it is needed, huh?" She laughed as he lifted her over her pile of literature, book still clutched to her chest. "Perhaps later we can test out how long you can sustain yourself."

"You are crass, Mian. How does anyone ever tolerate you?"

"Some people tolerate me very well," he said.

"What people? Barmaids and tavern wenches?"

His eyes sparkled with mischievous glee. "More like nobility and gentry."

Guards pulled open the doors to the library, eyes forward as they fell in behind Mian and Pria.

She coughed a laugh. "What nobility finds you tolerable?"

He leaned down close to her ear. "Nobility like…Lady Sorana."

Her jaw dropped. She stared up at him, incredulous. "Lady Sorana? She's ten years your senior!"

"What can I say, she likes younger men." He shot her a playful wink as she rolled her eyes.

"You are a complete degenerate."

"Some people like that in a man."

She laughed as he followed her out into the hall. "You can try to be a little less repugnant in public."

"Perhaps, but it wouldn't be as fun." He slid the book from her arms and tucked it into his elbow. "I'm not always repugnant; even you have to admit I have some good qualities."

She stared at the book in his arms. "Some, I'll grant you, but they are so deeply hidden among your vices that it would take a scholar to find them."

He laughed as they turned into the dining hall, smiling at the servers who rushed to set a table. He pulled out a chair and pushed her into the table before leaning close to her ear. He laid the book beside her and made his way to the seat next to her. "And I will be watching what you eat so if you read and ignore the food, I will take that back."

She flipped the book open and dropped her eyes to the pages. "You might try."

"Mian?" A tall brunette rushed over in a graceful cloud of sweet perfume and the delicate swish of silken skirts. "I thought you were out on a raid! When did you get back?"

Mian embraced the tall woman before offering her his chair. "Well, turns out I had an important dignitary to watch after for our dear prince. Lady Tara, this is High Priestess Pria."

Tara brightened as her eyes fell on Pria, whose gaze had just moved from the book in front of her. "Honestly? *The* high priestess?" Her hands began to race around her hair and clothes. "Had I known I would be meeting the high priestess I would have made sure to make myself more presentable."

Mian pulled another chair over and dropped into it. "Tara is Jeran's betrothed."

Tara blushed as she dropped her eyes. "Our families have been allies for years."

Pria kept her face stoic as Tara smoothed her hair self-consciously. "There is no need for primping, Lady Tara."

"Priestess, your reputation is legend. My family has an estate outside the Lorien—we summer there. Our house staff have family that work in the school and we heard so many stories about you!"

Pria cleared her throat, her eyes stern. "I'm sure they were all conjecture and rumor, nothing for nobility to concern themselves with."

Tara's face fell. "I…I… They were nothing defamatory, I can assure you. Our people would never dream to slander the high priestess."

Pria remained stoic in the face of Tara's anxiety. "Even so, I'm sure you will not be spreading or listening to such stories anymore."

"Of…of course not, Priestess." Tara stood and dropped a deep curtsy. "It was a genuine pleasure getting to meet you, and I apologize for any offense."

Mian sighed as Tara ghosted away from them. "Well, that was openly hostile."

Pria's attention returned to the book. "I do not need people seeing me as some rumor-grown image, Commander."

"Are you worried about what she could have heard about you?" He searched her visage for some sign of the woman who should be there, the woman his Pria should have grown into.

"Don't be ridiculous."

Lips pressed between his teeth, Mian drew patience into his body. "Pria, what could it have hurt to have been nice to Tara?"

"It is *Priestess* to you. Nothing she could have heard would be truth. The stories of me that spread through the Silver City were bloated lies wrapped in a glimmer of fact. They were foolish tales spread by people grasping at any tidbit of gossip about someone they considered celebrity. That woman was looking at me as if I was her childhood idol."

"You *are* her childhood idol." Every second her eyes remained on her book, his anger flared higher.

"I don't need some woman treating me like we are childhood sweethearts sharing old stories."

This was not his Pria. The woman he faced was the emotionless product of priestess training, a pretty face hiding a heart of stone. "Tara is a good woman, bright and warm. All she wanted was to meet someone she looks up to."

"And she did."

Servers piled trays around them with nods and smiles as Mian grinned up at them. They drifted away and he began lifting the lids to reveal the food beneath. "You don't have to be quite so mean to people. Perhaps if you weren't so cold to her, she could see that you are the priestess and not the stories she heard about you."

She pulled a tray toward her and tore off a strip of pheasant meat. "Or she could get more enamored and, in her excitement, spread the stories she heard. I will not be some fairytale."

Mian rubbed his forehead in sad resignation. "Pria, I miss the old you." He stood and moved away.

Pria felt relief rush through her as Mian moved away. Of course she would run into someone who remembered her exploits as a rebellious child. She had worked so hard to overcome that vision of herself as reckless and impetuous. Her post was already so tenuous, all she needed was for the Lorien to be reminded of those rebellious days—or worse, for some fabrication to be spread of such behavior occurring now.

It was bad enough that she kept finding herself so affected by Mian that she slipped back into foolish, childish ways. Maybe the Council was right, maybe she wasn't ready for this responsibility. The words on the page before her faded out of focus as fear settled over her. Was she really balancing her families' lives on her foolish pride?

Her hand began to shake and she slapped it to the table to steady it. She had to keep it together, she was visible. She couldn't let people see her panicking. She deepened her breathing, swallowed the lump in her throat. She could do this; she had been trained for this. Stillness settled over her. She could fail herself; she couldn't fail Trimera.

She just had to focus. No difficulty there, not when she was facing a foe that had control of the horde. She just had to calm down and focus on what needed done. She couldn't control what others did or thought.

But how was she expected to perform to her best capacity with her head on a chopping block? A vice clamped around her chest, squeezing her heart tight. She laid her hands flat on the table, pressed her feet into the floor. The contact helped her ground herself, stopped her from running from the room. Would it look strange if she just walked out? It definitely would to that woman Tara. Might even encourage her to spread stories. Mian was right, she should have been nicer. She should have tried to form a connection with her so she wouldn't be tempted to conjecture.

There was nothing for it; she had to sit here and calm herself. That was one thing Mian had always been good for, helping her calm down. If only she could lean on that now. But he didn't understand. She didn't know how to make him understand.

She let her finger trace the swirls in the surface of the table. Mindless and repetitive, she forced her breath into the same looping pattern. In with one direction of the swirl, out with the opposite.

Back to work. She had to focus on work.

The hall around Mian was its normal buzz of chatter and noise as the house occupants and guests ate and socialized. Long tables lined the hall among the columns that were carved with trees and animals. Soldiers and nobles nodded as he passed, and he tried to return the smiles of the ladies and maids who waved at him. People sat in groups chatting—everyone but the icy priestess at her solitary table.

As he made his way across the room, he finally spotted the table he was looking for. Tara blushed as he dropped into a chair beside her. "Mian, I am sorry if I insulted the priestess; it was not my intention."

Mian felt the rage rush back up to flare in his eyes. "Don't you be sorry for her; she's a stubborn, heartless shell where a human used to be."

Tara blanched. "You mustn't say such things, Mian. High Priestess Pria is an inspiration in bravery and honor! Of course she doesn't want some silly girl falling at her feet; she is far too important."

Mian smiled at the woman's open pride in a person she barely knew. His anger subsided in the face of her sweetness. "I would love to hear the stories you heard of her, Tara. Would you tell me?"

Tara dropped her eyes. "I don't think I should, it might anger her."

Mian grinned mischievously. "I can only hope it will."

Tara sat forward and pressed her hands over his as her eyes flashed with excitement. "Ten years ago, she showed up. The city was all abuzz. It had been years since a high priestess had entered the lists of the Lorien."

"Lana."

"Yes, High Priestess Lana. My parents told me of when Lana sent word to the Lorien of Pria's birth. The halls erupted in excitement and conjecture. When she finally came to the city, her reputation was already so blown out of proportion that the girl herself became a symbol of hope and unity. We would go to the Lorien and hope to see her. She was a precocious girl, always sneaking past the security into the city; the shops and townspeople always watched for her. She was so beautiful. Nothing ever fazed her.

"One day she was traveling the streets at night and came upon a man being robbed. It was a large group of men, but she did not flinch. They saw no harm in such a young girl, but she tore through them with little effort, leaving them all tied in the alley for the watch and stashing their loot with the poor man they were robbing."

He smiled. "Sounds about right. She never knew when to back down and wouldn't let anyone get hurt if she could stop it."

Tara's eyes flashed. "And that is only one! There are so many more!"

A low chuckle rumbled up from his chest. "I'm sure there are," Mian dropped his gaze looking to soften his words. "Tara, Pria is…difficult. She's afraid that people will not see her as the priestess."

Tara nodded seriously. "I can see why. She is a beautiful young girl in a position of power and duty. It must be hard for her to interact with others without feeling that they are judging her on her looks alone. She was quite right to stop me. It is an open area and many people can see us. Me acting starstruck is not what she needs."

Mian cocked his head. "Are all women crazy, Tara? Seriously, they seem to think on lines that make no sense."

"You only say that because you haven't met one that will make you crazy yet."

He glanced at Pria, still engrossed in her manuscript. "I wouldn't say that; our high priestess is a fair bit on her way right now."

"Is she now?" Tara's face bloomed into a knowing grin.

Mian met her grin with a flat stare. "Not like that, Tara. Just plain, incessant insanity."

Tara's smile was warm and open as she held his gaze. "Mian, I have seen you with many women."

Mian rolled his eyes to the ceiling. "Is this going to be a lecture on depravity? I've been having enough of that lately."

"Not on depravity, no. I have never seen you quite this aggravated with any woman before."

"That's because you haven't seen me around Pria. The woman is maddening," he said.

"I can see that."

He raised his hands. "Why does everyone seem to think that I am in love with Pria?"

"Perhaps because they know you."

He huffed. "I don't want to talk about it anymore. How are the arrangements for your wedding going?"

She sighed with a pretty pout. "Slowly. It is hard with Jeran always being dragged off for some duty or another."

"I know, I'm sorry. He worries you are getting angry with him." Mian's face twisted with sympathy.

With a smile, she dropped her gaze to the table. "I could never be mad at him. He is so perfect. I could never be angry at my sweet angel."

He giggled. "Sweet angel, I like that. Might have to be his new nickname."

She gave him a gentle shove. "You stop!"

His laughter sparkled across the room. "Okay, I won't call him 'sweet angel.' In front of the other men. Not all of them anyway."

He sat back with a glance over at Pria, who turned the page of her book. "I had better get back to my charge; if I don't watch her closely she will likely use that food for a bookmark rather than eat it."

Her smile drew his own wider. "Don't let her make you too crazy, Mian. A pretty face was always your weakness."

"Everyone with an opinion on my life," he said, kissing her fingers before crossing the room.

Pria didn't even glance up when he sat next to her.

"Doesn't look like you've eaten much since I left," he said.

"Did you go somewhere?"

His brow drew down. "Start eating or I'll take the book."

She slid her chair over and laid the book down in front of him, tracing a finger along the neatly written type. "There are few instances where any magical creature has been able to gain control of a horde of grinlo."

"This has happened before?" He drew a deep breath as she leaned closer to indicate another passage in the book and his head filled with the scent of oils and flowers. Soft waves of hair slipped from behind her ear and dangled between them, and for a moment he had the mad idea to run his fingers through it.

"Not often, but yes it has." She grabbed another strip of meat as she scanned the page again. "It takes a great amount of sacrifice to gain control of them—as well as incredible power." She tapped the page. "See here—Anondrin, he was able to gain control of a horde by sacrificing seven of his children to gain more power. Foomab"—she pointed to another place—"tore out his own eye and allowed them to drain his power before he could take control. This will not be some mere magical being we are dealing with; anyone who has the strength to do this will be twisted, not only by the act itself but even by the attempt."

He shook his head as she smiled up at him. "So how do we identify this twisting?"

She sat back with a heavy sigh. "It all depends on what they paid to gain power over them. I have no way to tell you that."

He gestured to the open page before him. "It's more than we had before."

Her eyes sparkled as she pulled the book back. "That's what I'm here for."

"How about some more pheasant?" He nudged a tray toward her. "I will have Janu come to the library after you eat and we can discuss this further. Is that all right?"

She waved him off. "Whatever you want."

Mian bit his lip pensively as he watched Pria's eyes scan the page. "Pria, what do we do when we…find this person?"

"What do you mean?" she asked.

"What is our next move once we are able to identify the twisted magical being that has control over the horde?"

Her eyes met his as they rolled up from the text before her. "We find them and we stop them."

He sat forward. "You don't mean we, do you."

She met his gaze. "*I*. I will find them and stop them."

"That does not sit well with me."

"Sit well or no, that is what will have to happen," she said.

"Why?"

"I am not going to argue this with you." She glanced around at the table. "Have I eaten enough to return to the library?"

With careful consideration he took in the small portions removed from the trays. "I guess it'll do for now."

She stood and tucked the book in her arms again. "Good. You know where to find me."

His eyes trailed her as she left, knuckles white from his clenched fists.

"Been arguing with her again?" Jeran sank into a chair beside him and eyed the food left scattered around the table. "You two seem to do that often, don't you think? I thought you dragged her from the library so she would eat."

Mian rubbed his hand down his face. "She ate as much as she was going to eat. Keeping her here longer would have just created a public fight for which she would have inevitably blamed me. With a woman like Pria, it is all about compromise: How much are you willing to bleed for what you want her to do."

Jeran laughed as he sampled some pork. "Isn't that most women?"

"No Jeran, there are no women like Pria, thankfully. One of her is decidedly enough. Where is Janu?"

"He is going over maps with some lord or another; who can keep track of them all?"

Mian leveled a finger at him. "If you wish to command one day, you should take a care to learn. Those lords pay your debts." He snatched up a crust of bread as he stood. "Try not to let this go to waste, would you?"

Mian kept his eyes focused as he walked, not even glancing up at those around him. He didn't like Pria's implications about their foe. He was Battle Leader; combat was his area. His every action, his every thought was to protect Trimera, protect his prince. How was he supposed to sit back and let Pria go fight for the fate of his kingdom and the citizens he was stationed to protect? He wasn't—that was all there was to it. He wouldn't just sit idly by; he would be at her side, come what may. Of course, *come what may* could easily include her attacking him to get him out of the way. But no matter, Battle Leader stands between his people and danger—and that's what he was going to do.

He shoved open the door to the solarium and brushed the crumbs of bread from his shirt. The large oak table in the room's center was surrounded by well-dressed men, each absorbed with Janu, who stared down at the map before him deep in thought. Mian slid in at his side, sure not to draw attention. The lords always got angry when he drew attention, never mind the fact that he was a lord in his own right, or would be once his father left this life. Though, darkness send, that not be anytime soon. Not that he didn't want to take over his father's estates, but with the horde already on Trimera land and looking to take more, his place was at Janu's side, not overseeing estates.

Janu tugged at his upper lip, a common habit he had when mulling over something important. His eyes were hazy, assuring he saw nothing around him. Finally, his hand darted to his hair and raked it back. "We do not have the men to protect the fields; all of our soldiers are committed to fighting. We will have to move the fields back. There is no other way."

Tall, gray-haired Lord Gydir shot him a horrified glance. "But Majesty, that would leave our most fertile fields barren. Where would we find land as suited to crops?"

Janu's eyes rolled up to meet Mian's before dropping back to the map. "If memory serves, when my father was prince, we cultivated the Volstep. It has been used for horses for years; the fields should have had sufficient time to recover."

Coulsto jerked visibly. "And what of my horses? Majesty, our mounts bring much revenue to the royal coffers. Where will I graze them?"

"Your horses, for now, are needed here, Coulsto—every mount that is not with foal or gestating. Any others will be moved onto other farms, where your people will care for them."

Coulsto's eyes glistened painfully. "Of course, my prince, it will be so."

Janu pushed the map away. "Good, see to it as soon as possible."

The lords kept their eyes down as they filed from the room. Under normal circumstances they would have fought tooth and nail for such a statement to be uttered, but such foolishness they had long since learned would not be tolerated by their prince. Not with the horde at their back door.

"You come from Pria?" Janu asked Mian.

"I do, my brother."

"I could use some good news."

"I'm not sure I have any that would fit the description. She is in the library still; I think it best heard from her."

Janu nodded sadly. "She has changed much, hasn't she? I missed her so much it pains me to be away from her, but it pains as much to see her absorbed in problems so past her years."

"She always was old for her age."

Janu leaned forward and pressed his palms to the table. "Mother was so giddy when they discovered that she was to be a high priestess. My baby sister, born with the ability to be one of the strongest magical beings in all of Reia."

Mian smiled. "I remember. I do believe she dragged my parents from their beds for a party."

Janu's mouth tightened. "I wonder if she knew the price of such a gifted child?" He sighed. "The depth of her eyes is a bottomless chasm of pain where once a girl lived. I feel I have lost my sister in gaining my priestess."

Taking Janu's arm, Mian turned him toward the hallway. "Do not believe that. The girl we love is in there still…just afraid to step out into the light."

"This life will be the death of all things, I am foolish to mourn."

"It may be, but I mourn her as well. Narita is the only one who seems not to be sad for the loss, and I think that is only because Pria allows her to see what she hides from everyone else. Does she not trust us?" Mian asked.

"I would have scoffed at that once, told you what a fool you were being." Janu's eyes dropped to the floor, lidded and somber. "I wish I could still."

They stopped and stared at the library doors. "This life will be the death of all."

Mian pushed the doors open and they stepped into the library. Pria's pile of books still littered the center of the floor but the woman herself was nowhere to be seen. Janu spun in a circle. "Pria?"

A loud snap resonated through the large room, echoing into infinity around the high ceiling. Mian's heart seized as he took off toward the back of the library, Janu tight on his heels. They slid to a halt on the marble floor and stared in shock at a twisted metal gate as Pria calmly walked past them, laden with a stack of books that looked to weigh more than she did. "Why are you two so out of breath?"

Janu waved a finger at the gate. "What happened to this?"

She glanced back at it. "I couldn't get the lock off so I blew it."

His forehead wrinkled. "You couldn't ask for a key?"

"Don't worry, I'll fix it," she said.

Mian jumped back as a part of the gate crashed to the ground. "Fix it?"

"It's not that damaged, honestly."

She moved off and left them to rush after her. Janu slammed his hands down on the table as she dropped her stack of books. "I believe that part of the library was closed off by Lana. Can you tell me why you found it necessary to tear through a gate she put up to protect people from their own curiosity?"

Her smug smile was flat as she handed him a folded parchment. "Because Lana told me to. Would have been nice had she told me where to find the key, but the note suggests that she kept that on her. Likely lost forever now." She pulled down the top book, waving off the cloud of dust that lifted from its cover. "She had been looking into control over the horde when she was captured. She always was sharp."

"Tongued too." Mian nodded toward the book she was flipping through. "She left you a note to find more books?"

"She left herself a note to keep track of her thoughts. It was quite helpful."

"She wrote notes to herself?" Mian asked.

Janu laughed as he refolded the parchment. "She did that a lot. I've found them all over the castle. It's like she's been giving me help even after she died."

"It's a good idea. I might pick it up myself, just in case."

Two sets of eyes shot to her. "In case of what?"

She pulled a second book from her latest pile, shuffling pages before she turned to walk back to the center of the room. Janu raced after her. "In case of what?"

She blinked as she glanced up from the book in her arms. "In case I die. Or get captured. It will help whomever the Lorien sends to replace me."

Mian coughed a laugh. "You are not going to die, I promise you that right now."

She rolled her eyes. "Seriously Commander, are you telling me you have now stopped death itself?"

He crossed his arms over his chest. "You are not dying on my watch."

She dropped to the floor and laid the book in her lap. "You have no ability to contain my actions, Commander. I will do my job despite your meddling and interference."

"Your job is not to die."

"My job is to fight and protect my people," she said.

Mian leaned over her and jammed a finger at his chest. "My job is to fight."

She turned her eyes to Janu, ignoring Mian. "Janu, it will not be easy to identify whoever is controlling the horde. Until I am able to do so, your men are going to have to be able to anticipate higher intelligence from the grinlo."

Janu sighed as he glanced over at Mian's angry glare. "Your advice is to tell them that someone is controlling the horde?"

"It will have to be done sooner or later. Better to have them prepared than to let them get caught off guard. I'm sure you can find a way to soften it so that it won't be such an impact on them."

He laughed. "Yeah, I'll just tell them not to worry; you are prepared to die to take them out."

She eyed him. "Now *you're* starting?"

"Where exactly will we be if you get yourself killed?"

She slammed the book closed on her lap, which released a cloud of dust that enveloped her. "You two act like I am the only priestess who can hold this position! If something happens to me, the Lorien will assign you a new priestess."

Janu crossed his arms and moved toward Mian so they made a collective front. "A new priestess, but not a high priestess—and not you. You know these people, you know us."

"And all you two see is Pria."

They both blinked. "What does that mean?"

"You let Lana go with you on raids," she said.

Mian shook his head. "That is really not the argument you want to go with here."

"The point, Commander, is that you let her do her job. You are not going to stand between me and my station."

Mian took a step toward her, back bent to glare down at her face. "No, but I'll sure as hell stand between you and death, and there is nothing you can say to stop me."

"Mian, please, I am not a child—"

"You are my friend!" he bellowed.

"I am your priestess!"

They both jumped as Janu dropped a large book to the floor, rattling the wide walls with the resounding *smack*. "That is enough of that. I will not have my high priestess and my Battle Leader fighting like bickering children." He leveled a finger at Pria. "Mian is my Battle Leader, and part of his duties is seeing to your safety as well as mine." His finger shot to Mian. "I of all people can understand wanting to protect Pria, but her duty is to our people and we are both going to have to learn to respect that. Now, does anyone have a suggestion between you killing yourself and you locking her in her room?"

Pria dropped her eyes to the floor. "I know my limitations, Janu. If the person controlling the horde is stronger than I can handle, the Lorien is but a message away. I know what is at stake and you know I will not throw away all I have worked for without reason."

"Then maybe when you feel you need to do something, you share that reason with us? Not because you have to, but to ease our minds a bit?"

Her eyes slid from Janu to Mian and back again. "I'll try, but there is no guaranteeing you'll understand."

"Then try."

She drew a deep breath. "Anyone who can control the horde—anyone who is willing to do what it takes to gain that control—they would be the kind of person who has no empathy. An emotionless hull. There is no telling what they will do, what they will be capable of. A person like this is not someone I want near anyone I care about. As a priestess, it is my responsibility to ensure that this person is stopped. You can handle the horde; you can protect the people from them, but this person only I can stop. No strength of military can handle it, no might of arms. This is not something either of you can handle, and you need to accept that as a fact."

Mian crossed his arms. "So you are saying all we can do is watch."

"No," she said, "I'm saying if you try to go against them, you will die. You do not want to watch me die; I do not want to see you throw your lives away against something you have no hope to control. The horde is your problem to bear and it should keep you sufficiently busy. Whoever is controlling them is mine, and mine alone." She settled back. "I would like to review the registries from the gates."

Janu scoffed. "Which ones?"

She looked up to him seriously. "All of them."

Mian took a step forward. "What will that do?"

"Possibly nothing. I won't know until I look."

"How far back?" Mian asked.

"How far back do they go?"

His expression fell. "I'll bring you what they have." He stopped as he turned away. "Would you like someone to help you go through them?"

She coughed a laugh. "I wouldn't have any idea what to tell them."

He nodded. "Jeran and I, we may not be educated, but we're pretty quick on things." He searched her face.

She held his gaze for a moment, her expression an unreadable mask. "Thank you, Mian, I would greatly appreciate it."

He left to hide his smile as Pria returned her attention to her book, his chest swelling with pride.

Pria glanced up as Jeran dropped the pile of registries onto a nearby table. "What exactly did you want these things for?"

She jumped to her feet and shuffled through the top ledger. "I'm not sure yet."

Jeran spread his lips into the semblance of a smile as he silently cursed Mian. "Okay." Her bright eyes lifted to his face and Jeran let himself measure the woman he had heard so much about. The youth left a heavy impression, he couldn't deny it, but her eyes held such intelligence and strength that it wasn't overwhelming. She held his gaze with a bold confidence that was intimidating despite her youthful beauty.

He stared down at the pile of ledgers. "You are trying to find who is leading the grinlo?"

"That's the idea."

"You think they have been here? Inside the walls?" he asked.

"I'm sure of it."

Jeran let his mind mull over the possibility that this creature had been inside his town, around his people. He tried to comfort himself by thinking the high priestess was just following all possibilities, but he couldn't bring himself to think she would waste this much time on something frivolous. There was a practicality that radiated from her, an efficiency that demanded no energy be wasted and it stole any hope he had that this could just be a wild chase through the woods.

Pria rested her fists on her hips. "Jeran." She lifted one of the ledgers and pressed it to her chest before glancing up into his eyes. "I don't know what to tell you to look for here. I'm not even sure we will find anything."

He sighed. "So, you want us to look through these ledgers for anything that stands out."

"Stands out, feels wrong, even just catches your attention. If something draws you, mention it."

Jeran stared down at the ledger in her arms, his mind embroiled in thoughts of his beautiful Tara even now walking these halls unprotected. If this creature was near her… "Priestess, what happens if we do find something? If we find something and there is someone here now?"

"We consider ourselves very lucky and figure out how to kill them."

He searched her eyes as he let the practicality of her words and voice sink in. He stepped back and watched as men dragged in chairs. "Lucky, right."

A young page ran toward them, laden with another pile of ledgers. Pria pointed him toward the table. Jeran grabbed the top ledger from the pile he had brought down. "No time like the present, I guess."

With a slim finger Pria tucked a hair behind her ear and began reading, letting each name resound in her mind as her eyes passed over it. She had been secluded most of her life and gone from her home for ten years, so very few names looked even remotely familiar. A surname here, a family house there. So many strangers all counting on her to keep them safe. Beside her, Jeran's eyes never left his pages; he was diligent to his task as any soldier should be. He seemed a good man.

Every few minutes or so, a page would enter the room, burdened with yet another pile of ledgers. The stash upon the table was looking quite onerous when Mian finally returned with his own stack. He let his load drop to the table with a crash then bowed low to Pria and shot a wink at Jeran before dropping to the third chair.

Jeran turned his page noisily, one eyebrow raised. "You owe me big."

Mian smiled over his own book. "The joys of rank."

Cool, distant eyes drifted toward him before sliding back to the book in her lap. The never-ending list mocked her. She had set them a nearly impossible task. There was still the off chance that whomever had taken over the horde didn't have a spy among them, but she was sure they did. Even Lana had mentioned it in one of her notes. They would never have been able to so successfully track Lana otherwise. No, Pria was sure there was no way anyone who was controlling the horde had not infiltrated their strongholds, but how to find them?

No one could gain control of the grinlo without magical talent—it wasn't possible. That meant the possibility of training at the Lorien, but not the necessity. She had sent her suspicions to them already and had some of her trusted friends searching for possibilities there, but she didn't hold out much hope. The lists at the Lorien were exhaustive, including women and men from all over Reia and beyond. There was no way to narrow down age, sex, not even extent of training. They could have dropped out, been thrown out, or even graduated and entered the ranks of the priestesses; there was no way to tell. No, the most likely path to their identity lay in Austeria.

She drew a deep breath. A sheer cliff wall loomed before her and the only way to maintain her position was to climb it bare-handed.

Mian glanced over at her. "I think we need to start locking these gates."

Jeran laughed, eyes darting to Pria before returning to his book, smile still bright. "Maybe we'll get lucky and lock this person inside with us." He sat forward. "Going through every name is impossible. Perhaps we can narrow it down some? Like, I think we can skip over any lists that include our patrols. That will save a bit of time. I mean, even if they are a part of the patrols they will have to go out and come back by themselves eventually."

"Unless they are leaving the patrols after they are outside the gates," Pria said with a wave of her finger.

Mian shook his head. "That's not possible. No patrol is large enough that an absence wouldn't be noticed."

Pria sat back and stared at the ceiling. "Okay then, patrols can be skipped. Anything else that won't likely be necessary?"

Mian shared a grin with Jeran as they leaned toward her. "We transfer men a lot, between here and Kyneira. Their ranks are checked between here and there."

"Are any groups of soldiers passing through these gates large enough not to notice anyone escaping them?"

"Only when there is an offensive, in which case no registries are recorded anyway," Jeran said.

Pria pulled a parchment from the table before them. "Okay, movement of soldiers can be skipped for now. Are merchants guarded by our men?"

Jeran tucked his finger into his ledger to hold his place. "Some of them—we offer escort if they ask it. Most avoid any routes that would need it."

"So, we can rule out any merchant who leaves with a palace guard."

Jeran waved the book at them. "It would seem to me that a person who would go through so much trouble to gain control of something like the grinlo would be someone who thought something of themselves. I'd say they would be posing as someone with power of some kind—not a laborer, I would think, but at least merchant if not gentry or nobility."

Pria searched his face, her eyes narrowed as she tapped a quill against her lower lip. "It is a good assumption, but not one we can completely rely on. They may think themselves better, but a smart perpetrator would wish to draw as little attention as possible. A commoner can come and go with much less fuss than a noble."

Jeran nodded thoughtfully. "Maybe we'll get lucky and they are stupid."

She smiled over at him as he shook amused at his own joke. "Is our entire army nothing but jesters?"

Mian chuckled. "You like him, admit it."

She rolled her eyes as she turned a page. "He's tolerable, I suppose. Much more so than you."

Mian winked at Jeran. "In Pria terms, that is a glowing endorsement."

"*Priestess* Pria," she growled.

"No, from Priestess Pria, that is the equivalent of a marriage proposal."

Pria smacked him hard across the wrist. "That is enough out of you! These ledgers aren't going to check themselves."

"Forgive him, High Priestess, he tends to babble." Jeran's brow wrinkled. "Who is Lord Huran?"

Mian glared at him. "Jeran, you are pathetically hopeless! Huran is Narita's father!"

He held the book out to Pria. "But this is from this month; Narita's father hasn't been here for a year."

"That would be completely ignorant or impressively confident." She touched the register with her fingertip. "The gate guards record the names themselves, yes?"

"Usually."

"Mark this page and keep an eye out for anyone else that shouldn't be here," she said.

"Of course, Priestess."

Mian leaned over. "There could be many reasons for someone to pretend to be a lord."

"Yes, but how many of those reasons would come with enough nerve to utilize the lord of the estate?"

Jeran rubbed his face. "It is one thing to believe there is someone controlling the horde, but actually looking for them is creepy."

"Welcome to a life of privilege."

He waggled his finger in the air, sweeping another page of his ledger over. "Can I go back to being a poor man again now, Commander?"

"No."

"Tyrant."

"Lay about."

"Deviants!" Pria's bellow broke across the domed room.

They both smiled as Pria cocked an eyebrow and rapped her fingers along the leather cover.

The light through the windows traveled steadily across the floor beside them as they sat focused on their work. Seven more lords who had visited while they were away had been found, all prominent. It was too much of a coincidence to not pay attention to. Something was definitely going on—hopefully not more than what was already suspected.

Mian's head was already lolled against the chair in sleep and Jeran was not far behind him, but she couldn't rest yet. There was so much more to do.

"I think you definitely did them in."

She didn't turn as Janu approached. "Soldiers do not seem to be very sympathetic to the drudgery of bookwork."

"Were they at least of some help?"

"They were of great help, until they fell asleep," she said.

"They do not have the stamina of their priestess." He shoved a few ledgers aside so he could jump up on the table before her. "Pri, how are we going to figure this out?"

"Through hard work, Janu."

"Not…this!" He waved his hand. "This you will sort through like it is some child's game. You never did find a task you couldn't overcome." The smile wilted from his face. "I meant…us. You, me, Mian. I love having you back, but you're right, I see you as my sister and there is nothing I will not do to protect you."

She sighed and tucked the ledger into her lap. The struggle in Janu's eyes sent a sharp pain straight through her heart. Princess Pria cried out to confide in him everything: her struggles to gain the station, the tenuous grasp with which she held on to it, the faction of priestesses looking for any reason to remove her from Trimera and post someone with more experience and less connection. If she shared this burden, would it make the situation better? Would the knowledge ease the tension between them or turn him against the priestesses and undermine what little credit she had been able to garner? No, it was her burden to carry, not his. She would have to shoulder it alone.

"Janu, I will always be your sister. That will never change. Still, I am not *just* your sister. I am willing to share my plans with you, Janu, and even try to explain them to you, but you have to let me do what I was trained to do."

He sighed heavily. "I know. I'm sorry we haven't been very sympathetic to that since you've come back. Lana's disappearance really hit us hard. Mian wouldn't speak for a month, our men were so demoralized that most of them had to retire…some never did recover. Lana was a symbol to them; she was their protector, a being of legend and awe. With her gone, everything fell to us. There was no more buffer. I don't think anyone but Mian and myself had ever even talked to her outside of the context of her office. She was an image to them, and that is all they saw, so when she was gone they didn't know how to function without her."

"Lana was an amazing priestess," Pria agreed. "She was strong and brilliant."

"She wasn't real to them. I don't want you to be that. I really don't think we can survive the loss of another priestess, definitely not when that priestess is you. We limped along without her, but the wound it left festers still. Without the knowledge and skill of a priestess, recapturing the Seat and pushing back the horde became an unsurmountable obstacle. Without a priestess, the idea of victory is nothing more than an unattainable dream to them." His voice was desperate, fearful she wouldn't understand.

Pria fought to hold back her own concerns. Would her own reassignment be seen as a loss? Would her failure to hold the post of priestess in Trimera push back victory even farther? "So, what do you want from me other than to sit here and be a living statue?"

He rubbed his forehead in resignation. "I just want you to understand why we act as we do. It is not just that you are you, it is the knowledge of how much pain we went through the first time when Lana was no more to us than the embodiment of an office. The thought of losing another priestess is more than I can bear, and that doesn't factor in it being you."

She held out her hand and smiled as he took it. "Do you think I would survive losing you either?"

He laughed. "*You* would survive. You wouldn't let anything take you down as long as there were people depending on you, and there always will be."

"Which is the same reason you will be able to go on if something happens to me," she said.

He shook his head. "It won't happen."

Her lips curled devilishly. "Have you grown so pathetic that you can't survive without your baby sister?"

Janu rolled his eyes and waved. "I was more worried about Mian really—he holds you in pretty high esteem, you know."

She chuckled. "I'm sure."

He smiled at his shoes. "Do I get to keep being a little overprotective as long as I don't interfere with your duties too much?"

She pulled her fingers from his and sat back in the cushioned chair. "As long as I keep the right to ignore you when it suits my purposes to do so." Her eyes sparkled as she stared up at him. "Now, am I going to have to ask Narita, or are you going to tell me what is going on?"

His own smile was warm and open. “Pri, Narita has stepped up so much since her father has left. She of anyone, save Mian, has held this kingdom together despite any stupidity I might have enacted.”

Pria drew her arms across her chest. “Are you trying to sell Narita to me, or are you just defacing yourself?”

“You are not going to make this easy on me, are you?”

Batting her eyelashes, she sat forward and dropped her chin on her hands. “Why, whatever do you mean, dear brother?”

He laughed and ran a hand back through his hair. “I miss you being insecure and clueless.”

“I was never clueless.”

Janu dropped his head and smiled. “Pri, I would like to ask Narita to be my wife, if and when we can ever settle this kingdom to something less than complete anarchy and chaos.”

She smiled as a warm wash of joy rushed through her body. “That is fantastic, Janu! But why wait? With so much going on around you, it would be a wonderful distraction. A gift to your men and yourself for all of your diligence and hard work.”

“It wouldn’t seem frivolous?”

“It would be a beautiful celebration of life among the daily struggle of death,” she said.

He laughed as he shook his head. “You always surprise me. I try to anticipate your stricture to practicality and I still miss.”

“It is very practical! People need to be reminded why they are fighting!”

“But to pull so many resources just for a wedding?” he asked.

“Janu, honestly, are you going to argue this with me all night?”

He put his hands out in front of him. “No, no, I can tell when I am beaten. Has your torment of these two borne any fruits?”

“We have a few leads.”

Janu cooled his excitement and returned to a regal calm. “What can we expect out of this…person?”

She shrugged. “Hard to tell really, but it should be impressive.”

“Why don’t you take a break for the night, let my men get to their beds?”

She waved absently. “I’m not holding them.”

He knelt before her. “You can’t do everything tonight.”

“I will be fine missing one night of sleep.”

He pulled the book from her lap. “I’m calling in a brotherly override here.”

The exasperation rushed from her lips in a sigh. “And just how many of these do you expect to get?”

“A fair few.”

She raised her hands. “Fine! Take your men! I’ll go find my nice soft bed and sleep like some common princess.”

Janu smiled as he came to his feet, fists on his hips. “Be sure you do. You *do* realize that Narita will be looking to you to help her with this wedding, don’t you?”

“Are you worried I won’t be able to keep up? That sounds close to criticism.” She leaned over and jerked Mian’s arm. “Wake up, deviant! Your prince wishes you to get your rest.”

Mian launched to his feet, the forgotten ledger crashing to the floor. “What happened?”

“Ever vigilant,” Pria said, her voice light with laughter.

Jeran started at Mian’s yell. “Swords to the front!”

Pria cocked an eyebrow at Janu. "I feel so safe with these two on duty."

Janu helped her to her feet as Mian and Jeran shook the sleep from their minds. "They really are good soldiers when you haven't turned them to mush."

"If you say so." She turned back toward them. "Get some sleep, gentlemen."

Jeran rubbed his eyes as Janu and Pria glided off through the room. "Did I mention how much I don't like you?"

Mian rolled his head back on the chair behind him. "I wouldn't have volunteered you if it wasn't important."

"You could have gotten further without me."

"Three sets of eyes read faster than two," Mian said.

Jeran's grin was evil. "I didn't mean the ledgers."

"That isn't funny." Mian glared at him. "I could find dozens of girls to fall for before Pria."

"Maybe, but she is very beautiful. You knew her before she left, didn't you?"

Mian lifted a ledger from the floor, his hands sliding across the cover. His eyes became distant as he remembered the girl he knew, the girl who would follow his lead wherever they went. He remembered the girl who always had a smile to meet his. "Knew her back when she was human."

"She's still human."

"Glad you think so," he said standing. "Come on, she won't give us long to sleep in. We better take advantage of it while we can."

The night around him was alive with crickets and night birds. Raber had spent the hours since dusk staring up at the sky. The smattering of stars visible through the low clouds had been enough to keep his churning mind awake. Their gentle twinkling pulled the memory of *her* out of his subconscious. The perfection had waltzed into his life atop her gray steed. Of course, Commander Mian had snapped at him; even he could feel the importance of what had happened.

His father had always said it was like a lightning bolt, meeting "the one." Raber had always thought the man a foolish romantic, until now. Those eyes, that angelic face, the second she had ridden among the soldiers…it was like a physical blow. Of course he would have to be cautious; women of great power always required caution.

To his left a twig snapped, signaling the position of the current watchman. Raber poured his energy into his position as a soldier. If one was going to do a thing, one should do it well. His father was always saying that. Raber struggled for years under his father's shadow, straining for the light. There was no point; he would never escape. Even becoming a soldier had been his father's idea. Never know what you were capable of until you put yourself out there.

So here he was, out there. He went from under one thumb to another. Nothing changed, but if he could manage to catch the attention of a high priestess…neither his father or even the prince himself would be able to short guess him ever again.

THE SCENT OF MAGIC

The forest around him was silent and still as the man who called himself Neram clung to the branches. Below him hovered nearly a thousand of his thrall, each staring up at him in abject adoration. Before him was a field empty but for a small group of armored men far off toward the north. Small, but teasing. They were bait, a decoy, trying to pull out any hunting parties that might be lurking. The larger group would be along soon with whomever they were trying to hide, and he could wait.

He could still remember the residue of magic in the forests around Austeria. Not since he had captured the last priestess had he tasted magic in this kingdom and the flavor lingered on his tongue. He would need to be more careful with a new priestess around—no more flaunting the ignorance of the men surrounding him.

The small group was beyond his sight now, horses mingling with the far-off trees. There would be a group following them, larger and containing whomever they were trying to protect. He wet his lips and sniffed the air that was blowing steadily from the south. Could this coming patrol contain that tantalizing magical being he had scented so recently? He could only hope.

He heard the whining below him as the grinlo listened to the approaching horses. They wanted the release of tearing bodies apart but the patrol wasn't close enough yet. They would enjoy themselves soon enough, but for now they would have to wait.

Mian pulled his horse around as Narita trotted up to his side. Her mount's graceful neck curved as she adjusted her reins, her heavy braid swaying with the change in momentum. Their patrol trotted lazily across the open field skirting the nearby forest. Her face was tense as her eyes scanned the surroundings. "Something troubling you, my lady?"

She glared at him. "Don't call me that. Do you think it a bit frivolous to be traveling all the way to Kyneira just for fabric?"

Mian held up a finger. "For fabric, yes. But this is not for fabric."

Narita leaned back from him. "Oh, well enlighten me."

"This trip is for my prince's future wife's bridal garment," he said. "That is something worth a little time and effort."

She swatted him across the shoulder. "Pri is right—you *are* a fool!"

He rolled his eyes. "You know she loves me."

"The attachment is uncanny."

His brilliant smile sparked her laughter as he waved her off. "She's just holding to that frigid priestess persona. Doesn't want anyone to think she might be a real person or anything."

"You do seem to throw off her composure more than anyone else."

"Exactly, because she loves me," he said with his characteristic grin.

"You are going to get yourself hurt, and I am going to laugh at your pain." Mian eyed her hands, which were draped around her reins, and

Narita smiled. "Lovely, aren't they? Pria brought them back with her." She flashed the lace gloves.

"They are quite nice."

"She brought something for you too," she teased.

Mian's smirk tilted playfully. "Did she now?"

"She did."

"I bet it is expensive, to show how much she cares."

She rolled her eyes. "You are a complete lunatic."

"You know I'm right," he said.

"Pri has agreed to be my maid, you know. You two will look quite handsome together."

"I'll try to keep the blood to a minimum." He winked. "But I can make no promises for the high priestess."

She pressed a palm to her face. "What are we going to do with you two?"

"Don't look at me; I'm usually just an innocent bystander." His eyes snapped to the field around them as a horn blared.

Two soldiers rode up to him. "Grinlo, sir, from the north."

Narita's brow furrowed. "They didn't fall for the decoy party ahead of us?"

"Apparently not." Mian pulled his sword. "Looks like shopping is going to be delayed." He raised his voice high over the men riding around him. "Form up, we have incoming!"

Narita pulled her bow from her quiver, nocking an arrow as she scanned the trees around them. "So much for our pleasant ride."

Janu smiled as Pria picked through a pile of fabric swatches. They had spent the morning cooped up in this sitting room inspecting fabric. Well, she had. He wasn't quite sure why he was there, as his opinion was never asked before she rejected everything before her. The room was one of the smaller available and the fire blazing next to them kept it warm among the drapes and cushioned benches.

Pria shook her head as she looked up from the table. "No, no, these are not right."

"Pria, seriously, this is the seventh set of swatches you've rejected." He was starting to think that Pria had no actual goal in mind.

"They are not good enough. You should have gone with Narita."

He put up his hands. "I am not going all the way to Kyneira just for fabric, and I cannot believe you talked Narita into it!"

Pria waved her finger. "If she intends to marry the prince, she really needs to put in the effort."

"By going on a two-day trip to get cloth?"

"By putting forth the image of propriety," she said.

He put his arms across his chest as the much-abused servant carried the latest rejected batch from the room. "Are you really going to tell me that Narita isn't good enough for me?"

Pria blinked at him. "I would never do such a thing. I love Narita, possibly more than I love you. She is a bit less irritating." She turned her back on him as she left the table for the nearby fire.

He laughed. "So, she's perfect, then why does she need to go to such lengths to get material for a dress?"

She pivoted to face him. "Because she is marrying the most amazing brother a girl could ever have, and that is how it must be."

His eyes rolled up to the ceiling. "So now I'm amazing. A minute ago you loved Narita better than me and now I am the most amazing brother. You truly are fickle."

"This is where she is less irritating." She glided across the room.

"There's that mood change again." He pushed off from the wall and followed.

"Jayjay, it simply won't do. You must look perfect."

His face scrunched into a scowl as his irritation hitched higher. "Pri, I hate it when you call me Jayjay."

She froze and spun back to face him, her eyes agog with shock. "I didn't call you Jayjay."

He raised his eyebrow. "Yes, you did. Just now."

Her body deflated as her eyes dropped in contemplation. "Well that is strange. I'm sorry."

"Not so strange," he said. "You are my sister, as I recall. It is only natural that some old endearments slip out once in a while."

"Yes, but not here. Someone could have heard."

Janu threw his head back with a laugh. "Heard what? Heard that you actually care for your brother?"

"Janu, truly, as prince you should understand the intense pressure that I am under. I cannot allow anything to tarnish the image of my station."

He grabbed her arm as she glided past. "Pri, the people of Trimera are completely enamored of the high priestess and Pria. They have lived with the legend of your greatness for so long that your presence now is like a living dream. You could walk among them dressed as a fool spouting soldier ballads and it wouldn't scratch the awe they feel toward you. You are not a person to them—you are a brilliant vision of hope. Seeing you as a real person once in a while is not going to ruin that."

She sighed as she let him draw her into his arms. He felt her tension ease as she melted against his chest. "The Lorien didn't have any advice on how to deal with people who knew me as a child, on how to change how they see me. Janu, I can't afford to be seen as anything less than a priestess."

"I know this is hard on you; it's not easy on us, either. I know you hate us being so protective of you."

She remained still in his arms for a while until a whisper slipped out. "You think I'm weak. Why else would you not allow me to study the grinlo?"

He pushed her out to arm's length. "Pria, we do not protect you because we think you are weak. We protect you because we are afraid to live without you."

She blinked at him, her face unreadable. "Janu, you cannot protect me in this. No one can. I must put myself in harm's way."

"I know that. It doesn't mean that I have to like it," he said.

She turned to glide away again. "Now we really must find you something better, dear brother."

His head dropped as he followed behind her. "Of course, precious sister, of course."

Narita swiped at an arm that grabbed at her before she jumped back to Mian's side. Somehow they had been separated from the rest of the men, forced deeper into the trees. Thick trunks crowded around them and made it hard to see more than a few feet in any direction. Mian grabbed her wrist and dragged her around a tree. Her heart raced as she stared down at the tears in her coat. They were after *her* for some reason. Had Mian noticed yet? She was sure he had. The vice around her wrist was proof enough of that.

She could hear grinlo as they shuffled through the trees around them, getting closer.

Mian pressed himself against a tree as a group ambled past. "Which way is south?"

Narita glanced up at the sky. "My left."

He tightened his grip. "Are you ready?"

"No, but let's do this," she whispered.

He glanced into her eyes before he pushed off the bark and jerked her behind him. He darted through the trees, deftly avoiding the monsters.

She could just make out the edge of the forest—about to sigh in relief—when she felt something clamp down on her free arm. With a gasp she turned to stare at the lone grinlo who sniffed excitedly at her hand. Its gray skin was moist and clammy, coated with thick, bristling hairs. Humanoid, its face was twisted with long yellow fangs that jutted out below its jowls. Rudimentary armor covered its chest and a filthy cloak draped across its back.

She froze and held her breath. The creature was engrossed in her hand, making no move to slash at her with its razor-sharp claws, and she was afraid to draw its attention to the rest of her.

Mian faced her when she stopped and stared in shock. She mimed him to stillness with a flat palm. He leaned close to her. "Can you take the glove off?"

"I don't know." She pulled and nearly cried as the glove slipped from her fingers. The grinlo pressed the freed garment to its nose not even glancing up at them as they backed away.

When they were several feet from danger, she murmured, "That was strange."

Mian jerked the other glove from her hand and threw it on the ground behind them.

"Why did you do that?"

Anger had replaced the anxiety in his eyes. "They smell her, don't you realize? They smell Pria on the gloves. It's why they were after you."

They broke from the trees and rushed toward the soldiers that were still fighting off a smaller group. Most of the creatures seemed to be searching the forest for them—for Pria, to be precise. Mian cut down a grinlo and threw Narita ahead of him into the circle of soldiers. She stared down at her hands as he moved toward her.

"Pria—they were after Pria," she said.

He pulled her into his arms as her chest shook with sobs. "It's okay now."

"Mian, they know her scent! How can they know her scent?" Her voice inched close to hysteria as she stared at him.

He grabbed her face and gave her a quick shake. "Narita! Now is not the time to worry about that!" Her wide eyes focused on him as he faced the men around him. "Everyone mount, we are getting back to Austeria now!"

Narita stumbled as Mian pushed her toward her mount. She drew herself up into the saddle. She would be okay, she had seen worse. Her mind was tormented, but that was for later, when everyone was still alive.

It wasn't until her horse was at a full stride that she allowed herself a deep breath. Her eyes had yet to lose their haunted glaze by the time they had made the road, but she kept pace and watched the trees around her. The torrent would come, but for now she held.

The man who called himself Neram snatched the gloves from the monster as it cowered before him. "You lost her." He pressed the fabric to his face and inhaled. The intoxicating smell called to him, drew him like nothing else could. His tongue darted out to wet his lips as the blood rushed throughout his body, awakening long-forgotten senses. He opened his mouth, let the scent coat the back of his tongue. His irises shot wide as his face went slack.

"Wanted scent, brought scent."

His eyes snapped back to the sniveling creature. "Scent?" He held the gloves out toward the creature at his feet. "This was the only thing with the scent in that party?"

A clawed hand gestured toward the gloves in his fist. "Brought scent."

He stared at the gloves that lay so tantalizingly across his fingers as the thought took shape. "It was not her. It was not her, but she held these. Held them for a long time." A smile crept across his face. "You did well, pet."

He strolled away from the grinlo. They had done precisely what he had asked, but that was the problem with the grinlo—no imagination, no thought. They did as they were told, nothing more. They didn't have enough insight to go beyond that. He could give them the semblance of intelligence, but not any actual thought.

He would have her eventually, just like the last one. She would be his, might even come to him of her own choice. All he had to be was patient.

Wind blew in through the open casement and ruffled the light-colored hair of the young boy who leaned on the sill, staring off across the field beyond. The golden grass swayed in waves in the wind. Something dangling above trailed across his forehead and he swatted it away.

"Undano! Be careful!" A tall, full woman barreled toward him like a thunderstorm. "You will break the cualla!"

A cloud of flour and fresh herbs enveloped Undano as the woman reached over him and steadied the swaying decoration. It was his least favorite thing in the commune. Every house had one, hanging in the north-facing window.

His mother's arms pulled him back into her warm embrace. She gave the cualla a tap to send it spinning. It revolved and pulled his gaze away from the field beyond. The cualla was traditionally created from a turnip, carved and dried in the rictus of a death mask, but recently the materials were whatever the maker had on hand. Undano's was made of scrap fabric, beet-dyed sheep's wool, dried leaves, and some chicken bones. Together, they formed a rustic chime that rattled and danced in any breeze. Undano's oldest brother had carved this one. Undano did not like looking at it. When he was younger, the face had haunted his nightmares to the point that he refused to enter the room. Now, the cualla served to chill his blood.

Its traditional purpose, of course, was to ward off the grinlo. The tradition was more common in northern Trimera but had traveled south with refugees fleeing the horde. Now there wasn't a country home within Trimera without one. Farmers were nothing if not superstitious.

Undano shifted in his mother's embrace, trying to ease the itch of fingers down his spine. Just when he started toward comfort, the arms around his chest tightened down painfully. The world around him quaked and he cast around for a culprit for his mother's alarm.

Her lips brushed his ears. "Undy, hide."

His eyes shot wide as his mother stood and spun away from him. The silence of her movements heightened his anxiety as he ducked beneath the window and skittered across the floor on his hands and knees.

There was a loose board beneath the kitchen table. He had found it while playing hide and seek with his brother. The board squeaked as he angled it up and dropped beneath it. Cobwebs snagged at his skin and his head filled with the musk of the dirt beneath the house. The board snicked into place and the world dissolved into darkness.

Xiana crouched behind the door that led to the back pasture. She pressed her ear to the door. Beyond, she could hear the livestock: sheep, goats, a milk cow. They were calm, content in their grazing. But how could that be?

A butcher knife was cold in her hand. It was the best weapon in the house. If she could make it to the barn there were axes, shovels, a pitchfork—but the barn was past the livestock pen, through the open. The knife would have to do.

She needed to secure the door, to buy time for the men to return. She scanned the room for something to secure it. There was a heavy chest along the wall but she would never be able to move it by herself.

Outside, the livestock were agitated now; she could hear them jostling in the pens. She was running out of time.

She slipped to the window and inched her eyes over the sill. Beyond, all was quiet now. The animals were calm, still grazing—but hadn't she just heard them frantic not moments before? And what of the creatures that were advancing on her home? They must have circled around to the south side of the house.

She dropped back to the floor. They wouldn't catch her unawares.

Undano strained his ears to hear beyond the echo of his panicked breath in the small enclosure. Dust swirled around him with every step of his mother's feet. What was happening up there? What had she seen? The gnawing in his stomach told him it was near dark, but time was unchanging in the black nook. If it was near dark, his father and brother would soon be home and they would be safe. They just had to hold out. Just hold out.

His entire body convulsed as a door slammed and footsteps crossed the floor above, showering him with debris. His mouth went dry as a high, feminine scream erupted above him. His fists jammed to his mouth as the cries of his mother were subdued. Was she dead? Taken prisoner? His eyes burned but he stifled the cries. There was no way whatever was up there would find him. Once they were gone, he decided, he would find his father and rescue her. It was a good plan. He nodded to himself.

He cringed into a ball as his mother's scream tore at his ears. "No!"

His world flooded with light as the board creaked open and he was lifted into the blinding torchlight.

Narita's hands shook as Mian rushed through the halls. The walls flashed by. "Mian…"

"I know." His response was short and terse. He hadn't spoken to her since they had escaped the grinlo in the field.

"What are we going to do?"

He grabbed her by the forearms. “She won’t let us protect her.” He spun from her, continued down the hallway. “I don’t know, I really just don’t know.”

“When they took Lana—” she began but couldn’t finish. She didn’t want to draw the connection fully in her mind.

“You don’t want to know about that.” His voice was rough, hard. Nothing like Mian.

She couldn’t heed his warning, not where it concerned Pria. “Was it like that?”

He stopped and stared off into the distance. “It was similar. They were, I don’t know…more insistent.” With eyes closed, he drew a deep breath. “It was like once they had her, we were no longer important.”

Narita swallowed. “That’s why… That’s why you have so much trouble with her.”

He turned away from her. “Partly, yes.”

She touched his shoulder. “Mian…”

He waved the worry away. “It’s all right. Let’s just…find her.”

She took his hand and gave it a gentle squeeze. “Of course.”

He started off again, his strides so long she nearly ran to keep up. When he came to Pria’s room, he kicked the door open and rushed in. The blankets flew to the foot of the bed as she shot up in shock at the noise.

“Mian! Are you mad? What is going on?” Pria demanded.

His anger and fear were such a tangled mess that he couldn’t form a response. Narita stepped before him. “We were attacked.”

Pria shook the sleep from her eyes. “The grinlo did not fall for the decoy?”

Narita sat on the edge of Pria's bed, glancing at Mian, who crossed his arms. "They were waiting for us. For…something more. Pria, they were waiting for you."

Pria shook her head. "If they were waiting for me, they wouldn't have attacked. I wasn't there, remember?"

"No, you weren't," Narita said, "but your scent was. I was wearing the gloves you bought me. They singled me out immediately, had Mian and I completely alone in the forest. Only they weren't after me." She held up her bare hands. "They wanted the gloves. The gloves that you carried, the gloves that still held your scent."

Pria laid a hand on Narita's cheek. "I'm sorry, I didn't even think."

Mian lobbed a tray across the room. "You didn't even think? Is that all you have to say?"

She glared at him. "What do you want me to say? Do you want me to profess fear that they know my scent? Of course they do—magic is what they look for!"

Mian stared into her eyes, and the honesty there only served to fuel the rage that burned in his. "I don't believe this! Were you ever planning to tell us about your insight?"

Pria met his ire with cool determination. "There was and is nothing you can do about it besides worry. I am sorry not to have thought about the impact on Narita, but other than that I stand by my decision."

He raised his hands. "Of course you do! Little Pria, an army unto herself!"

Pria rubbed her forehead. "What would you have me do, Mian? Would you have me hide here in the castle? Watch my people die around me because I fear to face my duty?"

A quake started at his feet and rocketed up his body. "Don't you dare spout that nonsense at me! Not me! You could have told us this, but you deliberately hid it. Why?"

"I told you why," she said, her voice cooling.

"You only tell me what you want me to know!" His voice grew louder but he didn't rein it in.

"I tell you what you need to know."

He was boiling close to breaking now, his face displaying open rage. "I don't need to know that the horde knows you by scent?"

"No."

"Why not?" he growled.

"Because such knowledge would likely lead to you doing something foolish."

Wracked by laughter, he began a circuit of the room. "Oh, that is always so convenient for you, isn't it? Men are foolish so I don't have to tell them anything."

"I never said men are foolish."

He spun on her. "You imply it with your every breath!"

"Why are you yelling at me? I wasn't even there!"

The energy drained from his body and his voice dropped to a whisper. "I thought you would be better than this."

The change caught her off guard. "What does that even mean?"

He stopped before the dying fire, his eyes burning with emotion. "Lana kept secrets. From me, from Janu, from everyone. Things that might have helped save her life, things that might yet prove to be useful, but we'll never know of them because she never saw fit to tell us." He crossed the room and crawled up onto the bed, his hands out in supplication. "Is that something they teach you at the Lorien—to think that all men are stupid and should be kept in the dark?"

She blinked at him. "I do not think you are stupid, Mian."

"You sure act like it," he said.

She drew a deep breath as she slid one hand into his and the other into Narita's. "I'm sorry. I should have told you. It was a mistake. I knew it would worry you and there is nothing that you can do about it."

Mian scoffed. "Your every breath worries me."

She kicked him off the edge of the bed. "I concede your point. I will agree to be more open with what I know...*if* you agree to be reasonable with your reactions."

"Define reasonable," he said, still lying prone on the floor.

Pria's eyes narrowed. "You are not allowed to treat me like glass when I tell you something that might be of danger to me."

"Like this?"

"*Exactly* like this."

Mian's shoulders sagged. "So, there is nothing we can do about this?"

"Nothing save for defeating the horde." She shrugged.

His grin popped wide. "Now that is something I can do."

She waved him off. "Yes, go; defeat the grinlo with your wit and charm."

Narita smiled at Mian and nodded toward the hallway. She held her silence until he shut the door before turning her full gaze on Pria. "He is very frightened for you."

Pria threw her hands up. "Which is precisely why I didn't want to tell him. He is worried needlessly."

"It is not needlessly. You are in danger."

"I am in danger every day, and so is he," Pria said.

Narita nodded as she stared down at her hands. "You are going to be more open with them?"

"I will tell them my every dream, if I ever get to have any more."

She gave Pria's hand an affectionate pat. "You are going to be careful, right? I know you have a job to do but it stretches past defeating this person."

Pria stared at her. "I do not intend to throw my life away needlessly. If there is a safe way to do something, I will do it. Conversely, if it comes to my life or saving my people, I will not hesitate."

"I could ask no less of you, I suppose."

"Can I go back to sleep then, or are you going to take up Mian's rant?" Pria demanded.

Narita kissed her on the forehead. "You had better take care of yourself. I have grown very accustomed to your and Mian's fighting. I would miss the entertainment."

"You are a sick, twisted woman and I don't know why my brother likes you."

Narita smiled and dropped her head meekly. "Pri, do you think I could…"

Pria waved with a laugh. "Of course you can stay."

Orotid pulled the fargazer from his eye as he scanned the land below him. At his back sat four men, the closest young Raber. The boy wasn't bad, despite Mian's misgivings. He was easily distracted, but many his age were. Not all men his age had been handed the upbringing Mian had. Mian had been in his twenties when the battle for the Seat began in earnest. A young man had to grow up fast.

Raber, on the other hand, was from a small village south of Kyneira. The boy had barely seen a sword, let alone held one, before he had volunteered for the army. Naive he was, but also eager. Orotid had seen good soldiers come from worse men.

Orotid gathered his reins and turned his mount from the crest of the small rise. Rocks and clods of dirt broke free and raced his horse's hooves down the incline. He slipped the fargazer into his coat pocket as the soldiers formed up around him. Despite beginning the patrol with a skirmish, he hadn't seen hide nor hair of a grinlo since. Back in the days of Prince Inan's rule, he could remember entire campaigns going by without seeing a grinlo. They were there, to be sure, but they stuck to the shadows and rarely challenged any company of decent strength. But following the fall of the Seat, the grinlo were like the trees of the forest. One was hard-pressed to avoid them.

He glanced again at the empty landscape around him.

"Do you think it is a trap, sir?"

Orotid glanced back at Raber. The young man's eyes moved to Orotid's face when they found nothing of interest among the landscape around them. Orotid returned his attention to the rolling hills before him. "I'm not sure. Something is definitely wrong though."

Raber's face turned toward the sky. "You should never question the gift of peace." His bright blue eyes sparkled as they lowered to Orotid. "That's what my dad always said."

Orotid barked a laugh. "Quite the piece of wisdom, young man."

A chill wind gusted down across them from the north, snapping cloaks in its wake. Orotid shivered and hunkered down in his coat. If there were one wives' tale about a north wind, there were a dozen. Some said if you listened hard enough to a north wind, you could hear the dead. Even more said a north wind was an ill omen. His personal favorite was the one that said a north wind would sour milk and leave women barren. Whatever the portent, the wind brought with it a frigid edge sharp as a blade.

Orotid jerked as Raber again broke into his thoughts. "Very exciting, don't you think? A new high priestess."

"Had to send us one sooner or later. Can't go forever without a priestess."

"Did you know Lana? I never got the pleasure," Raber said.

Orotid sighed as he stretched in his saddle. "High Priestess Lana was quite the woman. Fearless wouldn't be an incorrect term to put on her."

"I wish I could have met her," Raber continued. He did like to talk. "That would have been something, meeting two high priestesses. Not many can say that."

"Not many outside Trimera," an older soldier said beneath his breath so Raber couldn't hear him.

The soldier was right, of course. Many in Trimera had the pleasure of meeting the high priestesses, but why burst the boy's bubble? He was just amusing himself, no harm in that.

The boy had a crush on their new high priestess, that much was obvious. And who could blame him? Were he a young man, Orotid was sure he'd find himself smitten. He allowed himself an indulgent smile at Raber's enthusiasm. He had no trouble whatsoever with his feelings, unlike some Orotid could mention.

Poor Mian. He'd never seen him so tangled up in his own emotions. Orotid wasn't deaf; he'd heard the ladies of the court talk about the commander. He was considered quite the catch, if elusive to the hunter. He had more important things on his mind than women and marriage. Romance and vying for ladies' attention was a young man's game, and Orotid was well past those years.

Raber had moved on from Lana now and was well into his speech about his plans for a stable. Orotid had heard the story enough times to have it memorized. He wished the boy luck; he had a talent for horseflesh. Maybe he'd make a go of it.

Mian drained the goblet in his fist as he stared into the roaring hearth. His mind had grown blessedly numb from the wine, but it was only a temporary solution. He had spent three days in a drunken stupor after Lana was taken, but when it faded the pain was even more acute.

Head back on the chair, he forced his eyes to stay open. Sleep brought horrible visions he would rather not experience again; the first bout had been horrible enough. He snatched up the bottle and filled the goblet again, draining it in one long draught.

He didn't twitch as his door flew open. "Mian!"

"What." His voice was heavy with wine but not yet slurred. He would have to drain the rest of the bottle.

Janu sighed. "I just received news that you had returned. Is everyone all right?"

He waved his arm. "More or less. We didn't lose anyone, if that is what you are asking. Today I was able to retain my entire patrol." He grabbed for the bottle but Janu moved it out of his reach.

"You mean yesterday," Janu said. "If you didn't lose anyone, what are you doing?"

Mian sat up with a sudden jerk. "They went after Narita. Like she was a juicy steak laid out for them. I was barely able to stay close to her. Do you want to know why?" Each word was punctuated with a wild wave of his arm.

Janu watched him impatiently. "If you have a reason, spit it out."

He held up his hands. "Her gloves. Her gloves that your dear sister carried back from the Lorien. A gift that made her a target."

Eyes pressed closed, Janu lowered his head. "They know her scent. Did you tell her?"

Mian pulled himself up from the chair, feeling the room spin around him. "She knew before I had any reason to utter it to her."

Janu's eyes tightened. "Ah, I see."

"Yes, you see. Janu, I won't do it. I won't watch them drag her away. I won't go through this again, not with Pria. Not. With. Pria." He punctuated each word with a sharp poke to Janu's chest.

Janu smashed the bottle of wine into the fireplace. "Come, my friend. We will find a better occupation for that mind of yours." Janu grabbed up Mian's hand, steadying him on his feet.

"My mind, dear prince, is already occupied with thoughts of chaining your sweet sister in the dungeon and never letting her out. I bet that would make her right angry!" Mian stumbled around the room, his mind still abuzz with nerves.

"I'm sure it would; tell me," Janu asked, "are you planning on trying this?"

Mian stared at him for a moment as he fought the fog of wine. "I think I will."

Janu laughed as Mian spun on his heel and snatched at the door for balance before staggering out into the hallway. "Yes, this should go quite well."

"Don't try to stop me!"

The prince stepped back to avoid Mian's arms as he flung them out wide. "Wouldn't dream of it. I'm quite looking forward to it myself." He followed Mian's jagged path down the hallway.

"Arrogant girl! Thinking she can keep something like this from me. How am I supposed to protect this kingdom if she keeps lying to me?"

"Lying is not precisely the same as omitting."

Mian waved a testy finger. "Don't defend her. You were as angry as I when we discovered Lana's deviances."

"I think you mean deviousness."

"Whatever," Mian said.

"Mian, neither Lana nor Pria hid anything from us to hurt us. You know that."

"But it did hurt us, didn't it? Lana's lies left us without a priestess for years, Pria's nearly lost us Narita. I won't stand for it, not one second longer!" He crashed into Pria's door.

"Yes, I can see this going very well indeed."

Mian extended his hand and tapped until his fingers found the latch. "Do not try to stop me."

"I doubt I will need to," he said.

He pushed the door open and staggered into the dark room. He tore at the sheets on the bed, tossing them about before dropping to the floor. "Where is she?"

Janu laughed. "She and Narita have been in the library for over an hour now. Would you like to go back to your room now or are you still of a mind to make a fool of yourself?"

"Now you're on her side?"

"Mian, you're upset and you are not thinking clearly. I daresay the gallon of wine you swallowed might have a bit to do with it," Janu said.

"I am not that drunk."

"Of course you're not. Go to bed and sleep it off. I will have Jeran take your duties for tomorrow."

"I do not intend to let this drop. I will remember when I'm sober," Mian said.

"I'm sure you will, but I am hoping you will be a bit more rational." Janu took his arm and led him from the room.

"I can't sleep," Mian said. "All I see is her being dragged off."

"I understand."

"No, you don't—you can't. I know you went through the loss of Lana as well, but you didn't see. You weren't there. Janu, I've dreamed of it every night since Pria's return. I can't get it out of my mind. I am not strong enough for this." Mian drew a deep breath. "I think it is time to seriously consider—"

"No."

"Janu…" Mian's eyes were wet with tears.

"I'm not replacing you. You are the best commander I have by far, and I will not settle for less."

"Jeran is a brilliant man," Mian said.

"But he isn't you."

Mian cringed. "I am damaged, Janu. You need someone more focused."

"You would really abandon me with all that is going on right now?"

"You'd have Jeran and Pria; you'd hardly be abandoned." Mian felt his stomach clench, his heart rend again. He and Lana had never seen eye to eye but they had eventually come to an agreement of sorts. In the end, he thought she might have even started to like him. He paused for a moment and his traitorous mind was in that field again, sword clashing as he fended off another attack. In his mind's eye, he turned to Lana but the face that greeted him was Pria, her eyes wide as she was jerked backward from her horse… He shook the ghosts from his head. "Janu, I can't survive that again."

"You won't have to."

"You can't promise that."

"Pria is a bit more sensible than Lana ever was. In some ways," Janu amended.

"Some ways. In others she's worse."

Janu turned him down another hall, laughing as Mian bounced off the corner. "She's always had her quirks, but she is reasonable, you know that."

"You call that reasonable? She's a stubborn, bullheaded, ill-tempered harpy," he spat.

"Anyone we know?"

Mian turned to face Pria and Narita as they came up behind them but tripped over his own feet and dropped to the floor.

Pria stared down at him in confusion. "What is wrong with him?"

Janu helped Mian back to his feet. "He's having some troublesome memories."

Mian shook himself free of Janu's arms. "There is nothing wrong with me!"

Pria blinked and he growled to watch the priestess take over her eyes. "Is this the example you set for your men, Commander?"

Mian leveled a finger at her. "I set a fine example for my men, Pria."

"You call this a fine example? And just how often do you allow yourself into this condition?"

He put up his hands and staggered to keep his balance. "Forgive me, perfect Priestess, if I do not live up to your standards! It is such a terrible crime to have allowed myself to become drunk *twice* in my entire career!"

Janu took his arm, then tightened his grip when Mian tried to shake him off. "Come on, Mian, let's get you to bed."

Narita pushed past Pria to grab Mian's other arm. "You will sleep for me, won't you?"

Mian gave up his struggling and allowed Narita and Janu to drag him into his room. Pria followed them, glancing around as they slid him beneath his blankets. After Janu tucked the blankets up around Mian's chin and stepped back, Pria moved in to kneel on the bed. Mian swatted her away as she tried to take hold of his face, but she moved his hands away and laid her fingertips on his cheeks. "Just sit still. You know I'm not going to hurt you."

"What are you doing?"

"I'm just going to ease the burden on your body some," she said. "You won't likely wake up feeling too sunny."

He closed his eyes. "Have anything for dreams?"

Behind her, Janu and Narita slid from the room. "Do your dreams bother you?"

"I'm not a drunk."

Pria brushed the hair from his forehead, her fingers tingling. "I never said you were."

"You are thinking it. You always think the worst of me."

She suppressed a twinge of hurt. "That is not true."

"Could have fooled me," he said.

A hollow opened in her chest. "Mian, why were you drinking?"

"Because I couldn't stop seeing her."

"Her?" She stroked his eyes closed with the tips of her thumbs. The muscles of his face relaxed and she held a hand to his cheek, her mind flooding with memories filled with him.

"Lana."

"Do you often see her?" she asked.

He took her hand in his and tucked it to his chest. The movement sent her heart racing. "Please don't be like her. You don't have to hide from us."

"You need to rest, Mian. I'll make sure you don't dream."

"Can you give me pleasant ones?" he asked.

She laughed. "I can allow you to rest without any."

"Will you stay?" His voice was small, almost frightened.

"Mian…" she warned.

"Just until I fall asleep? Please, Pria."

She squeezed his hand. "All right." A soft warmth built in her stomach, one all too familiar. There was no denying that Mian was part of her home, part of her family—she knew it every time she was near him. She pulled the warmth up from her depths, coaxed it along her arm, and out into her hand. She could use the calm he gave her to calm him.

The palm of her hand burned with an intense white light that suffused into his cheek. His breath slowed; the fervent dancing of his eyes settled beneath their lids. She smiled as his muscles relaxed. This at least she could give him.

"It's my fault isn't it? Why you are like this now?" she asked.

"You're the smart one, you tell me."

She laid her cheek on his chest. "Just rest, Mian. We'll talk when you wake up."

He coughed a laugh. "Don't you mean argue?"

"Shut up and go to sleep, you deviant."

His free arm rose to rest across her waist as she lay listening to him breathe. There had always been something comforting about Mian, even when he was driving her mad. The gentle tide of his chest was an impossible opponent as she lay in the silence of his room. Not even the brightness of daylight was enough to keep her eyes open, not while his warm breath pulled at her.

He was asleep now and all she had to do was slip from his side and get up. She glanced around the room and flexed her fingers as she tried to ease her hand from his but his grip tightened. With a sigh, she slid her free arm down and took his wrist gently, trying to slide his hand from her waist. His arm stayed fast.

"Even in sleep you are stubborn." She twisted but his grip only tightened further. "Fine. You win, again."

His lips curled as she relaxed against his chest. "Yes, yes I do."

She punched him in the ribs. "You are such a jerk! Let go of me!"

He sat up and pushed her back by her forearms. Despite the wine, his eyes were sharp. "Please don't leave us like Lana."

She sighed and leaned her forehead against his. Every sense heightened, focused. His hands were strong on her arm, his body warm against hers. Through the haze of wine she could smell his clean skin, the scent of home, the scent of her childhood. "Mian, I cannot promise that I won't die—I have little control over that. All I can do is promise to do my best."

"And no more secrets. Not from me, not from Janu."

"I'll promise no more secrets if you promise no more drinking," she said.

He dropped back to his pillow and propped his head on his arms. "The last time I got drunk was the day Lana was taken."

"Then why today?" she asked, her hand resting on his stomach, tense beneath her touch.

"Because I saw it unfolding again."

She rolled to her back beside him. "I know it has been difficult for you since I have returned." She turned her head to look at him, blue eyes searching depthless green.

He took her hand in his and pressed it back to his chest. "You have some large expectations to fill around here."

"I do. Finding a balance between who I am and what I am is not as easy as I had hoped."

"Just don't lose Pria to find the high priestess." His hand stretched out to trail along her cheek, leaving a spark like lightning across her face. "I like Pria better."

She rolled her eyes as he stretched contentedly. "Are you happy now? Can I leave?"

He shrugged. "What's holding you?"

She jabbed him in the ribs as anger rushed in. "You are unbelievable!"

"That's what they tell me."

Arms thrown into the air, she stormed from the room, growling as she caught sight of Narita and Janu waiting for her in the hall. "That fool deserves to be caned!"

"I do hope you weren't too harsh with him." Narita's voice was soft but her eyes were stone.

"Too many crimes would be involved in giving him what he deserves!"

Janu smiled as he fell in at her side. "He was always one for flair. He does have a point—we do need to address this new complication."

"There is nothing to address. All that can be done is to anticipate it."

"There is no way to mask your scent from them?" Janu asked.

"You are thinking too literal, Janu. It is not so much a scent, but more of a residue of magic. All I could really do is lessen it by ceasing any magic, but even that will not erase it. My body itself puts off enough for them to follow."

"And this is why you didn't tell us?" Janu said.

"Yes. Mian's response was not very encouraging, to say the least."

Narita dropped her head and watched her feet as she walked. "He was frightened, Pri. We were, both of us, almost captured. Lana really hurt him deeply. He saw it as his failure. He wouldn't talk to anyone for over a month."

Pria fought hard to rein in her frustration. It was none of their fault, any of it. Lana's loss, her own nerves at being scrutinized in her post, the possibility of being stripped of her role for being nothing more than herself. Not their fault, but they had to deal with it anyway. "That's part of the problem, you see. You cannot be so attached to me that my loss will jeopardize Trimera."

Janu slid an arm around her waist. "It's a bit late for that. And anyway, we have people like Jeran and Orotid who are capable and willing to step up should the need arise. When Mian needed time after we lost Lana, Jeran took his post. He could properly deal with Lana's death in his own way and return to us whole. You are the only person we can't offer respite to."

"We have a replacement prince as well?" she quipped.

"We do now."

She met his mocking grin with a glare. "That's not even funny."

"Wasn't meant to be." Janu clasped his hands behind his back. "I would like to suggest that you limit any travel outside the walls. There is no need to tempt too much."

"I have enough to keep me busy here for now. When I know more about who we are dealing with, I will decide on a safe way to draw them out."

Janu tried to hide his smile behind his hand. "I think that sounds like a good idea."

"Of course you do."

"Perhaps," Janu said, "we should implement a little more scrutiny at the gates. You can find a hundred names this spy has used, but that does not get us any closer to finding him."

She regarded him for a moment. "And what do you suggest?"

"Mian said you had eliminated patrols as easy access, as there was little chance a missing soldier wouldn't be missed. We could hold individuals and smaller groups entering and leaving Austeria until their identities can be verified. There are not that many travelers these days, so it should only be a slight imposition and well worth it for the increase in safety."

Pria could feel the warmth spreading across her face as she smiled up at Janu. "I think that a very fair idea." She spun on her heel. "He will be okay, won't he?"

Narita's grin was evil. "Would you like to go back and sit with him?"

"I'd sooner sit with a rabid cave monkey!"

Janu nodded. "It would likely be better behaved than Mian when he's drunk."

Pria smiled at him appreciatively before turning back down the hall. "I'd better get back to the library. I'd hate for Jeran to get frustrated and set something on fire." She glided away without looking back.

"They are always interesting together, aren't they?" Narita smiled at Janu.

"Yes, you can say interesting because you aren't as likely to get caught in the crossfire."

Narita stepped toward him and twerked his nose between her fingers. "Awe, poor Prince Janu! So mistreated! Should I draw you a warm bath and rub your feet to soothe your frazzled nerves?"

He slid an arm around her waist and pulled her to his side. "Actually, yeah, that sounds lovely!"

She swatted him on the shoulder. "You stop!" She slinked against him. "So now what am I to do for my bridal gown?"

"We can always have fabric sent here."

She tugged at her lower lip as her eyes walked the floor. "Perhaps, but they'd have to be sure to stay with the main roads. I'd hate to endanger anyone."

"I know. Perhaps Pria would rethink her stipulations, given what has happened."

"No, she's right, it must be special!"

He laughed. "Okay, we'll figure something out."

She slipped her fingers into his. "I'm glad we waited. It wouldn't be right without Pria here."

"No it wouldn't." He sighed. "I'm afraid you will have to wait a while for your bridal gift, though. Your future estates have a bit of a vermin problem."

"To say the least." She pulled him tighter to her side. "I've got the only present I need."

"This battered old carcass will have to do, I guess," he said.

Narita lowered her gaze. "What are you going to do, when she finds whoever is leading the horde?"

"Take up drinking with Mian, I suppose." He smiled at her tight glare. "I don't know, Narita. I'm trying very hard not to think about it."

She pulled from his arms. "I'm going to see if she needs any help."

He stared after her as she slipped down the hall.

Orotid scanned the herd of cattle grazing in the field. They were maybe twenty or thirty either cropping grass or chewing their cud in the sunrise. No shepherds tended them, no farmers stood guard, but neither did they scatter at the sight of the riders approaching. Several feral herds had been lost in previous raids never to be reclaimed, but they fled soldiers and farmers alike. These were not feral cattle, which begged the question of why they were untended.

The hair on the back of his neck rose to attention—something wasn't right. His men waited around him, patient and silent as they awaited orders. He pulled his map from its case and referenced the land around them. The last communal farm on the list rested just beyond the horizon. The locations for these communal farms hadn't been chosen at random. No farms in northern Trimera were ever truly indefensible, but these groups had all been gathered to the most defensible locations available. What that meant to Orotid was there was no safe approach that would keep them out of sight for anything that may be waiting at the farm.

Frustrated, he chose the tallest hillock around. Perhaps they could at least get their own eyes on what was going on. He left his men to gather up the cattle as he headed for the rise; no need to advertise their numbers. He left his horse at the base of the rise and continued afoot. The grass whispered against his breeches, brushing almost as high as his thighs. Near the crest, he ducked to keep his profile among the reeds. Crouched and alert, he had a partial view of the makeshift village.

The cluster of buildings below sat in silence. No occupants were visible in what had become the green. No chickens or dogs either. The guard wall around the buildings stood uninterrupted. The dirt was unscarred other than in the patch of garden.

With a glance at the sun, he settled down to watch the building. His eyes scanned for movement; his ears strained for sound. He watched birds flock among the buildings, alighting along the eaves, and in the grass. Satisfied that nothing untoward awaited them among the village, he returned to his men.

Glove tucked behind his belt, the man who called himself Neram melted into the crowds of Kyneira. He was safe here, so far from any of the skirmishes, free to wear his own face, free to go without disguise. Soldiers patrolled the streets around him, armor gleaming in the sunlight, but they were more for crowd control than protection. The citizens smiled and chatted, oblivious to any peril that might be going on outside the walls. He could catch snippets of gossip as he passed among them: talk of the prince's marriage, rumors and conjecture on the newly instated high priestess, quiet whispers about the horde.

Vendors called out to him from their stalls, tried to entice him with their wares. He ignored them. Feeling a slight brush, he shot an arm out just in time to catch a wrist. He snatched the lifted glove from the would-be thief's hand and shoved him away angrily. He stared at the lacy garment and fought the urge to press it to his nose and inhale the fantastic aroma in its tangled pattern.

"A lady friend, Master?"

He crushed the glove in his fist as he glared down at the skinny man beside him.

"We have the finest fabrics in Trimera. Rumor has it the prince's future wife herself is looking to buy from us for her wedding."

His eyes narrowed. "What do I care about princes and fabric?"

The merchant motioned the man toward his shop. "A fine lady who would appreciate a garment of that caliber knows the value in a fine fabric."

His face twisted into an unaccustomed smile. "She is a fine lady indeed. You say the prince's future wife wishes to buy from you? What of our new high priestess?"

"Don't get much heard about her. Very secretive they say, though as beautiful to behold as a sunset in spring."

"Would such fancy, fine fabric entreat one so secretive as she?" he asked.

The merchant smiled. "Only if the high priestess knows quality when she sees it!"

His smile crept wider across his face as he shook a large coin purse hanging at his side. "I'd like to see the best you have."

The guards at the gate buzzed with an almost hectic energy. Janu had been observing the registry since dawn, traveling from gate to gate, and each stop was met with the same frenzy. He had never visited the gate specifically to inspect registry before and each unit wanted to make a good impression.

He watched each arrival with suspicion. Each merchant, farmer, refugee, visitor…could this be the culprit behind the grinlo? There was no way for him to know, of course, not according to Pria, but that didn't stop him from looking. Or wondering. One merchant kept glancing over at him; was he nervous of being caught or just curious as to why the prince was overseeing the gates? A pretty noblewoman hesitated in answering the soldiers; was she thinking up a lie or tired from a long journey? A man could go mad with speculations.

He shook the suspicion from his mind as a guard handed him a neatly written sheaf of parchment. Name, occupation, origin, and duration of stay. He had delegated a group of soldiers to conduct a census to compare the gate lists to. He had already ordered all citizens to report prior to any travel.

He handed the parchment back to the soldier. This was only half his plan. The second half was not going to go over well but it was the only thing he could think of. He had already drafted the orders and delivered them as he made his rounds. The order was simple: No one was to leave without his written permission except on patrols. It was going to bury him in paperwork but it would increase oversight of traffic in and out of Austeria. With any luck it would nab them this spy.

The air was crisp as he stepped up into his saddle. The horse caught his nerves and danced sideways before he could pull him back under control. His guard formed up around him as he started back down the street.

Tara flared red as Pria floated into the room, a book cradled open in her arms. She dropped a deep curtsy as Pria glanced up and acknowledged her and Jeran. "Lieutenant Jeran, Lady Tara, I did not expect to see you here."

She dropped her eyes. "Forgive me, High Priestess, I was just bringing Jeran some snacks."

Jeran smiled at her warmly. "She is too good to me."

"Anything new since I left?" Pria brushed past them and trailed a finger along several open ledgers.

Jeran shot Tera an apologetic smile as he faced the high priestess. "A few more entries. I still don't see how cataloging each will help."

"It may not; we won't know until we do." Pria kept her eyes locked to the ledger, as if Tara was not even present.

Jeran's face tightened. "You do realize that is an annoying answer?"

"You do realize whom you are addressing?"

Tara flushed. "Priestess, forgive him! He means no disrespect. I'm afraid living among soldiers has made him forget his manners." She turned a harsh glare on Jeran but the fool man ignored her warning.

Pria laid her book on the table. "Commander Mian says you are to be married soon."

Tara's smile was brilliant as she beamed up at Jeran. "As soon as Prince Janu can spare him."

"That could be quite some time."

"I realize, but some things are worth waiting for," Tara said.

Pria pulled a ledger across the table. "Jeran, I could use some quiet to think."

Jeran's eyes searched her face as she looked up at him. "Of course, High Priestess. I will check in with you later." Pria waved them off as she returned her attention to the books around her. With a shake of his head he took Tara's arm and led her from the room. He pulled the door shut behind them, drawing Tara into his chest. "I'm sorry, Tara, the high priestess… She can be a bit distant."

She smiled as she pulled from his arms. "Why is it you men assume I will take offense to the high priestess?"

He raised an eyebrow, lengthening his stride to catch up to her. "I've been around her a bit and I must admit she can be hard to take. Sometimes she seems bright and funny, but just when you start to get comfortable with her, she snaps an impenetrable coldness around her."

She rolled her eyes. "Is that what you think she did?"

He waved an arm behind them. "Are you serious? She was coming close to acting like she cared about us and then she went all cold!"

Her smile was long-suffering. "Jeran dear, she didn't go cold. She didn't send us away because she was opening up to us. She gave you a break from a difficult task as a reward in a way that wouldn't make you feel guilty for taking it."

"What are you talking about?"

She took his hand in hers and patted it. "It's so cute when you get confused. She made the excuse that we were distracting her so that you could take a break because she knew you wouldn't ask for one yourself."

His brow twisted in confusion. "Is that what happened?"

She pulled him into a small garden and snaked her arms around one of his. "She is quite amazing, you know. She is truly the bravest person I've ever heard of."

"Must be a family trait." Jeran chuckled.

"You wouldn't understand, you've been sequestered up here for too long. If you knew half of the things she did while at the Lorien…"

He turned to kneel and pluck a yellow lily. "The last thing I want to do on the rare moment alone with my beautiful betrothed is talk about the high priestess."

She smiled as he tucked the flower behind her ear.

Orotid knelt by the road, trying to decipher the chaos of prints in the dirt. There was nothing he could point to that was concerning. The strangest thing was a mass of fresh tracks. It appeared that the entire population of the makeshift village had left at once. There was no single print he could find that would indicate a raid. He could pick out dogs, cattle, horses, men, but no elongated footprints or claw marks to indicate the presence of grinlo.

But if no grinlo had attacked the farms, why would everyone leave?

Still, that appeared to be exactly what had happened. Not a sign of life remained. His men had discovered tracks from chickens, but so far, no birds. They had, however, found furniture and personal items left as if awaiting the return of the owners. They found little in the way of food or clothes. It was as if the entire populace had packed for a trip with every intention of returning, but why?

"Orotid!"

The shout disrupted his inspection of the tracks and drew him to his feet. A younger soldier waved from a house at the edge of the buildings. He dusted his uniform and made his way toward the farmhouse.

"What is it, Leer?" he asked.

The soldier indicated the entrance. Orotid blinked at the young man as he stepped into the house. He had entered other houses in the group, and apart from a lack of supplies and clothes, nothing had been out of place. Beyond this threshold, however, were obvious signs of struggle. Behind the door, discarded on the floor, was a butcher knife. Chairs had been knocked aside and abandoned. Items were scattered haphazardly across the table.

The hairs on his neck snapped erect.

"There's more sir," Leer said from his shoulder. The other soldier pointed beneath the table.

Orotid knelt and felt a chill rush down his spine. Beneath the table, several boards had been pried away, revealing a small space barely large enough for a child.

"Bring me a messenger bird; we need to get word to Prince Janu."

Orotid stared at the disordered space around him, the only sign of anything untoward in the village.

Raber stepped up behind him and knelt beside the misplaced boards. "Looks like something happened here, but it's awfully localized to incite a full evacuation."

"My thoughts exactly," Orotid said. "Where would they have gone?"

Raber stood and stared off out the north-facing window. "If I were them, I would head for Kyneira."

Orotid shook his head. "Why Kyneira? There are no defensive walls and there would be no outposts to resupply on the journey."

Raber smiled at him over his shoulder. "Kyneira has no defensive walls because there have been no attacks on the city. Seems like that would be pretty tempting to someone seeking safety."

Orotid scratched his chin. Was he thinking too much like a soldier? Would frightened farmers seek peace over defenses? It was definitely something they needed to explore.

Raber tapped the cualla hanging in the window beside him, a superstitious charm many of the northern farmers had adopted. "I'm no expert in magic, but maybe the high priestess would be able to tell us more."

Orotid berated himself. The boy was right on both counts. He was too old and stubborn to think right.

"Let's go."

Out in the bright morning sun, he waited for his men to gather around him. "First off, Raber, you will return to Austeria and inform Prince Janu of what has happened. The rest of us will split up. Half will ride for Kyneira; the other half will continue to check the surrounding farms. If his was an attack, we need to know. This would be the furthest incursion the grinlo have chanced and we cannot ignore that possibility." He met each man's gaze. "We need to find these farmers, find what happened to them. Get moving."

Janu held up his hands to stifle the chorus of shouts and growls. "Enough!"

The roar of voices petered away into a silence. The small greeting room was packed inch to inch, breath to breath, with nobles, merchants, farmers, and traders, each more outraged than the last. Janu gave the silence a moment to settle before addressing the crowd.

"I am quite aware that requiring permission to leave the city walls puts a strain on everyone, not the least of whom myself. I did not set these strictures without reason."

"And what are those reasons?" a voice shouted from near the back of the crowd, well protected by anonymity.

"You cannot restrict commerce!" This from a noble near the front, outraged but not disrespectful.

Janu rubbed his temples. "It is for the safety of everyone, and anyone found trying to shirk the stricture will be tried for treason against the crown."

A wave of whispers rushed around the room. Again, Janu waited for the room to return to the rustle of silk, wool, leather, and linen. At his right shoulder stood a slim man who stood nearly a full head taller than the prince. Janu gestured to him with a wave. "Steward Lessel will take your names and details. If everyone can just be patient, we will try to work this out as quickly as possible."

Janu fled the backlash into a small office just off the meeting room. He would hide here, buffered while he let Lessel take the brunt of his people's aggression. It churned his stomach, but it was the only way it would work. He couldn't fend off aggravated citizens and effectively scrutinize each request. It was quite possible he couldn't scrutinize each request by himself even with Lessel fending off the petitioners, but what other choice did he have? What he needed was a council he could trust, but most of those he could trust implicitly were needed elsewhere. Was it worth the risk to bring in someone he wasn't sure about? He knew this intruder was using the names of nobles and others to enter Austeria, but what else was he capable of? Was he able to disguise his very appearance as well? If he could, was there anyone he could really trust?

Janu dropped into the desk chair and closed his eyes, forcing the questions back. There were only so many things he could deal with. Suspecting everyone within his own house was not going to help anything. Deal with what he could, which meant restricting traffic in and out of Austeria.

Lessel entered the office with a handful of parchments and a crash of voices before they were cut off by the closing door. "First batch, my lord," he said as he laid the stack of parchments on the desk before him. "I took the liberty of sorting the petitioners by importance of need. I assumed that would be what you wanted."

Janu felt a tension ease across his shoulders. "Thank you, Lessel."

The man gave a faint smile before melting back into the chaos of the adjoining room. Maybe he wasn't quite so alone in this as he thought.

Narita rubbed her temples as she sat back in her chair. Pria turned the page of the ledger in her lap. "Are you planning another trip to Kyneira?"

Narita stared at her incredulously. "You're joking, right?"

Pria glanced up from the book. "Why would I be joking?"

"Pri, I was nearly captured!"

"But you were not and you know what happened. I do not see the problem," Pria said with a shake of her head.

Narita coughed a laugh and dropped her head back on the chair. "I am not risking any more lives for fabric! We do not know how much contact it takes for them to scent on you. It doesn't seem worth it to me to risk the trip a second time."

"But you will still go on patrols."

"That's a little different," Narita said.

"Perhaps, but we cannot let ourselves be cut off from Kyneira."

"I will go on our next supply run," Narita ground out. "Will that appease you?"

"Don't feel obligated."

"Pria! What is this obsession you have with my wedding clothes?"

Pria searched her face for a moment before setting her book aside and leaning forward. "Narita, I have missed so much while I was away. It feels like a different world to me here. Everything I missed, everything that has passed, this…*this* I will have." She tapped her finger down on the table. "This is what I have to make up for all that I have missed."

Narita blinked as she fought tears. Pria jerked back and snapped the book open on her lap, refusing to meet her gaze. "I'll see if Mian can take another patrol, make sure that I don't have anything that has been near you with me," Narita said.

"That sounds good." Pria's voice was tight but she never looked up.

Narita sighed as the doors opened, admitting a conspiring Mian and Jeran. Pria dropped her book into her chair as she jumped to her feet and glided to the shelves at the opposite end of the room. Mian nodded in her direction. "What, she's going to ignore me outright now?"

Narita shoved her ledger into his chest as she came to her feet. "You know, Mian, not everything is about you."

Mian spread his hands as he and Jeran watched Narita rush from the room. Jeran smiled. “Two for two, pal.”

Mian glanced toward Pria, who continued to scrutinize the tomes before her. “Not my best day.”

Jeran shifted closer and dropped his head, covering his mouth. “Mian…” He trailed off.

“Yeah?”

“Is she really as cold as she seems?”

Mian tucked his thumbs behind his belt and watched Pria as she ignored them. “Pria is anything but cold.”

Jeran followed him to the chairs, keeping a close eye to the woman across the room. “She dismissed me like I was bothering her. Tara is convinced that she sent us off as some reward so that we could spend time together.”

Mian pulled a book open. “What were you talking about, before she dismissed you?”

His brow furrowed. “Tara was talking about how busy I am.”

Mian’s eyes slid to Jeran.

“Is that some secret woman thing? How is a man supposed to decipher that?”

“She seems to think that in order to be a good priestess she has to appear…” Mian waved his hand as he searched for a word.

“Emotionless?”

He tipped his head and hand together. “Distant.”

Jeran shook his head. “Is she worth the effort to decipher all this insanity?”

Mian's smile brightened as Pria glided back toward them. "Definitely."

She didn't look up from her new volume. "Definitely what?"

"Definitely time for you to have a break."

Her eyes jerked to his. "I just had a break."

"How is your dress for Janu's wedding coming along?"

She waved a finger at him. "I will not be in a dress; I am the high priestess."

"Then you'll be wearing your silks?"

"I have several fine formals on the way here," she said.

"Seems a shame."

Pria's eyebrow rose and he threw his hands up in surrender.

"Not that your robes aren't," he amended. Her jaw tightened as his eyes ran the length of her body. "But a dress would be a bit more fitting, don't you think?"

Jeran nodded in agreement. "It is more traditional."

Mian sat forward, framing her with his hands. "I think a soft blue would go fantastic with her eyes."

Jeran tapped the arm of his chair. "And match your suit."

Mian waggled a finger between them. "We are on the same page, sir."

"Are *we* done with this foolishness?" Pria dropped the book to the table. "There is still a spy to find."

Mian sighed. "Come on, Pria! It has been a rough couple of days here. Let's take the day and shop. We don't even have to buy anything, just walk around with me?"

Her arms drew up to cross her chest. "Mian, I need to finish this."

"Not today. Besides, Janu said you agreed to let him increase scrutiny of travelers at the gates."

"Mian," she growled.

His lips curled evilly as he rose to his feet and snatched her hand in his. "Today you need to relax, with me."

She rolled her eyes. "There is no day I need to relax with you."

"Jeran, fetch us some horses. We are going to the merchant district!"

"No Jeran!" She pulled away. "I am not going shopping when there is so much work to be done."

Mian kept his grip on hers and headed toward the door, the high priestess in tow. "The day is shot anyway. Can you really focus on ledgers after almost losing Narita and myself?"

"That argument isn't going to work with me."

Mian turned and tucked her fingers into his elbow. "You don't think so? Seems to me that if it wasn't going to work you wouldn't be out in the hallway now."

She glared up at him. "You are a jerk, you realize."

He shrugged. "One day that name might start to offend me."

She straightened her neck and lifted her chin high. "I doubt that. You seem to cultivate it." Her eyes darted to his face, her lips curling. "It is very exciting, isn't it?" She tightened her grip on his arm as she leaned toward him. "Do you really think I should wear a dress?"

"Do you really think you should attend your brother's wedding as the high priestess?"

She glanced up at him through her eyelashes. "You know I hate it when you're right."

"That's what makes it so very fun."

She stretched into an easy glide next to him. Beyond the doors, the courtyard opened into a wide expanse of stone with a short wall surrounding it. In the center was a garden filled with bright flowers in the spring and summer, although now it lay dormant waiting for the sun to return. Guards swarmed around them as her soft slippered feet crunched on the stone walkway. "I wouldn't expect you to know much of fabric shopping," she said as Mian led her from the grounds into the city proper, guards a constant haze around them. The courtyard fell away, replaced by shops and alleys; carts and stalls dotted the streets.

He stroked her fingers absently as he glanced at the buildings in the near distance. "You would expect correctly."

"How, then, do you expect to locate me such a fabric that will be befitting the sister of your much beloved prince?"

"Well…" His eyes narrowed as he scanned the streets.

"If it is fabric you are seeking, my lady, you will find none better."

Pria turned as the guards around them parted to reveal a stall in a narrow alley. Behind the stall stood a tall slim man in dark clothes, a steady smile on his face. Mian eyed him suspiciously as Pria glided toward the stall and her eyes searched the cloth displayed there. "They are very fine, to be sure."

"Newly arrived from Kyneira, my lady." He beckoned her closer. "Come and let Neram take care of you."

She turned back. "Mian, come look!"

Mian kept an eye to the merchant as he moved to Pria's side. The man put his hand out. "He is right to hesitate, your man is." He bent and pulled a bolt from beneath his stall, still wrapped in brown parchment. His long fingers spread across the package. "This, this I have saved for that special patron." He flattened out the wrapping to reveal a sleek, brilliant purple silk that shimmered in the evening light. "If I may be so bold as to say it, the color would pick up your fine eyes nicely."

She slid the fabric from his fingers, her hand brushing against his. "This is fantastic." Mian felt a darkness twinge inside him as the merchant brought his hand toward his face before noticing Mian's scrutiny.

The man smiled. "The lady knows her fabric."

"We'll take it."

Mian ran a corner between his fingers. "You haven't even looked around yet. How do you know that this is what you want?"

The merchant smiled, bright blue eyes never leaving Pria. "I assure you there are none finer to be had."

"Mian, this is Lorienian silk! Handcrafted by the monks of the Lightbringers. There is nothing else!"

He tried to return her excitement but couldn't shake the twisting in his stomach. Something about the man was off. "And just how much does one charge for so fine a cloth?"

"Sixteen gold. Special price, for the lady."

"We'll take it," she said, her voice rushed.

Mian held out his hand. "Wait, sixteen gold?"

Pria was already fishing among her silks for her purse. "Mian, even in the Lorien this cloth is nearly thirty gold."

"For fabric?"

She leveled a flat glare at him. "Commander, *you* were the one who wanted fabric. Now this is what Narita will have for her gown. No arguing."

The merchant's face jumped, his smile losing a shade. "The Lady Narita?"

"So you intend to buy more cloth after this woven masterpiece?" Mian asked.

She waved him off. "Do be quiet, Mian!"

The merchant began to fidget with the fabric in front of him, eyes darting. "Perhaps I have something that would please the lady for herself? Truly you will find none better."

"Or more expensive."

"Hush, Mian," Pria hissed.

The merchant dug through his swatches. "This golden hue, yes? To pull the highlights from your hair?"

"I'm not so sure about that. I don't want to pull attention from Narita."

He draped it up her arm and let it fall across her shoulder. His fingers brushed along Pria's arm, tracing down to her wrist as she stared down at the fabric swatch. The hair on the back of Mian's neck jerked erect as he watched the man's intense stare. Mian grabbed his wrist roughly. "That's close enough."

The man dropped his eyes but not before Mian caught a flare of emotion. Could it have been rage? More likely jealousy. "Forgive me sir, I meant no offense."

"It is a lovely color." Pria's voice was soft and distant.

"Lovely color for a lovely lady." The man's voice left an oily feel across his skin.

Her eyes snapped back. "We'll take it."

"Now wait a minute…you just said—"

"I want this." She indicated the fabric with a nod.

"You don't even know how much he wants for it, and considering what you paid…"

The merchant jumped in. "I will throw it in, free of charge, if the lady would permit a humble merchant to kiss her hand."

Mian tightened and pulled Pria to his side. "That is enough! Now, I'll hold my tongue if you want to sell a palace to buy cloth, but I'm not about to stand by while this man paws at my high priestess!"

"It's hardly pawing," Pria said, "but I must insist on paying, sir."

The merchant's eyes grew wide as he backed away and dropped to his knees. "Forgive me, my lady! I knew not whom I was addressing!"

Mian eyed him as he folded the golden cloth. "And just how much for both, merchant?" He didn't bother to hide his hostility and ignored Pria's angry glare.

"For the honor of having my cloth grace my beautiful priestess, I will give both for the sixteen gold."

Mian shoved the cloth at the nearest guard and pulled his purse from behind his belt. "Sixteen gold, to keep my priestess happy." He dropped the gold on the table and locked an arm tight around Pria as he drew her away.

"The nerve of that man! Asking a kiss for fabric! From the high priestess, no less!" Mian growled.

"It was only my hand, Commander, and I can refuse for myself."

Mian glared over his shoulder. "Your *hand*! He had more than your hand in mind."

"Not everyone is as much of a deviant as you are."

He sighed in resignation as she slipped his hand from her ribs and tucked her fingers into the crook of his elbow. Hand laid over hers, he forced his breath to slow. Nothing too terrible had happened—what was he so upset about? Pria glided along at his side, the perfect image of a high priestess. The crowded streets parted before them to stare in awe at the living legend among them. Whispers scattered out from the circle around them, fingers pointing toward them, toward *one* of them. Children rushed forward through the crowd of legs, eager to be able to say they had laid eyes on the high priestess. How could Pria not see the reaction she caused?

"So…we have fabric. Ah…"

"Seamstresses. Experienced ones," she said.

"Seamstresses. Right."

She glared up at him. "Just follow and look like you know what you are doing."

"Like always."

Her voice was bright with laughter. "I hope you've gotten better at it."

"Where do you get these memories anyway? I'm not that hopeless!"

Her full laugh broke across the crowded street and drew the eyes of soldier and citizen alike. "What a selective memory you have, dear friend!"

He stared down at her, enjoying the mirth that sparkled in her eyes.

"Why are you looking at me like that?"

He smiled sheepishly as he shifted his eyes to the buildings around him, then raised her fingers to his lips and kissed them. "That's just the first time you've called me your friend since you've come back."

She waited for his gaze to return to her. "Mian, I hardly think it would need to be mentioned. If, after all these years and all that we've been through together, you do not understand how much you mean to me, then I do not know how to make you see it. You have always been there for us, and I will never forget that."

Mian blinked down at her as his lips spread into a smile. "Pria, that is the sweetest thing you've ever said to me."

She rolled her eyes. "Try not to let it go to your head."

"Don't try to take it back now. You *like* me."

For her response, she elbowed him in the ribs.

"Well, High Priestess, I have to admit that you inhabit a special place in my heart as well."

"Thank you, Mian."

"You are welcome, High Priestess." He bent down close to her ear. "Don't look now, but I think you were just acting like a person, not the high priestess."

"What do you mean *gone*?"

Janu stared at the young soldier that stood before him. He'd just shown up out of nowhere and demanded an audience with Janu. Now here they were.

"Gone, sir," Raber said. "They abandoned their livestock and most of their belongings."

Janu dropped back into his chair. Gone. It was madness. Where would they have gone? And why? "And there was no sign of grinlo attack?"

"No sir," Raber said. "Everything was well shored up and secured. In all, there was only a couple of things out of place in one house."

Janu rubbed a hand down his face. "Tell me about that."

Raber turned his attention to his boots. "It wasn't much. Not enough to warrant an evacuation. An overturned chair, some broken items." His eyes returned to Janu's face. "The really strange thing was there was a nook in the floor. The floorboards were pulled up, as if something was hiding in there."

"Hiding…" Janu whispered.

"Orotid split up the patrol. He took half to Kyneira; the other half was to see if they had moved on to one of the other communal farms."

Janu came up short. "You said you had already checked the other communes."

"Yes sir, but the tracks were fresh; there was no guarantee of overlap," Raber said.

Janu dropped his face into his hands, calmed his breathing. "What is going on?" He pulled a quick breath. "Kyneira?"

Raber's eyes widened. "Well…" He swallowed. "Seems logical, right? The city is close; there hasn't been any reported activity there." He paused. "There was also a thought that maybe, with magic, something else could be detected."

Fear crushed his chest. "No."

"But sir…"

Janu lurched to his feet. "I will not send another priestess into danger! I will not lose Pria!" Janu closed his eyes, pulled his anger back. That wasn't the prince's reaction. The prince needed to put his people first, and that meant utilizing every advantage he had, no matter how dangerous it may be. "Forgive me. You are right. Of course, you are right." He drew himself up and raised his voice. "Lessel! Find me my Battle Leader!"

Pria tugged at the straps for the armor she had been given as she stepped from the guardhouse of the courtyard she and Mian had been summoned to. It was Narita's and didn't fit as well as it could. She made a mental note to commission her own armor as soon as they got back from this next task, whatever it was.

A mass of soldiers awaited her, all neatly lined up and ready to ride out. She had yet to be told what was going on, just that she needed to be ready to leave once Janu arrived to address them. Mian and Narita waited at the head of the group, each with a horse at their side. Her own mount stood patiently beside Mian, one back leg cocked in tethered boredom. Mian passed her the reins as she joined them.

A commotion beyond the courtyard entrance announced the arrival of Janu and his entourage. Every muscle in her body tensed as he rounded the fence, Raber at his side.

Mian took a step closer to her. "What is he doing back here?"

Pria just shook her head as she tried to read Janu's expression. She remembered a time when it had been so easy for her, like second nature. Now it took effort. He avoided eye contact as he dismounted and approached.

"Prince Janu," Pria said, "what is going on?"

Janu glanced around at the men gathered around them. It was a large number of soldiers, mostly made up of Narita's command with a handful of other commanders' men. Janu pulled his shoulders back and propped his fists on his hips. "Orotid found one of the communal farms abandoned."

Pria glanced at Narita and Mian, but no other explanation seemed to be forthcoming. "Would someone like to fill me in on this little piece of information?"

Mian pressed his lips together. "When the Seat fell, many farmers collected their families and moved farther south or to one of the cities for protection. A handful chose to stay with their land. We managed to convince them to form communes for safety."

Narita took up when he stopped. "Our patrols incorporate a circuit of these farms to make sure they have what they need and to chronicle any incidents."

Pria turned back to Janu. "So one was attacked?"

Raber stepped out from behind Janu. "Not exactly, High Priestess," he said. "There was no sign of grinlo. It was more like they packed up and left."

"And how do we know that's not exactly what happened?"

"Each of these communal farmers had to sign a contract with the crown," said Janu. "Until we know exactly what happened, we must assume foul play." He drew a deep breath before continuing. "I would like you to lead these men and discover the fate of these farmers for me."

Pria cocked an eyebrow. "I thought you didn't want me leaving the estate? This hardly sounds like something you would need me for."

"Things change, Pria." Janu stared down at his boots. "It is where I would want my priestess. Maybe there is something there you can detect that our soldiers cannot. Also, it was pretty nice getting that message while you were out with Mian. With you there, if we do find something, I'll be able to communicate immediately with my men."

Pria leaned toward Narita. "These men only want me around when I am of use to them."

Narita laughed. "You should be used to it by now."

GONE WITHOUT A TRACE

Pria crouched atop the stone fence, watching as Janu's soldiers milled about the farm below her. Trees swayed in the gentle breeze at the horizon as lazy clouds slipped across the sky. Her ever-vigilant guards stood to either side of the fence, neither willing to risk any lapse in focus. She stood and walked along the fence; the thick soles of her boots gripped the rocks. Mian and Narita ghosted beside her.

"Would you like some flags to wave while you are up there?" Mian glanced up at her, eyes hard. "Draw a little more attention to yourself?"

Irritation bubbled up as she glanced down at him. "Is that your way of saying you would like me to come down?"

"Yes. Yes, it is."

With a fist to her chin, she knelt beside him. "It is scent they key on, Mian. Being hidden among soldiers will not mask that."

He held out his hand and helped her to the ground. "You do realize that in no way makes me feel better?"

Narita dropped to the ground beside her, arrow nocked and eyes searching. "He's right. You stand out up there to any creature thinking to attack us. From a distance, your scent could be anyone's."

She rolled her eyes as she made her way toward the old farmhouse. "I would like to point out that coming on this little venture was not my idea."

Fields rolled out around them, lined with stone fences and spotted with trees. A cluster of buildings were encircled with a mound of dirt topped with spikes. Crops swayed in the breeze, weeds poking up through the soil. To her right, a churned-up field screamed of livestock that no longer inhabited the space. Raber had told them that the cattle were roaming free just over the rise. An ominous forest covered the hills several rises off. Inside the house she glanced around at the few scattered belongings that remained. A plain rustic table with a smattering of plates stood toward one wall; a short bench sat under a small window. Faded curtains fluttered in the wind and a stained rug lay before a cold hearth. Beneath the table, several displaced boards revealed a hollow beneath the floor.

"This couldn't have been a raid. They packed clothes, food. Nothing is really broken. They were not forced from this house and none of the other homes show any sign of damage."

Janu crossed the room toward her. "If they had decided to leave, someone would have told us. They would have mentioned raids."

"But a messenger can easily be intercepted. We are within a day's ride to Kyneira. I'd say Raber had a good idea of checking on Kyneira. I'm sure Orotid will return with word that they are safe within the city."

"Then why leave? They were so fervent to stay here. Why leave now?" Janu asked.

Her smile was crooked as she strolled past him. "Things change, dear brother," she said, repeating his words back to him. "Perhaps they grew tired of the constant fighting. There are numerous reasons they could have left."

Janu rubbed his face. "Mian, I want these farmers found."

"Of course, sir. Orotid will have made it to Kyneira by now and the men he sent to the other communes should be returning soon. We will determine our next move once we get their reports."

Janu nodded. "Pria, I want a report the second you know anything."

Pria watched him for a moment just to be sure she had heard him correctly. "We will find them, I can promise you that."

Mian cleared his throat, choosing his next words with care. "Are you sure you wish to expose Pria for this? When we know the horde is after her and we have no reason to worry about these men yet?"

Janu's eyes screamed the fear he wouldn't voice. "It is where she is needed." He shook his head. "I need her knowledge. I cannot travel with you and still coordinate Trimera. This way Pria will be able to communicate with me with no lost time and no possibility of a fallen messenger, and I will be able to direct our men." He pulled in a breath.

She was sure he was trying to convince himself more so than Mian.

"I need her with the action, to be able to draw knowledge directly," he finished.

"Then that is where she will be," she said.

Pria turned as Jeran entered the room. "Jeran, we need to write a missive." She wandered off, Jeran in tow.

The creatures around him groveled as the man who called himself Neram watched the woman through his fargazer. He could pick her out even among the mass of soldiers in dusty traveling clothes. Glove pressed to his face, he inhaled its sweet lingering odor as she ticked off points to a tall young soldier who was following her around.

"Where are we headed, my sweet pet?" he murmured. He watched as two more soldiers joined her, both greeted with comfortable familiarity. The feel of her skin still played along his fingers and tingled his senses. He had rejoiced at that touch, at being so close without her realizing what he was. She was strong, so much stronger than the last. "Don't worry, I'm already waiting to welcome you."

Everything was working perfectly. All he had to do was be prepared.

He lowered the fargazer from his eyes and stared at his hand, remembering the sound of her voice as it had washed over him. Her presence was so powerful he could taste it on his tongue even now.

With a slight shake, he licked his fingers, his body alive with anticipation. She would be his.

It was only a matter of time.

Pria tightened the collar of her coat before she started off across the camp, nodding to salutes and bows from the men. "High Priestess."

She turned to see a young soldier smile down at her. "Raber?"

He gave a deep bow. "That is right, Highness." She jerked as he lifted her hand to his lips. "I am glad we have a moment to talk."

She ripped her hand from his, her face a blank mask. "Soldier, you will watch your manners around me."

His smile deepened. "Or course, Highness, I was just overwhelmed. I am not used to speaking with such a beautiful woman."

Her eyes went cold. "Soldier, I am your high priestess."

He rubbed his neck as he stepped closer to her. "That doesn't intimidate me. My family… You see, they have a bit of magic in their blood—oh, nothing compared to you of course."

She let the strength of her frosty attitude chill the air between them. "Of course."

"Dad, you see, he went to the Lorien for training too. Thought maybe I'd have the touch, but with Dad dropping out and all, he didn't figure it would be worth it." He ducked his head in the semblance of deference. "Not that you would know my dad, he's a fair bit older than you."

"Soldier…"

He took a step toward her and she felt her spine stiffen as he towered over her, much too close for propriety. "I'm just saying, if there are things you need to share that…others…may not understand, there are some you can confide in."

She sighed, turning her back on him. "Soldier, you need to see your commander on proper behavior concerning—"

"I understand. We will keep it quiet."

She straightened as she felt his breath brush her ear before he walked away. Rolling her eyes, she growled at the retreating man.

Narita jumped at Pria's angry glare. "What is wrong with you?"

"I think I will walk around with a large stick to keep from screaming at someone."

Narita laughed. "Funny, I didn't see Mian close to you just now."

"Strangely enough, it wasn't Mian this time." She crossed her arms stiffly. "Impertinent fool."

"That is strange," Narita mused.

"Let's not think about it. If I have to beat some sense into a few soldiers, I will just have to do it."

"Doesn't sound very priestess-like," Narita said.

"No, but it sounds very Pria-like."

Mian laughed as he crept up on them. "Then it sounds lovely to me. What are we talking about?"

Pria shot him an evil smile. "Teaching your soldiers some manners."

Mian laughed but it fell short. "You're not talking about me, right?"

She shook her head and shoved him away. "It's a given that you always need to be taught manners."

Mian straightened his hair with a rake of his fingers as he directed his gaze away from the women in front of him. They were camped at the farm; the soldiers were cooking dinner, and the air was filled with a slight haze. He caught Pria's gaze as she faced him. "Why is Janu so worried about these farmers? What makes their disappearance so worrisome?"

Mian sighed. He had wondered when she would get to questioning him—he had expected it the moment Janu had left with his guard. "The farmers that remained with their land were a stubborn, resilient lot. Nothing would make them see reason. It would have taken something rather drastic to change their minds. He's worried about something drastic enough to make them leave being so close to Austeria and Kyneira. He just wants to be sure there is no reason to worry."

Pria cocked an eyebrow. "Considering what the horde has taken over already, I'd say he has plenty of reason to be worried."

"Yes, but more than usual. It will not take us long to receive word from Kyneira, and it will make him feel better."

"He worries almost as much as you do; I think you are a bad influence."

He rolled his eyes. "Pria, which of these men are you intending to terrorize and why?"

Narita laughed. "I'm sure you'll be able to tell by the tears."

Pria raised her chin. "I do not need your protection, Commander."

"Who says I was going to protect you?" He jumped back as she swung an elbow at his stomach. "Your aim still needs some work, though."

"I'm sure you'll help me improve soon enough."

The man who called himself Neram smiled at his genius, for he was a truly brilliant man. Kyneira was the perfect play. He had been planning on moving toward Austeria next but the arrival of a high priestess changed everything. Austeria was well protected, nestled in the mountains behind her walls. With the added protection of a high priestess, it would have been impossible to route the city. He needed to pull her from the fortress, to make her fight where he chose.

He reveled in the noise around him, the carnage of people who had thought themselves safe. His minions swarmed the streets searching for stragglers, citizens who hadn't fled or died in the initial attack. He had already laid the groundwork, spread enough breadcrumbs.

The best part was she was already on the way, his prize. Everything was set.

From among his robes he pulled a sphere, perfect and delicate and glass. His body pulsed with magic at the center of such a large mass of grinlo, not to mention the creatures the grinlo controlled. The Lorien had vilified the creatures, made them out as grotesque, monstrous, but each one had its own beauty.

The sky above him darkened as he inhaled and pulled strength from the surrounding grinlo. Twilight fell over Kyneira as his hands floated over the surface of the sphere. Clouds materialized and churned within the glass, swirling in a raging torrent as tiny sparks of lightning flashed across the small globe. Within the glass, a glow built among the roiling haze. His palms sparked a bright brilliant white that pulsed into the sphere and erupted in a bright line toward the sky. The line of light shot straight above the buildings and towers then mushroomed out and expanded into a thin shell that draped in a dome over the entirety of Kyneira.

The line of white flashed out but the sphere maintained its mysterious lumination.

Nearby, a grinlo cradled a plain wooden box in its arms, unadorned, its only feature leather straps. With a wave of his hand the box snapped open to reveal a nest of wool-stuffed velvet. He nestled the sphere within it. The magical dome it had created would protect the city from all but a straightforward attack. The grinlo shuffled away to secure the generator.

He turned back to the destruction around him. A chorus of screams broke from the buildings around him; they had found another pocket of survivors. He paused to enjoy the terror and pain of the slaughter before sweeping back toward the trees. He had more work to do if he hoped to succeed in capturing and turning his high priestess. Together they would sweep Reia with his army of minions at their backs. His eyes sparkled with anticipation.

Narita flexed her hands in her gloves. The cold bit hard this morning.

She made her patrol around the camp, the men with her silent as they ghosted through the trees. The thick forest around them did little to cut the icy wind.

They had been waiting for two days with no sign of the half of Orotid's patrol that had been sent to check the rest of the communes. Mian was beginning to get antsy, but there was nothing for it. They would waste more time searching for them than waiting for them to return, so here they were.

The air rushed past Jeran's lips in a huff. "Raber said his patrol never saw a single grinlo. I can't even remember the last time I heard of a patrol going without at least one skirmish."

Narita felt her stomach twist. "I have heard that."

"Mian seems pretty concerned about it," Jeran said.

"I know exactly what he is thinking." Jeran raised an eyebrow at her. "They have something more exciting occupying their attention. They are after Pria."

"That would explain why it worries him."

She smiled at him. "Watch where you say that, they are living in denial."

"Glad I am not the only one who sees it," Jeran said.

"Dear, everyone sees it; you just don't mention it in front of someone with the power to have you executed."

"Commander, Lieutenant." They turned as Raber approached. "There is a rider approaching."

Narita threw her head back angrily. "Finally."

Jeran went to meet the coming scout and Narita moved to follow him but Raber grabbed her hand. "Commander, can I ask you a few questions?"

She eyed him. "What is worrying you, Raber?"

"Not worry so much, just interested."

She hesitated. "Interested in what?"

"You are close to the high priestess, yes?" he asked.

Narita drew a deep breath. "Close as you will find."

"How…how would a man…" He forced a laugh and dropped his head shyly.

Narita smiled, understanding. "Raber, you are a nice young man…"

"But."

She faced him. "The high priestess is not an ordinary woman. She is not likely to view any intentions on her heart kindly."

"You are saying she is difficult to entice," he said.

"No… Raber, your attentions are going to anger her. I'm not saying she will require work to catch her attention, I'm saying the only attention she will give you will be anger. I'm not saying this as a high-ranking officer of her high priestess—I am saying this as the childhood friend of Pria: She would not consider a relationship with you."

He stared at her and she was sure she could see white-hot rage in his eyes before his face blanked of emotion. "I realize I may not be a noble, but my family is far from poor. I will inherit a respectable estate—"

She held out a hand to halt his rant. "I'm not saying you are not good enough for her. You are a good man—any woman would be lucky to have your eyes on her—but Pria is not for you."

His forehead wrinkled in thought as his eyes conducted a feverish search of the ground. Her heart went out to him. "You are too nice for her, anyway. She takes a stubborn hand."

"You are kind to say so." He sighed and glanced around them. "I just…she's so beautiful and mysterious, and being high priestess…" He coughed a laugh as he tucked his chin, his sweet face flushing in a handsome tinge of color. "You must think I'm a fool."

Narita snaked an arm around his shoulders. He was truly a sweet boy. "I would never say that, Raber." She jerked as she thought she caught another flash of rage in his soft eyes, but that was foolish. The flash was gone just as quickly as it came and he was the same fresh-eyed youth again. All Pria's talk of spies had her jumping at shadows.

"I am a fool to think someone as amazing as the high priestess would ever be interested in someone like me." He kicked at the dirt with the toe of one shoe.

Narita waved him off, chiding herself again for the foolish flight of fancy. Really, thinking sweet Raber could be hiding a dark side! "She's boring once you get to know her, so save yourself the trouble. Find a girl who will enjoy your attention and leave Pria to her mysteries."

His eyes were hollow when he looked up from the ground. "Thank you, Commander."

Pria felt her stomach fall away. "Kyneira?"

The scout before her struggled to stand at attention against his fatigue. "Yes, High Priestess. We were lucky enough to run across some tracks on our way to check the city. When we looked for a vantage from which to observe the city safely, we saw grinlo wandering the streets."

Pria dropped to the chair behind her. She, along with the officers, had taken over the farmhouses. It had been three days with no sign of either patrol. She had started to worry that both had fallen to an ill fate, yet with the truth before her now she longed for the worries of ignorance. Jeran and Mian stood behind her, a wall of comfort and stability. She leaned on that thought now as her mind struggled to grasp the thought of Kyneira under attack.

Kyneira. This wasn't the heart of Trimera, this was south, well south, farther than any attack before. Whoever was controlling the horde was putting effort into showing his strength. This was a statement. Now, she only had to hope she was strong enough to match it.

"We need to send word to Janu immediately." Her mind jerked in a flurry of directions so fast that she couldn't focus on any one of them.

Narita ducked into the house, her bright expression falling at the sight of Pria's face. "What's going on?"

Pria waved to the scout, her mind still at war with itself working to determine what action to settle on first.

The scout stared from one woman to the other. "Commander, I came from Orotid's patrol to Kyneira. The city is under attack. We found tracks and discovered grinlo among the streets."

Pria's hands twitched as her thoughts circled on where to land. A hand landed on her shoulder, comforting, familiar. Pria centered herself on that contact. It could only be Mian. He would recognize the signs of anxiety in her body. She closed her eyes, calmed her breathing, let her thoughts slow. She needed to contact Janu and the Lorien. She moved to pull parchment from her travel supplies.

"Let's get the men prepared to move," Pria said. "Mian, select a crew to remain behind and collect the rest of Orotid's patrol."

"Yes, High Priestess." His hand vanished from her shoulder, leaving a chill on her skin. He slipped from the house and the other soldiers followed. She didn't need to worry about them; they were the best Trimera had to offer. She just had to live up to their trust.

Mian rubbed his temples as Jeran swept the forest around them, an arrow nocked to his bow. Pria had wasted no time in setting out for

Kyneira. Messages were sent to Austeria and the Silver City requesting men and sharing information, respectively.

Pria had scouts range ahead of the main party each day, searching for signs or pitfalls of any kind. Mian tried to be a part of them as often as was feasible. It felt good to be useful. Today he and Jeran were doing just that—not that anyone had found anything yet. Just stretches of land marred by nothing more than wildlife.

"We haven't seen a single person from that farm," Mian said. "This has to be connected to Kyneira, don't you think? Too coincidental otherwise."

Jeran glanced back at him before returning his eyes to the trees. "Not my place to say, sir."

"There has to be a connection. Something moved them from their homes. We've never had anyone even hint at leaving those farms before, and now one vanishes without so much as a word or a trace and at the same time this...*person* makes a play at Kyneira. That's too close for me."

"If it is connected, we are on the right path." His sweep froze. "I see something."

"What is it?"

They crept forward, ghosting around the trees as they closed on the dark shadow lying at the foot of a small rise. Jeran knelt next to the form and shifted it with the tip of his arrow. The mass was raw, shredded, a skinned carcass left to the flies. The ground around the body was stained dark with blood. "That look human to you?"

Mian's jaw tightened as the knot of worry in his gut dropped lower. "Unfortunately, yes. Any way to tell who it is?"

"No clothes." Jeran tapped something with the tip of his arrow. "Looks like a buckle." He slipped it from the mass of chewed flesh. "Looks like our issue."

Their heads snapped around as a branch cracked behind them. "Jeran, we need to move."

"We should bury him; he's one of our own," Jeran said.

Mian grabbed his shoulder and pulled him back from the body. "We'll come back with the full company. We can't dig a grave and watch our backs at the same time." He spun around at shuffling to his left.

"Mian…" Jeran started.

"I know. I want to be with her in case something *does* happen. At least we can die together."

Mian drew his sword, his eyes in a constant scan of the land around him as he rushed along behind Jeran. He turned at a noise behind him, instinct keeping him on his feet. Jeran put a hand out and stopped him with the pressure. "They're in front of us."

"And behind."

"How many?" Jeran asked.

"Enough."

"Close and fast? Our men can't be more than a few yards ahead."

"Let's hope all of Pri's training pays off. This is a bad place to stand." Jeran moved his hand as Mian drew a deep breath. "Let's do this."

Jeran started forward, his footfalls softened by the dead leaves that carpeted the forest floor. Mian followed and tried to keep his breathing quiet, his focus on the shuffling around them and keeping his eyes moving. A rattling growl paced him to his left but he couldn't see the creature that produced it. Jeran slipped around a trunk before crouching low to the ground. "Can you see any of them?"

"No," Mian whispered.

"Why can't we see them?" Jeran swept his bow along the small opening around him. "I'm sure the high priestess would know why we can't see them."

"We can ask her if we live to see her again." Mian raised his sword as he heard a twig snap to his left. "I'd really like to make that happen."

Jeran rose to his feet and rushed across the small clearing. "Shouldn't we be able to see the men by now?"

"Did we get turned around?" Mian asked.

"No. It's not possible." Jeran pressed his hand against the tree beside him. "This tree feels strange."

"Strange how?" Mian turned in a circle. "You think this could be a trick?"

Jeran stood up and lowered his bow as he stepped out into the clearing. "If it wasn't, would we still be hearing grinlo and not be under attack?"

"What do we do?"

Jeran shrugged. "How are we supposed to fight an enemy we cannot see?"

Pria opened her eyes as she wrinkled her forehead. "You can't smell that?"

Narita's glance was concerned. "All I smell is the mass of sweaty, tired men around us."

Pria drew a deep breath into her lungs. "No, I definitely smell—" She stopped suddenly. She wasn't about to admit to Narita that she smelled Mian. It was too ludicrous. "Something. I definitely smell something." She turned in a circle as her eyes searched the camp around her. The men were all settled down for the night, taking advantage of the last of the light. Mian and Jeran should have been back hours ago.

Her breath caught as she felt something brush her arm and the strong scent of Mian filled her senses again. "This isn't right." Hand out, she felt something jump away from her fingertips where there should have been only air.

Narita was on her feet in an instant. "What is going on?"

Pria knelt and spread her fingers over the mossy ground. It pulsed with magic. "I don't know. Someone is here."

Narita's voice was anxious. "Someone? Who?"

She stood; the tips of her fingers tingled. "Mian." She whispered it, soft like a prayer. She felt something brush across her palms.

"Pria, you're scaring me," Narita said. "What are you feeling?"

"Magic. Mian and Jeran are here—I can feel them—but something is keeping us from seeing them." She drew on the magic around her, draining the spell from the ground. Narita gasped as the air began to shimmer and shift. Deeper she pulled, eyes closed as her stomach tilted. "Mian!"

She felt something grab on to her outstretched hands and she closed her fists. Her eyes rolled open and she smiled to see Mian's washed-out image materialize before her. His face was shocked and confused as he solidified at the end of her arms. A smile slipped across his face. "Well, it's about time you found us."

Jeran stared around himself, wide-eyed as the camp began to gather. "Never saw Lana do that."

Pria dropped Mian's hands self-consciously as he stared down at her.

"Do you know what happened?" She cursed the flare of red that flushed her cheeks.

Jeran still held his bow ready as he kept a constant eye on the camp around him. "We found a body. I *think* we found a body. Was that real?"

"You're asking the wrong person there, brother." Mian moved over toward a campfire. "I'm not sure what we did see after leaving to scout. On our way back to find you we heard grinlo, but we never saw any. They hounded our every step, but never within sight. Then we were just wandering around this glen till I heard my name. Someone was calling me, softly. We just followed that here."

Pria cleared her throat. "You found a body?"

"Maybe," Mian said. "There is no way to tell until we go back. It could've all been an illusion."

Pria stared at him. "Why would someone bother to set this trap? We're already suspicious that our men are gone, so it wasn't to keep the body hidden. Why go through all this trouble just to keep you two from returning to us? Two men, even the two of you, aren't going to make much difference."

Mian held her gaze. "Maybe it was because I was one of your guards."

"Don't be ridiculous, Commander." Pria glanced at some soldiers as they passed close by. "Let's get you warmed up."

She took his arm and led him to her secluded fire. In a harsh whisper she said, "What are you thinking making a statement like that with so many ears around?"

He sank to the ground and spread his fingers to the glowing warmth. "You going to tell me you're not thinking the same thing?"

"Of course I'm thinking it! Removing you and Narita would be a logical first step in getting to me, but giving it voice is only going to cause panic."

Narita kept a close eye to the soldiers that still milled about. "You don't think it could just be a coincidence? A trap set to catch anyone who happened by?"

Jeran shook his head. "It would be too random; there would be no way to guarantee that anyone would stumble onto it."

"Even if it was to hide the body?" Narita prodded.

"If we even saw a body! If the forest around us was a mirage, the body could easily have been as well," Jeran said.

Narita cradled her head in her fingers. "For this person to have been after Mian, that means that they were not only watching us at the farm but also pacing us to here just to wait for the chance that he or I left the camp."

Pria met her eyes as they watched each other across the fire. "There is nothing we can do about any of that. What we do now is up the watch. I'll be sure to set up some barriers around our men. We'll have to keep the scouts with the main group until I can think of something to keep them safe in case this was not set up to catch Mian."

Mian sighed. "And what do we do about you?"

She closed her eyes. "I will have to be careful."

"You will have to remain glued to Narita and myself." His voice was gruff, almost angry.

"I will stay close to my guard dogs," Pria said.

Narita smiled. "I am not a dog."

"I'm a dog," Mian snapped. "I'm a very territorial dog. You had better not give me reason to act on it."

Pria rolled her eyes. "I would definitely hate to see that."

Jeran jumped to his feet. "I'll see that the guards are ready for anything that might arise."

Pria glanced back at him. "No one leaves the boundary of camp."

"Of course not, Priestess."

She shivered as she stared into the flames. "It was a bold move." She pulled her breath through her teeth. "How far away was this body?"

"Not far. If there really was a body, we'll see it before noon."

"The body could have been a lure. Something to get you close enough for the spell to ensnare you," said Pria.

"I thought of that."

She forced a laugh. "Of course you did, you're not a fool." She rubbed her face. "I'm sorry, Mian."

Mian grinned. "Sorry that you thought I was a fool or that you almost got me lost?"

"It is not funny, Mian. First Narita, now you. Who's next? Janu?" She threw her head back and jerked away as Narita patted her shoulder. "No. I cannot allow you to keep putting yourselves in danger for my sake. This has to stop."

Mian watched her, his face calm. "It will stop. As soon as we are able to defeat the person behind it."

"That is not good enough! From now on I go without guard. If the enemy wants me, I don't want the grinlo to have to kill anyone to get to me."

"That is never going to happen," Mian said. "We cannot afford to risk losing you."

"Well, we'll just kill you and Narita instead; I'm sure that will be much better."

Narita grabbed her hand. "Pria, just calm down. Mian is fine, Jeran is fine. No one got hurt and you found them. It is just one more thing we need to watch out for."

"How did you find your way back to camp? If the forest around you was an illusion, you would have no way to determine where you were."

Mian rolled his eyes. "Jeran has an incredible sense of direction, always has."

"Even without any landmarks to guide him?"

Mian tipped his head. "The Battle Leader's command gets the best, present company excluded."

Narita smiled evilly. "Better be."

Mian dropped his head and sat for a moment. "I could hear you." Pria's eyes shot to him. "When we were lost, we kept hearing things moving around us. We thought they were grinlo but we couldn't see anything. Then I heard you calling my name."

Pria felt the flare of a blush on her face. "The spell I used to draw you back…it only works with a strong connection, deep emotions. The spell was calling you to me."

He couldn't hold the smile that broke across his face. "Good to know you can always call me home." He sat forward. "This person definitely knows that he wants you. Pri, none of our lives are worth yours. There is no one here I will not risk for you. No matter what happens, you need to stay alive to stop this person, whoever they are, before he destroys all of Trimera."

She sighed. "You know I hate it when you're right."

"You must be miserable a lot." Her glare didn't even faze him as he smiled at her. "So how do we keep you safe?"

"I don't know."

Jeran dropped to the ground beside them. "We are as good as we are going to get." He glanced over at Pria. "So what do we do with you?"

"All we can do is go on with what needs to be done. Keep everyone together and get to Kyneira." She met Mian's eyes. "We'll all do what we must for the safety of our people."

He watched her from behind the wall of magic. She couldn't see him; the magic masked his presence from her. To see him she would have to cross the barrier, step into the trap…but she wouldn't do that. Not yet. Soon she would come to him. He just had to be patient.

The man who called himself Neram had been watching her for some time now while she studied his magic. He flattered himself to think she was impressed—with what he accomplished, with his ambition. And it was ambition. He would be the first man to not only take control of the grinlo but to use them to take over Reia, to topple the priestesses forever.

His hand brushed along the magical barrier tracing the line of her jaw, the soft curve of her neck, the supple line of her waist. She would help him do it. With her at his side there was no way he could lose.

His gaze drifted toward the soldier at her side. The man she had pulled from his trap. He was too close, too familiar and this angered the man who called himself Neram. This foolish boy thought himself close to the high priestess, but she wasn't for him. The man who called himself Neram would joy in watching the soldier's death. It would be slow, he'd make sure of it.

Pria walked along a barrier visible only to her eyes. She kept her arm out behind her to keep Mian and Narita out of the trapped area. "It is a wide area to set, would take a lot of power." She laid her palm along the wall of magic and let the resonance tingle along her skin. A chill crept along her spine, raising gooseflesh on her arms. Anything could be beyond that barrier and she would never know, unless she walked through it.

Mian's face twisted as he guided her back a step. "Lovely. I wasn't worried enough."

"It's okay, Mian, it will not pull me in. You have to walk into it."

"No need to take any chances though," he said.

Raber rushed to her side. "We kept to the ring like you said, High Priestess, but we couldn't see anything. The area is large enough that something could be beyond our sight."

Pria's eyes shifted toward the distant trees. "Yes, that is true."

Mian clamped his hand down on Pria's shoulder. "Well, guess we won't know."

Her gaze moved to his, her eyes wide with pain. "Mian, we can't just leave someone out there."

"*If* there is someone out there. We have no way to know if there is even a body there."

Pria dropped her head, let her hand trail along the barrier. "It wouldn't be worth risking lives to retrieve a body that may not be there."

His fingers massaged her shoulder. "No, it wouldn't."

"This trap is large and elaborate. Whoever did this could easily have done something similar on that farm to draw the men out. They could very well be caught in this trap or even a similar one elsewhere."

Mian nodded, keeping his smile as he glanced at the men behind him. "We can't take that time right now. We need to get to Kyneira. These farmers may be caught in this trap, but there are thousands in danger there. For all we know, those farmers may be there as well."

Pria felt a wash of anxiety crash over her. "Can we really abandon them if they are out here?"

"We have no idea if they are or not. If and when we find out they are out here, then we will worry about it." He turned her from the trap. "We will keep it in mind, but we can't stay out here exposed. Not with you."

She shook, feeling secure in Mian's comforting embrace. "So we head to Kyneira."

"We head to Kyneira."

KYNEIRA

Mian brushed his hair back from his face as Pria lowered the fargazer from her eye. Kyneira lay below them, its towering buildings and crosshatched streets empty of the normal bustle of citizens. In their place were throngs of grinlo patrolling in haphazard groups. A glimmering domed shield rose above the city, encasing it entirely. No birds crossed it, no wind-blown leaves passed through it.

"How many could be trapped?"

"Thousands." Mian moved closer and pitched his voice low to keep from being overheard. "There is likely a large number holed up inside the temple; it's the most defensible structure."

"That's a lot of distance between us and them."

"And a lot of grinlo." Narita leaned on her bow as she stared down at Kyneira's streets, which swarmed with monsters. "At least now we know why the farmers left. Probably were getting raided. Doesn't explain why they didn't send us word."

Pria handed Mian the fargazer. "Whoever did this would want us blind to it. There is a lot of distance to cover sending a messenger to Austeria, lots of places to lay a trap. Once they got here, they would have been too busy trying to keep the horde out of the city. With no wall, it would have been impossible."

Mian ran his hand down his face. "With that shield over the city, we won't be able to mount a proper offensive."

"We're not losing those people."

Narita brushed her hair behind her ear. "I don't see how we are going to get to them."

"If we can get the shield down," Pria said, "we should be able to sweep the streets."

Mian's eyebrow rose. "And just how do you propose to do that?"

Mian felt his nerves jump as Pria girded herself. "A shield this large couldn't be sustained by an individual—it would take too much focus, energy. There has to be a generator. I'll have to go in and disarm it."

"We won't be able to get even a small force past their guards." His hand dropped to his sword hilt, knuckles white with tension. Mian could see where she was going and he didn't like it.

Every muscle was tight as Pria faced him. She had to know this would be a test for him. Could he allow her to do her job in the face of obvious threat? Darkness knew he had to, but would he be capable? Her voice was gentle and soothing when she continued.

"No, but Narita and I should be able to slip past them unnoticed."

Jeran grabbed Mian's arm. "You are not honestly considering this?"

Mian studied her impassive face, the struggle clear on his own. "How would you find the generator?"

"Once we are inside, I should be able to sense it."

Mian nodded as he stared at his feet and warred with himself. His mind wandered to the innocents trapped inside the city below them: the families, women, children. He couldn't let them die, couldn't ignore that they had a chance to save them. "You know what the horde does with magic, how they hunt it."

Narita scanned the edge of town. "We'll need disguises, just enough to shelter us to casual eyes."

"There should be some dead grinlo from the fighting; we can use them. Will help mask our scent as well."

Jeran planted himself in their path as Pria and Narita started off. "There is no way you are going in there."

Each woman patted a cheek as they parted around him. Mian ran his eyes across the town below him. "Pria?" He waited for her to turn to face him. "Come back to me."

She held his gaze, her face unreadable. "Always."

Jeran rounded on him. "You're going to let them, aren't you?"

Mian stared after the women as they disappeared around a stand of trees. "What gives you the impression that it is in any way my choice?"

Pria knelt over the stinking pile and shifted it around with a stick. "Do you think the cloaks will be enough?"

Narita cupped a hand over her mouth. "I think it might be too much. What about our armor?"

"We'll keep it, just be sure it is covered and secured. We don't want any clinking giving us away." She freed a cloak and snapped the dirt loose. "Size might be a problem."

"We'll have to be sure to stay away from anything that will give away how small we are."

"I'll take that one," Jeran said.

Narita stared at Jeran as he took the cloak from her hands. "And what do you intend to do with that?"

"I'm going with you."

Pria stood and pulled another cloak free of the twisted bodies. "Fewer would be better, Jeran. We'll be fine on our own."

He swung the cloak about his shoulders and grimaced at the smell. "How much time did you spend in Kyneira before you left?" he asked. "Couldn't have been much. I was born here. I know every nook this city has; you're going to need me."

Pria held his gaze. "This won't be a battle, Jeran. We'll need to avoid attention. It won't be pretty and it won't be safe."

He shrugged himself deeper into the fabric. "I could say the same to you."

She nodded grimly. "Secure your armor. Be sure your sword is hidden."

He knelt and helped her search the bodies. "Mian is going to create a distraction on the north side of town. There is a large sewer that drains out of the west that should cover us quite nicely."

"You'll want to dull up your armor."

She put action to words and grabbed a handful of what she had to keep repeating to herself was mud. Jeran watched the two women and smeared a handful across his own breastplate.

Pria stood. "I think we are as good as we are going to get."

Narita nocked an arrow to her bow and crept along behind them as Pria shifted the short swords hanging at her hips. Narita shifted closer to Pria. "What about…your scent? What are we going to do about that?"

Pria glanced up at Jeran who looked forlornly down at the city below them. "We will just have to hope for the element of surprise. If they aren't expecting it, hopefully they won't notice it. Besides, the generator should be creating enough low-level magical residue to mask me as long as I keep my distance." She stepped forward. "Lead the way, Jeran."

Mian rested his hand on his sword hilt as he surveyed his men. He had caught sight of three shadows ghosting toward the city just a moment ago so he had very little time. With Jeran off, his second was Orotid, who rode toward him.

"Everyone is set sir."

"Good. Remember, no arrows until the shield is down. We will have to fight our way in and draw them until Pria gives us the signal."

Orotid nodded as he reined his horse around and moved into place. Mian jumped onto his own steed, sword drawn as his eyes searched the shadowed streets. He raised his sword high and waited for Orotid to mirror him before kicking his horse toward Kyneira.

Pria pressed her hand against Jeran's chest to hold him against the wall as they listened to the shuffling at the head of the alley. He hoped she couldn't feel how hard his heart was beating. Some protector he was, cowered behind a wall scared to death.

The shuffling moved on down the street and Pria's hand fell from his chest. Eyes closed, she drew a deep breath. "It is in that direction." She pointed to the left.

"How…" Jeran swallowed. "How far?"

"It's weak," she said. "I'd say at least four hundred yards."

"Okay." He drew a deep breath. "Follow me."

She fell in behind him and moved in a staggering amble that perfectly mimicked the horde. He tried to copy her but was sure he just looked drunk. Narita scanned the streets around them, her own sway more than convincing as they stepped out into the street. He tried to keep his shoulders slumped to hide his height and keep from showing how short the women with him were.

He could feel his nerves twist his stomach but, searching their faces, he couldn't find any sign of fear in the two women. They moved about their tasks, stoic, as he struggled to contain his own fear and anxiety.

Jeran drew his breath and concentrated on moving one foot at a time. One step he could do. One step was possible so long as he didn't let his mind wander to the impossibility that followed.

Pria moved up to his side and nudged him to keep them headed in the right direction. He turned down a narrow alley—and froze as Pria was jerked away from him.

He lunged forward, and Narita grabbed his arm, motioning him to silence. His body ached to tear into the creature that dragged Pria toward it. He clamped onto Narita as he struggled to maintain control, quiet. He couldn't fight a battle here alone, and if he attacked the grinlo holding her, that is exactly what he would face. His mind screamed coward but he held—priestess help him, he held.

Long, savage claws dug into Pria's arm as she allowed the beast to pull her into a building.

"Who you?" Its voice was rough and slurred as it drew her scent toward it. "Smell funny."

She laid a hand on its chest and a tiny pulse of light flashed out through her palm. "I am like you; all you see is what you expect."

A tusked snout poked from the cowl of its hood, snuffling as it moved toward her face. A rough tongue slipped from its mouth and ran along her cheek, leaving a trail of slime and filth. "Master says we move north."

"We will follow you."

Her arm slipped from its grip as it moved back out into the alley and away from them.

Jeran felt his body liquefy as Pria inspected her arm. He shook his head. "Tara said you were the bravest woman she ever heard of, but she is wrong. You aren't brave—you are completely mad." He hissed, "What possessed you to do this?"

Pria watched him calmly; a hint of the tarnished pride glinted in her eyes. "It needed to be done."

"By you?"

She blinked and when her eyes opened again, they were devoid of the tightness that was there before. "Who else would have been able to?" She waited for his mind to work through the answer before she continued. "Now if you are quite finished with this rant, we need to keep moving. Mian cannot pull them forever. We have to get this shield down and get to any survivors."

His body quivered as he glanced around the warehouse the grinlo had pulled Pria into and nodded. This was not the place or the time. They would return to this argument, her gaze told him. "Okay, let's get moving."

Narita nodded and ducked back outside then searched the alley before motioning them to follow. As they slinked along the streets, avoiding groups of patrolling grinlo, he felt like half of his life had worried away. His body was exhausted when Pria finally motioned him closer. "It is just beyond that wall."

He grabbed her arm and rushed toward the building in the hope of getting this insanity over with. The door stuck and he crashed into it loudly.

They both cringed as a group of grinlo turned toward them in curiosity.

Pria and Narita faced the approaching unit. Pria growled back at him, "Get the door open."

Eyes closed to the monsters behind them, he jerked a dagger from his belt and knelt before the door. The slim blade slipped between the door and jamb as he searched for the latch. He could hear the grinlo draw closer but pushed them from his mind. All that existed was the door.

The knife caught and he slammed it upward then kicked the door wide.

"Get inside!"

He turned back and started with a jerk. The small group of grinlo stood slack-jawed and drooling before Pria's outstretched hand. Beside her, Narita kept watch for others.

"Darkness save us, girl, that is just creepy."

"Get inside; make sure the building is safe." Pria's eyes never strayed from the monsters that swayed before her, ensnared in whatever magic she used. He stepped to her side and the hair on his arms stood on end as sparks strayed along his skin.

Narita nodded and ducked into the open door. "This room is clean."

He stared up at the grinlo frozen in Pria's grip. Three at the front were close enough to stretch out a clawed arm and snatch Pria away. Drool dripped from their slack jaws, puddling at their feet as every muscle twitched as if sparks danced along their skin. Each gaze was hazed with a gray distant stare.

"Jeran." Her voice jolted him.

He nodded, blade raised toward the grinlo. "I'll follow you."

"If I loosen my grip on their minds they will attack. Get inside."

A violent battle erupted inside him. To argue with her would put her in danger; to agree left her open to danger. There was no good choice.

Enraged and filled with a feeling of impotence, he prayed for the best. His fist quaked around the dagger's hilt before he leapt inside. His breath raced as the door shut behind them.

"I think it is upstairs." Despite the ordeal outside, Pria was calm and collected.

Narita had her ear pressed to an inner door. "I can hear movement." She kept her voice urgent but under control.

"Likely a guard for the generator." Pria moved to her side, palm flat to the doorway.

"It's heavy. Could be trouble."

"'Cause we haven't had any till now." Jeran slowed his breathing, fought to get his racing heart under control. How could they be so calm? They acted like they were on a shopping trip. He pushed aside his fear; it did him no good here.

They paused and listened as a group clamored by outside. Narita glanced up from the door and nodded before pushing it open. Her breath caught as she stepped aside. Pria shambled in after her followed again by Jeran's stagger. He was sure his heart stopped beating when his eyes fell on the guard at the bottom of the stairs.

The floor creaked with its weight as the crouching grinlo turned to eye them. His cloak had been discarded, leaving its grotesque form exposed. If it stood up, the grinlo would be taller than the ceiling. Its long savage claws scraped the floor as it shuffled about clumsily. Huge stained tusks jutted out from under its fat lips to frame a snout-like nose. Its body was covered in short fine fur that was caked with filth and gore.

It swung a huge gnarled fist at them. “No one to be here!”

Pria held a hand out behind her. “Master sent. Let us pass.”

“No one to be here!”

She jumped back as it chopped at her again and snagged her cloak with a claw. It straightened, head crashing through the ceiling to rain debris down around them. “He’s protected,” Pria said. “We’ll have to kill him.”

“Finally.” Jeran jumped forward and threw his cloak back over his shoulder, sword drawn.

“Quietly, Jeran. We can’t draw attention.”

Narita drew her bow, blossoming an arrow in the grinlo’s throat. Jeran eyed her angrily as he jumped forward and slashed at a claw that flashed out at him. A second arrow sunk into its chest and the grinlo staggered backward through a wall and crashed to the floor. Jeran leapt on its chest and slashed down. Pria appeared at his side, short swords in hand to add her weight to his as Narita fired into the red reptilian eyes.

Both hands wrapped around his sword’s hilt, he stabbed down with all his might and felt his blade bounce off a rib before it pierced deep into the chest cavity. A clawed hand snatched at his shoulder and tore his flesh. Jeran clenched his jaw tight against the pain until the beast beneath them stilled.

Narita rushed to his side. “Don’t move.” She pried the claws from his skin and let the arm smash to the floor beside her. She lifted the cloth aside to inspect the wound. “It’s not deep, you’ll be okay.”

Pria jerked her swords from the bulk beneath her as she scanned the room. “We need to get moving before one of them comes to check out the noise.”

"Your compassion humbles me, Priestess." He bowed from his perch on the body before he jumped down and winced at his jarred shoulder. Hand out, he helped Pria down and looked around the trashed room. "Where now?"

"We need to find stairs. It is still above us."

"Well, let's not just sit around here waiting," Jeran growled.

"Just cut it off!" Mian struggled to move as he lay prostrate on the ground. "It's crushed and I can't breathe with it on!"

Orotid slid his knife along the edge of the armor and sliced through the closures. Mian gasped as the older man jerked the mangled metal from his chest.

"You might have some broken ribs."

"We'll worry about that later." He struggled to his feet and cupped a hand to his bruised side. "We need to keep pushing."

Orotid wanted to argue, especially as Mian nearly collapsed back to the ground but his commander was a stubborn man. No amount of arguing would beat sense into his head. Mian leaned on his sword as he caught his breath and surveyed the burned-out houses around them. Inside the shield the city was devastated: walls crumbled and scattered out into the streets, buildings smoked and creaked as they collapsed. He forced his breath to slow as he stood up straight, sword gripped tight in his fist. "Let's get back to the front."

They picked their way through the littered bodies and tried hard not to notice the humans among them. There were no survivors yet, but they didn't expect to find any at the edge of town.

Orotid turned at a loud wordless cry, sword ready to face the charging grinlo. Mian's bare chest glistened beside him with sweat and blood as he blocked their blows, struggling to keep up. His arms jarred with each block as he faced the creatures and ignored the cuts to his skin. One by one they fell to his blade as he danced among them, trusting Orotid to his back. Soldiers poured around them, cutting down any that had yet to fall.

Mian glanced up to the sky.

"She'll be all right. Jeran is with her."

Mian smiled back at Orotid before he raised his sword high. "To the temple!"

Men roared around him as they charged down the streets in search of more grinlo to slaughter.

"Bring me a horse."

A young soldier darted off back toward the treeline. Orotid watched Mian. "Maybe you should go back to the overlook. Be easier to see her signal from there."

"And easier for me to rest?"

Orotid shrugged. "Wouldn't be a bad thing."

"I will be fine. A horse will allow me enough rest to command from down here."

"There is no one here for you to impress, boy. A body doesn't get anyone," Orotid said.

"I'm not leaving this city until she is by my side." Mian inspected the edge of his sword then pulled out a cloth to wipe the blood from its length. He caught Orotid's knowing smile and glared at it. "Can't leave my prince without his priestess, now can I."

"Whatever you say sir, who am I to argue with you."

"Shut up."

The man who called himself Neram watched as the trio slinked along the street. He couldn't help but be impressed. Never would he have thought that the high priestess would risk herself and come into the besieged city. But what an excellent opportunity it offered. She may have made it into the city, but she would not make it out.

He turned from the street and made his way into one of the nearby buildings. He couldn't have planned it better himself. The building resonated around him with soft, cooing calls. It was time for his next move.

Pria laid her hand against the door and a quiet hum vibrated from her lips. "It's here, but there are guards."

Jeran crept backward. "How many?"

"Enough to cause a problem," she whispered.

"We'll handle it." He felt a rush of excitement at the thought of finally facing the enemy head on.

"Not yet."

He glared at her. "Why not?"

"You have so little patience, Jeran. Tara needs to train you better." She ran her hand along the wood grain and changed the note she was humming. "They aren't protected—the magic would interfere with the generator this close. I should be able to"—several loud thumps came from behind the door and she smiled as she pushed it open—"put them to sleep."

Jeran glared around in aggravation. "Where is the fun in that?" His irritation flared at the loss of the one task that he would be capable of accomplishing during this trip. He was surrounded by two of the most important women in the kingdom, women vital to the survival of everyone he loved, and he was completely worthless to them.

Narita patted him on the shoulder. "We did tell you it wouldn't be pretty."

Pria picked her way around the sleeping mounds toward a small box set against a wall. Box in hand, she rushed back toward the door. "Let's get moving."

Jeran gestured at the box in her arms. "That's it? That's what is making the shield covering the city?"

She hefted the box. "That is what is *maintaining* the shield over the city. Whoever is controlling the grinlo would have had to create the shield and then transfer the spell into the generator, but yes, this is it. Or, it is the case the generator is contained in. The generator itself will be nestled inside."

Jeran waved at the box in exasperation. "Aren't you supposed to do something with it?"

Narita darted down the stairs, Pria close behind. "The second the shield drops, their master will direct them toward this building after us. We cannot be here when it falls."

"First rational thing you've said this trip."

The building creaked and settled as they crept down the stairs. "How far is the temple?"

Jeran paused and pressed his ear to the outside door. "This is the Lower District; the temple is in the Middle. Barring any more issues, we could be there in a heartbeat."

"The sooner the better."

With a nod, he cracked the door and glanced around. "Street's clear." He stepped aside as Narita followed him, eyes never slowing their scan of the town.

Pria settled her cloak over the box as best she could. "We will have to be more careful with you bleeding. They will smell the blood."

Jeran nodded with the satisfaction of a choice in this mad job that he could justify. "If it comes to that, I'll lead them away and you two go on."

Narita scoffed. "And do what, get lost? You said it yourself, we don't know this town."

"We'll deal with it when it arises. For now, keep moving." Pria swept a hand toward the road ahead of them.

Jeran shook his head as he resumed his staggering with a little more haste than before. If they intended to die with him, he wasn't going to give them as much of a chance to do it.

They could now hear the sounds of battle off to the north. With the shield up, the army would have to push their way in with no archery support. It should have been slow going but from the sounds of it, they weren't doing too bad. Mian must not have been so calm to let them come as he pretended.

Jeran jumped as a wall beside them collapsed under the weight of its abuse, sending up a cloud of debris and dust. Every few street crossings they would encounter a group of scouting grinlo but so far none had turned their way. His heart pounded when he caught sight of the temple's towers over the surrounding buildings.

"We're close—just a few more streets." He turned to check on Pria and Narita but they were both stopped staring back down the street. "What is it?"

Pria shook her head. "Something is coming."

Jeran looked to Narita. "What does that mean?"

"I don't know, that's all she'll say."

Pria closed her eyes, breath even and steady. "It's closer now."

Jeran grabbed the box from her arms and took her wrist in his hand. "Then let's not be here when it arrives, huh?"

Her body was stiff as he pulled her along. Narita glanced around, her eyes never pausing. It was the first sign of unease he had been able to detect in her and it built a knot in his stomach.

Pria jerked to a halt. "It's here."

Narita and Jeran turned to face the street behind them that now was blocked with a large group of armored grinlo. They had no cloaks, just mismatched, battered armor. Each held a chain that ran behind them to a beast that scrambled along in their midst. The creature walked on four long spindly legs; its body jerked and bounced with each stride. A long neck ended in a small head with a trunk-like nose that waved around as it scented the air. A whip-like tail twitched as it focused on them.

"It wants me to go to it." She took a step forward.

Jeran tightened his grip on Pria's arm, stopping her. "Well, it had better get used to disappointment."

He jumped as the thing threw back its head and emitted a high-pitched wail that rattled the walls around them. Pria jerked against him but he held firm. Narita pulled her bow to her ear but Jeran shook his head. "No, we can't fight with Pria entranced like this. Who knows what that thing will do to her."

"Then what do we do?" Narita's voice was laced with worry.

Jeran steadied his nerves as he stared at the creature again ambling its way toward them. Pria's enthralled stare was a force beside him but he couldn't let it distract him. Fearless and crazy she may be, but she needed him now and he couldn't lose his head. "We run. The temple is just around the corner."

"What if we can't get in?" Narita asked.

He met her eyes, praying they didn't betray his fear as he handed her the box then jerked Pria over his shoulder. The wail behind them dropped into a horrid piercing roar followed by loud rattling as the group raced after them.

He focused on the road in front of him, watching where his feet landed to keep from tripping and falling. Narita was at his side, box cradled to her chest. They slid around a corner and broke out into the main street at the front of the temple. He lengthened his stride over the cobblestones. Guttural growls sounded from several different sides as more grinlo caught sight of them and gave chase.

Pria still struggled to go to the monster behind them. She strained atop his shoulder as he crashed into the door and rejoiced as it gave way and swung open with his momentum. Narita grabbed the handle, let her speed whip her around, and slammed it shut. Jeran tossed Pria to the ground as he searched the room and shoved a heavy dresser in front of the door.

The building rattled as something crashed into the door behind them; Jeran slammed his full weight against the barricade.

Narita shoved a large chest toward them and they added its weight to the dresser. "We need boards, nails, anything to close off this door."

She started as she turned.

"Who are you!" An older man glared at them as he held a knife to Pria's throat from behind. Pria's eyes were still hazed and she twitched with her need to go to the creature outside.

Jeran kept his weight against the barricade as Narita put her hands up. "We're here to help you. Just let her go."

The old man glanced at Pria's face. "What's wrong with her?"

Narita took a slow step forward, hands low and open. "She's entranced. She is the high priestess. I am Narita of Austeria, this is Jeran of Kyneira."

Jeran grunted as another crash sounded from the door. "Sir, we really need to secure this door. You can still kill us after that if you wish."

The old man glanced around at them then removed his knife from Pria's throat. Narita caught her as she glided toward the door and pulled her out of the way. The older man shouted over his shoulder. "Bring supplies; we need to shore up the door!"

Narita wrapped her legs around the struggling Pria as men and women flooded the room, carrying boards and supplies. They set to work and secured the door, ignoring the crashes from the other side. Every now and then they glanced back at Narita who was using her full weight to keep Pria still. "Jeran!"

He rushed to her side and lifted Pria from the ground where she couldn't gain purchase as she flailed. "What are we supposed to do with her?"

Narita jumped to her feet. "I don't know." She slapped Pria hard across the face, snapping her head to the left. She jumped back as Pria's eyes returned to her, fire burning from them. A terrible screech tore from Pria's throat as she threw her head back. Her legs and arms took on an unnatural strength as she flailed against Jeran's restraint.

"We'll have to kill it." Jeran growled as Pria landed a strong blow to his gut. "And quickly."

Narita looked at the older gentleman. "We need to get to the roof. Do you have any weapons? Bows, spears, anything?"

"I'll show you to our arsenal. Will she be all right?" The older man gestured to the enraged Pria, a tiny storm of fury in Jeran's arms.

"Do you have any rope?"

Narita started. "Jeran, you can't!"

"You'd rather I let her beat us all to death?" He struggled to speak as Pria clawed and fought for her freedom.

A young boy ran to him with a coil of twine. "Will this work, sir?"

"It's going to have to. Do we have any weight-bearing support beams?" Jeran asked.

The boy pointed. "In there."

"You think you can tie that rope tight while I hold her?"

His eyes bulged.

Jeran smiled wickedly as he remembered every rude snipe and irritating comment. "Come on kid; let's commit some high treason here."

Narita dug through the pile of weapons and handed several to the men around her. "There is a creature outside; the grinlo are holding it with chains. We need to kill it, however we can. If we can kill it, we have a chance to get this shield down and the army will try to free the city."

The older man stared at a spear that Narita had handed him. "How will killing this thing remove the shield?"

She stood as Jeran rushed into the room behind them. "Hopefully it will free the high priestess and she will be able to disarm the generator."

"And if it doesn't?"

Jeran tossed his cloak to the floor. "We'll deal with that when it comes to it. For now, let's kill this thing."

Narita nodded as she faced the older man. "The roof?"

He turned to lead the group up a spiraling staircase, Narita and Jeran close on his heels. The building creaked as they spilled out onto the rooftop. Jeran ran to the edge and peered over, Narita just a step behind.

Below them, a mass of grinlo clogged the small courtyard in front of the temple, and at its center, the gangly pink creature trailing its handlers from the multitude of chains. The older man stopped beside Jeran and he pointed down into the throng. "That. We need to kill *that*."

"What is it?"

"Doesn't matter." Narita loosed an arrow and smiled as it sank into the creature's back. It reared up, tearing its claws from the wood of the door and roaring. The grinlo around it pointed up at her and they had to duck and jump as a volley of rocks and primitive weapons flew at them. Narita jumped back up and loosed three more arrows before she dropped and rolled aside. Crouched low, she crawled around to a tower ledge and stood with her back to it. She moved around until she could see the creature. Her next arrow bloomed in its eye and it staggered and knocked down several of its handlers.

Its head snapped up to her, eyeing its target. It hunched down on its stomach, then launched itself up the building, long sharp claws making short work of the climb. The remaining grinlo handlers lost their grip on the chains and stood staring up as it climbed.

Narita gasped, darting back from the wall. She faced the monster as it lifted itself onto the roof, a rattling cry bouncing off the towers of the temple. Jeran was at her side in an instant, sword drawn as the creature closed on them, chains loose behind it. Slumped low, it twitched its long trunk of a nose and took in their scents as it approached.

A spear flew past her shoulder and dug deep into its side, creating a spray of thick black blood across the roof. She continued her assault, peppering the pale body with arrows as Jeran led a charge of armed men toward the beast. Slashing and cutting, they surrounded the creature and she had to pick her shots carefully to avoid hitting any people. She could hear a scream from below now as the creature tried to call Pria to it again.

The fiend before her reared back on its hind legs. She fired a shot into its chest as Jeran sliced up into its gut, sword spilling putrid intestines onto his boots.

Narita ran down the stairs, her heart pounding with anticipation. She slid to a halt and stared at Pria slack in her restraints, still tied to the support beam. The boy watched her from the edge of the room, his eyes wide in terror. "I didn't mean to. She was wailing so awful then she started to struggle and the ropes…they were cutting into her skin."

Narita ran a hand across his hair. "It's okay son, what is your name?"

"Armen."

"Armen, can you help me cut her down?" she asked.

He nodded and she moved to support Pria's body as the boy cut her restraints.

Body laid on the floor, Narita cupped her cheek in a palm. "Pria?" She slapped her face before she turned to the boy who still stood, cut ropes clutched to his chest. "Do you have a healer, an herbalist, anything?"

His lip jutted out in a pathetic pout before his face brightened with a sudden smile. "We have smelling salt!"

"Can you fetch it for me?"

Armen darted off.

She inspected Pria's head. "Well old girl, you'll have a headache but you'll live. That boy sure put you in your place. You can face down the horde but not a twelve-year-old with a board."

She smiled as Armen darted back into the room beaming. "Thank you."

"They kept it around for the ladies that got overexcited during worship," he said. "Do you ever pass out?"

She tapped him on the nose. "Haven't yet." She took the vial and uncapped it then jerked back. "Pria, if this doesn't wake you up, nothing will." She waved the vial under Pria's nose, ready to force her back to the ground if she needed to. She held her breath as Pria jerked and stirred. Her eyes fluttered open then focused as Jeran entered the room followed by the older gentleman. "Pria? Are you okay?"

She sat up and pressed a hand to the back of her head. "What happened?"

Jeran knelt beside her to inspect the large lump that had formed beneath her hair. "The grinlo had some weird creature with them. It was like it searched you out, put you in a trance."

"You kept trying to go to it. Then you became violent and we had to tie you up so we could kill it." Narita moved behind her and cradled Pria's head in her lap.

Pria looked around. "Then why does my head hurt?"

Narita smoothed the hair back from Pria's forehead. "You were hurting yourself. You had to be knocked out."

Pria inspected her bloody wrists before she pressed her hand back to her head. "Next time, let me tear my hands off."

Narita laughed. "Don't be so dramatic! Are you going to be able to disarm the generator?"

Pria sat up and pressed a hand to her mouth. "What did it look like?"

Narita shared a confused look with Jeran. "I'm not sure, it was in a box."

Pria took a deep breath as she fought to curb the headache induced irritation. "The creature…with the grinlo. What did it look like?" She swayed and put out a steadying hand.

Jeran shrugged. "Long pink nose and claws."

She nodded. "Bring me the generator."

Jeran darted from the room as Narita laid a comforting hand on Pria's back. "Are you sure you can do this? That thing threw you for quite a loop."

Pria leaned back on Narita's shoulder. "It was a listril. Its call is entrancing to anyone with a magical gift. As long as my head doesn't cause me any issues, we should be fine."

Narita smiled at Armen, who looked increasingly nervous in the corner. Pria closed her eyes as she remained propped against Narita's shoulder when Jeran returned with the box. He set it on the floor at her feet as she leaned toward it.

With a wave of her hand, she bombarded the lock with an explosive spell that sent rusted metal clinking across the floor. She lifted the lid to reveal a pulsing sphere that she raised from its case and held before her eyes. The very air seemed to buzz as shafts of light shot from the ball, sending shadows jumping around the room, and cracked the walls wherever they landed. Pria's eyes slid shut, her brow wrinkled as the moments stretched out with nothing but the crash of angry grinlo outside to accompany it. The sphere pulsed one last violent glare that forced all in the room to shade their eyes before it went dark.

Pria's body gave out and she dropped the generator then collapsed against Narita's lap. "We need to signal Mian."

The older man stepped forward. "What is the signal?"

Narita shifted and pulled a shaft from her quiver. It was nothing more than a thick rod of silver metal but it rang like good steel across a whetstone the second her hand touched it. "This is a Kaleer rod. It needs to be fired straight up into the sky."

He took the rod from her hands. "Porthos?"

A handsome youth stepped forward to take the rod from him then left the room. Pria took a deep breath and reached toward Jeran, who pulled her to her feet then held her steady until she caught her balance. She faced the older man. "What is your name?"

"They call me Farner, ma'am."

"How many men do you have here?" Pria asked.

"There are maybe three hundred that can fight."

She jerked a nod. "Take me to the roof; I'd like to see our situation."

Jeran grabbed her arm and earned himself a raised eyebrow. He would have to pay for that. Pria could be very lax in private, but in the public eye she could be excessively prickly. "What if another one of those things is out there waiting for you?"

She eyed his hand and he dropped her arm. "It is unlikely they would have had time to bring another listril, and if they have, it would be better to know of it before we move to the streets, don't you think?"

"Yes, High Priestess." He suppressed a sigh as he followed her out of the room.

Narita fell in beside him with a sympathetic smile. "I won't tell her it was you who tied her up if you don't tell her it was the boy who knocked her out."

The man who called himself Neram froze among the trees as he watched the shield wink out above Kyneira. It wasn't possible. She couldn't have gotten away, but there was no other way for them to have taken the generator down. His lips curled. She was even more impressive than he had anticipated. He had expected to have the benefit of the shield until the army was able to push through the city to get to it.

His hand tightened into a fist as his mind ran over his plans. It was all right, he could still make it work—and best of all, he could increase the ambition of his plans for when he had turned her to his side. Between his strength increased with the horde and hers, there was no one who could stand in his way.

Who held Kyneira was of no consequence. The point was she was *here*, away from the walls and defenses of Austeria. She was vulnerable to him…and once he had her, the blow of losing a second high priestess to him would crush its people and its prince. Trimera would crumble and there would be nothing in his way.

Excitement boiled beneath his skin as he turned back into the forest. A group of grinlo swarmed around him, eager and expectant. His connection to them shared his mood and they pranced around him in a circle. He would need more numbers now, but there were several already on the way. Once he had gathered their numbers from the city he would regroup and prepare for his next move.

Janu tugged his gloves tighter onto his hands before he fished the note from his pocket again. He had it memorized: *Kyneira has fallen, send help.*

Pria's neat hand trailed across the parchment. He had been at his desk attempting to concentrate on work and not dwell on Pria, Narita, and Mian. His friends, family, out searching for who knows what. One second he was staring at requisitions then a folded note flashed from the air before his eyes and floated down to rest between his palms.

The note was warm to the touch as he lifted it and read the short message. *Kyneira has fallen.* Kyneira. The grinlo hadn't even made a move toward Kyneira—why would they suddenly turn so far south? Austeria was closer to the Frontier and to the warfront. Kyneira was defenseless, sheltered from the war. He couldn't imagine the chaos and terror any attack would have caused.

He shook his head. "Mount up!"

The courtyard and streets surrounding the palace were packed shoulder to shoulder with soldiers and mounts. The air rang with armor and hooves as the mass moved to their horses. His own mount shied away from him in the steward's hands.

He paused to collect himself. Better to seem hesitant than to show the churning worry inside. A third major city gone. The Frontier hadn't progressed so far in generations. He was losing Trimera, failing his parents, letting down his citizens… He slowed his breath. Trimera wasn't gone yet. He could still turn this around.

His hand was steady as he stretched up to grab the horn of his saddle. This wasn't where he should be. He should be with Pria, he should be on the front line, but instead he was stuck gathering soldiers. He was the backup while his friends were taking the real risks. As a ruling prince with no direct line of lineage, he had to be careful what situations he put himself in. Any succession that wasn't set out would end up with a legal battle that would be a disaster for the kingdom already in turmoil. So, it was his obligation to hide on the sidelines, to be the kind of ruler his father had always taught him to hate: the kind that let other people die for him.

He let his horse follow along with the flow of soldiers and guards. Even when they arrived at Kyneira he would still be in a buffer of protection. Pria had no idea what it was like to be truly coddled. No idea at all.

Mian ducked a savage slash from a hooked blade then, spinning with the momentum, cut the grinlo's arm from its body. They had already encountered seven of the larger grinlo. They seemed to be leaders of some kind and were much more difficult to kill in the open. Sweat wiped from his face and chest, he turned back from the alley down which he had forced the large grinlo. His body was beginning to feel the hours of fighting.

A piercing cry shattered the sounds of fighting and he searched the sky frantically and caught sight of the bright flashing trail of the Kaleer rod. With a glance back at the surrounding hills, he smiled as archers rushed toward the front line to set up support. They knew their orders and would adjust them according to the situation. The sky darkened with the first volley of arrows soaring high over his men to rain deep into the city of monsters.

Heady with renewed adrenaline, Mian rushed back to the front and crashed into the oncoming horde with wild abandon. He shouted over the din of battle. "Advance the line! Push them back!"

The men around him responded in an eruption of enthusiasm to his new energy. The enemy line cut back; his men roared with the heat of battle. Orotid was at his side in a blink, a knowing grin plastered across his face. "Anyone ever tell you how annoying you are?"

"Only people who know I'm right."

"You're not right. And even if you were, it wouldn't matter." Mian punctuated each word with another blow of his sword.

Orotid swept his sword low and dropped his opponent to the dirt. "Of course it matters. It matters to you, doesn't it?" He kicked a grinlo square in the chest and cut another across the gut then swung his sword over his head to gain himself some space. "High priestess she may be, but she is still a woman."

"You an expert on women now?"

He bowed low over his sword. "I am an expert on everything."

Mian growled as he was charged by a group of four grinlo. He and Orotid made quick work of them, slicing and cutting as they pushed on down the street. Mian inspected his blade as he waited for the next wave to reach them. "A woman she is, but she's also one who thinks I'm a childish fool. Nothing more than her brother's goofy friend."

Orotid belted a laugh as he dodged a spear aimed for his thigh. "Then maybe you should show her who you really are."

"So she can throw me in the stocks?"

"So she can appreciate you for the man you *are* rather than who she remembers you as," Orotid said.

"And then she can throw me in the stocks."

Pria scanned the streets with her fargazer as she watched the progress of their soldiers through the city. "Mian didn't waste any time."

Jeran leaned toward Narita, his voice low. "Helps when your sights are on a prize better than a city."

She glared at him reproachfully but wasn't able to hide her smile. Pria turned from the edge of the building. "Do you know of any other people in hiding?"

Farner straightened as she stopped to face him. "Not for certain, no, but I have a few ideas on where like-minded groups could have made a stand."

She nodded. "Good, bring me maps." She turned to Parthos. "We'll need an exit from this building but we'll also require a distraction and support from the roof here."

"We already have most of our projectiles up here from earlier, but arrows will be a problem," Parthos said.

"Do you have water and pots? We can build fires up here. Heating oil would be great."

He nodded. "Yes, I think I understand you."

He darted off and she turned to Jeran. "I want you to get with Farner; you two will be leading his men from this building. We will give you cover from here. Narita, how are you on arrows?"

She patted her quiver. "Getting low myself."

"Collect what remains of their arrows and gather a few of their best archers; we'll need you up here as well."

"We won't hold here for long."

"We won't have to. Once Jeran and the others are free of the building they will descend on the grinlo gathered below, allowing us to join them and those staying behind to secure the building," Pria said.

Jeran glanced around to ensure no one was within earshot. "I'm not sure leaving people behind is such a good idea. What if we don't free the city?"

"It can't be helped. They will be too exposed if we take them with us. We'll record every building we leave people in. If we can't retake the city, we'll have to collect them after we regroup with the army."

"Okay," he nodded as he met her eyes, "it's a battle then. I followed your rules in, you follow mine out." He stepped toward her and lowered his voice. "Know that there are no limits to the number of men I will sacrifice to ensure your safety. I want you to remember that every time you get some fool notion in your head of something that needs to be done by you. Do we have an understanding?"

She blinked up at him innocently. "What makes you think I will do something foolish?"

He suppressed a growl and turned to Farner as he returned laden with maps. Farner's eyes darted from Pria to Jeran, unsure of who he should address.

Pria nodded. "Farner, Jeran is an excellent soldier and a good leader. I want you to work with him on getting us to the next likely place for survivors." She moved off as Parthos returned at the head of a group of people carrying wood and pots.

Jeran leaned toward Narita as Pria drifted away. "There is no way she's going to listen to me, is there?"

"I wouldn't hold your breath." She slapped him on the shoulder before she snagged the sleeve of a passing man.

Farner eyed him. "Forgive me for intruding, but I can't help but notice that there is some tension between you and the high priestess."

Jeran coughed a laugh. "You ever try to protect a woman who thinks she's invincible?"

The older man nodded. "I thought she had that feel."

"Yeah, well this one has the power to have me executed if I make her angry, but if I don't protect her, my king loses his sister and priestess." Jeran cooled his irritation at being incapable of the only task his prince wanted of him, the only task that mattered: protect his kingdom's most precious weapon and asset.

"In her position she must project nothing but power and confidence. Being seen allowing you to protect her would tarnish that vision, but it doesn't mean she doesn't need it, or appreciate it."

Jeran smiled. "What is your profession, Farner?"

"I'm a mason."

"How did you come to be in charge of these people?" Jeran asked.

"We needed someone and they all looked to me. Never really made the choice."

"What kind of fighting experience can I expect here?"

Farner looked around at the men spread out around them. "They have potential but little experience. They are good men all and they know what is at stake."

Jeran clapped him hard on the shoulder. "That's all we can ask."

Pria clenched her fist and turned as a grinlo dropped to the road, dead. Young Armen grunted as he and a boy she didn't know dumped a pot of lamp oil over the edge of the roof. With a flick of her hand she sent a wave of flame after it, then ducked as it flared up in a massive fireball to consume a dozen of the creatures still scrabbling at the door below.

Narita loosed an arrow before she dropped from her perch along the guard wall. "They're coming!"

Pria pivoted to the men. "Okay, fighters, get ready to leave. Those staying behind, prepare to barricade the doors." The clash of swords and armor rang out as they rushed down the stairs to where four men guarded a small side entrance. Pria turned with an encouraging smile for the group of children and elderly, who would be left behind with the injured. "We will come back for you."

The guards formed up around her, keeping a respectable distance. She could easily bully her way past them with little effort if she needed to. Narita was at her side in an instant, smiling at the men around them. Pria nodded in greeting. "Let's go relieve Jeran's worry. I'd hate for him to have to come looking for me."

"He's a good man."

"Don't remind me," Pria growled.

"You like him too, admit it."

She drew her short swords and glared at the street around her. Rubble and debris littered the street and smoke choked the air. "He's tolerable, I suppose."

"Mian's a good man too, you know."

Pria blinked at her in shock. "What does that have to do with anything?"

Narita shrugged. "I'm just saying. He's made quite decent progress into the city, don't you think?"

Pria glanced at her. Surely she wasn't going to start this old argument in the middle of a besieged town. Mian was the last thing she needed to clog her mind at the moment. "I guess. He should be good—he's Janu's Battle Leader."

Narita smiled and shook her head as they rounded a corner and caught sight of Jeran and the other men just as they finished off the final grinlo.

Jeran ran to them, a wave of men at his back. "Are we ready for this?"

"Don't really have a choice." Pria glanced behind him at the bodies that littered the courtyard. "Good work, Jeran. How far to the first building Farner indicated?"

"Just a few streets over. We sent Arino to scout for us; he should be back here in a second."

She smiled up at him. "Let's get going then."

Mian leaned against the temple wall as he kept watch in the street while soldiers evacuated the building. A knot of worry jostled around in his stomach but he pushed it away. He didn't have time for it. The horde was being pushed back and they were evacuating groups of survivors.

Orotid returned to his side. "They were here, Commander, but they moved on."

"Then we keep looking."

"Of course, sir," Orotid said.

Without waiting for his men, Mian crossed the courtyard toward a wide street. He could hear something in that direction and it was as good as any. He could hear Orotid and other soldiers rushing behind him as he caught sight of another group of grinlo. A spin of his sword to loosen his wrist and he rushed toward the group, intent to vent his frustration. He tore through them and moved on to the next street, looking around before he continued on. He caught sight of a group of grinlo as they ran away from him several streets away and he took off at a sprint, ignoring Orotid's warning shout.

He slid to a halt at the edge of a building, heart pounding he caught sight of a group of soldiers pinned against a large warehouse. He could hear his men rush to catch up behind him as he crossed the street toward the fighting. A smile spread across his face as he caught sight of Narita among the group. The grinlo didn't even notice his approach as he began to cut through their backs. His men charged up behind him and tore the monsters down with ease.

A large grinlo fell at his feet to reveal Pria, who stood with her hand out. Her bright blue eyes sent a wave of relief along his body as she stood before him, perfect and fierce. She looked up at him with a smug smile.

He stepped over the body, cupped a hand behind her neck, and pulled her mouth to his.

She stiffened against him, her free hand to his chest as she swayed with his momentum. Tension fell from his body in a wave as he wrapped her tight to his chest, safe where she belonged. His Pria.

Her eyes were wide with shock as he let her heels drop back to the street and turned to cut at a grinlo as it reached for her. She stepped back from him, her chest heaving as the soldiers around them finished off the small group.

Jeran cleared his throat. "Uh, Commander?" He pulled a folded map from behind his armor, careful to avoid looking at Pria. "We have buildings marked on this where there are still survivors holed up."

"We have already evacuated the temple."

"Good. The horde seems to be retreating from us now," Jeran said.

Narita eyed Pria before she shifted a glare to Mian. "They will not be able to hold long, not with you meeting up with us. They'll likely start burning before they retreat."

Mian swept his hair back from his forehead. "Let's not give them time. We'll push them through the streets fast enough that they won't be able to stop and burn anything."

"Well that will help, but you know it won't prevent all of it."

"It can't be helped. Let's get moving." Mian faced Pria but she had vanished to the edge of the group.

Orotid crossed his arms as he stepped up beside them. "I told you to show her who you were, not slap her across the face with it."

Mian sighed. "Still annoying."

Jeran stared at his feet as he lost a battle to hide his smile. "Could be worse..."

"Listril!"

They turned at the scream to see an older man drag Pria back toward them, her hands clapped over her ears. Narita jerked an arrow from the body of a grinlo and nocked it to her bow. At the end of the street, a grinlo led a lanky listril toward them, its long trunk nose twitching with excitement.

Narita loosed her arrow and ripped another from a nearby body. Pria had curled herself on the ground against the building, hands clapped to her ears as she kept her back to the approaching creature. Soldiers blew past Narita and ruined her line of sight to rush the listril and its handler before it began to affect Pria.

A hand laid to her friend's shoulder, Narita watched the street and waited. The listril's high-pitched cries were piercing even to her, but every wail sent a ripple through Pria's tense body.

A moment later, the listril's cries faded as the soldiers cut it to pieces. Narita could feel Pria's shoulder relax beneath her palm as the men returned to them.

Mian's jaw was set firm as he knelt before Pria. "Pria? Are you okay?" Her eyes rolled open but remained hazed and unfocused. He cupped her face in his hands and his eyes searched frantically as her body collapsed against him. "What's happening?"

Narita shook her head. "She said the listril only entranced her, she should be fine!"

His eyes became distant as he thought, Pria slumped against his chest. "Unless it was a distraction."

Narita launched to her feet. "I was watching her the whole time! Nothing got near her."

A trickle of blood escaped the corner of her mouth to trail down across her cheek and along her jaw. Her head rolled back on his shoulder and he slid his hand behind her neck. His hand jerked back and he stared at the drop of blood that bloomed on his finger. Narita crouched beside him and pulled a dagger from her belt to shift Pria's hair aside. Clutched to her neck was a tiny creature, its teeth sunk deep into her flesh. Membranous black wings capped its back as it wrapped tight around her neck and back. Huge ears twitched and jerked as they swiveled to catch every sound. Large black eyes studied each of them with great interest. Spindly limbs tipped with tiny claws latched into her flesh.

"What is that?" Narita's voice rose with her panic.

Mian's face paled. "Get it off her."

Narita's mouth worked but refused to produce words. "How… How do I…"

"Just kill it!"

Mian's voice rose to a shout and Narita's anxiety rose to meet it. "It's latched on to her neck. I might hurt Pria!"

Jeran lifted Narita aside and dropped to his knees on the pavement. "I did warn you." He met Mian's gaze and nodded before he turned to inspect the small life that drained Pria's blood and energy. "Let's see how badly I can hurt myself."

He jabbed the creature with a finger and its eyes shot to him. Large eyes narrowed as they followed him with intensity. He poked it harder, jabbed at wings and legs until it raised its head from Pria's neck and hissed. It swatted at his hand, shrill cries growing louder. He moved to jab it again and it launched itself at his hand, teeth and claws slashing. He jumped back and snatched madly, snagging it from the air. The creature flailed and latched onto the web of flesh between his thumb and index finger, claws a whir as it struggled to break free of his grasp.

"Narita, knife!"

Narita's eyes were wide with shock as she grabbed his wrist and held it down against the street. The creature's flesh resisted the knife and its cries shattered across the streets to rattle the windows. Grinlo roared in response and rushed in from several directions. Narita leaned her full weight on the knife as grinlo crashed into the soldiers around them, fighting to reach the tiny black monster.

The blade slipped and severed the creature's spine, ending its horrible cries.

Jeran's hand shook with pain from the uncountable cuts as he dropped the dead body from his grip. "That thing had nasty teeth." He shook his hand, splattering blood onto the street. "I'm going to say it has venom too—my entire arm just went numb."

Narita stood as she wiped thick, bright blood from her dagger. "And I say you're done for the day. You and Mian can watch over Pria while she recovers. Orotid and I can handle this."

Mian opened his mouth to argue but Orotid glared him down. "I have been lenient with you today but we both know you are spent. We'll sweep this city clean for you."

Mian's eyes fell to Pria's pale face, her cheeks smeared with blood and her eyes closed. "Come on Jeran, this battle is practically over anyway."

Orotid and Narita nodded as they moved to help fight off the wave of grinlo that still raged.

Jeran held out his good hand to help Mian to his feet with Pria cradled in his arms. Jeran eyed his mangled hand and coughed a laugh. "If she's still upset with you when she wakes up, you can tell her what I did and she'll be angry with me instead."

"I might just take you up on that," Mian said. "I intend to let her recover in my tent."

FALLOUT

Pria stretched before she pulled the blanket to her chin and rolled onto her side. She felt comfortable despite how dead tired she was. She cracked her eyes and saw she was in a strange tent. Sitting up and looking around, she felt her jaw tighten as her eyes landed on a sleeping Mian, who lay against the folding table, silk shirt unlaced, feet bare. A jolt ran through her body as memory came rushing back. Breath struggled to free itself of her chest as her mind filled with his strong touch, his soft lips…how every fiber of her being had wanted him to never stop. She was a foolish girl, a silly princess with her head full of romance and too foolish for her station. If the priestesses at the Lorien had any inkling of her feelings for him, or the thoughts he inspired in her mind, they would not wait for her to make a mistake. She would be snatched from her post before she could even explain. Relationships were not unheard of among priestesses, but they were close enough to border on taboo.

She pulled the cloak of priestess around her, that cool confidence she had worked so hard to project. She had to get her wits together, force this foolishness from her mind. It was Mian, just Mian, her brother's Battle Leader, and she was his high priestess. That is where it ended. That was where it *had* to end. It didn't matter what he wanted. It didn't matter what *she* wanted.

When she was confident of her composure she allowed her gaze to return to him. She had to admit he was handsome with his soft waves of red hair and his tall, lean frame. He was everything a woman could want in a man, but she couldn't afford how weak he made her, how vulnerable. Why couldn't he see the danger he represented? Why couldn't he understand what was at stake? He only wanted what he wanted; he couldn't see where it might lead to. She would just have to protect both of them from this madness. She may lose a friend but she would keep her Battle Leader.

She threw the blanket off and glared down at the soft silk shirt she wore that left her legs bare. She jumped to her feet but her body couldn't support the movement and she dropped to the floor, jerking Mian awake. He shook his head as a slow smile spread across his face.

"It's good to see you up…" He waved a hand at her. "So to speak."

He rolled to his feet. "Would you like a hand, or are you mad at me?"

She jerked the shirt to pull it down around her hips then struggled to stand. "Why am I in your tent?"

He knelt beside her and ignored the flash of rage in her eyes as he brushed her hair aside to inspect the back of her neck. She tried to ignore the spark that jolted through her at his touch but she was too unsteady, too weak. "You were attacked; some little black thing with nasty teeth." Her hand strayed to the back of her neck just to jerk away as it brushed his. "You needed to rest, and my tent is the most comfortable."

She rolled her eyes as she pushed herself up off the floor. "You didn't think I would be more comfortable in my own tent?"

She wobbled and swayed dangerously as he caught her arm. "I thought you would be uncomfortable if you woke up and found me in your tent."

"Ha! Look at that, you got something right." She jerked against his grip. "Would you let go of me?"

"You want me to let you fall back to the floor?" he demanded.

She growled. "Phisher—I should have expected that." She glared at him. "Must have been distracted."

His devilish grin widened as he shrugged and pulled her toward him. "Are you saying I distracted you?"

"Let go of me."

"You can't stand on your own." He swept her off her feet and carried her back across the tent. "So I'm afraid you are stuck with me a bit longer." He nestled her into a padded camp chair as he knelt at her feet and rested his palms on her bare knees.

She glared down at his hands and rage flashed from her eyes. "Where is my armor?"

He sighed in resignation. "Narita was kind enough to get you out of it and wash off that fantastic odor you had worked so hard to create."

She shifted as an unwelcome flood of appreciation swept through her. "Thank you."

"You're welcome." He stood and moved to a table. "Tea?"

She felt her pride tweak. "You don't have to watch over me, I'll be fine."

"I know." He kept his back to her as he poured the tea. "If I remember correctly, jasmine with honey is your favorite."

She blinked. "It is. How did you know that?"

He shrugged as he leaned against the table and handed her a cup. "I know a lot of things."

"I doubt that," she said.

He coughed a laugh as he set his cup on the table behind him, face serious. "Pria, I'm sorry—not that I kissed you, but that I let it go so long."

Her eyes widened and her body froze. A tremor traveled down her spine as her mind flashed to that moment when her eyes locked with his, when his long legs carried him over the body of the grinlo between them and his arms lifted her from the ground. Her head swam. She snatched at the chair beneath her.

He pushed off from the table. "And since you are up, I should probably take some time to check on my men. At the very least Jeran has had a rough week."

Pria tried to stand but finally gave up. "What happened to Jeran?"

Mian ran a finger down her cheek. "He saved your life."

She stared after him, the smell of his soft skin lingering in her nose. Her eyes trailed his tent, searched the tidy and comfortable belongings. So much of her world was tangled up in him, dependent on him. She couldn't afford for him to distract her, couldn't be split in her loyalties. The faint memory of his lips played across her mind and her stomach dropped to her knees. She couldn't afford—

She nearly screamed as Narita ducked into the tent. Narita's smile was teasing as she crossed the space toward her. "And how are we feeling?"

Pria rolled her eyes in annoyance. "I'm fine—you can all stop coddling me now."

Narita's grin grew wider. "Oh, is that what has been going on in here?" Pria's flat stare promised violence as Narita threw her hands up in surrender. "Seriously, you scared him. He hasn't left this tent for three days."

"I've been out for three days!"

"If it wasn't for Orotid, he'd have likely been worse than you when you woke up." Chair pulled close, Narita dropped beside her and whispered conspiratorially. "He was looking rather handsome this morning, don't you think?"

Pria slammed her palm into her forehead. "I am the last sane person in the land."

Narita giggled. "Okay, Mian is off limits. What do you want to talk about?"

"Arrogant, stubborn man. What could he possibly be thinking?" Pria moved to stand before she remembered how weak she was and dropped back to the chair.

Narita raised an eyebrow. "Do you really want me to answer that?"

"Shut up." She dropped her eyes and turned the cup in her hands. "What happened to Jeran?"

Narita took Pria's cup and set it on the table behind her. "He got that thing off your neck. Tore him up pretty good. That was a tough creature." Pria's hand drifted back to her throat. "You going to be all right?"

She smiled. "It will take more than a phisher to take me out."

"I bet."

"What of Kyneira?" Pria asked.

"The city is mostly clear. We've been finding small pockets here and there and with reinforcements we should be able to sweep the town thoroughly and resettle everyone."

Pria's back straightened and Narita recognized the shift from friend to priestess. "I wish to be informed the second my brother arrives. Has anyone started a census to see how many were lost? We may need to bring in supplemental workers to repair everything."

Narita stood bowing low. "It will be done, Priestess."

Pria nodded as she struggled to her feet. "And find me some proper attire. I can't command in one of Mian's silk shirts."

Narita's grin took in Pria's exposed legs. "I don't know. I'm betting the men would do anything you say dressed like that."

Pria glared in mock reprimand. "Go, Narita."

Narita bounded from the tent with a bright giggle.

"She's right; I've always found your legs to be one of your best features," Mian said.

Pria kept her back to Mian as she stumbled, testing her feet. "Will you always be a delinquent? You shouldn't have your mind or your eyes on my legs."

He crossed the tent and stopped behind her. "I keep forgetting the almighty priestess is not allowed to be human." She cringed as he slid his hands down her arms but was too unsteady to pull away. Couldn't force herself to want to pull away. "Not allowed to be seen as a woman."

She closed her eyes as he pulled her to his chest and wrapped her in his arms. The tremor that wracked her body had nothing to do with her injury. "It's not right, Mian." She hated how weak her voice sounded.

He buried his face in her neck as she turned her head away. "What's not right about it? There are no laws forbidding a priestess to marry."

The word sent a jolt through her body. She stiffened and pulled from his grip her face stern. "There is no law, but a priestess traditionally does not marry." Arms crossed, she tried to ignore her exposed legs. "I cannot afford to be distracted right now. Janu needs me. Trimera needs me."

"I would never come between you and your brother," he said. "You know I would never do anything to hurt Janu."

She held out her hand as she waited for him to go silent. "I cannot afford for you to be distracted either."

He threw his hands up and paced the length of the tent in a rage. "Don't do that—don't handle me like I'm some commoner you are trying to placate! Don't keep me at arm's length!"

She let his emotion fan her resolve. "I need you to calm down now, Mian."

A growl rumbled from his chest as he rushed across the tent and shook her by the arms. "I will not calm down! You can't…" He drew a deep breath then loosened his grip on her arms as she struggled not to jerk back from him. He pressed his forehead to hers, her face cupped in his hands, and his eyes rolled up to meet her gaze. "No. I'm calm. I'm not going to let you just ignore this because you think I'm acting crazy." He dropped a hand to the small of her back, pulled her against his chest, and pressed his mouth over hers. Her back stiffened before she melted against him.

Pria's head swam with his smell, his taste, the strength of his arms around her. Her heart raced in her chest and she wondered how his touch had ever made her calm. He stared down into her eyes as he pulled back, her fingers hovering above his chest.

"I do hope I'm not interrupting…" Narita's grin was mischievous as she crossed the tent, folded clothes pressed to her chest. "I can always come back later."

Pria stepped around him, her face unreadable. "There is no need for that."

Narita sighed in resignation. "I brought some clothes and a steward should be arriving soon with some food."

"Excellent, thank you Narita." Pria took the clothes and laid them on the table as she kept her back to Mian. "Commander, run and fetch Jeran, I would like to see him."

His eyes sparkled with anger as he paused at her shoulder. "Anything you wish, Priestess. We can finish this discussion later."

"We will *not*."

Her body jerked as he ran the back of his fingers along her arm. His lips brushed her ear as he leaned close to keep his voice low. "Fine with me, I prefer action to words anyway."

Her face paled as he nodded to Narita and slipped from the tent. Pria snapped out the breeches, her knuckles white. "Stubborn, irritating man."

"He does seem to be quite irrational."

"How many times do I have to tell you to shut up?" Pria snapped.

"A few more to be sure."

Pria blocked her out as she dressed. "I'm completely alone, truly the last sane person in the kingdom. Honestly, how am I supposed to work under these conditions?"

"Oh, poor High Priestess, she is so tormented!"

"You can leave now," Pria said.

"No, I don't think I will."

Pria turned toward Narita, eyes narrowed. "Are you refusing a direct order?"

Narita's head tilted thoughtfully. "That wasn't a direct order—it was an allowance that gave me permission to stay or go, and I choose to stay."

"Fine." Pria jerked her laces tight. "Then *I* will leave." She jumped back from the tent flap as Mian ducked in. "What are you doing back here?"

He glared at her as he dropped into a bow. "I believe my high priestess commanded me to fetch Jeran."

Pria straightened and stepped back. "Proceed, Commander."

Mian rolled his eyes as Jeran stepped in behind him and glanced around in uneasy curiosity. He bowed to Pria. "High Priestess."

"Let me see your hand, soldier."

His brow wrinkled as he looked up at her. "Pria…"

Her eyebrow rose in a silent threat.

"Priestess…the healer already looked at my hand;" he continued, "I assure you it is fine."

Her hand, out before him, did not waver.

He laid his wrist in her palm. "Pria, it's fine."

She ran her fingers along the angry cuts. "*Priestess*, Jeran. Mostly scratches—you are lucky I got most of the venom. It definitely could have been worse. What were you thinking?"

His eyes searched her face for a moment as if he wondered what viperous retort brewed behind her stolid face. "I was thinking that my prince's sister and priestess was dying in front of me. What would you have had me do?"

"Phishers do not kill—they only drain, make you weak so you can be handled. They will, however, kill non-magical creatures that get in the way. You were lucky." She turned to leave. "I wish to be informed the second my brother arrives. Narita, send the steward to my tent when he comes. I do not wish to be disturbed otherwise."

Mian slammed his palm to his forehead after the tent flap fell back in place behind Pria. "Why couldn't I be in love with *anyone* else?"

"She does seem to be acting a bit excessively." Narita paused. "But I do think you should take heart in how strongly she feels she has to fight you. 'Course that doesn't mean it's going to be any easier."

Mian grinned as a steward pulled the tent flap back. "Commander, we brought food for the priestess."

"Bring it in."

Narita eyed him as he took the tray of food and guided the steward from the tent. "What are you up to?"

He spun as he raised his hands in dramatic flair. "My priestess wants pomp and propriety, so that is precisely what I intend to give her!"

Jeran shook his head. "I think you are going to lose Janu a commander, fool."

He winked before he moved to a chest in the corner and rummaged through the clothes within. "We'll see, won't we?"

Pria pulled her feet beneath her, sinking into the thick cushions. The firestone beside her filled the tent with a pleasant heat as she searched the book perched on her lap. *A History of Service* had been required reading in her classes—a study of the reigns of past priestesses was supposed to keep you from making their mistakes. So many of these women's actions had seemed so logical but still had resulted in disaster. So much pain and suffering could result from her smallest decision.

She rubbed her face as she felt the tent flap shift behind her. "Set it on the table, please."

"As you command, Priestess."

She rose with a sigh and faced Mian as he set the tray down. She cocked an eyebrow at his brilliant pristine dress uniform and the deep bow he offered her. "I said I didn't wish to be disturbed."

"The priestess said she did not wish to be disturbed except for food and the prince."

"And what happened to the steward?" she demanded.

He stepped forward as he pulled a folding camp chair over to the table and snapped out a linen napkin. "As you so emphatically pointed out, you are the high priestess and the high priestess should be attended by someone who complements her station. As ranking officer and Battle Leader, who better than I?"

"Fine." She rolled her eyes in annoyance.

She dropped into the chair but he grabbed her arm before she could touch the tray. "Today we are featuring pheasant with a raspberry sauce, roasted potatoes, and carrots. Would the priestess like some wine?"

She glared, her mind searching for what he could be up to. "No, tea will be fine."

Pressing the linen across her lap, he said, "I will start the water." He brushed her shoulder as he passed to set the tea kettle onto the firestone. The touch heated her skin well after he'd moved on. The stone itself was no more than a rock imbibed with a spell to radiate heat. The spell made the rock glow with a soft yellow hue. "I didn't know these existed outside of the Lorien."

She sampled a piece of pheasant and wiped juice from her chin. "It is a simple enchantment. I could make you one if you'd like."

"I would like that very much." He lifted the boiling pot from the stone and sprinkled in some leaves from a pouch in his pocket. He set a saucer down beside her along with a bowl of honey. Returning with the tea, he filled a cup and set the pot aside.

Her head was filled with the warm musk that had filled her childhood, ruled so much of her life. She pulled it deep into her lungs, let the memories calm her as her heartbeat sped beyond her control.

His gaze burned along her skin, left a tingling that lingered, made her worry about her clothes, her hair. "Is there anything else I can get for you, Priestess?"

"I am fine, thank you," she whispered.

He brushed a stray hair behind her ear and drew his thumb along her cheek. "You need your rest. I'll leave a guard outside at all times if you should need anything. Sleep well, my priestess."

He stood to leave but she jumped to her feet. "Mian wait!"

His worried green-eyed gaze pierced her very soul. She crossed the tent and pulled his mouth down to hers, a tangle of his hair in her fingers. His arms snaked around her back to lift her feet from the ground. He forced her mouth hard against his—

She jerked up, heart pounding as her eyes darted around her deserted tent. The blanket tucked around her was strange and the tent was full of the smell of venison. A polished tray sat abandoned atop her camp table. *A History of Service* was laid atop her travel chest.

A soldier poked his head in through the flap. "Priestess, are you okay?"

She eyed him skeptically, not even trusting her own memories. "I'm fine, why are you guarding my tent?"

"Commander Mian said to be sure to take care of any needs you might have. Do you need anything?" he asked.

"No, thank you."

She dropped back to the cushions, her sheets and clothes clammy with sweat. She grimaced in distaste as she threw the sheets off, waving a rekindling spell at the firestone and stepping out into the night.

She ignored the guards as they ghosted along behind her, sure to keep their distance. Most people lived in reverent fear of her. She was a symbol of power and protection, a living weapon to keep them safe. She had been groomed for this. From the day she was born she had been drilled with selfless duty and sacrifice. Her entire life was about the greater good.

Her eyes focused on the tent before her, and she was not surprised to see Mian's snarling wolf in scarlet. She threw the flaps aside and charged in, glaring down at the offending man as he slept. Of course he was having no trouble sleeping—he wasn't about to lead his people down a path of destruction, the likes of which had never been seen before.

She kicked him in the ribs and smiled in satisfaction as he doubled over, coughing. He stared up at her incredulously, his arms wrapped around his bruised chest. "What was that for!"

She paced around the tent, arms flailing in exaggeration. "You think the world should just fall into your lap because you wish it? You couldn't even begin to comprehend the pressure of duty and sacrifice. No! You just walk in and expect me to fall into your arms!"

"I never said that!"

"Well you've got another thing coming, soldier! My brother needs you focused and if I have to beat sense into you, I will!" she said.

"Pria, calm down!"

"I am not excited!" Her angry scream shattered the silence of the tent. He stared at her from the floor. Her face fell. "Sorry."

Untangled from his blanket, Mian stood and shook his hair back from his face. "It's all right." He pulled a chair out for her then dropped into another. She kept her eyes on the table before her as she played with the cuffs of her long sleeves.

"It's not a good idea."

"So you keep saying," he replied.

She snapped forward. "Do you know much history?"

He studied her face leaning forward to meet her. "Mostly military, but I'm not completely ignorant."

She raised her eyes to his as she spoke. "In school, we must learn the complete history of the ruling priestesses. For five hundred years, peace and stability.

"Hanoria of Trent was the first of the priestesses to get married. The civil war of her reign decimated the population. None of her children survived. The second to attempt marriage was Lenoria of Prull—her reign was marked by famine and disease." She sighed. "In all, seventeen priestesses have gotten married; fifteen of those reigns brought ruin."

He watched her as she stared at him, her expectant eyes trying to pull an answer from his guarded face. "How many disasters befell those who didn't marry?"

Her anger jumped. Of course he wouldn't understand, wouldn't see the benefits of logic, reason, caution. "It doesn't matter! The point is they let their loyalties be split and brought destruction on the people they were supposed to protect!"

"Pria, I really think that is generalizing too much," he said. "You don't know what else was going on at those times. It could be a coincidence."

She slapped her hand on the table. "It's not a coincidence, Mian!"

He sighed. "I don't buy it. If they were so sure that marriage destroyed those reigns, they would have made a law against it, and they didn't."

"No law, but years of tradition. Could you really sacrifice lives?"

"Would you really sacrifice your happiness?" he pressed.

She raised her hands. "What makes you think I'm not happy?"

"You shouldn't be afraid to let your heart feel."

"My heart feels plenty," she said.

Mian smirked. "This is the best reason you could come up with?"

"The destruction of my land and people seemed to be a pretty good reason."

He watched her as the energy drained from her face. "I don't buy it. Even if I distracted you from your duties or you made a poor judgment, you don't really think Janu wouldn't catch it? He's not an idiot, Pria."

"He shouldn't have to!"

"You're his advisor, not his ruler," he said.

She guffawed. "You'll never understand!"

He leaned forward, waiting for her eyes to meet his. "I do understand. What I want you to understand is you can't put such high expectations on yourself. You can't expect to not make mistakes."

"But I don't have to knowingly walk into them either!"

His lips twitched. "Did you just call me a mistake?" A smile curled across his face, eyes alight with amusement.

"Can't you ever be serious?" He held her gaze, never losing his amusement and drew a curve across her mouth. She broke out in laughter. "I hate you!"

He leaned back from her, a satisfied grin on his face. "No you don't."

She dropped her head. "I could lose the post in Trimera." She waited in the silence before her fear forced her to look up at him.

"Why?"

"They don't think I have enough experience for such an important post," she said. "What if this is the last tick? That last piece of evidence to show that I shouldn't be here?"

"Then I'll follow you wherever they post you." There was no question in his voice.

"And leave Trimera unprotected?"

He waved a hand. "Trimera has dozens of smart, talented commanders with years of experience on me."

"I'm serious, Mian."

"So am I," he said. "You are home. Tell me I am not yours and we can drop the conversation now."

"I can't do that." She could feel the force of his grin without looking at him. She pulled herself up straight and glared him down. "You listen good, soldier: I will not have such foolishness from my prince's Battle Leader."

He rolled his eyes. "Fine. Jeran's been bucking for a promotion, he can have it."

Her face became stoic as she sank back into her chair. "If it came down to you or him, it would always have to be him."

His smile vanished. "I wouldn't have it any other way."

"And I'd expect the same from you if the positions were reversed."

"I will not promise that," he said.

Her brow dropped. "What?"

"I can't." He shrugged. "I already promised Janu that I would protect you over him. I can't break a promise to him."

She slammed her fist on the tabletop. "That conniving little snake! How dare he ask that of you!" Her jaw snapped shut as he raised an eyebrow at her. "That is completely different!"

"Of course it is, because you came up with it."

"Don't be so smart," she snapped.

His grin bloomed again as he stared up through his eyelashes. "I can't help it."

She shook her head and stood. "As entertaining as you think you are, I for one need my rest."

He stood with a smile as he watched her cross the tent. She turned back and eyed him appraisingly, thinking, before she swept back toward him.

Balanced on her toes, she snaked a hand behind his neck and pulled his mouth down to hers. His fingers drifted toward her waist, but she dropped back to her heels and turned to leave.

A triumphant grin bloomed across his face. He pumped his fist before he dropped to his bedroll, smiling up at the roof above him. "I win."

Pria leaned her head on her knees, arms wrapped around her legs. She had been sitting like that all night, unable to sleep. Every time her eyes drifted shut, her mind filled with visions of kissing Mian while Trimera burned around her. Now she sat slumped in her tent, berating herself for being foolish, for letting her emotions endanger the people whose lives were entrusted to her. Perhaps the Lorien was right in their worries—perhaps her connections to her family were a danger to her post.

"Well, baby sister, they told me you were recovering nicely from your attack," Janu said as he ducked inside.

She slumped in misery. "I have failed."

"Is that so?" he asked.

"If I stay I will have doomed us all, brought ruin to all our parents fought and died to leave us!"

Janu bent to inspect the stack of books beside her. "Curious. How precisely did you do that?"

"Don't patronize me, Janu. I know you well enough to know that you've already talked to Mian."

Janu dropped to a cushion at her side and stretched out his long legs. "Just because he's my friend doesn't mean we are conspiring against you." He pulled her to his chest and gave her back a soothing rub. "He always used to say that he was going to marry you, guess he wasn't joking."

She pulled away from his chest and brushed her hair from her face. "I'm going to resign my position."

"You've got to be joking! Over this?"

Her chest wracked with a sigh. "You don't understand—once they learn of this, once the Lorien learns that I have fallen so far as to risk my own people for the sake of a romance, they will strip me of this post anyway. The land of Reia cannot afford to have a frivolous girl positioned in Trimera. I will resign my position to retain some modicum of dignity and they will assign you a priestess who is not a foolish girl."

"You're being ridiculous. Why do I keep having to have these conversations? I have the best minds in the kingdom helping me but all they do is try to talk me into others."

"I am being *practical*." She faced him, her serious eyes laced with anxiety. "Janu, the only reason I was given this post is because it traditionally goes to the strongest living priestess. As a high priestess, it should have been mine without contest, but as it was my home there were many who did not think I would be able to hold it. They thought my connections to the people would create a conflict and distract me from my post. Obviously they were right. I will return to the Lorien until I have my wits about me. They can reassign me then."

He stared at her in confusion. "I don't understand. You've done nothing wrong."

"Haven't I?" Her eyes were awash with pain as she stared up at him. "I nearly got Narita and Mian killed. Kyneira fell right beneath my nose and now I am mired hip deep in ridiculous thoughts of romance!" The bite on her neck twinged with her agitation. "And let's not forget that I nearly got myself taken by the horde!"

"Lana had no connection to us and she was taken by the horde!"

Pria rubbed her eyes with her fingertips. "But that only goes to further my point! She had her head on straight and she lost herself to the grinlo! I have no hope to hold this position. My only chance to maintain any respectability as a priestess is to willingly vacate my position to one of leveler head and more stable disposition."

The silence stretched between them. Janu was forming his argument for her to stay, but she had already made up her mind. She would not allow her foolish heart to destroy her home and her family.

He lifted his head and pinned her with a piercing gaze. "So you'll run? You'll show them all that you are the foolish girl you are trying so hard to prove you are not. A real woman could face her fears and stand despite them."

"A real woman acknowledges the dangers of her choices and decides based on logic," she said.

His gaze sharpened. He smelled blood, and like a lion, he honed in on it. "Logic would dictate you not leave us with a weaker substitute. *Logic* is not why you are running."

Her lidded eyes dropped to her hands. "The chances of my leading Trimera into disaster increase exponentially if I fall victim to my starstruck heart. I can't just stay here like nothing has happened."

His eyes grew wide in astonishment. "I don't believe it. You're afraid of Mian."

She stared at him flatly. "Now who's being ridiculous?"

"I never thought I'd live to see the day. Since when are you afraid of a mere soldier?"

"I am not afraid of Mian, and he is much more than a mere soldier."

Janu shook his head, face twisted with disgust. "He's a lackey and an all-around louse! You are royalty and a priestess—he's not good enough to lick your boot heels, yet you're afraid of him!"

"I am not afraid of Mian! And you know as well as I that he is a fine commander and a great man, if a hopeless scoundrel."

He waved a hand at her. "Phaw! He's a hopeless fiend. His family couldn't have less than three-fourths the estates we do." He leaned toward her, hand cupped to his mouth. "Plus, I hear most women find him less than attractive."

Eyes rolled to the ceiling, she felt the conviction rush out of her. "You are trying to make me defend him, see that I like him."

"I'm trying to make you *think*!" he said. "You only villainize Mian because you know you like him and you don't want to appear vulnerable."

She dropped her chin to her knees with a pouty huff. "When did you get so smart?"

"In the ten years I didn't have you watching out for me. Had to learn to think for myself—it was rough."

Her eyes hazed with anxiety. "He eats at my mind, Janu. You need someone who is focused."

"I need you! You are stronger than this." Janu shook his hands.

"I'm afraid I'm losing my grip."

"So let go," he said.

"Janu…"

"Pria." He shrugged. "What's the worst that could happen?"

Pria spread her hands before her. "Trimera could fall into complete ruin, destruction could rain on everyone I love, and the people I love and the people I protect would all die a horrible death."

"I'm glad you have such faith in me."

"It has nothing to do with you!" She jumped to her feet and paced the tent in agitation. "How can I guide and advise you if my mind is addled with thoughts of Mian? Not to mention the fact that if the Lorien learns of this, there is a long line of priestesses that will argue I am unfit."

He snagged her arm as she passed and jerked her back to the floor beside him. "The Lorien will not let anyone tear you from your post unless you prove yourself unworthy. Besides, your mind is pretty filled with him now. Maybe what you need is to fill your life with him as well."

"And what if that only makes it worse?"

"What if ignoring it makes it worse?" he asked.

"Why are you on his side?"

He gave her slim shoulders a gentle squeeze. "I'm on the side that keeps both my sister and my friend. I can't afford to lose either."

She buried her face in her hands as she muffled a scream.

"What, they didn't teach you anything about romance at the Lorien?"

"Strangely I think I missed that," she mumbled into her hands.

"Well, think of this as field training." He cocked his head to the side. "You going to make it now?"

"No."

"Nonsense." He came to his feet and held out a hand. "Come on, I need my priestess."

"What you have is an emotionally compromised, physically unstable sister."

He shrugged as he pulled her up. "It'll do for now." He tucked her hand into his elbow before he stepped out into the bright warmth of afternoon.

Pria's back straightened, head held high as she glided along at his side. "I don't know how to handle this."

"It's just a briefing, you've been through dozens."

The camp swept past them in rows of tents and campfires. They passed soldiers among the tents but for once their eyes didn't put her on the defensive. Her mind remained focused on Janu. "Don't be dense, Janu. I meant courting. I don't know how to handle courting. There isn't really any protocol for it."

"Then I say you get to decide your own rules." He paused outside of a large pavilion-style tent and looked into her eyes. "I have faith in you both; I know you will find a balance where you can both be happy."

She drew a deep breath as guards lifted the tent flaps aside. "I may kill him, you know."

"I think you'll be pleasantly surprised."

Everyone in the tent stood as they entered then bowed low to the floor. Her eyes locked with Mian's as he stood and something tugged at her soul. "I doubt it."

Janu took his place at the head of the table next to Mian and guided Pria to his opposite side. When they sat as one, the rest of the room took their ease. Narita dropped into the chair next to Pria and grasped her hand beneath the table. Pria didn't let her eyes drift but she felt some of the tension drain from her body.

Mian rapped on the table to draw attention to the front of the room. As he stood he nodded first to Janu then to Pria. "Your Majesty, Priestess. I am pleased to inform you that our scouts report the city clear and surrounding land patrolled and guarded. I will defer to Farner for a casualty report."

The older man hesitated but stood and bowed. "Your Majesty, High Priestess." He mimicked Mian, unsure of the attention. "I would like to begin by thanking you and your men for clearing our city." He lifted a parchment from the table before him. "These numbers would be considerably higher had you not."

His eyes dropped to the lists in his hands. "The Lady Narita escorted a small group into Kyneira to locate census records. There were twenty thousand citizens living in and around Kyneira. So far, known survivors number around one thousand. Many were able to flee before the siege took hold and several more may still be in hiding, but our estimates are pretty optimistic at five thousand." He sank back to his chair.

Pria sat forward. "The lives lost here will not be forgotten, nor will those saved. Kyneira will not be lost."

"We will be moving in supplemental workers to help rebuild the city." Janu met each gaze with determination. "I will be stationing several top commanders in the city itself to be rotated out on a later determined schedule. We will keep a constant line of defense along the northern border."

Mian nodded. "We know they will not give up, but we do not intend to lose Kyneira."

"Commanders Mian and Narita have already volunteered to remain here." Janu glanced to Pria and she nodded. "The high priestess and I will also be staying. Master Farner, I would like you to be our personal advisor."

Farner paled. "I am honored, Your Majesty, but I have no credentials to warrant such a position."

"Master Farner, I am quite aware of your station. I have been informed that you were instrumental in rallying the survivors when the high priestess disarmed the shield."

Farner shook his head. "I answered a few questions."

"And that is all we are going to ask of you now." Janu stood. "We will need all the firsthand experience we can get, as much knowledge as we can gather, about the city and what happened during the siege. This is what we must now ask of you. Master Farner I will need you now; Commander Mian, will you see to arrangements?"

The tent emptied as Pria stared at the table in front of her. Mian was watching her when she looked up, her face unreadable. "How are you feeling?" he asked.

"I'm not sure yet."

He stood and offered his arm. "Come on, I'll see you to your tent."

Her heart jumped as her fingers slid into his hand. Her mind wouldn't focus as he tucked her hand into his elbow. His arm was tight beneath her fingers, the slick silk cool to the touch. Soldiers bowed and saluted as they passed among them but she didn't notice them, couldn't notice them. She had spent years building a dam to hold back her emotions behind the confident decorum of a priestess, but in one swift act Mian had torn open the floodgates. His presence was a downpour she couldn't ignore. She dropped his arm as she glided into her tent, her heart pounding like thunder.

"I'll be sure to inform you when I've found you rooms, Priestess."

"Thank you… Mian." Her lips curled as her tongue formed around his name.

His crooked grin was genuine. She held out a hand toward him, unwilling to trust her feet. He slipped toward her, his fingers cupping her hand and pulling it to his lips. All she could hear was the rush of blood through her veins as his mouth met her knuckles. She jerked her hand from his grip and wrapped her arms around his waist as she pulled herself to his chest. His hands crept to her back as he rested his chin on top of her head.

Her mind cleared but the feel of his body was intoxicating. "It must be a secret, Mian. I cannot jeopardize the image of the priestess."

He nodded as she pulled away to meet his gaze. "I understand. I will let you be a rock for them as long as you're yourself with me."

She tilted her head toward him as he ran his thumb down her cheek. She slowed her breath for a moment as she tried to remember why she was speaking. "If…" He cupped her cheek in his palm and she pressed her eyes closed and inhaled. "If…either of us shirk our duties, it's over. No second chance."

He stared down into her eyes. "If it comes to that, I will end it myself."

She pressed her forehead into his chest, tangled her fingers in his silk shirt. "I must be crazy."

"I've heard that said about you." He chest quaked with mirth as she jabbed him hard in the ribs.

"You are still a jerk."

"You are still a brat." He pulled back from her reluctantly. "And speaking of shirking duties, I believe I better get to settling these men."

"Yes you should, Commander."

He whimpered as she brushed her lips across his.

"You'd better hurry, Mian."

He backed through the tent flaps with a growl. "That is not even fair."

The smile wouldn't leave her lips as she moved through her tent. She changed into her silk priestess suit; if Janu intended to rule from here they would need as much normalcy as they could project. If people see what they expect to see, she knew, it helps give them faith and keep them calm.

Her hair fell loose around her face and shoulders as she stepped from the tent and the guards took up their customary shadow. She made a loop through the soldiers, being sure to project an air of confident knowledge to dispel their worries of her injury.

Appearance made, she set out to find Janu and Farner.

She stopped as her eyes fell on a man at the edge of the soldier's camp. His eyes never wavered, his gaze bold and unafraid—he wanted her to know he watched. The cool breeze shifted his long scarlet robes. His gaze burned across her flesh and left a slimy film that itched.

One of her guards stepped up behind her and whispered in her ear. "Is there something wrong, Priestess?"

Her head shook but her mind was too engrossed in this man. There was something about him that tickled at her memory and lifted the hair on her arms. She watched as the man raised his arm toward her. "Everyone down!" She jumped forward and threw a shield in front of the soldiers, rocking back as a wall of green fire crashed around the invisible wall. The stranger took off running and she broke after him, ignorant to the shouts from the startled guards. Her opponent's long legs easily outdistanced her. He was lost in the trees long before she made the edge of camp.

She slid to a halt and searched the trees as her guards formed a bristling wall around her. Her chest heaved with exertion as she knelt to inspect the ground where the man had stood. She pressed her palm against his footprint and closed her eyes. The residue of his strength was amazing as it tingled up her arm.

She stood and scanned the trees again as more soldiers rushed up behind them. She didn't turn as Janu stepped to her side. "You shouldn't be here."

Janu tucked his thumbs into his belt. "Doesn't seem like it's me they were after."

Mian's body was tense. "Are you all right?"

"He was just sizing me up. The attack was only to slow me so he could get away."

Both men's eyes turned to the trees. "Who was that?" Janu asked.

Pria eased the tension in her muscles. "I think it is safe to say that 'he' was likely the magical being behind the grinlo."

Janu nodded. "I want you to return to Austeria. Mian, you take her."

Mian had grabbed her arm and was already pulling her away before she could jerk loose. "Honestly, Janu. If I leave, you and your men would be defenseless against his attacks."

"I am not letting you prance around here waiting for him to come after you again."

"He could be watching us right now, plotting how to kill you or take you from us," Mian argued.

She laid a comforting hand on Mian's arm and started at the tension in his muscles. "I felt him leave. He wouldn't risk staying or attacking while I'm alert and ready for him—that would be stupid."

"Pria, please!"

"Prince Janu, these are my people and it is my sworn duty to protect them. How do you propose I do that crouching inside a castle?" Pria snapped.

"You can't protect anyone if you are dead."

"I have both the training and the strength to protect myself and I will not cower to make you feel better." Mian's arm trembled beneath her fingers now. "I suggest we work on getting these people safely inside the city and setting up guards. I will contact the Lorien and confer with my peers. I have been keeping in contact with them—maybe they might have something of use to us. Commander, do you have a room where I might have some privacy?"

"Of course, Priestess." His eyes flashed to Janu and they both nodded before Mian offered her his arm.

He kept his silence as they picked their way toward the city.

"I do not intend to throw my life away needlessly," she ground out. "You can breathe."

"That was much too close, Pria. Losing you would be more than any of us could handle."

"You *would* handle it and you would protect our people, as is your duty as well," Pria said. "You must focus on the big picture and remember the people who rely on you for protection."

He drew a ragged breath as they entered the city proper. The streets were strewn with debris, but most of the bodies had been removed. His jaw was tense as they turned down a side street then entered a large inn. He stopped in the common room as the soldiers that had followed them swarmed past and poured through the rooms and halls.

Pria raised an eyebrow. "You brought me to an unsecured building?"

Mian glared down at her incredulously. "Don't be ridiculous. Just making sure we didn't miss anything."

She shook her head and tried to hide her smile. "Are you this bad with Janu?"

"Yes, but he never gets mad at me for doing it."

She laughed and gave him a shove as a soldier trotted down the stairs toward them. "The first room on the right is clear, sir."

"Thank you Audren." He led Pria up the stairs, nodding at the guards posted at the door. He guided Pria inside, slipped into the room behind her, and secured the door.

He jerked her into his arms and held her to his chest, his breath labored. "Tell me who I'm after. I'll hunt him down and kill him."

She molded against him, slipping her arms around his waist and let his warm comfort fill her body. "I know you would, Mian."

"Then permit me."

She pressed her cheek against his chest. "Why do you smell so good?"

He grabbed her face and pressed his forehead to hers. "No diverting."

"Mian, even if I knew who he was, you would not be able to handle him."

He shrugged. "I don't know. I realize that I may not have any powers, but I could surprise you."

She laughed as she tangled her fingers in his shirt. She couldn't show him how worried she truly was. If he had even the slightest inkling of the level of anxiety she had, she would never keep him from doing something foolish and dangerous.

The truth was the stranger's attack was more than a test. He was not only bold enough to confirm her fears of someone controlling the horde but also confident enough to show his true intent. There was no way to deny it now: His intent was to capture her just like he had captured Lana. None of that changed her obligations to her people, though. "Mian, I have trained for years for this kind of thing. You have to trust that I can handle it."

She pulled on him as she rose up on her toes but hesitated just before her lips touched his. She dropped back to her heels and straightened his shirt before she stepped back from his arms. "I will contact the Lorien. They will advise me on how to proceed with our visitor."

His eyes were unreadable as he watched her. He turned to leave but stopped, his hand poised on the knob. "Why did you do that?"

She blinked in confusion. "Do what?"

"You started to kiss me but then you stopped. Why?"

Her skin flared red as she took an involuntary step back and dropped her eyes to the floor. "I don't know what you're talking about."

His grin slipped as he leaned back on the door. "Priestess, are you afraid to kiss me?"

Pria rounded on him, pulling the full weight of her station around her as her robes swayed with her legs. "Commander, I believe you have duties to see to."

Hands clasped behind his back, he took a large step toward her. "I do, and I will get right to them…after you kiss me."

She leveled a no-nonsense glare at his mischievous grin. "Mian, duty comes first."

"Then I suggest you get to it. I'm waiting."

She crossed her arms. "You are still completely intolerable."

"You only seem to say that when I'm right and winning an argument."

She held her arms stiff to shield herself from his searching eyes. "That is ridiculous. You are never right."

He pursued her across the room, reducing the gap between them. "So, if I'm never right, then you shouldn't have trouble kissing me."

Her mind raced as she struggled to find an escape. "Maybe I don't want to kiss you." She bumped into the wall behind her and stared up into his eyes.

"Oh…you want to kiss me." He brushed his nose up her neck and across her cheek. "We'll just see how long you hold out." He crossed the room and bowed from the door. "Priestess."

She glared after him. "You are still insufferable."

When she was alone, she glanced around the room to take stock of what was there. It had been tossed, with furniture flung about, but not damaged overmuch. She righted a chair and moved it over to the cold hearth. She gathered several discarded logs and stacked them in the fireplace before setting it ablaze with a touch.

Arranged comfortably on the chair, she sat a moment to let the flames warm her body. She pulled a small flame from the fire to cradle it in her cupped palm and stared into the pulsing orange.

She focused until a warmth began to grow at the base of her skull. She always associated the feeling with being home. She waited there, poised on the brink of a breakthrough.

The minutes stretched by before she heard a soft chime.

"Pria?" The word was a gentle buzz that stretched across her mind. "What is wrong?"

Pria felt her lips curl. Nae was Head of Articulation and in charge of all communications in and out of the Lorien. She had taught many classes when Pria was enlisted. Nae, who Pria had always thought had a warm motherly air about her, had been a firm supporter for Pria's stationing in Trimera. Her voice lifted the knot in Pria's stomach.

"I need the resources of the Lorien, Nae." Pria's eyes hazed as she sent the memory of the man from earlier to Nae's mind. "I have never encountered him before."

Something shuddered. "I will see what I can find for you. How is your home?"

"We are fighting to hold Kyneira, and the horde pushes us at every turn. Someone is leading them."

"You think this man is the one?" Nae asked.

"I'm sure he's not a friend."

"I want to send someone to help you, if you wouldn't mind." Nae's voice was gentle—was she probing for something? Not Nae. Nae wouldn't be gathering information to hurt her.

Pria remained silent for some time as she weighed her options. The fact was she needed help. She couldn't be everywhere at once and there was no telling when this man would show up again. She let her breath rush from her chest in a huff. "I would appreciate any help you could give us, if just to have more protection for my people."

"I will get back to you with what I find on your visitor."

"Thank you, Nae," Pria said.

Pria blinked and pulled her eyes back to the flame flickering in her palm. She exhaled and sent it floating to the hearth as she stood and arranged her robes. A small riverstone sat on the hearth. She cupped the stone and sent it to Nae. The resonance on the stone would tell her where to send help.

She left the fire burning as she swung the door wide, not surprised to see Mian still milling about among the soldiers in the hall. He made his way to her side as he noticed her, his bow deep and courtly. "Priestess."

"I will require two men to guard this room and bring those who arrive here to me immediately."

Mian's brow wrinkled but he nodded. He didn't bother to give a command; his men were good enough to know what was expected of them. She smiled as Mian fell in at her side. She kept her voice low as she glided along the hallway. "That didn't look much like what you were supposed to be doing."

"Maybe not to you. I had scouts running the whole time you were in there. Would you like to see your rooms?"

"Have you settled Janu yet?"

"Right beside your room." He walked without speaking for a moment as he glanced at the men around him. "Opposite of mine."

She glanced at him sideways. "Delinquent."

"Just making myself handy, in case I'm needed. I've already taken the liberty to move your things from your tent. If this man returns, I want a solid structure—"

"For him to set on fire?"

He glared down at her. "Cute."

"You really shouldn't worry. If he thought he had the strength to take me, he would have tried."

He waved at the dusty hall around them. "What do you call what he did?"

"He was testing my strength, gauging my abilities. It would have been foolish to make an actual attack while I was protected among military. He would never be able to fight me and the soldiers."

"I'm glad you're so sure," he growled.

She grabbed his arm and turned him to face her as their escort formed up around them. "I am sure, Mian." He kept his eyes from her face as she tangled her fists in his shirt. "Mian, this I was trained for. This is what I spent ten years at the Lorien learning to do."

His arms clamped around her as he drew a slow deep breath. "We'd better get you inside."

When he turned to walk away, she shook her head and straightened her robes as she slipped into her well-practiced glide. Her own mind was full of enough questions. Fighting she had seen, battle she had seen, but magical fighting was something she had only ever encountered in the protective grip of the Lorien. Something about the stranger had seemed familiar, like the memory of a dream. Had she met him before? Quite possible, with the man slipping in and out of Austeria whenever he pleased. Bold.

Mian paused at a large estate and allowed the men around them to flow forward and search the building. She laughed as she glanced up at the man beside her. "You are tearing me up with this."

"Security is my responsibility. If I have to accept your responsibilities, you will have to accept mine." He smiled down at her but his eyes were still tight. "If you have to face an unknown evil by yourself, then I will spare no effort in keeping you alive to do so."

Her mind fought between amusement and affection. Ridiculous he may be, but she had to admit there was something comforting about the knowledge that Mian would jump between her and any danger that might present itself. Still, she couldn't help but tweak him some. "So, what you are saying is that you are going to be worse now than you were before to compensate for some unintended slight on your manhood?"

"Pretty much."

"Great. I am so glad we could reach this understanding," she said.

"Me too."

He rocked up onto his toes. "High Priestess, if this…gentleman…were to attack, what…"

She felt her face blanch and she tucked her head. "The temptation to overtake the horde comes from the incredible boost to one's power once you have it. The more that is sacrificed, the greater the increase in power. From what I've seen that he has done, he was either incredibly strong to begin with or he has given up something very precious. If he gains the confidence to attack, I may be hard-pressed to hold him."

Mian's arm stiffened beneath her fingertips. "What are the chances that he will?"

"I don't know, Mian." She drew a deep breath as she glanced around the littered street. "The only comfort I could give you is that, historically, there is no precedence of any direct attacks. They have all preferred to come at the priestesses sideways."

The soldiers piled back out of the building and a grizzled lieutenant gave a grim nod. Mian led her into a large open sitting room, his eyes sweeping the emptiness. He really was going to be intolerable. He moved on to a wide curving staircase and slowed as he began to climb. Their rooms were on the third floor, which appeared to not have been touched by the destruction of the raiding. The guards outside her room nodded as Mian approached, doors swung wide for them. She was not surprised when he closed the door behind them.

"You wanted something?" She searched the books piled atop a nearby nightstand and pulled one from the stacks.

He stared at her. "I just…I don't want to…"

She smiled as a tingling grew in her stomach. "You don't have to leave."

He returned her smile in relief and followed her to a couch, pulling her to his side when they sat. He leaned his head back and closed his eyes as she opened her book.

As she stared at the inked pages of the tome in her lap, she found she couldn't pull any meaning from them. Her mind was too focused on the rhythmic breathing beside her. She hated to admit even to herself how comforting his presence was. So much of her life was wrapped up with him and somehow along the way he had become home to her. The very thought was ludicrous, but it was her new reality.

She nestled back into his embrace.

The man who called himself Neram smiled at the soldiers that marched past him. Today he wore the face of a common soldier—not his preferred disguise, but it did help him blend in. Soon, he promised himself, soon he would be able to walk the world with his own face. All would know and fear him. The world would tremble at his feet and no one would ever dare stand against him. But for now, he wore the visage of a lowly soldier. It turned his stomach.

Pride was for later, though. Today he must focus on work.

He strode along the edge of the encampment, eyes alert for his high priestess. He didn't expect to run into her—she would be heavily guarded after his attack. It would take her some time to convince them to allow her back out in the open.

A group of soldiers marched by and he stared into his own eyes as they passed. Perhaps it was time to tighten the noose some, but first, a little surprise.

He continued his trek around the edge of the camp until he came to a patch of scorched grass. The conflict of magic bombarded his senses and danced along his skin. She would come back here, he knew, to study the residue of his magic. When she did, she would find more than she bargained for.

THE WELL

Pria smiled at the men as they passed by. Narita had her charge today; her men swarmed around them like a hive.

Narita's confident smile never faltered as they walked the littered streets of Kyneira. Nervous citizens mingled with the watchful soldiers as all worked to clean the debris. Janu had already sent for workers to help restore the city but it would take them a while to reach it.

"High Priestess." Mian approached with a small group of men. "You have visitors. I have set them up in your room."

She forced a smile. The Lorien must be very worried to have responded so quickly. "How many?"

"Three—very stuffy, unfriendly; I'd say Lana would have loved them," he said.

Pria shook her head as she glanced up at him. "Here I thought you and Lana got along very well."

Mian grinned as he winked at her. "We had a special relationship, didn't we?"

"It is not every woman who can handle you, Mian." Narita flashed a roughish glare. "Apparently it takes a high priestess to do so."

He glared back at her before he gestured toward a side street. “If you are quite finished, your visitors are waiting on you.”

Pria took his arm. “Lead the way, Commander. I’m sure they will warm up to you after you have been properly introduced.”

“I can’t wait.”

“Have we had any more strange instances of note?” she asked.

He cocked an eyebrow. “Strange instances?”

“Try to remember your station.” She glanced at him.

He covered his mouth in a struggle to stifle his laughter. “I have had no reports of any more incidents. Our patrols haven’t seen any grinlo or otherwise.”

“Good.”

He chewed his lip. “Will they really get better after you introduce them?”

She spun to face him, her robes a swirl of color. “Commander Mian, these people are the highest and brightest magical beings this world knows. They are charged with the protection of all who reside here and must by design retain a certain decorum.”

He waved his finger back and forth in front of her. “So you’re saying no.”

“Precisely.”

“Well, I’d hate for them to dry out up there alone. We’d better get to them,” he said.

Pria laughed as he spun her around and tugged her toward a tall building. The guards at the door parted as they approached, their expressions stressed.

The blazing fireplace left the room warm and inviting, with her books in neat piles along the furniture and bookshelves. The curtains were pulled back, flooding the room with sunlight and illuminating the few unbroken items that remained from the former occupants. A small group of stiff people sat around a table, each with a steaming cup of tea. A thin weaselly man with short mousy hair stared into his tea with an expression like he was sucking on a sour prune. Priest Peetare. Her heart sank at the sight of him. He had been one of the most stringent opponents to her being stationed here. The two women with him were severe but stately, one matronly with gray-streaked hair, the other with a stern emotionless expression. It was the second woman that drew her attention and brought a smile to her face. Priestess San returned her smile with a nod. All wore well-made flowing silk suits with simple decoration, though well cut. They turned as one and came to their feet as Pria stopped before them.

The tall gray-haired woman sank to a knee, followed by Peetare and San behind her. "High Priestess, I am Priestess Aliat. My companions are Priestess San and Priest Peetare."

Pria nodded her head. "I bid you welcome to Kyneira." She gestured behind her. "My attendants are Commander Narita of Austeria, and Commander Mian, Battle Leader of Trimera."

The three rose to their feet and eyed the commanders. "Priestess Nae informed us that you have encountered a rogue," said Priestess San.

Mian sighed as Pria indicated the table behind them. "We should sit; there is much to discuss. Nae said she would research the image I sent her. Was she able to find anything before you departed?"

Aliat glanced behind her at Mian and Narita who remained beside the door. "She sent us with a few files for you to look at and will be sending more." She leaned in close to Pria's ear. "Are you sure you can trust these two?"

Pria kept her face stoic. "There is nothing to fear from either; they are as dear to me as family."

Peetare didn't bother to hide his distaste as he glared at Mian and Narita before deciding to ignore both. "It has been many years since anyone has gained control of the horde. What makes you believe that is what is happening now?"

Pria could feel her pride bristle at his tone. She allowed the cool arrogance of the high priestess to fill her mind. "I realize what I am asking you to accept is both outrageous and frightening, but I would never have called you here if I was not sure."

His eyebrow rose. "Is your surety from your own experience or the observation of others?"

Pria felt the smile on her face but didn't bother to rein in its hostility. "My dear Priest Peetare, I appreciate your help and experience, but if you continue to disrespect my people I will be forced to put you in your place."

Peetare blinked before he lowered his head. "I will rephrase my question, Highness. What makes you believe that this horde is under someone's control?" Pria glared at him until he began to shift in his seat. "Forgive me for any perceived slight, High Priestess, as it was not intended."

Pria blinked as she pulled her gaze back from Peetare. "We have encountered numerous instances that can only be interpreted as traps. The horde is displaying a level of intelligence that they cannot possess. We have also encountered a man I believe is the perpetrator."

San blew on her tea. "Have we discovered what happened to the high priestess Lana?"

She felt Mian cringe and saw Narita take his hand.

"Lana was lost in service to her people. It is my belief now, and I believe hers before she was lost, that the being controlling the horde was hunting her." Pria laid a hand over San's. "I'm sorry San; I know you were close to her. She didn't let anyone or anything stand between her and her duty."

Aliat stood and drew all attention to her. "I want to see where you encountered this man."

"Of course."

Mian helped her to her feet. He pulled her close to his side as they led the way from her room. "Well aren't they just…frigid. I will never complain when you go Priestess on me anymore."

She smirked and rubbed her thumb along the back of his hand. "Not as bad as you thought I was?"

"You are a sweet, perfect doll."

She rolled her eyes. "Well I'll try to refrain from their behavior if you cannot treat them like you did Lana."

He drew a deep breath and glanced behind them at the floating statues that followed. "Lana and I had a special relationship. I will refrain from annoying your stiff new friends."

The street around Pria and Mian was choked with a guard over twice her normal size. A shake of her head and she glared up at the man beside her. "I don't even want to know how you accomplished this. I would, however, love to know why Lana let you get away with the attitude you always had toward her."

Her eyes narrowed as he smiled down at her with a mischievous wink. "Lana and I came to a little agreement a long time ago."

"What kind of agreement? You don't think I will be foolish enough to let you get away with that!"

A grin slid across his face as his eyes sparkled. "No, we will have a completely different kind of agreement."

Her eyes narrowed as she pulled from his grip and turned to the three stoic faces behind her. "My only interaction with this man was here at the edge of our camp. He was watching me and attacked once he realized I had noticed him."

Aliat knelt and laid her palm to the grass. "How long ago?"

"Yesterday."

Her eyes rolled up to Pria as she stood straight before her. "There is new magic here."

Pria nodded. "I felt it. He must have returned during the night."

San moved closer and pushed Mian back with a palm. "Bold. He knew you would come back to investigate."

"He knew someone would."

Mian's eyes darted around them as a wave of fear washed through him. "What is going on?"

Peetare brushed him off. "Nothing for you to worry about, soldier."

"Commander, take your men and get them back inside the perimeter of camp." Pria's voice was cold.

Mian's eyes flashed as Narita rushed to his side. "I'm not leaving you."

San circled Pria. "There is nothing you can do here but interfere."

The air around Pria shimmered for a moment before it snapped back. "Do as I ask," she pleaded.

Narita grabbed his hand before she motioned her men back. "What can we do?"

Pria glistened again as she drew a deep breath. "Protect us."

Narita nodded as she dragged Mian back from the group and the three newcomers surrounded Pria, each taking the other's hands. Mian shook as they made the edge of camp.

Narita waved to the soldiers. "I want a ring around the high priestess! Keep your distance and no one gets by!"

Men flowed past them as she turned back to Mian, who appeared to have stopped breathing. Green eyes locked on Pria, he took a staggering step toward her. "I can't leave her to face this by herself."

"We don't have a choice." She took his hand, her own breath ragged. "She'll be okay." Even as the words left her mouth she couldn't tell if they were more for Mian or herself.

Pria's lungs burned as she feared to draw breath and clung to the world around her. Every second the trap grew stronger in its attempt to force her away. The world around her shimmered in and out as she fought. She could feel the tethers hastily thrown up by the circle around her as they bought time to disarm the spell before it overwhelmed her.

Eyes open, she could see strange hazy stones begin to form beneath her feet. This place wasn't strong enough; she had no connection to it. She closed her eyes and imagined her rooms back at the Seat, each cherished detail down to the green-eyed boy. Boy? Her eyes flew open and met his as they watched in helpless fear from across the protective ring of guards. Her home away from home. Mian. Those eyes held her.

She shifted her magic as she released its hold on the lifeless earth beneath her and locked it onto the green-eyed boy. There was nothing in her world but those eyes and the way their gaze made her feel beautiful.

Wind tickled across her cheek and filled her with the memory of soft red hair.

She blinked as San touched her face. "Are you all right, High Priestess?"

Pria drew a tentative breath as she let her eyes drift to the blissfully green ground beneath her feet. A rush of relief raced up from her toes. "We did it."

"Thought we were going to lose you there for a minute, but your magic shifted. What did you do?" San asked.

Pria's cheeks rouged. "I found something stronger to hold me." Her gaze rose. "The green-eyed boy."

San smiled as Peetare blinked. "The green-eyed boy? I don't believe I am familiar with that technique."

Pria cocked an eyebrow as she stepped to the edge of the trapped area. "I don't think that technique is for everyone."

"Priestess?" Narita stood far back, her hands folded at her waist. "Is everything safe?"

Pria drew a deep breath and closed her eyes as she stretched her mind outward. She glanced around at the circle. "Anyone?"

San nodded. "The energy is fading."

Pria glanced behind Narita to smile at Mian and Janu as they stood, bodies tensed and stock still. "You may inform my guard dogs that all is safe."

Peetare watched Narita as she returned to the soldiers. "Bold. He would have had to set this up after your men were alert to him."

"He's followed us before. Set traps to capture my guards, separate me from my protection. This is what happened to Lana. Prince Janu never mentioned it, but she wouldn't have wanted him to worry when he couldn't do anything."

Aliat scanned the edge of the forest beyond the soldiers. "Are you saying this man is targeting high priestesses?"

"Maybe. Maybe it's just anyone in his way that can stop him."

San arched an eyebrow. "You don't believe that."

Pria's eyes dropped to her shoes. "No. It feels too personal. I can't explain it, but it feels more like he's testing me, tempting me."

San's eyebrow rose as her eyes lifted to Pria. "You don't think Lana could still be alive?"

"It has been years. There is no history of any priestess being held captive by the horde." Peetare crossed his arms.

"None that we know about." Pria smoothed her features and lowered her voice. "Nothing is said to the others." She smiled as Janu stopped beside them, Narita and Mian to each side. "Prince Janu, I would like you to meet Priestesses Aliat and San, and Priest Peetare."

Janu nodded his head to each in turn, his face calm but his eyes a rage of emotion. "We all thank you and the Lorien for any help you can give."

Peetare regarded him coolly. "We all have our duties to the high priestess. Her true place is at the Lorien."

San's glare was open. "That is not your place, Priest, and this is not the time to discuss it."

Janu's eyes tightened but he held his tongue. "What happened?"

"Nothing to worry about." Pria smiled at him with a reassurance she didn't feel. "Just another little game with my new friend."

His breath was ragged but his voice held steady. "I'll have the… We'll search the… What can I do?"

San straightened her robes. "You can provide us a guard."

Pria nodded. "Yes, if this man is bold enough for attacks this close, we will need to patrol ourselves."

Janu swallowed. "Is that…really necessary?"

"There is no other way to keep everyone safe," San said.

Mian drew a deep breath. "I will set up a rotation of men to watch over each of you." He met Pria's eyes, his face hard and resolute. "How often?"

"Constant. One of us will patrol while the others work on how to capture this man before he can do any more damage."

San nodded. "I will take the first patrol. Commander Mian, would you accompany me?"

"It would be my pleasure. Narita, do not leave their side." He stabbed a finger at the woman in question.

She nodded in acknowledgment. "I am a barnacle."

"We should get back to my rooms; I want to get a look at the information Nae sent us." Pria turned to San. "Keep them safe."

"Every strength in me. We will do all we can, have faith in that."

The man who called himself Neram clung to the branches of an old frost oak. The bark was rough against his skin but it afforded the perfect perch from which to watch his plan unfold. He didn't expect for his high priestess to be caught in his trap, though it would have been a delicious bonus. Oh, she was strong! He could almost see the ebb and flow of her magic as she struggled to hold against the pull of his trap. She nearly lost her grip a couple times, almost fading to invisible before she managed to fight her way back.

There were others around her now, drones from the Lorien, looking to keep his prize from him. Looking to ruin everything he had worked for and keep him squashed under their thumb. When he had his high priestess secured to his side, they would be the first to die. He felt when his trap sprung open and his prize managed to break free.

His lips curled. They would close ranks now. Secure the safety of his prize and lull her into a false sense of protection.

He slipped down from the tree and gathered his thrall around him. Soon it would be time to begin his full offensive, but first there was one more piece to get into place.

Mian took San by the elbow. "Come with me, Priestess. We'll find you a proper guard." He forced himself not to look back. If he caught Pria's gaze he would lose his nerve.

"The only way to keep her safe is to catch this man," San said.

A jolt wracked his body and his spine snapped straight at the knowledge in her voice. He chewed his lip as they weaved their way through the tents. "I don't know what you're…" He glanced down at San's flat stare, his forehead wrinkled in anxiety. "That obvious?"

"Young man, I have worked with High Priestess Pria since the day she arrived at the Lorien with Lana." She smiled up at him through her eyelashes. "I must say Lana had some rather…colorful stories about you."

"I would bet so." Mian's voice burst with pride.

"I heard many more from young Pria. You seem to be quite the scoundrel, Commander."

He shrugged. "I try my best."

"I have it on good authority that you led the patrol from which High Priestess Lana was taken."

He dropped his eyes to the ground before him, his body deflating. "I did."

San lowered her head. "She was a good friend of mine, Lana, wrote to me often. There was many a time she lamented giving you such free rein. Whenever she would start on that I would tell her of Pria's progress. She truly is the most amazing child—and I can still call her a child; I am old enough for that."

Brow lowered, he eyed the woman beside him. "And you're telling me this why?"

"You are very important, to everyone involved here. If I want to make any effect here, I will need to be on your good side."

He couldn't hold the mischievous grin that spread across his face. "And if I don't have a good side?"

In a swirl of silken robes, she faced him. "No one who can hold Pria so well that she used him to sustain herself in that trap would be without a good side."

Mian's head cocked as his eyes narrowed. His heart jumped at the thought. "She used me? How?"

San stepped close to him and trailed a finger down his cheek. "Green-eyed boy. You do realize the strength of the tradition she is going against for you? The risk she is taking?"

Green-eyed boy, he definitely liked the sound of that. Mian stepped back and glanced up at her. "She mentioned that a time or two."

"Of course, she is very thorough."

A heavy sigh slipped past his lips as they curved into a raucous grin. "Yes, that she definitely is." He chewed his lower lip as he watched her. "Is this where the lecture comes?"

"No lecture," she said. "I told you, I want to be on your good side."

He shrugged. "If you were close to Lana, you know how she got on my good side."

San laughed as Mian's eyes sparkled with an evil glee. "Yes I do, and I also know the grief you put her through. A priestess always learns from her predecessors, young man. I will not give you that freedom with me, but I will give you a promise." His muscles tensed as she took a step toward him. "I promise you that I will not only keep your secret but I will also put everything I have into finding this man and keeping him from hurting anyone else."

"No lectures on decorum and propriety?"

She coughed a laugh. "No lectures, as long as you treat me with respect."

He rolled his eyes to the sky. "That's asking an awful lot from me."

"I'm sure those lovely shoulders can handle it."

He squared himself toward her. "Pria will only be safe after this man is dead. If you can bring him to me, I will give you more respect than you can handle."

San's smile was triumphant. "She chose well." His grin deepened. "You do have lovely eyes. Let's get some guards so we can work on finding this man before he takes another priestess."

"He's not getting Pri." Mian waved a soldier over to them. "Audren! We need at least twenty guards, from my men. I also want you to hunt down Narita and make sure she has access to the soldiers she needs."

The man took off at a run across the camp.

"And find me Jeran!" Mian called after him. "Fool man is never where I want him to be when I need him."

"Were you there when this man attacked?" San asked.

His jaw drew tight at the memory. His purpose was to protect her and he had failed. "I left her. I left her and he tried to kill her."

San's expression was incredulous. "You cannot be with her every second and I doubt your presence would have changed the outcome."

"I will not give her up."

"I would not ask you to," San shot back.

He jerked a nod. "Pria said the Lorien looked down on marriage."

"The Lorien does not encourage relationships, no."

"So…" he pressed.

"Why am I not talking you out of it?" San smiled at him. "Have you ever heard of a Well?"

"I will assume you do not mean the kind with water at the bottom."

San's glare was flat as she stared up at him. "I can just imagine the torture you put Lana through. No, not a water well. A Well is something very personal to the priestess that she can use to focus her strength and allow her to do more than she could normally."

Mian's brows drew down. "Do I want to know where this is going?"

"I felt the spike when her power shifted."

"So you think I am a…Well?" he asked.

"I think you are Pria's Well, my green-eyed boy, and I will not only refrain from lecturing, I will encourage you to spend as much time as possible with her."

His eyes sparkled as he watched her, a smile spreading across his face. "San, I think I'm going to like you."

Jeran eyed San warily as he approached Mian. "You needed me?"

Mian clapped a hand to Jeran's shoulder. "San, this is Jeran, one of the best men you are going to meet. Jeran, we are going to be providing a guard for the priest and priestesses as they search out the high priestess' new friend."

Jeran's smile was painfully forced. "Oh, good. How many would you like, sir?"

Mian turned back to San. "Twenty sound good to you, enough to keep you safe but not enough to get in your way?"

San allowed a slight smile at Jeran's obvious unease. "Twenty for myself should be sufficient."

Mian nodded. "But if Pria asks, you tell her you had fifty."

"Fifty?" San's eyebrow rose in amusement.

"Don't look too smug. This guy tries for you and I'll bump you all to a hundred. I'll give you twenty for now."

San laughed. "I do hope the high priestess knows what she's getting into with you."

"The sad part is that she does."

Pria rubbed her eyes as she sat back in the cushioned chair. Aliat and Peetare had Janu cornered across the room as they picked through his memories like an old tome. The exhaustion that gathered around his eyes was plain. She herself poured over the information sent by Nae. San was due back any moment. With Mian as her guard, anyone stupid enough to stand against them would be in for a wash of pain.

Aliat approached and took the stack of parchment from her lap. "Why don't you go rest, High Priestess. We have things here under control."

"But someone will have to replace San when she returns."

"It is not going to be you—not yet, anyway. Go lie down, we'll send if we need you," Aliat said.

Pria's eyes searched her face for a moment before she released a heavy sigh. "Fine, but only for a couple of hours." She glared at the woman's smug smile as Aliat made her way back to Janu.

Resigned to her forced rest, Pria made her way out into the hallway and nodded to Narita as the men fell in around her. "Here I thought Mian would only be comfortable if I were surrounded by his own men."

Narita bowed. "He wouldn't be, these are his men, but he was gracious enough to give me their charge."

Pria's eyes rolled toward the ceiling. "He's such a fool of a man; I really don't know how I am to tolerate him."

Narita gave a playful wink. "Well if you need any suggestions…"

Pria smiled despite herself. "My brother has turned you into a deviant."

"I'd say it was more likely the influence of my soldiers than Janu. And where are we off to?"

"My chambers. The high priestess has been ordered to rest." Her face twisted in distaste.

"Such a rough life you lead."

"And just when was the last time you rested? Or Mian? Or Janu? Why am I the one sent off to bed? I feel like we're children again and Lana is hovering over me like an old hen!" Arms crossed across her chest, Pria glared at the hallway around them. Her face smoothed as a couple of the guards glanced back and smiled.

Narita shook her head. "*We* were not attacked by multiple magical creatures in the past few days."

Pria huffed as they rounded a corner to her room. Two men stood outside her door, and one darted inside at the sight of their approach. The second laid his hand against her stomach and forced her to stop. Raber smiled out at her from beneath his helmet.

"Sorry, High Priestess, but Battle Leader's orders. The room will be searched before you are allowed to enter."

Pria's eyes narrowed as his fingers lingered on her stomach. "Insufferable man."

"I do hope you have recovered, I had heard-tell that you were attacked again."

She stepped back from his touch, being sure to project a serene frostiness. "I can assure you that I am quite fine and that all this fuss is bothersome and unnecessary."

The first guard returned with a sharp nod and Raber lowered his hand for them to pass. Narita followed her inside and closed the door behind them. "You have to give him props—the boy has courage."

"He'll have a stump if he doesn't watch it." Pria spun and settled her silken robes in a practiced flourish about her sides. "Are you going to watch me sleep?"

Narita's face twisted in an evil grin. "I am at that, Mian's orders. Of course, I could always have Raber come in and keep an eye on you."

"That is not even funny."

Pria jerked awake.

The room around her was dim with only one candle burned low far over on the mantle. The room was still but something had awoken her. She crept to the edge of the bed. Narita must have given up and returned to her own rooms or back to guard the study. She calmed her breathing and studied the room around her, but the silence held. Must have been the guards outside. Tension wracked her body.

How long had they let her sleep? She could see the faint outline of the pale moon on the sheer curtains of her window. In a huff, she stormed across the room and grumbled as her foot caught on something on the floor, sending her toppling into the darkness. She sat up and groped around as she tried to discover the obstacle in her way when her hand fell on soft hair. Frozen, she fought to draw breath. She flung her hand wide and sent tiny flames around the room to the candles in a wash of warm glow.

Crumpled on the floor before her lay Narita, her eyes closed and a small trickle of blood along her hand.

Pria's eyes darted about the room as she pressed her hands to Narita's limp body. Her flesh was warm—she was still alive. Pria leaned down and kept her eyes alert. "Narita? Are you all right?" She tapped her cheeks to try to draw her awake. "Na?"

She jumped at a shuffling over near her bed. Something small she could hear but not see. It scrambled closer; she could hear claws as they scratched along the floor. There was a shadow now, flitting in jumps and skits across the floor. Something sparked in the candlelight: two large over-sized eyes. Her heart raced as she watched the shadow skirt the light and creep closer, the tiny wings snapping in excitement.

There was no way to get to the door—any action at all would draw its attention and she would be down in an instant; phisher venom was strong and fast acting.

It stopped, tiny head cocked to the side as it listened to the guards outside.

Pria pulled Narita closer as she heard a quiet knock on the door and it cracked to reveal a sliver of the hall beyond. "Priestess? Are you okay?"

She never let her eyes drift from the phisher in front of her as Raber poked his head into the room. He pushed the door wide as he caught sight of her crouched on the floor next to Narita. "What is it?" He rushed to her side and pulled his sword.

Her hand rose to point at the tiny creature as it watched from the shadows. The movement drew it closer. Raber jumped and shifted in front of Pria. "We have to get you out of here."

"I will not leave Narita."

"It's after *you*," he hissed.

"I know what it is after, and I will not leave her!"

They both gasped as it jumped closer. Raber drew a deep breath. "Okay, how do I kill it?"

"It has venom—that is what happened to Narita. Don't let it bite you. Phishers are tough, their skin thicker than it seems like it should be."

His brow furrowed. "That isn't very helpful or comforting."

"Sorry," she whispered.

Sword kept low toward the creature, Raber took Pria's wrist and pulled her along behind him as he circled the phisher. "Stay with me, Priestess." Her pulse raced beneath his fingers as she grabbed at his shirt. "We have to draw it out, away from Commander Narita, to where I can get at it."

She pressed her forehead against his back. "It will follow me; it can smell the magic in me."

He followed the pressure of her hand as she backed toward the door and slipped into a small pool of light from the candles. The black shadow crept along the line of darkness in their wake, its focus never waning. A tiny squeal grew as it placed one clawed hand into the light.

"Put your hand out," Raber said.

Pria shot him a glance.

"Put your hand out, pull it closer."

Arm still secured in his grip, Pria stretched her fingers out toward the darkness. The beast's nose lifted and strained to catch her scent as it crept forward. His grip on her wrist grew painful as the seconds ticked by.

The phisher pulled back into the shadows as it hunched down beneath its folded wings. Raber's fingers bit into her flesh as she felt him tense beside her. Everything froze for an instant as if the air itself held its breath—and then the room erupted.

With a piercing screech, the phisher launched into the air and snatched at her hand. Raber reacted like lightning as his arm convulsed to throw her behind him and he slashed down with his sword. The steel rang out against the tough hide of its target as it swatted the tiny form to the floor. Pinned with his boot, the phisher clawed at the leather, teeth gnashing as Raber struggled to force the blade through its skin.

Pria could feel the bruise that radiated from her hip as she pulled herself up. Raber was stronger than he looked.

The phisher's cries died out as his blade broke through the flesh. She jumped as Raber's hands clapped to her face, pulling her eyes to his.

"Are you okay?"

She nodded. "I'm fine, just sore. We need to get help for Narita. She'll need treatment. Priestess San will know what to do."

"I'm not leaving you."

"The other guard," she prompted.

He pointed at the floor between her feet. "Don't move."

She glared at him as he moved toward the door. "Everyone my keeper now?" Her eyes moved toward Narita, lying motionless. Pria held her position, listening intently, but all she could catch was Raber and the guard at the door. She crawled back to Narita and drew her head into her lap.

When Raber returned, he rested a hand on her shoulder as he stood watch over the room.

She glanced over her shoulder around the darkness. "How long have I been sleeping?"

He shrugged. "Few hours."

She shook her head. "Why had no one come for me?"

"Someone came a couple of times. Narita spoke with them."

She felt an ire rise in her gut. "I am not a porcelain doll. I am needed here; they can't just keep me ignorant."

"Narita wanted you to rest."

A heavy breath rushed from her lips. "You did well, Raber." She looked up at him. "You saved our lives."

He smiled at the floor. "I did my job, Priestess."

She clapped a hand over his. "No, Raber. Thank you."

His eyes sparkled. "You are always welcome, my priestess." He let his thumb run along her hand. "I am sorry they do not understand you." He knelt down and his gaze searched her face. "They see you weak, but you are stronger than any of them."

"They have trouble seeing me as more than just family."

"No, Highness. They do not understand what you are, what you can do, the power you possess. They fear you make them obsolete, and you do. You could end this perpetual battle. Draw on the power of the Lorien; they will follow you," he pressed.

"Raber, we are not warriors, we are protectors."

"You are raw power harnessed. Why not use it?" he demanded.

Her heart ached as she stared into his eyes so full of awe and expectation. "For all of our power, we are vulnerable to the horde. No amount of strength can overcome it."

"You can. You can overcome them. My father used to say there are people who have been able to control the horde."

Her eyes widened but he stood as soldiers burst in, followed by San and Aliat. The priestesses rushed to her side and checked Narita as Pria watched Raber back away from them, his eyes still aglow with intensity. San grabbed Pria's arm and drew her attention back. "What happened?"

"She was attacked by a phisher."

San smiled as she patted her cheek. "Do not worry, we can help her."

"Do whatever you have to."

"We may need your aid," San said.

"Anything."

San waved to a couple of soldiers. "Lift her from the floor. On the bed there." Aliat delved into a bag that hung at her side. "Give us the room." The soldiers filed out and pulled the door shut behind them. "How did a phisher get into your room?"

"I don't know. The windows were all secure, guards at the door, men patrolling the streets. I can't imagine how we could be more diligent."

Aliat handed San a vial then inspected Narita's wound. "We will have to set up barriers. This man seems quite set on you; we will need to ensure your safety at all costs."

San cradled Narita's head as she poured the vial between her lips. "This will help dilute the venom. We will give it a moment to take effect then we have a few tricks to help her fight." Her smile was warm and comforting. "She will be fine, I promise."

Pria nodded as the three women watched Narita's chest rise and fall deep in the grip of the phisher's venom. There was only the one bite on her hand; she likely never even knew what happened. Narita was not the intended target—she was only in the way. Thankfully she was only seen as an obstacle, the tiny creature could easily have killed her. Aliat nodded as she climbed onto the bed and laid her fingertips along Narita's arm. Pria and San mimicked her, each only making contact with the very tips of their fingers.

Aliat drew a deep breath. "First, we will use *niswara.* Do you remember?"

Pria nodded and closed her eyes as she focused the spell through her fingers into Narita's forehead. "Come on, Narita."

A slight glow began to spread along Narita's skin and warmed their hands as they worked. Aliat raised a tone in her throat, changing from *niswara* to *pingar* and a slight darkening spread from her fingers. San lowered her tone into a deep rumble that radiated throughout the room. Sparks jumped from her hands, arcing down toward Narita's body to land on the lightened areas and the dark alike in a dance across her skin. Pria remained on *niswara* to feed strength into Narita's body as Aliat burned the venom and San targeted any damage done.

Color seeped back into Narita's skin and her breathing steadied, but she still had a long fight ahead of her.

The three priestesses sat down for a long wait as the full extent of their exertion began to set in.

Janu paced the hallway outside of Pria's room. A low deep rumble spilled out over the doors as they waited. The soldiers were anxious as they kept a wary eye to him. Unable to restrain himself, Janu swept over to the guards stationed outside of Pria's door.

"What happened?"

A tall young man from Mian's command gave a smooth bow. "My prince. The high priestess returned for rest several hours ago. All was quiet with only a few callers that Commander Narita spoke with and sent away. There was nothing of note for a while, then I heard a soft thump so I went in to check on it and found Pr…the high priestess kneeling over the commander. Something she called a phisher had attacked Commander Narita and was coming for her. I was able to kill it before it could hurt her."

"You killed it?"

"Yes sir," the young man said.

Janu searched his face for a moment. "What is your name, soldier?"

"Raber, sir."

He pulled the man to his chest in a warm embrace. "Thank you, Raber." Janu clapped a hand to his shoulder as he stared at the closed door. "How did that thing get in there?"

"I do not know sir. It was small… Could we have missed it?"

Janu rubbed his face as he glanced around the hallway. "The real question is how do we prevent it from happening again." He turned back to Raber. "We will need to coordinate our men with the priestesses to see if there is anything more we can do." He watched Raber's reaction but the man gave little away. "I would like for you to see to that. Would you be willing?"

Raber's lips curled into a small smile. "To protect the high priestess, I would do anything."

Kyneira flashed past Mian as he ran, heart pounding. He had left Peetare in Jeran's hands when he heard about Pria's attack. He could feel her slipping from his grip and he couldn't allow that, wouldn't allow that. If he had to hunt this man himself, he would protect her.

The front doors crashed open as he ran through them without slowing. Janu stared at him wide-eyed as he stormed into the hallway full of guards. He didn't wait but rushed past them into Pria's chambers, only stopping when he met her eyes over Narita's sleeping form.

"Do come in, Commander." San's eyes sparkled as she stood from the bed.

Janu was at his elbow in a flash, his face twisted in concern as he stared down at Narita. "Will she be all right?"

Pria held out a hand with a warm smile. "She will be fine, thanks to San and Aliat."

"You as well, Pria." Aliat settled a blanket over Narita as Janu sat gingerly at her side.

Mian brushed his hair back. "What was it? How did it get in?"

"Phisher, and I don't know." Pria smiled up at him and he had to fight the urge to rush to her side. She would not want such a strong display in front of so many strangers.

A tremor rocketed through his body fueled by his impotent rage. "What do we do about it?"

Janu nodded behind him. "We work with the priestesses. I have asked Raber to get with them and see what can be done to secure against this."

Raber stepped to his side with a nod to Mian. "There is no need for worry; we will do all we can."

Pria's eyebrow rose but whatever thought had provoked it remained unspoken. "In the meantime, I believe all of my rest has been for naught. I am more tired now than I was before."

Mian nodded. "Good, you can rest here with Narita. I want three men in this room, including myself, an additional ten in the hallway. Full light, no mistakes."

Pria watched him incredulously. "I am supposed to be able to rest in full light in a room full of men?"

"That's how it is going to be. Raber, you go with the priestesses and you find a way to secure this room, keep her safe."

Raber's eyes lingered on Pria as he turned to follow Aliat and San from the room. Pria shook her head as the room emptied.

Mian snapped the second the door shut. "How can you sit there so calm?"

"Mian, please do not get upset. If the people see you like this, panic will spread."

Janu's body shook. "She's right. If they know how much danger she is really in, there would be chaos. The loss of a second priestess would crush their spirits—we'd never recover from it. We will find the hole in our security and we will do our best to fix it."

"They could have both died!"

"But we didn't. Mian, please, sit." Pria held out her hand and he reluctantly slid his fingers into it and let her draw him down beside her. She leaned her head on his shoulder and stiffened at his trembling. "It'll be all right, Mian."

He jerked her into his lap, crushing her to his chest. With his face buried in her soft hair, he rocked her as the tension left his arms and she slid from his lap.

His eyes were still wide as she made her way across the room and touched a finger to each candle to set it alight. "You don't have to look quite so frightened."

Janu shook his head. "The man has every right to be frightened."

She spun back to face them, her eyes lingering on Narita. "I don't have any words to make this better. All we can do is prepare."

"Prepare? You call this *prepared?*" Janu waved a hand at Narita.

Pria pointed a finger at the ground. "This we learn from. This is why I contacted the Lorien. Give us time."

Mian jumped to his feet and shook Pria by her shoulders. "Time is something we don't have. This man is after you—don't tell me you can't feel it!"

"I know. I mentioned as much to San." She lowered her eyes. "I found more notes from Lana, before we left. There was a lot she never shared. She knew it was her they were after in the raids. A little time and hopefully we'll know if this man is after anyone with magical talent or specifically high priestesses."

Janu sighed as he dropped his head. "And how long did you intend to hold on to this theory of yours?"

"It had only occurred to me recently, and other subjects seemed to take precedence," she said.

Janu rose. "You need to rest; I will go and see what is keeping your guards."

Pria returned to lighting candles as Janu shut the door. "How have you been getting along with San and Peetare? I do hope you do not treat them as you did Lana."

Mian's laugh was deep. "I do think San actually likes me, though it might pain her to admit it. Peetare is convinced I am some villainous rascal who needs to be scraped from his boots."

"He is a difficult man, always has been."

Mian leaned on a post of the bed then glanced up at her through his eyelashes. "San said you talked about me when you were at the Lorien."

She tapped the last candle then returned to stand before him. "Most of my life revolved around you—that shouldn't be so shocking." She brushed past him as she moved to arrange the blankets on the bed.

"What does 'the green-eyed boy' mean?"

She froze mid-fluff, blankets still dangling from her fingers. "I'm sure I don't know what you mean."

He glanced back at her over his shoulder, mischievous grin painted across his face. "I think you do."

She returned to her task then slipped into the bed. "Where did you ever hear such a statement?"

He tapped the back of his thumb against his lip as he watched her squirm. She had learned to ignore much at the Lorien, and the fact that he could still break through was thrilling. "Did you really use me to hold yourself in that trap?"

Pria's cheeks flared red. "San told you."

"That she did."

Pria flopped her arms down atop the blankets as her eyes lowered in a glare. "Miserable woman."

He slid a hand behind her neck and locked his lips hard onto hers. "You use me however you need to as long as it keeps you safe." He jerked back as a knock came at the door and several guards rushed in.

Pria closed her eyes with a moan at the racket as they set themselves up around the room.

"Sleep well, Priestess. Nothing will get to you now."

San clapped in satisfaction as she opened the bag Nae had sent. "Perfect."

Young Raber stepped closer to look over her shoulder. "These rocks will help us protect Priestess Pria?"

The boy was young and naive but he was also brave and diligent, and he drank in anything she said. She couldn't deny how much that pleased her. "These are Andarian crystals. They will absorb whatever magic we cast at them and create a barrier that will keep any nasty little surprises out."

He snatched one up, inspecting it skeptically. "We are to trust her life to rocks?"

She shook her head. "You boys think you are the only ones to hold her dear. High Priestess Pria means more to us than any of you can imagine. A high priestess does not just come along every day."

He lowered his striking blue eyes as he handed her the crystal. "Forgive me, Priestess San, I did not mean to second-guess you."

With a pat to his cheek she carried the bag of crystals over to a nearby table. "I will need our full concentration to set them. How long before Aliat returns?"

"Prince Janu said he does not want any one of you out for more than four hours at a time."

She nodded. "We will set them before Pria leaves. She should be rested by then."

Young Raber hitched his shoulders, reluctant to voice his concerns again so soon. "Do you think that wise, letting her go on these patrols? If she is the target, it puts her out like bait."

"We can only hope that it does. If we can force his hand, it puts us in charge." She smiled at the tightness in his eyes. "We have already discussed this among ourselves. We will all be at the ready during Pria's patrols. If anything happens we can be there in an instant."

His eyes narrowed. "I was not informed of this plan."

"No one was," she said. "It didn't seem necessary."

Peetare eyed the young boy before ignoring him. "These soldiers seem to think highly of themselves for wanting to connive out every thought from our heads."

"Do not be so petulant, Peetare. They are worried for Pria."

Raber again inspected the crystals. "Can these mask her? Keep her from being found? Perhaps if she carries one with her it will keep her from being as much of a target?"

San took the crystal from him and set it back in the bag. "Soldier, we will do everything we can. Your worry is physical; we have the magic under control." His eyes swam with questions even as he nodded. "I am sure Prince Janu would thank you greatly for your diligence."

A smile spread across his lips. "My only concern is the high priestess' safety." He bowed low before he gathered his notes and made his way from the room.

Peetare was at her side in a blink. "Seems a bit casual with us, does he not?"

"He was not disrespectful in any way. There is no need for you to be so harsh."

"That was not harsh. These people seem to think that our every thought is their concern," he snapped.

She glared at him as she shouldered the bag of crystals. "Just because they wish to be in the loop does not mean that they do not respect us."

"That's what *you* say. The high priestess is too soft on them, gives them too much rein with her. She should show them their place."

"Lana believed in her and these people. You should respect that," San said.

He watched her leave, his face tight with anger.

Pria tried hard to ignore Mian as he hovered a mere arm's length from her side. Her brush ran through her hair with ease, leaving it in a soft cascade down her chest. Narita's eyes were still hollow as she sat slumped on the edge of her bed. Pria drew a deep breath as Mian stepped closer. *I will not snap at him, I will not snap at him.*

"There is no need for you to go on patrol."

She glanced up at him with pursed lips as she fluttered her eyes. "Is there somewhere else you would like me to be?"

"That's not fair."

"Stop being such a hen, Mian. San, Peetare, and Raber have been holed up for hours working on ways to keep us safe. I have complete confidence in them," she said.

Arms crossed, he stepped back. "I'm glad you do."

His eyes widened as she laid a hand along his cheek, not even glancing at the men around her. "You need to trust them too. I have given you my faith and allowed you to see to some of my safety. All I am asking of you is to understand when I tell you what else is needed."

He held out his hands to his sides. "Now, safeguards I am all for. I just don't see how parading you around like a lamb for the wolves is in any way safe."

She shook her head. "We better get going or Aliat will think I have completely abandoned her." She stood and made her way to the door. "Feel free to rest here as long as you wish, Narita."

Narita rubbed the back of her neck. "This has to be the worst I've ever felt."

Pria paused at the foot of the bed. "It'll wear off, I promise. Soon it will be little more than a bad memory."

Narita scoffed prettily. "What memory? All I can remember is standing guard over you then waking up just now."

Mian glanced around the room. "Maybe she shouldn't rest here. What if this man tries again?"

"The phisher only attacked Narita because it knew I was in here. She should be safe with me gone." Pria swung the door open and forced herself not to flinch as Raber smiled down at her, stunning blue eyes piercing.

"High Priestess, you are feeling better?"

She smoothed her face before anyone could take notice. "Yes. Has Priestess Aliat returned from her patrol?"

Arm held out toward her, he stepped back from the door. Overly conscious of Mian's eyes on her, she laid her fingertips along Raber's arm and let him led her out into the hallway.

"She has, and all are awaiting your arrival. Priestess San sent to the Lorien for some special rocks to help safeguard your sleeping chambers," he said. "She said they would need your help to set them."

"Andarian crystals? They shared their plans with you?" She tilted her head, her brow furrowed.

Raber beamed as he grinned down at her. "Prince Janu gave me specific instructions to devise a way to fill the gap in our security."

Pria kept her hand very still on his arm. "That is quite an honor for you."

"One I do not take lightly."

"You better not." Mian's comment was soft and breathy, meant only for her ears but she caught Raber's glance at him anyway.

Raber lowered his voice leaning down a bit toward her ear. "Have you thought any, on what I said before?"

Her heart stopped and she hastily enveloped them in a cloud of magic to deaden any sound. "Raber, you must not say things like that. What you speak of is a vile, evil act. You must promise me you will not mention this ever again."

He blinked, his face masked. "I did not mean to upset you, Priestess. I just thought—"

"Don't! I don't know what stories you have heard, but you will promise me never to mention it again. Swear it!" She kept her face stoic though her voice was acid.

An indulgent smile curled his lips as he lifted her fingers to his mouth. "I will swear by my priestess never to mention controlling the horde again."

She jerked her hand free and pressed it to Mian's chest as he jumped forward, eyes flashing. His body wracked with tension but obeyed her silent command. "We have spoken of that before, Raber. I will not warn you again."

He raised his hands innocently and risked a quick glance back at Mian, still outside of the sound bubble. "Of course."

She let him continue, allowing the sound barrier to dissipate without removing her hand from Mian's chest. His eyes sparked when she met his gaze. "You kept me from hearing what you said. Why?"

He moved up to her side as she moved off down the hall. "It was of no one's concern but ours."

"I should have had him mucking stalls the day he broke rank to give you that flower." Mian's eyes shot daggers at Raber's back.

"Commander Mian, I have Raber well in hand and have no need of your meddling or interference."

His fingers flexed. "I'd like to get him in hand."

She sighed as she pulled back her irritation. "Are you angry at your soldier for overstepping his place with a priestess or at a man for being forward with your woman? Please clarify—I would like to know why I am going to be angry with you."

Her eyes met his impassioned glare with cool serenity. "That's not fair."

"How is it not fair? If the one, I highly doubt that you of all people telling him he should not view the priestess as a woman to chase is going to be effective. If the other, I am not your property and am quite capable of deflecting unwanted advances on my own."

His eyes rolled to the ceiling but at least they left Raber. "I wish someone would explain to me why I had to fall for you of all people! I could have had some vacant little high-bred lady who spends her days reading the great love stories and would swoon to see me defend her honor!"

She patted his cheek with a rough slap. "Keep it up, you still could." She didn't even acknowledge Raber's bow as she glided past him into the small meeting room, Mian close at her heels.

San, Peetare, and Aliat all rose as they entered each a different level of coolness. The room was pleasantly warm with a fire near the back.

San nodded in greeting then again in approval at Mian as he remained flush to Pria's side. "High Priestess, I trust your friend has recovered."

"She could still use some rest, but she'll be fine soon enough."

San clasped her hands at her waist. "That is good to hear. I trust young Raber filled you in on the basics."

"What pittance of it his mind could grasp," Peetare huffed.

San glanced a reprimand at him before turning to a table piled with large crystals. "There should be plenty to secure each of our rooms with a couple left over for here."

"This is a large sum to set." Pria scanned the table skeptically. "Are you sure we'll be able to?"

San's eyes jumped to Mian so quick that Pria nearly missed it. "I believe it will be easier than you think."

As Pria inspected the crystals, San motioned Mian aside and pitched her voice low. "I want you to remain in the room when we set the crystals. Once the ritual has begun, take your bare hand and lay it against her skin, wherever you can. It is unlikely that she knows that you are her Well, but her power will recognize and take advantage of it."

"You are sure that won't distract her?"

"What won't distract me?" Pria asked.

San smiled at Pria as she turned to watch them, suspicion heavy in her eyes. "Nothing dear, just talking security." She dropped her voice again. "Not enough to break the ritual. A Well is a very difficult concept to teach, but she already knows how to use it—she just has to let her mind in on the fact." She patted his cheek fondly. "Trust me on this."

Aliat stepped to the opposite end of the table, her back stiff. "Give us the room."

Soldiers flowed out in a silent wave. "I have asked Commander Mian to remain to deal with any unforeseen complications," San said with a wave.

Though her face remained stoic, Pria's eyes glistened. "And who will keep him from causing those unforeseen complications?"

"We know it won't be you." He jumped as she cracked the air with a snap of wind.

Aliat hissed, "Let us focus. To make the crystals most effective and to help prevent any tampering or masking, we will each imbibe them with a different ward of our own choosing." She waved her hand. "Pria, if you would begin."

Pria drew a deep breath as she spread her fingers above the table. Something deep inside her resonated in tune to the crystals, and a faint pink glow spread across the face of the stones. Eyes closed, she began to whisper.

"*Intaro prenara.*"

Her body jerked as she felt fingers circle around her wrist. A flood of power rushed through her body and the glow from the crystals grew painful behind her eyelids. As the spell was absorbed into the crystals she opened her eyes nervously.

"What happened?"

San smiled but it was Peetare, staring wild-eyed at Mian, who spoke. "The soldier is a Well! How is that even possible?"

Pria's eyes snapped to Mian at her shoulder.

"That is a discussion for after the work is finished." San spread her fingers over the crystals and closed her eyes. "*Mobtana rebalt.*"

A green glow began to pulse from the rocks to spread along San's skin, persisting for a few moments before fading away.

Peetare dragged his eyes from Mian though his glower remained. His hands spread out along the tabletop. "*Wingdom zeamab.*"

The table shook beneath his fingers. The shards jumped and skittered as they clouded an impenetrable black before clearing.

Mian's eyes were worried but he held his tongue as Aliat raised her hands to the table.

"*Benarlap.*"

The rocks began to sweat as if they would melt straight into the table. Pria knew if you were to touch one before the spell set, they would be soft and pliable like dough. She remembered doing just that at the Lorien out of curiosity when learning warding and being reprimanded for ruining the crystal. Each crystal absorbed the droplets back into itself as it returned to solid rock again.

Each of them returned their hands to the table, Pria still with Mian's fingers enclosed around her wrist. She pulled at her power tentatively as she focused her thoughts through an image of Mian. The torrent of magic tore a gasp from her lips and she threw her head back. She forced the violent wave into the crystals, setting each matrix around the wards hidden within them. She released the wave and dropped to the floor in a panting mass.

When her mind cleared she found herself engulfed in a warm familiar embrace. She shook her head as she sat up, bracing one hand on Mian's chest. "I'm okay—just caught me off guard."

Peetare huffed. "I would still like to know how a soldier becomes the high priestess' Well."

Mian took her hand and lifted her to her feet as San gathered the crystals into a pouch. "Peetare, you know all that is needed for a Well to develop is a strong emotional attachment."

Pria stared up into Mian's eyes.

Peetare crossed his arms. "I have never heard of a person becoming a Well."

Aliat circled the pair, keeping far back. "I don't believe anyone has. I would like to take him back to the Lorien for study."

Mian smiled, never letting his eyes stray from Pria's. "I'm afraid I'm a bit engaged at the moment."

"Well obviously!" He jerked away as she tried to grab his chin. "But I must insist! We cannot allow this to go unrecorded."

"It must be his decision to go—no one will force him," Pria said. Aliat stepped back. "But it is nothing to worry about now. Commander, I want you to go to your room and rest, I will see Jeran does as well. Orotid will be my guard for the day."

Mian rolled his eyes. "Not Raber?"

Pria's brow drew down as San shouldered the sack of crystals.

"Raber will be busy assisting us with securing the high priestess' room." San nodded to Pria. "You had better get to your patrol; we have things in hand here."

Mian's face drew tight as he stared into her eyes. "You listen to that difficult old man; he's saved my life more than once."

Her hand met his as a smile bloomed on her face. San shook her head as she opened the door to a very disgruntled Raber. His eyes darted over the room, hesitating on Mian before returning to San.

"I was told to be in on the planning for security," Raber said. "How am I supposed to know what is going on from behind this door?"

Mian barked a laugh. "Soldier, if you are going to insist on working with priestesses and priests, you had best get used to feeling worthless." He bowed to Pria. "If you will all excuse me, I must go and rest so that I may be fresh for when my priestess again has use of me."

Pria glared at him as he strutted down the hall. "Because he wasn't insufferable enough before! Where is Jeran?"

Raber beamed. "Jeran is below, High Priestess. Would you like me to fetch him?"

"Tell him he is to rest, he and his men."

"But who will lead My Highness' guard?" His voice was giddy with expectation. Maybe she should let Mian handle him.

She let an icy chill penetrate her tone. "After you have dismissed Jeran, you will bring me Orotid."

"Of course, Highness." His voice held a distinct note of disappointment. "Then am I to rest as well?"

"You will return to Priestess San and work on setting the wards. After that, you will set up guards for them if they wish to retire."

His eyes narrowed but he saluted anyway before he stomped off. San moved to her side as they watched him walk away. "He is an interesting little thing, isn't he?"

"Try to keep him out of trouble, San."

Confused eyes searched her face. "You expect trouble from him?"

"Nothing bad, but his good intentions have caused me grief before," she said.

Several tray-laden soldiers entered the hallway outside. A lean man nodded as deeply as he could without spilling his burden. "Soldier Raber ordered refreshments while you await your guard's return."

San waved them past as Pria's eyebrow raised in approval. "Of course, the boy is not without his attributes."

Orotid beamed as Pria approached amid a cloud of armored soldiers. "I am glad to see you are looking better."

Pria's heart swelled as she allowed the older man to pull her into a warm embrace. "I have had a constant barrage of nursemaids to see to it." He fell in at her side as they started off down the street. "I assume, as I haven't heard anything, that none of the patrols have run into trouble yet?"

"You would assume correct. We haven't even seen the horde for days." He lowered his head, judging the distance to the soldiers around them. "Do you think that means that this…person…has infiltrated our ranks again?"

She eyed him. "Mian told you?"

"I had my suspicions and brought them up to Mian and Jeran. This was long before you had returned. Mian told us of his and Prince Janu's suspicions. After this latest attack he mentioned the possibility of him being able to pass among us."

"You don't seem overly concerned about that."

The older man shrugged. "My father used to say the ant does not worry about the lion. This man is beyond my means." He leaned his head to the side and rolled his eyes over at her. "He is your problem to solve. But the horde I can do something about." He hefted his sword with a smile.

Pria's eyes sparkled. "Orotid, you are much wiser than your commander and my brother."

He shrugged self-consciously. "I just know my limitations." He turned his eyes to the horizon as they made the edge of town. "It's you he's after, isn't it? Just like with Priestess Lana?"

"It would appear so. I must be more amiable than I thought."

Orotid nodded. "You are strong. There is no telling what it is he wants from you. If he can turn the horde to his whims, who knows what he could do to a priestess if given the time and incentive."

She drew a deep breath to gather her courage. "Orotid, when this man makes his move, you will likely have to keep Mian and Janu from interfering. Do you think you can do that?"

He watched her for a moment in silence. "I will do what I can, but they are both very stubborn."

"I don't care what you have to do. Arrest them if you must. I will not have the ability to protect them while fighting this man. I do not want them to die needlessly."

"The problem is they do not see it as needless, but I will do what I can. The men will be reluctant to move against them, but they will do what I ask," he said.

"Thank you, Orotid."

Pria nodded to the guards massed around her door as she entered the hallway, Orotid at her back, but she wasn't headed to her room—not yet. She was exhausted from her patrol, staying out longer to allow the others to rest. It was strange that none of the patrols had yet to run into any trouble, but she was too worn down for that train of thought now.

She stopped at a door across from hers and waited while Orotid and his men formed up around her. She eased the door open and paused to allow her eyes to adjust to the darkness. Her slippers whispered across the floor as she took in the tidy, unadorned room. Armor was arranged on a nearby chair but appeared to be the only thing out of place. It hardly looked lived in at all.

The deep, rhythmic breathing brought a smile to her face as she tapped a candle by the bed, setting it alight. The gentle glow played across Mian's handsome features as he lay on his side in peaceful sleep. With great care she slid beneath the blankets, watching his eyes as they danced beneath their lids. His soft red hair fell in a fiery cascade across his pillow and she couldn't resist running a wavy lock through her fingers. She could remember those tresses tickling across her cheeks as he carried her around on his back when they were children. Every memory of her home had him in it some way or another.

She slid her fingers into his. Forehead wrinkled, he drew a deep breath and cracked his eyes. Their brilliant green was hazed with sleep as they focused on her face. A terrible smirk stretched across his expression and sparkled up into his eyes. "Why, High Priestess, whatever will the nobles say?"

She pulled his hand toward her and cradled it against her cheek. "Things are getting a bit wild around here; I just wanted to make sure you were okay."

She jerked upright as he sat up on his elbow, the blanket falling down around his bare waist. "Just what wildness were you worried about?"

"I just don't want you to feel awkward about what San said."

"The well thing?" She nodded and he sighed. "She told me when we were out on that first patrol, so I've had a while to think it over."

Her hands rose in defense. "I swear I did not do it intentionally! I don't even think you can create a Well consciously—it just sort of forms itself!"

He laid a finger across her lips. "It's okay." His devilish grin deepened. "I rather like it. Not only do you need me more but I now know just how much you care for me even if you won't say it." He slid his hand behind her neck and pulled her to his lips. Her timid response flared something deep inside him and he locked his arms around her form, pulling her down on top of him. Her shocked squeak bubbled laughter from his mouth as she leaned her forehead against his.

She balanced with her hands on his chest as he slid his fingers down her back. Her hair fell forward around her face, giving her a feral look as her panting slowed. He stretched up and nuzzled his face into her neck, walking his lips and teeth along her skin. Her cheek rubbed against him, her mouth finding his hungrily as he leaned back. Fist buried in her hair, he rolled her beneath him. He moved his attention to her chest and her fingers cupped his chin, guiding him back to her mouth, one hand slid behind his neck.

He pulled back and searched her deep blue eyes as a finger trailed along her cheek. "This room isn't safe for you."

She traced the muscles of his neck as her teeth flashed evilly. "Are you sending me to the capable hands of Raber?"

His jaw tightened, green eyes ablaze. His voice was strained as he stared down at her. "Would you go?" His brow furrowed as she let her hand run along his jaw.

"Where would I go? You're right here."

His laugh was deep and throaty as he dropped beside her and propped his head on his hand. "That's a pretty good answer."

She rolled her eyes as she sat up. "Pretty good?"

He shrugged as he slid his hand beneath the silk of her blouse. "Well, when compared to knowing that I am the single thing you care the most about, the bar is pretty high."

She punched his shoulder. "You are completely intolerable!"

He grabbed her wrist with a laugh and forced her back to the bed. "Apparently intolerable is how you like me."

She lurched against him and growled as a brilliant smile split his face. Bright green eyes held hers, stilling her body beneath him. "I really hate how you can do that. I want to be mad at you, deviant."

He rubbed his nose against hers and shook her head. "No you don't."

Her back arched up against his chest as he moved his mouth over hers, pulling soft moans from her throat.

"I say we have Orotid make Raber move your fancy rocks over here, because I do not want to let you go." He ran his teeth along her earlobe. "I want to spend the night with you in my arms."

"No," she breathed.

He jerked back and searched her face at the serious tone. "No?"

Her face melted in sympathy as she slipped her hand free of his grip and laid it along his cheek. "Mian, Narita stood guard over me and nearly died. There is no way I would let you sleep in a room with me."

"I don't like that I can't find an argument for that." He sighed.

Pria kissed him. She remained close as she opened her eyes. "Well, I do have to protect my Well."

He laughed as he pulled her fingers to his lips. "Just remember that excuse only works until we defeat the horde."

"Then that should give you incentive to see it done." She slid from the bed, deflecting his attempts to snatch her back and leaving him stretched across the mattress.

He growled in frustration and planted his face flat on the bed. "You are a vile, cruel woman."

She laughed as she slipped from the room. "Poor Mian! I think you'll live."

Orotid greeted her with a warm smile when she turned from shutting the door. "I take it the dear boy is well."

She arched an eyebrow as they moved off down the hall. "As well as Mian can be."

"Raber was not happy to see you go in there," he said with a lowered voice. "I had to send him back to his task three times."

Her irritation jumped as she straightened her robes with a haughty scoff. "Of course you did. He's a man and is incapable of being anything but completely ridiculous at all times."

She nodded to Orotid as he bowed and let Raber and his room guards envelop her for the last few feet of the hallway. Raber stood with his arms out in front of her as two men made a quick inspection of her room. His eyes darted toward her.

"It may not be my place, Highness," he said, voice low, "but I do not think it proper for you to be in a man's chambers alone."

She kept her voice cold. "You are right: It is not your place. I am the high priestess and I have every right to consult with whomever I choose wherever they may be. So unless you wish to question my honor, this is the last I want to hear of it."

He lowered his head in submission. "Forgive me Highness, I meant no insult." He drew himself back up. "To either of you, the commander is a good man."

She allowed herself a slight smile and he beamed foolishly. The two men rushed back out of her room and nodded. Raber swept his hand toward the door. "Priestess San assures me that the wards are all safely in place."

Pria stepped forward and indeed felt a slight tingle as she entered the protected ring. "Thank you, Raber."

He followed her into the room and waited at her bedside table. "Do you wish a guard in the room while you sleep?"

"That shouldn't be necessary for now."

"Are you—" he began.

She held up a finger in warning. "I do not intend to argue matters of magic with you. The guard at the door and the crystals should keep me safe."

He lowered his head. "Of course, Highness."

"Go and rest, Raber. You have done well here."

His low bow did little to hide his grin as he slipped from the room. She sighed as he pulled the door shut behind him. "Must everyone I deal with be so difficult?"

She slipped from her robes and replaced them with a thin dressing gown. She pulled a file from the bedside table and gave herself over to her research, allowing all other thoughts to fly from her mind. These were problems she could solve.

The neat, cramped writing of the files strained her eyes in the dim light of her room, and after only a few minutes her head dropped to her chest in a light doze.

A MATTER OF TIMING

Narita eyed the tiny bite that was healing on her fingertip. "Stupid phisher."

Peetare coughed a laugh. "They are quite a nuisance."

In truth the finger hurt much less than her pride. "I didn't even see it. She's my best friend and I couldn't even help her." Her hand curled into a fist. "I feel so worthless."

Peetare snapped his robes around himself. "What you people seem to fail to realize is that there are many things in this world that are beyond your control."

She watched the small man she had been sent to protect. He wasn't unattractive. Smallish but well-muscled, she could imagine some even finding him handsome if it wasn't for the perpetual sour demeanor he wore like a shroud. "Do you not have family, Priest Peetare? Anyone who cares for you?"

He paused in their slow circuit, his eyes searching the trees. "They understand that there are aspects of my life that they are not privileged to know. Any who did not accept that I had to sever contact with."

Her heart convulsed at his cold tone. "That's terrible."

He continued on along the outer edge of the camp. "That, Commander, is life." He stopped to inspect the area around where Pria had been trapped. From what she had heard from other patrols, this was common among them all. He knelt. "What do you know of this…Mian?"

Narita blinked. "You can't possibly think Mian is the one behind this? I've known him my entire life, and though he may be an incurable scamp he is one of the most honorable men I have ever known!"

Peetare stood, his face flat with ridicule. "Of course he couldn't. Lana was with that boy every day. If he had even a hint of magical ability she would have known."

Her forehead wrinkled. "Oh. Then why do you ask?"

Peetare stepped away from the trapped area, the patch only discernible to the four Lorienians. "He seems to have an inappropriate attachment to the high priestess."

Narita dropped her gaze to check the closeness of the other guards. "We are all very close to Pria; she is our family."

He held up a warning finger. "She is a priestess first."

"I don't see how it is any of your business what relationships Pria forms." Narita crossed her arms.

Peetare regarded her coolly. "You are speaking as a friend. I am speaking as a priest. It is our obligation to protect the people we serve."

Eyes narrowed, Narita drew herself up to her full height. "Are you trying to imply that High Priestess Pria is in any way incapable of doing so?"

He plucked a blade of foxtail and scrutinized it before tossing it aside. "The high priestess I knew was driven, focused. The girl I see now is distracted, scattered. It begs the question of what the difference is."

Narita let her rage flame. "Priest Peetare, I would like to see you watch your family and friends hunted like animals, your homeland ravaged by monsters. I would like for you to see half of what she has and be able to remain calm. How dare you even suggest such a thing! She has risked everything in the hopes of saving her people and you have the nerve to stand here and imply that she is distracted by a man who would gladly lay his life down if she asked it of him!"

His expression did not falter. "That is precisely why I was against returning her here. Such involvement complicates our position."

Narita was yelling now, uncaring of the eyes that watched them. "That *involvement* is the very reason she is working so hard! She is not distracted because she is attached to us—she is distracted because there is an army of monsters descending on innocent people led by a man who is after her personally. She is worried that she will not be able to keep everyone alive. I don't want to know the person who can stay unaffected in that situation!"

She stormed off toward the ring of guards, keeping her back to the priest at its center. Grizzled old Lenner kept his bow toward the trees as he ghosted to her side. His severe features always seemed to keep most people at bay but Narita found his unapologetic frankness to be comforting. The deep lines on his face spoke of a wisdom earned through a hard life. When she had first been given her command, she had worried that Lenner would feel slighted but he had taken to her leadership so naturally that no one else in the command would speak against her.

"Been a stressful week around here," he said.

"Only promises to get worse." Her tone was short as she focused on the treeline.

"I heard the prince say we are to be receiving seventeen thousand men from the Alacian Province."

Narita spun to face him. "When did you hear this?"

"Just before we came out here with Priest Personality there." He jerked his head over his shoulder.

She waved the man off. "What did Janu say?"

"He said once the men from the Silver City return, it will be time to turn to the Seat."

Her eyes flashed with excitement. "Finally!"

Lenner barked a laugh. "Yes, now the real dying starts."

"Don't you see? If we are on the offensive, that gives this man less time to concentrate on Pria and less time to set traps for our men." Narita shook her head.

"Perhaps."

She sighed. "What are you thinking?"

"This man has been bold enough taunting us from afar. Who knows what a direct attack could precipitate."

"It is a risk we will and must take." She glanced behind her at the priest who seemed quite unperturbed at her outburst. "Beats staying here with these emotionless statues."

The man who called himself Neram crouched low beneath the trees as he paced the robed man at the edge of the army. The man had yet to be able to sense him though his eyes often drifted toward the forest. A jet-black phisher sat perched on his shoulder, its large eyes sparkling as he watched the man from afar.

He stood from his vantage point and turned to the trees. It wasn't time yet. The man turned again to watch the patrol over his shoulder. No, not yet.

Several more phishers glided down to land on his clothes. They had their limitations but they were definitely useful. The same could be said of each of the creatures at his disposal, but as a mass they were an indestructible tool to crush anyone foolish enough to stand in his way. He had underestimated the girl's courage, which had cost him Kyneira, but the move had put her in a less defensible position. He would win in the end, he always did.

The soldiers felt themselves safe within the city but it had already fallen once. His horde outnumbered them. With an evil smirk he stepped into a clearing packed with waiting grinlo. There was no command they would not follow from him, he had made sure of that.

Very soon even the Lorien and the high priestess herself would bow to him.

At the center of the mass a listril crooned, its long limbs raising it high above its handlers. The phisher had failed but together the two creatures would fetch him his prize.

A grinlo shuffled up to him, its hand tangled in the swaddling gown of the infant that dangled from its grip. A stunned glaze painted the child's face as it swayed with the creature's movement but its body remained unnaturally still. The phisher's venom kept it comatose.

Smile plastered across his face, he took the snagged gown from its claws and let the burden drape forgotten by his leg. There was nothing he wouldn't do to keep his new station. Nothing.

Pria jumped as a hand fell on her shoulder.

"Tired?"

She faced Raber, who stood behind her chair. His voice was pitched low so as not to disturb the other people scattered around the table but she caught Mian's irritated glare none the less. The table was occupied with Janu and his commanders and littered with maps and orders. Heavy dark curtains blocked the windows and a ring of soldiers guarded the room. "More frustrated than anything."

"You need to keep up your strength. Without you we are completely defenseless."

She chuckled. "Hardly."

Jeran grabbed Raber's elbow and moved him back from Pria's chair. Her eyes narrowed at Mian's satisfied smirk. "If we attack, are you planning to keep Kyneira as your base?"

Janu shrugged. "Good a place as any."

Mian turned a page in the roster as he kept his eyes on the writing. "We'll need to build up the defenses, either way. Kyneira will not stand if we go on a full offensive. We'll need to send for workers to build a wall and some guard towers. Priestess, can you send the orders for us?"

"I will send whatever you write up, Commander." His brilliant green eyes met hers and pulled away any irritation she had. She looked away pointedly; she wanted to be irate at him and he had no right to alter that. From the corner of her eye she caught the evil grin that made sure she was aware that he knew what she was thinking.

"Thank you, Priestess." He signaled for parchment and set to his task. He may be intolerable but he was dedicated.

Janu slid the roster from in front of Mian as he perused the ranks himself. His eyes held a guarded optimism when he looked up to the men seated around him. "For too long we have allowed these monsters to roam our homeland. This cannot stand. It will not stand. No more cities will be lost to this ravenous scourge. This is a promise I make to you, here and now. With these ranks we will begin our retaliation. We will push this vermin from our land back into the darkness where they belong."

Pria allowed herself a proud smile. Every man in the room drank up his words like a fine wine, eyes aglow with patriotic pride. They would march into the jaws of death if he asked them; he was their prince and had earned their love and loyalty. He looked every inch the great prince, tall and lithe with a strong jaw and handsome face. He looked much like their father.

Men all around the room stood, whispering among themselves in preparation to organize their men for the work to come. Work for all of them. It would be up to herself and the priest and priestesses to protect the workers from attack—their enemy would not stand by and watch as they built up defenses.

She stood as Mian approached, taking the missive from his fingers. The letter flashed in a blink as she pulled her power through him, so much faster than she would have been able to accomplish without him. The self-satisfied grin on his face pulled a heavy sigh from her lips.

"Always impressive." He gestured for her to walk with him, nodding to Jeran as he and Raber fell in behind them. "We will need protection for the work crews while they shore up the city."

"I have already thought on this," she said. "We will of course keep the workers safe."

He hooked his thumbs behind his belt. "I don't like to put you or your people in this situation."

"I am quite aware of that. I am also aware that if you had any inkling of how to avoid it, you would."

Guards held the doors for them as they stepped outside into the street, the sun bright in the sky. "This will be no easy endeavor, shoring up Kyneira's defenses. I'm not sure how long it will take. We might have to keep it going after we start fighting."

"I will leave San, Aliat, and Peetare to watch them when we go."

He dropped his head, wavy red hair swaying down across his cheek. "I was hoping you would stay with them."

Her eyebrow rose. "You want me to stay behind while you go off to fight the horde and reclaim the Seat?"

"I want you to protect our people." His voice was quiet but urgent.

"That is not why you ask."

"You are a stubborn creature, Priestess," he growled.

"And you are an ignorant fool. How do you expect to protect your soldiers? The workers here will be looked after by competent, experienced priestesses. My place is with you, it is where I will do the most good. Kyneira will be less of a target without me here. Do you really intend to leave me here to face the enemy without my Well?" she pushed.

He tangled his fists in his hair as he spun on the cobbled street. "There is nowhere to keep you safe, is there?"

She laughed. "What did you think? That you could shut me away somewhere so that I would be sheltered?"

He chewed his lip as she stood watching him. "You find this all amusing, don't you?"

"I do not enjoy seeing you tormented so, but your stubbornness is entertaining." She took his arm and turned him back down the road. Soldiers all around them worked on rebuilding the city, fixing collapsing walls or tearing down dilapidated structures. The city was alive with the noise of construction, every man spurred on by the coming conflict. Several more worked outside the city itself, cutting down trees and working on the defensive walls to keep the invading army out. Mian made his circuit to check on each crew, a serene Pria at his side. Nothing but calm confidence to the public from the high priestess and Battle Leader.

The soldiers looked on in awe as they glided by in a haze of mystique, spreading confidence as they went. Everywhere they stopped soldiers bowed low before they jumped back to their tasks with enthusiasm. Pria smiled at Farner as he stood from the wall he was working on. He bowed low to Pria then nodded to Mian as he stood. "Good day, Priestess, it is a pleasure to see you."

Pria embraced him. "The pleasure is mine, dear Farner." She stepped back. "You remember Commander Mian and Jeran."

His lips curled in a smile. "Of course. We are making great progress on the repairs to Kyneira; the work crews are all doing quite well."

"It is good to hear that. Walk with us awhile, Farner," Pria said.

He glanced behind him at the work still awaiting his attention before he waved a younger man over and indicated the pile of bricks he had been working with. He waved his hand wide before Pria. "Lead the way, Highness."

Pria's long silken robes flowed around her as she glided along on Mian's arm. Farner tried hard not to fidget as he kept pace on her other side. Both Pria and Mian kept their silence as they continued out into the surrounding camp. Soldiers rose in a wave as they passed to fall in step as a massive guard. Pria shook her head in exasperation as she glared up at Mian who sported a satisfied smirk. "Is this your doing?"

He laughed. "No, it is not; they did this all on their own."

"Great." She faced Farner. "We are going to need you to refocus your men for a while. Kyneira is going to need a defensive wall as soon as possible. That will have to become the greatest priority for now. You will need to put your crews to that."

"We have several crews working on the wall already," Farner responded.

"I am quite aware of that."

Mian addressed Farner over her head. "We have gathered enough men to make a try for pushing the horde back. Prince Janu wants to try for the Seat, possibly even Amber Keep if all goes well before the winter."

Farner nodded. "So, we need to get the city defensible before the army leaves."

"Not the entire army, but a fair bit of it."

"We will not abandon Kyneira," Pria said. "Pushing the horde back will protect the city. The priestesses and the priest will be remaining behind to keep the workers safe."

Farner's eyes darted back to Jeran before returning to her. "You will be going with the army."

She glared at Jeran over her shoulder. "Something tells me I would like to know what you two talked about when I was not around."

Jeran's smile was innocent. "I don't know what you could possibly mean, High Priestess. Farner and I only ever discussed tactics."

"Arrogant men." She raised her voice back to normal but let it keep its irritation. "The horde will not leave our people alone until they are defeated; we cannot do that huddled here."

Mian patted her hand but it did little to soften her sharp tone. "What can we get for you?"

Farner wrung his hands as he glanced around the encamped soldiers. "Time."

"We will give you as much of that as we can afford, along with workers from Austeria and the Silver City when they arrive," Pria said.

Farner's eyes were large with anxiety. "How long before the soldiers leave?"

Mian's face showed his worry, it was a lot to heap on the man's shoulders. "We are waiting for our numbers to get here, could take some time. Until then, we will be sure to keep a guard around your men to keep them safe."

Farner nodded. "I will gather everyone I can and meet back here." He bowed again then hurried off toward the city.

Pria tossed her hair over her shoulders and raised her chin in satisfaction. Her body flushed with anticipation but a quick relaxation exercise brought her heart back under control. An ego boost was one thing, but there was work to be done. "We need to find San and the others. Get them out here to watch over the men."

Raber rushed forward. "Allow me, Priestess." He took off toward the city without even a backward glance.

Mian raised a hand after him. "He's definitely more exuberant around you."

Jeran laughed. "You're just jealous that he never ran that way when you gave him an order."

"Guess I'll have to keep my high priestess close so I can keep him in hand."

A blaring horn pierced the bright sky and shattered the sounds of construction around them. Mian grabbed her arm as he and Jeran glanced around the bustling camp. "Western perimeter."

Mian nodded then glanced down at the woman at his side. "I'm not getting rid of you, am I?"

Pria smiled devilishly. "Not if you wish to keep your arm."

He rolled his eyes as they took off at a run, soldiers swarming around them with swords drawn. The streets were abuzz with rushing men as they flew through the city. Jeran stayed flush to Pria's side his eyes toward the buildings around him. Soon the cacophony of battle began to swell over the rush of boots as they neared the western edge of the city. Mian slid to a halt, jerking Pria to his chest as they reached a line of combat near the end of town.

Monsters flowed from the trees, boiling toward the soldiers lining the city. Pria's heart seized as he realized the numbers that barreled toward them, they would be overrun. Pria took Mian's hand and pulled him forward as she pushed through the soldiers massed ahead of them. Mian tightened his grip on her hand as she was nearly jerked away. "Pria, what are you doing?"

"Stay with me!"

Mian shoved soldiers out of his way and rushed forward to her side sliding a hand around her waist. "What are you doing?"

Pria entangled her fingers in his as she tried to inch her way toward the line of fighting but the men would not give way. She growled in frustration, screaming to be heard over the din. "They'll be overrun, you know that! Get me to the front; I can help even us out!"

Mian's jaw tightened before he swore, drew a deep breath, and shouted over the fighting. "Make a path! Let us through!" Men glanced over their shoulders and struggled as far aside as they could to allow them to creep forward.

Pria stopped only three men back from the conflict before she pressed herself into his arms and wrapped them around her chest. Eyes closed, she rolled her head against his shoulder as she pulled through him. The contact not only made using the Well easier—it made the connection stronger and allowed more strength to flow from him.

Hand stretched up, she laid her bare palm along his neck filling herself with even more magical resonance. Her free hand lowered toward the ground, fingers spread as she sent the torrent into the street beneath her. It snaked out beyond the soldiers as they struggled against the overwhelming foe. Someone yelled but she left her physical body to the soldiers around her.

She let the spell spread in a wide wave creeping up from the depths in ropes and vines. The creatures saw nothing as they rushed past the buried magic beyond their senses. She snapped the tendrils and snagged several creatures into the air then sent them crashing back into their comrades. The second volley rained down upon new grinlo as they rushed in to fill the emptiness. She kept her mind blank; there was only the warm embrace behind her and the rain of death ahead.

Some of the horde turned to flee as she advanced her attack toward the soldiers. The men cheered as the line of magic approached them.

She was jerked backward; the sudden shock tore the spell from her fingers as she crashed to the ground. In a void over them was Raber, his sword slashing at a swarm of phishers. Pria's jaw tightened as Mian lifted her from the street and carried her back away from the fighting. As she watched over his shoulder she flung out her hand and swatted the tiny black devils from the air with a satisfied smile.

Mian dropped her to the ground and jerked her along behind him by her wrist never slowing. The sounds of battle faded away and still he ran. "Mian! I think we can—"

He slid around a corner and spun to catch her. Her eyes widened in shocked horror as a group of grinlo rushed toward them down the street.

Her heart raced as she struggled to keep up with Mian. Another turn and he stopped again snatching her backward into his arms.

The street before them was clogged with seven tall listrils.

Mian glanced behind them to the still-advancing grinlo, his arms clamped around Pria's shoulders. He rushed toward a door in a large warehouse that lined the street, using a heel to break it open. He tossed Pria further inside as he spun to secure the door with whatever debris he could find lying about.

Pria shook visibly, steeling herself as Mian faced her. "We need to find a way out," he said.

"No Mian." She hated how unsteady her voice sounded.

He ignored her as he paced the littered warehouse. "There has to be another exit!"

She forced him to look at her. "Mian, you have to go." He tried to shake her off but she held fast. "You listen to me! You have to go for help. We will not escape, not the both of us. They know I'm here—I am what they are after! You can get away; you can escape and bring help." She pulled his mouth to hers, savoring the sweet gentle caress as she willed him to listen.

His eyes screamed hatred as he pulled back from her. She forced the tears back. "They won't kill me, not immediately. They use magic. This will buy you time to find me." Desperation raised her voice until it rang from the walls around them. "There is no other way! They will follow my scent wherever we go! Without help we would never make it."

He pushed away from her. "I hate you for asking this of me! I hate you!"

A loud crash answered him from outside as the grinlo began work on breaking down the door.

"You are running out of time," she gasped.

He growled as he punched the wall before grabbing her and pulling her into an impassioned kiss. He pressed his forehead to hers one hand cupped to the back of her neck. "I will not lose you. If I have to tear through every grinlo with my bare hands I will find you."

She cursed the tear that slipped from her eye. "I will try to hold here as long as I can."

His muscles spasmed before he jerked away and took off at a full run. "Stay alive, I will come for you!" He crashed through a door along the far wall.

She was alone.

Her heart seized as her mind turned to the monsters that tore at the door. She could already see a crack in the heavy wood. She pulled a deep breath and focused on the warehouse behind her.

"Okay Pria, time to work."

She rushed around the room gathering as much debris as she could and piled it in front of the door. She crouched behind the pile and waited as the wood splintered with the abuse from the opposite side. Trapped she may be, but no priestess worth her muster was ever helpless.

Mian tried to keep his mind blank as he ran. He couldn't panic; if he panicked she was gone. So he ran on in a blissful fog. The streets around him were dead silent, all the soldiers fighting the horde to the west. He needed men, rested men and lots of them. He needed Narita.

He turned down a side street. Narita would be with the priestesses and priest; it was the only eventuality that he would accept.

His shoulders burned as he crashed through the door of a building and rushed up through stairways until he stood panting before the three Lorienians and a confused Narita.

She rushed to his side as he fell to his hands and knees. "Mian! What's wrong? Are you bleeding?"

"Cornered…need men!"

Narita launched into action. She was gone in a flash and he was left breathless as San forced a bitter concoction down his throat. Something boiled up from inside of him and eased the tense fatigue from his muscles.

Narita was back at his side in a blink. "Where are we going?"

"North, to the warehouse district." He waved at San. "Maps! In case I fall behind!"

Aliat rushed toward him with a street map of Kyneira. He studied it for a moment then pointed to the building he had left his heart in. She would pay dearly for driving him to it.

Narita nodded as she marked the map with a pin and stuffed it behind her breastplate. "Let's go."

Mian's mind was so occupied that they were three streets away before he noticed San at his side. He let his full anger at Pria surface. "Where do you think you are going?"

She shrugged, somehow still able to appear serene and calm even at a jog. "I assume it is the high priestess we are rushing to. You will need my help."

The slow pace only fueled his rage but they would need to fight when they got there. "I'm not risking both of you. We have already encountered a swarm of phishers and there is a pack of listrils waiting for us at the warehouse."

"I'm not going back."

"Is willful stubborn stupidity a class you teach at the Lorien?" he asked.

She smiled sympathetically.

Pria let the high-pitched wail flow from her lips as she cupped her hands to her ears. A listril crooned from behind the door to which she pressed her back. After she had set the first pile of debris on fire she had retreated to the next story of the building and held there behind another barricade.

When the advancing mass had made it through, she moved to the roof with nothing to block the door.

She scanned the rooftop one more time. She was running out of options. There was no permanent way to resist the listril, only deflect its call. Soon she would be ensnared and all her tricks would have been in vain. She cut off the scream and lowered her hands hesitantly. The crooning had stopped. Had Mian returned?

She spun and pressed her ear and hands to the door, listening. A hushed whisper met her straining ears.

"I know you are there, Priestess."

She jerked back, preparing a few nasty spells to choose from when the time came.

"You must be so tired, you've fought so hard."

She backed away to give herself space to fight.

"Oh no! Don't leave, little one. We have come here for you."

The door handle turned a bit but stopped—she had jammed it tight with a dagger. The best she could do in a pinch.

"Come now, little Pria, we both know you can't hold here. My creatures have your scent. There is nowhere you can hide. Come to me willingly and I will pull my army from this city. No more fighting. We are only here for you."

When she didn't respond, quiet laughter drifted toward her.

"But you still hold out hope, don't you? Do you really think they'll get here in time?" He punctuated his last word with a sharp blow that rocked the door between them. "You will not escape me!" The soft sickly-sweet cajoling was replaced by an enraged roar.

She flung up a hand to cover her face as the door shattered and rained splinters across the rooftop. Four grinlo rushed out onto the roof and shuffled aside as their master stepped from the doorway. He was hidden with the same hooded robe he had worn before. He spread his hands wide. "Hello Pria." He glanced around them. "But where is your companion? The one who pants at your heels?"

She wriggled her fingers as she settled on her first strike but still he didn't attack. On her guard, she was still a threat to him. He took a step toward her and she kept the distance. A deep laugh rumbled from his chest.

"Come now, pet, let's—" He spun as an arrow blossomed in his shoulder and she flung the spell from her fingers, sending him back through the door.

She brought up another spell but was torn from her feet as something crashed into her from her right. The grinlo roared as they rushed after her when she recognized Jeran at the end of her arm. He rushed toward the edge of the building. "Jeran, there's—"

The scream that tore from her lips pierced the sky as Jeran launched himself from the guard wall, jerking her along behind him. He rolled as he hit the roof of the next building cradling Pria to his chest before he tossed her back to her feet. She glared at him.

"Are you mad?"

He grabbed her hand and rushed across the roof toward a trap door. "I'm sorry, were you having a good time?"

"You just pulled me off a roof!"

He flung the trap door open, grabbed her by the forearm, and lowered her through it. "It was maybe a ten-foot drop! Honestly, woman!"

Her slippered feet hit the floor hard as he released her. He dropped beside her and took her chin in his fingers, tilting her head back and lifting her hair before she slapped his hands away. "I'm fine. How did you find me? Where's Mian?"

"I was going to ask you that. Didn't he take off with you after the phisher attack?"

She tapped a torch as he pulled it from the wall; the resulting flame danced shadows across the room around them. "We were trapped; I made him leave to get help."

Jeran's face blanched as he rushed through the darkness. "He left you alone?"

"There was no choice," she whispered.

"I doubt that made much difference to him."

She dropped her head as they raced downstairs. "He wasn't happy. It was the only way for both of us to live."

He pulled her into a hallway and broke into a run toward the far door. "The attack must have only been to pull you out; they drew back once you ran."

"He was waiting for us. Mian dragged me around for several streets when we ran into a pack of grinlo. When we moved to escape them, we were cut off by listrils. We ducked into the warehouse but there was no way we could evade them by ourselves."

Orotid held open a door ahead of them. Out in the street waited two hundred soldiers, swords out, eyes searching. Raber jogged toward them from around the corner. "You found her!" He slid into place at her side.

She rolled her eyes. "Reserve your worry for yourself Raber, I'm fine."

He wiped at a large scratch that ran down his cheek. "What are a few cuts in the service of my priestess?"

Jeran cleared his throat. "We need to regroup before the grinlo attack again." Orotid led the men off through the town.

The city around them was filled with a strange quiet. She kept her voice low. "He's going to be very angry with me."

Jeran's eyebrow rose. "What do you mean 'going to be'?"

"He won't have room for anger until he knows I'm safe," she said. "I don't know how to make this up to him or even if I want to."

Jeran glared at her. "Why wouldn't you want to?"

"Sending him for help was the right decision. Him staying with me would have gotten him killed or both of us captured. We had been outsmarted. I wasn't going to evade them, not with seven listrils. If I act like I did something wrong, he might not go a second time."

"I can't believe he went this time," Jeran said.

The soldiers ahead of them stopped and silence fell as they waited. Orotid pressed himself against the wall listening to something neither of them could hear. Several minutes passed before he waved them on.

"How did you know that roof was there?"

His glare was exasperated. "I told you, I grew up here. This is my city, Priestess. There is nowhere you could hide from me."

She laughed. "Well, I'm glad you're on our side."

He shook his head as Orotid stopped them again. In the silence they could hear the rattling cacophony of an army in full run through the streets. After a peek around the corner, Orotid slipped from sight. Jeran pressed Pria against the wall of the building. His chest heaved behind his breastplate as the minutes stretched out.

Every muscle tensed as footsteps rushed back toward them. The soldiers around her all drew their swords as a man slid past the corner, his eyes searching the men spread out there. Pria collapsed against Jeran's chest.

"Mian!"

Mian stood frozen as Orotid and Narita rushed up to him. Narita's frightened face broke into a brilliant smile as she rushed toward Pria and tore her from Jeran's protective embrace.

Mian had yet to move.

"Jeran."

"Do you need something?" Jeran eyed him warily.

Mian drew a deep breath. "How did you find her?"

"We followed you."

Mian nodded. "And?"

Jeran stuffed his thumbs behind his belt. "We saw you get cut off. I took our men down a few streets and left them there. I took an archer with me and climbed onto a building next to the one you two were hiding in. We could already see the fires when we started planning. Then I saw Pria on the roof. She was confronting a man in a robe. The archer opened fire as I jumped down onto the roof and slipped Pria out while he was distracted."

Mian's eyes drifted toward Pria, still ensnared in Narita's relief. "Your archer, did he kill this man?"

Jeran's jaw tightened. "I'm sorry to say it was just a shoulder wound."

Mian sighed as he nodded. "You did well, Jeran."

"Thank you, sir." Jeran watched him as he walked past.

Mian stopped halfway to Pria and turned back. "Jeran, find Prince Janu and inform him of what has happened. Orotid, how are the men?"

Orotid's eyes met Jeran's before they returned to Mian. "Tired, sir, but they will hold."

Jeran's head tilted. "They're coming."

"Jeran, go now," Mian said, pointing. "Narita, fetch your men. They will not recapture Kyneira."

Pria took a step toward him but he rushed back down the street. Narita and Jeran both darted off as Mian waved his men closer. "We need to set up a perimeter to keep the people safe. Where did Narita go?"

Pria's voice was steady. "You sent her to fetch her men."

He started but kept his back to her. "Of course." He pointed toward the street behind them. "They should be coming toward us down that street. We're going to need to push the horde back at least three streets. I don't want them this close to any inhabited buildings, and some of these warehouses are storing supplies." Narita led her men around the corner, San close at her side. Mian snatched her breastplate and dragged her along behind him. "Where did you put that map?"

Narita fished behind her armor and handed Mian the map. "Do we have enough men to hold them out?"

Mian snapped the map open then knelt and smoothed it along the road. "We're going to have to find a way." He pointed. "We can form a perimeter utilizing the narrow alleys. We can keep them out of the inner streets."

Pria knelt beside him. "We can't hold them like that forever."

He chewed his lower lip as he kept his eyes to the map. "I know."

Pria smiled up at San as she laid a hand along his tense forearm. "If you can hold on these alleys here"—she pointed at several intersections—"then San, Aliat, Peetare, and I can drop these buildings to form a barrier. A makeshift wall that will allow us to stand until reinforcements arrive."

His voice dropped to a whisper. "It's a good plan."

San sank down on his opposite side. "With multiple magical scents it would be much more difficult to focus in on the high priestess. They would have to know her physical scent as well."

He tilted his head. "And if they do?"

Pria sighed. "We'll take guards." She leaned close. "Mian, you know this has to happen. I know you don't want to put any of us in this position. We will take as many precautions as we can."

San leaned in on his other side. "We will stay on the go; it will be hard to pinpoint us."

"After we get married we are going on a long honeymoon," Mian said.

She stood and arranged her sleek robes haughtily. "I do not recall ever having a big enough lapse in judgment to agree to marry you."

Mian jerked her into his arms, cradling her head. His thumb trailed along her jaw. "For as long as I've known you, you have always been the standard by which I measure others. Beside you there is no one else. You are the only woman I want to fill my arms. I love you Pria, and only you." He pressed his forehead to hers, inhaling the sweet scent of her skin. "If you love me, tell me now, for I cannot bear to walk away from you again not knowing."

A tear slipped free as Pria stared up into Mian's emerald eyes, for once not concerned about the people that watched.

"Mian…you've always meant the world to me. My heart broke when I sent you away, knowing how much it hurt you. I do love you, Mian. You can keep that in your heart whenever I force you into something you don't want to do. Always know it hurts me as well." Her eyes brightened as she smiled. "We can spend the first week in the Silver City!"

"Then we can tour the museums in Schtaad."

"That sounds lovely," she said.

He cupped his hands along her cheeks. "Be careful."

She swatted him on the chest. "I'm always careful!"

"We'll see you to each building and leave a guard for you," Mian said.

Pria nodded. "Set up your men, Commander; we will fetch Aliat and Peetare."

Raber nodded when Mian met his gaze and grabbed a group of men then loped off after Pria and San. The boy was a pest but he would throw himself between Pria and death.

Narita rubbed his arm as he pulled a deep breath. "What are we doing, Commander?"

Pria's heart pounded as she raced to the next building brushing dust from her face as she went. Raber was close at her heels with a company of ten guards. She had argued it down to ten; they needed to be mobile. She picked out her next target and redoubled her speed as she crossed an open street.

She raised her hands as she stopped, ignoring the men that formed up around her. The foundation began to groan as she pulsed a destabilizing spell into it. The walls bowed and cracked as they gave way to the abuse and crashed down against the debris from the last.

She dropped to her knees and allowed her body some semblance of rest. She could hear other crashes as San, Aliat, and Peetare worked to form an unending wall of debris around the city. Arm out, she allowed Raber to pull her to her feet before she darted off to the next building. She could rest after everyone was safe.

Her knees began to shake as she brought down the next structure. This would have been much easier with Mian, but he needed to lead his men. With any luck, the grinlo's leader would assume she was with him and allow time for the priest and priestesses to do their work.

Her next step dropped her to the ground, and her skin scraped along the rubble. Raber didn't miss a step as he scooped her up into his arms. She pointed to the next building. "I can do one more!"

"You can't even stand!"

She didn't have the energy to spare for irritation. "I don't need to stand!"

"You've already done three more than you told San you could do." He motioned his men to a tall building beside the collapsed rubble. "I'm sure the wall is nearly complete."

"Where are we going?" she demanded.

"I'm going to take you to see your wall. Maybe if you see how much you've done you'll take a break." His pace never wavered as he climbed the stairs and stepped out onto the roof. The cool breeze felt good along her scraped skin as he sat her down beside a guard wall. He pointed out over Kyneira. "See? Already our men are pulling back behind your wall."

She nodded. "Let us go and check on Aliat."

"Yes, Priestess."

A group of soldiers rushed toward them as they made the street, an exhausted Aliat supported among them. Her tired eyes rolled up to Pria. "High Priestess."

"Priestess Aliat."

"I've worked down from the Glade District. Peetare was working toward Rader Street. Hopefully he has met up with San by now," Aliat said.

The city around them rocked with the collapse of another building. Pria pointed behind them. "We'll check the barricade back this way for any place that might get breached. We will meet back at the temple."

Aliat nodded. "Be careful."

Pria closed her eyes as Raber walked along the debris wall. "We can easily check this wall ourselves. You can go and rest."

"And if there is a breach? Can you drop a building to fill it as well?"

"I'm sure we can deal," he said.

"I'm not going, Raber."

"Stubborn," he breathed.

It wasn't long until the gentle motion pulled her to sleep in his arms. His lips curled as he juggled her arm up onto her stomach. There was no strength in her muscles as she lay draped along his chest. The wall stretched uninterrupted for multiple blocks to form a barrier nearly two men high of dangerous shifting litter. It wouldn't stop the horde, but it was better than the open streets. Mian would be by looking for her, as soon as he saw that she was not at the temple.

He nodded to the guard who carried San as she slept in his arms. Confident that the wall was uncompromised, he led his men down a side street, San's guard turned back the way they had come. Something small caught his eye but it was gone as soon as he noticed it.

He paused in the street as the world around him seemed to vibrate. The guards behind him dropped to the pavement as a robed man stepped from behind a pile of debris.

"I believe you have something of mine."

Raber cupped Pria to his chest as the cloaked man took a step toward them, his own eyes staring back at him out of the cowl.

"Took you long enough."

"Keep your voice down," Raber hissed. "You'll wake her up."

The robed man ran his thumb along her forehead, sucking the flavor off his skin. "Not likely. Our little priestess has been busy."

Raber scoffed. "She is a stubborn creature. Took her a long time to drain through it."

The man reached into his robes and drew out a phisher. He laid the creature reverently on her chest and it latched on to her neck.

"Come now, boy. The time draws near for us to crush this pathetic resistance."

THE CONNECTION

Mian loosened his reins again, patting his horse's withers. He saw Janu do the same beside him. His men stretched along the wall of debris, watching for any attempts to breach it. He felt his horse toss its head and again eased the tension that kept returning to his grip. He had already seen San and Peetare as they were carried off toward the temple.

Janu glanced up toward the sky. "We could have missed her. We didn't see Aliat."

Mian's entire body convulsed. "Then we check the temple?"

Janu's eyes swept the soldiers all waiting for hell to descend on them. "You go. Tell me she's fine and we are worrying for nothing. I can handle this."

Mian just released his hold on his horse, letting the animal charge away from the barricade. They had just missed her, that's what it had to be. Raber wouldn't have let her get hurt. He dropped from the saddle letting the horse charge on as he reached the temple plaza.

A handful of soldiers were gathered outside and jumped to attention at his approach. A deep breath slipped from his lips. "Report."

An older man saluted. "No incidents, Commander. The priest and priestesses from the Lorien are resting comfortably inside."

His jaw ached as the muscles tightened. "And the high priestess?"

The soldiers glanced around in confusion. "We assumed she would be with you."

He pushed through them. The temple was open inside but still cluttered from the attack. Near the center along the floor were San, Aliat, and Peetare, all comfortable and asleep. Mian shook San by the shoulders. "Priestess, wake up!"

Her eyes were bloodshot as they snapped open. "Commander? Did something happen?" she gasped. "Are…are we needed?"

He grabbed her face trying to force the fatigue from her with sheer will. "San, where is Pria? We haven't seen her."

San's head lolled as her arm jerked toward her companions. "Aliat spoke with her, she is fine."

"Where did she go?" he pushed.

"She will come here, probably has young Raber cornered somewhere arguing with him."

Mian released her back to the floor. "I'm sure you're right."

"Of course I am," she said. "Raber would never let anything happen to her. He pines so deeply for her, he's probably trying to get to clean her robes."

San rolled back onto the floor, her eyes sliding shut. His gaze locked on the door. Soon he was on his feet pacing the temple his mind full of a hundred possibilities each more horrible than the last.

Pria struggled through the heavy fog but nothing would budge the weights that kept her blind. Her head lolled to the side, resting on her arm as it stretched above her. Her body sighed pulling her already sore muscles tighter. A muted haze crept through her eyelids as they cracked open though she couldn't discern anything.

Hands caressed her face and tilted her head back. "Why, you are waking up, aren't you? Stronger than I thought you were, but no matter; you are still too weak to break free." He buried his nose in her hair and inhaled. "I am so glad you have come to be with us."

She forced her mouth to move but the only thing that emerged was a pathetic squeak.

The man ran a finger down her lips. "Hush now, pet, there will be plenty of time for that after."

A gentle flicker of fear began to bloom deep in her stomach and she latched onto it savagely. Her heart began to pound pulsing the mind dulling poison throughout her body. The fear would help burn through it quicker.

The man released her hair. Lips brushed her ear but she couldn't fight to pull away. Her body was too far gone for it.

"Do not worry, Priestess. We are going to show you true freedom." The voice stabbed deep and the fear was replaced with cold rage. Raber. "They will never think you weak again."

Something thick and salty was forced into her mouth; her mind reeled to spit it out but her weakened body let the metallic brine slide down her throat. A hand clutched her jaw as a tongue ran across her numb lips. It would have been infant blood, innocent blood, the collection of which twists the soul.

Her body shook as a chill settled over her skin. Her eyes flew open as white-hot pain snaked down her spine. Muscles tightened, pulling her body backward in an arc, her eyes staring up at the ceiling. A soft whimper escaped her lips but she couldn't draw breath for a scream.

Raber was at her shoulder in a blink, mouth close to her ear. "It hurts less if you don't fight."

She dropped in her bonds, her limbs going limp as the sweat poured from her skin.

He lifted her chin with his fingertips. "And you don't have to worry about your little pet Mian; I'll be sure he gets some extra attention."

The robed man returned with a bowl, dipping in two fingers and painting her cheek with the thick slime held within. Her body tried to cringe away but Raber held her tight. "It will help, just hold still."

Her cheek began to glow with a radiating warmth that spread across her face. Her eyes burned, flashing solid black before returning to blue. The breath whimpered from her lips, taking resistance with it.

Something in her mind railed as Raber held a goblet to her lips. She drew the liquid into her mouth, coughing as it burned down her throat. He trailed his thumb along her lip, wiping a drop of the elixir from her mouth.

"See, it's better already."

Mian's knuckles were white, his hands clenched in fists at his back. Nine bodies littered the street around them as the sounds of battle raged nearby. The lull had only lasted about an hour as the man razed the city for any sign of Pria. His men easily kept the grinlo from crossing Pria's debris wall; it was too difficult for them to climb. She always had been sharp.

His jaw was clenched as San inspected each body. "It was him, wasn't it? He took her."

San stayed diligent to her work. "We have no way to know that."

His rage boiled up. "You could feel him out there! Why is this different?"

She stood from the last body, her eyes tired but determined. "Traps must have residual magic to work, a trace is purposefully left. Whomever did this wanted to leave as little behind as possible. I cannot tell if it is the same or not."

"Raber is not here," he said.

"Then you cannot possibly think she is in any danger." San smiled indulgently. "That boy would not leave her side even if he was a corpse."

Mian sighed as his eyes searched the buildings around them.

"She was very tired—I bet he took her back to her room. Have you tried her room?"

He glared at her. "Do you seriously all think we non-magical types are stupid?"

San closed her eyes. "Have you tried his rooms?"

Mian froze. "He wouldn't. I'll kill him if he has."

He took off at a flat run and she waved a soldier toward her. "Fetch me Prince Janu and be quiet about it." She pointed to another soldier. "You there! Bring me Priestess Aliat and Priest Peetare; they should both still be in the temple."

She turned back to the bodies as the soldiers fled to carry out her orders. She could only pray they returned before Mian.

Her eyes were blank as they stared out, showing none of the soul-shattering pain that tore from her lips. Raber clamped his hands over his ears. "I don't remember the last one taking this long or being this loud!"

The man who called himself Neram waved off the grinlo as it delivered its latest burden, a newborn boy. The child was wrapped in a rag still coated in gore from birthing. It had his eyes, brilliant blue.

"The girl is very strong. She fights harder than I anticipated." He handed the child to Raber, who stared at him. "Had you informed me of her strength beforehand I could have prepared better. As it is, we are stretched to hold her."

Raber glared at the child in distaste. "They could have at least cleaned it."

"Have you done what I asked?"

Sarcasm dripped from his lips. "Yes, Father. I went to them as you asked, even made sure they were given the growth lapse serum. You don't think it will take that many?"

"They will always be needed later to maintain control."

"So degrading, you know I hate doing that," the boy whined.

Raber flinched as the man who called himself Neram swatted him across the back of the head. "You will do as I command. There is nothing I will not do to keep my power."

Raber pulled a dagger from his belt. "I just hope it works this time. Another high priestess is not going to just fall in our laps."

The man who called himself Neram knelt before the girl. She had stopped screaming and was convulsing again. He could hear the sharp cry as Raber continued his work behind him. "I will break you, pet. It is only a matter of time. No one can save you. There is no hope. Just give in and it all goes away."

She didn't respond of course, couldn't respond. She was too far gone for words. The process was going to begin damaging her mind. He needed a large push, something she couldn't fight, but what?

"I still don't see why I have to sacrifice these things. I brought you the girl—didn't I do my part?"

The man who called himself Neram slipped a blade from his sleeve. "Do not worry, my son, you will not need to do it again."

Grabbing the boy's chin, he thrust the knife up into his heart.

Raber's mouth dropped open in a strengthless scream. It was the same mouth as what graced the face of the man who called himself Neram. In fact, other than age, there was no difference between them except training. He couldn't allow the boy to gain magical talent; with the same strength, the boy could have one day grown to challenge him. But the man who called himself Neram would never allow that. Raber had been a tool, useful but disposable.

He met his own gaze over the boy's shoulder as the pulse that transferred to the blade slowed. The magic in his blood tingled along his fingers as he lowered the boy to the ground. "But you will help me. *Kandriano.*"

Raber's skin flashed a brilliant white, scattering shadows about the small cave and illuminating the dagger still embedded in his weakening heart. His eyes stared out accusingly as his lips twitched.

"I cannot just sit here and watch her slip away from me," the man who called himself Neram said. "I will not let this silly girl stand between me and my power."

The blade was a blazing beacon in his grip as all of Raber's strength leached into it. He wasn't dead yet, but a fog was gathering in his eyes already as the dagger withdrew from his back.

"I will have my power. Nothing will stop me."

San knelt along the top of the heap of debris, young Narita ever vigilant at her side. She glanced back at Mian, his eyes a raging tempest of anger and impatience. She had debated about bringing him. If the enemy was able to turn Pria, the last thing they needed was to give her more strength.

But if he had turned her, they would need the strength of their connection to bring her back—*try* to bring her back. In the history of the Lorien there were many cases of priestesses being turned. There were no cases where they were successfully returned.

She slipped to the next purchase. This had been a good idea for keeping the horde out. The climb was precarious and it was impossible to defend against attack while scaling it. None of that made her struggle over it any less annoying.

Finally, her soft slippered feet touched the firm cobblestones, Narita close behind her.

Her brilliant eyes were nervous but determined. "Do you have any idea how to find her?"

Mian crashed to the street beside her in a rain of dust and debris. "Pria could make a map. She made a map to find Narita from a piece of her armor."

San sighed as Mian helped Aliat down beside him. "We have already tried that. It was…unsuccessful."

"What does that mean?" Mian growled.

Peetare shook the dirt from his silk suit as he made the street behind her. "It means that this man is shielding her from us. It means that we should have removed her from this place when I suggested. It means that her attachment to you people has lost us the most powerful high priestess we have seen in centuries, and above all, it means that I was right in not wanting her to return here."

San grabbed Mian's wrist as he spun toward Peetare, murder dripping from his gaze. "Peetare, it was the council's decision to give Pria this post. They believed as I do, *as Lana did*, that it was in the best interest of all. We will not lose her."

"And just how do you intend to find her?" Peetare challenged. "And if we do, and this man has transformed her, I don't think I need to remind you of the history of the Lorien going against turned priestesses."

She glanced down at her grip on Mian's arm, contemplating letting him vent his anger. "Peetare, until Pria's return, I am senior here. If you intend to question me every step of the way while offering no helpful ideas, you can return to your rooms and go down in history as the priest who sat by while Trimera was being consumed by monsters."

Peetare's teeth snapped shut with an audible *click*. San nodded.

"Aliat, send word to the Lorien and inform them of our situation. Any advice or assistance would be appreciated."

Mian's wrist shook in her grasp, his voice soft and pained. "Priestess, how do we find her?"

The man who called himself Neram trailed his fingers along her throat, almost a loving gesture. He had planned so carefully, went through so much—he wouldn't lose control now. A glowing dagger protruded from his bare chest, its tip buried deep in his heart. His skin rippled with the force of his spell but still she balked. How was that even possible?

Enraged, he threw her away from him, growling as she rolled and flopped across the floor of the cave. Grinlo fled from him as he raged about the small cavern, her eyes staring up at him blindly as he stood over her. "Bring me another!"

Muted shuffling was the only answer he got as the grinlo rushed to avoid his wrath. Grabbing her jaw, he jerked her head up, glaring into her lifeless eyes. "You will fall to me!" She fell back limp to the ground.

She gripped the green-eyed boy's hand tight as he jerked her along through the hallway. The fourteen-year-old boy was the only other person she had seen in this strange place. He ducked into an alcove, pushing her into the shadows behind him.

Something large shuffled toward them, snuffling the air. Long black claws clicked along the tiles leaving deep gouges as it passed, red eyes searching. Its body transformed to smoke, wafting away into nothing as they watched.

But that was the way of this strange world.

The boy pulled her from their hiding place, glancing around the corridors. "Come on." He ran for the door, but it would be locked. They were trapped, somehow, she knew that. Sooner or later the creature would catch her and it would be over. All she could do was run.

Meeting the boy's brilliant gaze, she again wondered if he would be able to leave if not for her.

The walls around them gave a violent lurch and he jerked her into his arms as he backed along the hallway. "The East Garden—we'll climb down the lattice. One of the paths leads to a small gate…"

He took off at a run as the terrible snuffling began anew. The familiar corridors rushed past, but something wasn't right. Detail faded around the periphery, objects appeared when she thought about them, and the halls were devoid of life apart from them and the monster.

She gave the boy at the end of her arm closer attention. The hair wasn't right, it was longer now; he had always balked when his mother cut it. The red curls grew as she watched. His hand should be larger and calloused from weapons. She felt his fingers grow to fill her grip. He was taller now, more muscled but his eyes never changed. He turned toward her as he grew into the tall handsome man he should be.

"I don't know what's happening."

His smile was sad. "I know."

They pivoted at a noise behind them. "It's coming again."

"Then we will keep running."

"I can't run forever," she said.

"Then we fight."

"You're not real, Mian." The second it left her lips she knew it for truth.

He rippled between the boy and the man before becoming solid again. "I am as real as you need me to be."

She faced the approaching sounds. "That's not real either."

He touched his fingers to her cheek drawing her eyes back to him. "But it will hurt you."

"It will hurt me because it represents a real danger." She stared up at the ceiling. "What is going on out there?"

He followed her gaze. "I can't tell you that."

She pressed her hands to her temples pacing the hallway. "The monster represents something real, something that is trying to hurt me. If it can hurt me…" She stopped, staring up into his worried eyes. "Can you help me?" She put her hands on his chest. "Can you fight the monster?" She balled her fist, jabbing him square in the nose.

His eyes sparkled as he stared down at her. "Been wanting to do that for a while, haven't you?"

"You're not bleeding."

"I'm not real," he said. "Not in that sense, anyway. Neither is the beast."

"What does that mean, in that sense?"

"I can't tell you that," he said.

She jumped as something crashed into a door behind them. She took a step back. "Try the window."

The sparkle in his eyes faded but he moved toward the window. It slid open.

"Can you go outside?" she asked.

"You'll be alone."

The crashing came again. "Try to go outside."

He put his hand out of the sill and it vanished up to his elbow. "What if I can't come back?"

She smiled. "I will never be free of you, Mian. Just step out and back in."

He slipped from the window and vanished.

Her heart seized as the seconds slipped by. What had she done? Had she killed him? Forced him from this illusion and left herself alone? Eternity passed before fingers appeared on the sill and Mian emerged from the blank square.

The door behind them cracked as the creature tore at it. She grabbed Mian's hand, dragging him behind her as she raced away. This part of the

Seat wasn't as familiar to her; it warped and shifted. She turned down a side corridor, securing the door behind them.

"What did you see?" she whispered.

"It is hard to describe. I didn't see anything. It was more like I…dissipated. I just floated free and formless for a bit before I was drawn back."

She rubbed her temples. "There's nothing outside? How can there be nothing?" She stared at the wall beside them. "There is a painting that hangs here, do you remember?"

He nodded as she laid her fingers along the wall.

"This place, I can influence it. Try to see the painting hanging here."

He laid his hand beside hers, his forehead wrinkling. The painting formed along the wall, faint and blurry. Pria touched the canvas. "It doesn't look quite real, but it is there."

"What does that mean?" he asked.

"It means that though you may not be entirely real, some part of you is more than just a figment of my mind." A loud crash sounded behind them. "We'd better keep moving."

As they rushed along the corridors Mian kept flashing back to the young boy of her memories. Why wouldn't he stay?

She glanced at the hallway around them, slowing. "I know this place."

"There are few places in the Seat we do not know."

She shook her head. "I know it, but I'm not familiar with it." She rushed to a door, throwing it wide. She stepped into the room and crossed to the window. A small breeze wafted toward them from it.

There was no wind here.

Mian waved out of the window but his limb did not vanish this time. Beyond the pane was a small clearing and trees. "Why is this one different?" he asked.

Her eyes flashed. "It's the way out! It was our way out! This was the window you took me out of after my parents died." She leaned over the sill, glad the emptiness didn't press against her like before.

Mian stared out at the trees. "I can't go with you."

"I know. But you'll still be with me."

"The beast is waiting for you outside, and it's not alone," he said.

Nodding, she pulled him into her arms, remembering the warm embrace. He kissed her tenderly before stepping back.

She climbed up onto the sill, staring down at the ground far below her. There had been a rope last time, but even as she remembered it nothing appeared. She would have to jump. Glancing back over her shoulder, she was not surprised to see the green-eyed boy. His smile was full of mischief and love.

She let herself slip out into the air, hoping it wouldn't be the last time she saw him.

Her entire body jolted and she found herself staring up at the ceiling of a cave. She let her eyes roam the area, pausing on Raber's bloody corpse a few feet away. Her eyes darted toward movement to her left. Standing at a table was the robed man, his back to her as he mixed some concoction in a large bowl.

With great care she began to work her body, starting at her toes and moving up. She was weak and sore but she could move.

Easing onto her stomach, she pushed herself to her hands and knees, inching toward freedom.

Mian shook his head and forced himself back to reality as he found his mind again focused on the Seat. This time on an obscure painting that hung in one of the restricted areas. As children, he and Janu had snuck in often. He shook his head in anger. No knowledge of the Seat was going to help him now. He returned to his study of the tracks before him. There was heavy traffic on this path to and from Kyneira. Grinlo traffic. That was what he needed to focus on.

But still the painting intruded. It was stronger this time, more tangible. Tentatively his fingers stretched out, pressing against the knobby canvas. The forest around him vanished, replaced by a hallway. Beside his hand on the canvas was a smaller, more delicate one.

Gasping, he fell back onto the forest floor. Narita was at his side in an instant.

"Mian, are you okay?"

San rushed toward them, her pants soaked to her knees.

He sat up. "I just… I think the stress is getting to me."

"What did you see?" San asked.

"Well, it was home. I saw a hallway in the Seat. There was this painting. I could see it." His eyes shot to San as he said, "I think I saw Pria's hand. It was more, though." He looked at his fingertips. "I could…" His eyes flashed wide as he leapt to the side, clutching at his arm as it started to bleed.

Narita jumped to move but San grabbed her. "What did you see?" she persisted.

"It felt deeper. Something ran past me. I can't even…" He pulled a deep breath. "It means something, doesn't it?"

"There is a magic pulsing in you," San said. "I recognize the feel of the high priestess."

He let his eyes grow hazy. "I think I can go there. I think I can pass into it."

"No, Mian, that could be very dangerous. Mian!"

He didn't listen. His head slumped and he crumbled to the ground.

He spun in a circle, his heart pounding. He was home, why was he worried? It was his room—he remembered every detail. But the dresser was wrong. He and Janu had broken it when they were sixteen trying to hide some stolen sweets.

The drawer was suddenly hanging askew as it should.

His forehead wrinkled as he wracked his mind. Something was bothering him. No, he couldn't be at the Seat. The Seat was overrun. He ran for the door and stumbled out into the hall as it flashed open. He rushed to the other end of the corridor, to a door carved with trees and birds.

He pounded on it. "Pria!"

"You shouldn't be here."

He stared down at the beautiful girl. Her large eyes were flooded with anxiety.

"I don't know if it's gone," she said.

"What's gone? Where is this?"

"The monster," she answered in a hushed whisper.

He dropped to his knees taking her by her shoulders. "What monster, Pri?"

He shook his head pressing his eyes closed. She wasn't a child, not anymore. Her slim little arms changed in his grip, pulling his hands up above him. Opening his eyes, he saw Pria staring down at him. She laid her palm along his cheek. "It's not safe for you here."

"What is going on?"

"I can't tell you that," she said.

He tangled his fists in his hair. "What does that mean?"

"I am not real in that sense."

"You are even more maddening here than in the real world!" He growled.

She laughed and said nothing.

He put his hands out toward her. "Okay, you drew me here for a reason. What was it?"

"I did not draw you here; I do not have that power."

"What is this place?" he asked.

She smiled. "It is a connection."

"Between us."

"Yes," she said.

"You have been here?"

"I am always here," she said, shrugging, "as are you."

"Okay, can you bring her here as I am now?"

Her head tilted as she batted her eyes. "I do not understand."

"You are Pria, but not entirely. I need you to become her entirely, as I am now."

"I cannot do that. The monster is after her." Her voice held a chill that frosted his blood.

"What is the monster?"

"It is a danger we face." She ran her finger along his forearm. "One you've already seen."

"Where is she?"

"I cannot tell you that," she said.

"She was here, you can tell me that, right?" he prodded.

"She was, not long ago."

"Can you go to her? Take her a message?" he asked.

"I do not know," she said.

"How did she get out?"

She smiled up at him, a strange glow in her blue eyes. "You are going to send me after her? She never thought of that. She realized you could get out without her, but I never tried to send you out to yourself."

"Will it work?"

"I cannot answer that," she said.

He rubbed his temples. "This place hurts my head. Where did you…she… How did you get out?"

"This way."

He tried to keep his eyes forward; he couldn't stomach looking around and seeing details change as he thought about them. "Tell me about this monster."

"You cannot fight it for me. I do not think it can be fought here. It represents a real danger. Here it must be avoided. I cannot tell you what will happen if it catches us here, but something will be lost, possibly forever."

"Now that is comforting. What real danger does it represent?" he said.

"I ca—"

"You cannot answer that." He glanced at the walls around him. "Where are you taking me? This…this…" He spun, finger pointing. "We are in the section of the castle that was restricted when we were kids."

"Yes, we are."

He smiled as he trailed a finger along the wall. "You said this place was a connection, does that mean… Is it the same place for both of us? Does it exist in our minds?"

"This is a place of magic, Mian. There has never been a recorded instance of a person becoming a Well. I have no way to tell you where this place is."

He moved toward the open window. "There should be a rope here." He tapped the sill with a finger.

She shook her head. "Not here."

"You jumped."

"I jumped," she said.

He smiled back over his shoulder. "Always more courage than sense."

"She got out. This is the way."

He clapped, turning to face her. "Okay, see if you can leave through this window, if you can take and bring messages. Can you bring her back here to talk to me directly? I need to know how to find her and help her."

"I understand, but I cannot guarantee this will work." Without another word she climbed up onto the sill and slipped outside.

Pria's eyes searched the forest. Somehow, she had managed to slip from the cave without being noticed, dissolving into the trees before a loud angry growl echoed from the entrance. The robed man had rushed past her in his rage, bellowing for the grinlo.

She could still hear them crashing through the forest around her as her stomach tilted. She had already thrown up several times, trying hard not to look at what came up.

Pausing a moment, she waited as something snuffled past her. Could they not smell her? A nasty twist of her gut dropped her to her knees as she retched again. If they found her like this, she would be unable to fight.

She pulled herself to her feet, glancing up at the bright patch of canopy that was the sun. She had no way of knowing where she was, no way to know in which direction lay Kyneira, but at least she knew she wasn't going back toward the cave. For now, that had to be enough.

She gasped as she stared up into Mian's green eyes. His mouth opened to speak but he was gone in an instant, leaving her to stare at a tree trunk. She drew a slow breath, taking another step and starting as a hallway solidified around her. She spun, her eyes wide.

There was nothing but trees.

Breath held, she listened intently—but there was nothing within her senses but birds and small rodents. She focused on a small knot of warmth in the back of her mind. It expanded, swelling to fill her view and she gasped, letting it snap back. Still no noise of pursuit around her.

Lip pinned between her teeth, she cast about her for a sheltered spot. Satisfied with her location, she sat at the base of a tree, leaning her head against the bark. She surrendered herself to the sensation, allowing the warmth to fill her.

She was standing when the feel of the world around her changed. She blinked, her eyes focusing on Mian's face. "Took you long enough."

"Why did you call me back here?"

"What can you tell me of where you are? How do I find you?" he asked.

"Find…" Her hand drifted toward his face, fingertips caressing his cheek. Her eyes flew open. "Mian! How…"

"There's no time for that now. How do I find you? How do I help you?"

She rejoiced in the very touch of his skin. "I have no idea where I am. I…I woke up in a cave. I can't even give you a direction." She closed her eyes, trying to think. "Raber is dead. He…he was working with him. The man who is controlling the grinlo."

He kissed her forehead, pulling her to his chest but jerked back. "What is that? It's like fire!"

"Fire?" Her hand moved to her neck, eyes wide. "The necklace! Narita's necklace! It's a heartstone! Tell San, she will understand!"

His lips met hers and she was filled with a strong burning that raged through her body. She jumped back from him, meeting his own shocked expression. "What was that?"

"You're asking me?"

"This place—it's some bond between us," she said.

He smirked. "That's what you said." He snaked his hands around her waist. "You'd better be careful—I want to come back and explore this place when we have more time."

"Deviant. Come on, I have a monster to flee and you have a rescue mission to lead."

He cupped his palm to her cheek. "We are coming. Do whatever you have to."

She slipped her fingers into his as they turned back to the window. "You'd better get there soon; I won't be able to fight him without you."

He pulled her hard to his lips. "That is the most beautiful thing you've ever said to me."

"How did you get here?"

He kissed her hand, spreading fire up her arm. "I'll tell you when I see you again."

He climbed onto the sill beside her and they dropped into the void together.

WITHOUT A CRUTCH

Mian's eyes shot open, darting around in confusion as his mind wrestled with reality. He sat up, focusing hard to remember what had happened.

San rushed to him. "Mian, are you—"

He grabbed her by the shoulders to push her back as he came to his knees. "No time. Heartstone. She said to tell you she has a heartstone."

Her face contorted in confusion. "Who…" She shook her head. "Okay, okay! Heartstone. It's old magic, most consider it obsolete. Just a rock with a warming enchant—" Her voice faded away.

"What?"

She smiled. "It's old and doesn't use much magic. It would likely be overlooked."

"And that means?"

"That means, if he didn't notice the necklace or dismissed it as insignificant, he wouldn't have bothered to shield it," San said.

"So, you can find her."

"We can certainly try." She jumped up, rushing toward Peetare and Aliat who were watching from a short distance away.

Narita moved to help him stand. "What happened to you?"

His grin was a brilliance of playful mischief. "I took a short trip to the Seat, of course."

She glared at him. "You arrogant jerk, now is not the time for jokes!"

"It's not a joke, Narita," he said. "I talked to Pria. There is something inside of us that allowed us to talk. I can't really explain it."

Narita's brow wrinkled as she kept her hands on his arm. "This place was the Seat?"

"Yes, but in our heads." Her eyebrow shot to her hairline before she could stop it. He waved her off. "Come on, let's see if your childhood gift is going to save Pria."

San brushed her hair back from her face, her eyes wet when she met his. "It's not working. There may be too much interference, she may be too far away."

Mian nodded. "Okay. The necklace is out." He chewed his lip as his eyes swept the glen. "Narita, we need maps."

"Maps?"

"Terrain maps." He spun. "Where is Jeran?" He grabbed San's arm. "Send a message to Janu: I need men who know these woods and maps, preferably of the land."

She scribbled hastily and flashed the note away. "What are we doing?"

"We are looking for a cave."

Pria wiped her hands on a patch of moss. She had torn a strip of cloth from the bottom of her shirt to stanch the flow of blood but she was now covered in it. The added scent would cost her. Thankfully the grinlo she had run into had been alone. Unarmed and exhausted, she'd been hard-pressed to kill it, but she had fared better than she had expected.

The phisher venom was fading but fatigue was taking its place. She was running out of time.

A piercing howl shattered the forest around her as a grinlo caught her scent. She sighed as it was followed by the wavering call of a listril.

"Well Pri, this is quite the predicament you've gotten yourself into, now isn't it." She limped off through the trees. "Just have to do everything yourself. Now look at you." She glanced up into the canopy. "Soon I'll be no good to anyone."

Swaying, she grabbed at a tree trunk to steady herself. "There's nothing for it, woman. You have to keep moving." She shoved off the tree and on through the endless forest.

The trees broke before her and she stumbled out onto a small path. A listril called out behind her as she took up the trail.

Mian dropped from the tree, rushing back to the mounted men waiting a few feet away. Vaulting into the saddle, he snatched his reins from Jeran and they rushed off down the path. They knew better than to ask if he'd seen anything—they'd have heard about it if he had. He kept close to Jeran's side, trusting in his knowledge of the land. They would find her, they had to.

He had sent the Lorienians with groups of soldiers each led by a native of Kyneira. Every group but his. If they found her, she wouldn't need anyone else. Jeran turned from the path, slowing his mount as he began to twist around the trees. He slowed his horse and waved Mian forward.

Mian drew a deep slow breath as his horse stepped up beside Jeran's. "I was seeing some disturbances up here. I haven't seen any human tracks, but there are definitely grinlo."

"We don't have time for skirmishes, go around any we can avoid."

Jeran's eyes met his. "She'll hold out."

"I'm okay. Until we know otherwise, I am focused on finding her." He clasped a hand to Jeran's shoulder. "Good eye."

"Thank you, sir," Jeran said.

They eased their way back toward the path, letting their horses stretch out into a faster pace. They were close. He could feel it.

Pria could feel the blood dripping from her fingers, having already soaked through her makeshift bandage. It would need stitches. Well, it would need stitches if she ever got away.

A loud scuffling down the path in front of her, and she pressed against the trunk of a tree. They were closing in. Leaning her forehead against the bark, she stilled her body and listened to the approaching monsters.

A high-pitched krill resonated along her skin and the approaching noise stopped.

"Hello again, pet. That is you out there. I can feel you." He coughed a breathy laugh. "I can smell you."

She pulled back sliding down along the tree to crouch on the moss beneath her feet. "They won't find you. You have only evaded me by luck so far. It will not hold."

She froze as something brushed her arm, her breath catching. She drew the air through her nose, sifting through the dirt and fungus of the forest. Her lips curled as her eyes narrowed.

Unfolding from the ground, she stepped from behind the tree.

The robed man smiled. "That's a girl, pet. Nothing will disturb us here."

"Because you've pulled us into an illusion." She glanced at the emptiness around her. "Not even your monsters can tread here."

His teeth flashed. "They come when I call, but don't worry, they will have your tender flesh soon enough."

He took a step forward and she kept the distance, placing her feet with care over a large gnarled root. Fingers splayed, she circled to the right. "Is this what you envisioned—wear me out until I am too weak to fight?"

A deep chuckle rolled from his lips as he spread his hands wide. "Dear pet, this is not some ego-driven mission where I must prove myself greater than you." He slipped around a tree, his robe swaying around his legs. "All I want is your strength, your power. You can keep your dignity." He prowled forward. "You don't have to fight."

A familiar scent crossed her path as she stepped to the side. "Lana fought you too. She didn't give in."

His smirk slipped wider. "She was foolish, but in the end she gave in to me, just like you will."

She focused her mind into the pocket where she could feel the warm caress that was Mian. She threw herself into that heat, wrapping it around her mind and pulling it deep into her soul. Her heart calmed as his strength settled across her. "You have not seen foolish yet."

Mian slashed at the grinlo as it grabbed for his shirt. Something hazed his vision for a moment but it snapped back. He shook his head as Jeran appeared at his side. "There are several prints that could be human but it is hard to tell, they are getting trampled."

"This is the group that took her."

"This is a group that took *someone*," Jeran clarified.

His head jerked as a scent tickled his nostrils. "No, it is her. She's here. Somewhere."

A gentle stroke swept his thoughts, tugging at his heart. "Somewhere…" He swayed. "Jeran, I need you to watch over me."

Jeran turned back. "Why?" His eyes shot wide as Mian collapsed to the group in a heap.

Mian's eyes opened as he glanced around the empty hallway. Pria wasn't here, but she needed him. How did he get to her? His eyes fell on the window standing open before him and his feet were rushing before he had even decided what he was going to do. He leapt from the window, rolling as he crashed to the ground.

His eyes met a tall man staring at him in confusion from across a glen. He kept his breath even as he pushed himself up. Pria was in front of him in a flash, a wave of energy tearing up the mossy forest floor and throwing the robed man back through the trees. He was on his feet and running behind her as they crashed through the foliage. He jerked Pria to his chest, his breathing labored.

"What is going on now?"

She molded to him. "We need to keep moving; he'll be after us."

His lips brushed her forehead. "Where are we now?"

"One of his illusions."

"How did you know I could get to it through the Seat?" he asked.

Her laughter bounced off the trees around them. "I had no idea. Just took a chance. It is an altered reality. Since we were in the same place only separated by magic, I was just hoping that the connection of magic would allow you to pass through to me."

He stopped. "We can't run forever."

The strange filtered light sparkled in her blue eyes. "He's too strong for me by myself. He absorbed Raber."

"Good thing you are not by yourself, isn't it?"

A tear slipped from her eye. "Guess I do need you to help me handle my magical problems."

His smirk faded. "It'll be our own little secret."

Jeran's mind wouldn't comprehend the empty patch of ground before him. Mian had just dissolved before him, like he had melted into the ground. Where could he have gone?

The soldiers around him were wide-eyed with anxiety as they glanced around, wondering the same thing.

"All right. Mian says the high priestess is around here somewhere," he said. "We are going to clear this glen of the grinlo and make sure they will be safe when they return."

Pria glanced around her, keen eyes scanning for the robed man. "So the necklace worked?"

Mian's brow furrowed. "What? No, no it didn't work. He must have been ahead of us on that too."

"Or we were already in the illusion." She paused. "How did you find us then?"

"Jeran."

"*Jeran?*" she asked, her voice incredulous.

"He grew up around here."

She glanced back at him, her eyes rolling in exasperation. "Yeah, he might have mentioned that a time or two."

"Yes, well, when the necklace didn't work we had to think of something else. All I had to go on was the necklace and you mentioning a cave. So I gathered as many men who were raised in Kyneira as I could and set them to checking caves."

She stopped, turning to face him. "All the knowledge of the Lorien and you found us by looking for a cave?"

His grin darkened in self-satisfaction. "Jealous?"

"Impressed." She stood up taller. "And I'm ashamed to say, a bit humbled."

He shook his head, laughing. "Don't be too humbled—it took us a long time after Lana was taken for us to start finding ways to supplement the loss of magic. Once we get used to having you around, we'll go back to being helpless."

"You are never helpless." Sighing, her eyes swept the forest around them. "Is he hiding from us?"

"Maybe he's trying to figure out how you regained so much strength so fast."

"Perhaps. Which means he's probably watching us now," she said.

She giggled as Mian's grin flashed mischievously. "Should we give him a show?"

"Honestly, Mian. Our lives hang in the balance and you're cracking jokes."

He took her hand, pulling her closer to him. "If I die today, I am precisely where I want to be."

She leaned against his chest, her mind stilling. "We will not die today, not if I have anything to say about it."

He closed his eyes as he enfolded her in his arms. His voice was a breathy whisper as it caressed her ear. "I just heard a twig snap over my left shoulder."

She didn't hesitate or even look, just lifted her palm and sent a stream of air slicing through the trees behind him. The leaves and underbrush the robed man had brought to track her marked his progress as he crashed away from them but she cut him off, calling up a wall of flames in a wide circle.

Mian turned as she stepped from his embrace, keeping his fingers entangled with hers. The robed man's eyes burned as he watched them.

"You again," the man hissed. "Do you really hope to make some difference here?"

"Already have." Mian's fingers tightened on hers but it was the stranger who spoke.

"You truly are everything I could have hoped for. We will be unstoppable together."

"We will never be together," Pria said with a glower.

His lips curled as a spark brightened his eyes. "We'll see."

Fingers tightened around his, she drew her anger through Mian, the trees around them trembling with its strength. One to her left snapped, shards breaking off and spinning in the air around them. "You should never have challenged Trimera."

He raised a defensive wall of magic as she slashed at him, sending waves of splinters down toward him.

"There is so much I can show you," he ground out. "Why do you fight?"

She shifted her attack to eruptions shifting him around as he tried to avoid them. "What you offer is not worth the price!"

The blade in his chest flashed, sending a ripple of light across his skin as he dodged her latest attack. His hand moved in a circle, his lips moving silently.

Pria gasped as her skin sparked in pain. Her eyes watered but she pushed it away, anger fueling her strength. Mian stepped up behind her, his hand sliding beneath her shirt to rest along her bare stomach. A rush of strength roared through her body at the intimate contact and the spell she was preparing flashed from her fingertips and knocked the robed man onto his back.

He lurched to his feet, tearing the cowl from his head, revealing a bald scaled scalp. "He's your Well? A human Well?"

"Raber not tell you that? At least we know why you needed him. Couldn't really pass for human yourself anymore," Pria spat.

He scoffed. "Oh, that's not what I used the boy for. The transformation did not bar me to your town." His smile deepened. "Or even to you."

She pressed back into Mian's chest, taking the chance to rest. Mian allowed her to hold enough magic to fight but he did nothing to erase the fatigue. "Then why wait so long? If you could get to me, why not just take me?"

"I wasn't ready yet," the robed man said. "Had to shore up my supplies, be ready for when we took you. But I was wrong. How did you hold out against me? Not even Lana with her knowledge and experience was able to hold against me!"

Mian held her in the protective cage of his arms. "Lana wasn't this stubborn."

His eyes shifted to Mian. "She had a Well, did you know? Lana. The strength she gave me with it makes my mouth water to think of it." He licked his lips hungrily as he drank in Mian's face. "I couldn't pull you, but what would happen if I took him?"

Pria shifted, pushing Mian backward as she thrust up a wall in front of her. The attack was quick and short as the robed man opened two small portals to each side. A haze rose around him, solidifying into two pink listrils.

Mian's sword rang in the small hollow as he swept her behind him. His hand fell from her grip as he rushed forward, slicing the head from the monster to his right. Pria's heart stopped as the robed man reached up for Mian, his face twisted in an expectant smile.

The listril's head still tumbled as Mian spun for the second. She wasn't even aware of the spell forming in her hand, and startled when a vice clamped on the robed man's heart.

His eyes grew wide in shock as Mian danced past his outstretched hand, cutting down the second listril before the robed man crashed to his knees.

Mian flicked blood from his sword casually as he stared down at the man before him. "You couldn't take her, could never take her. She is mine and always will be." His sword stabbed down into the man's chest twisting with a sharp jerk of his wrist. The man's lips parted, a quiet wheeze hissing from his mouth as he collapsed back to the ground.

He drew the blade from the man's chest, turning the sword as he smiled back at her.

She rolled her eyes as she held her hand out toward him. "Satisfied with yourself?"

Shrugging he slid his fingers into hers stepping from beside the bloody corpse. "With the situation, yes I am satisfied."

"I'm glad you are. Meanwhile, Trimera is still overrun with monsters, who knows what is going on with our family, the Lorien sees you as their new mystery to solve, and we are both still trapped in a madman's illusion."

He cupped her cheek and leaned his forehead down onto hers. "Then I guess you'd better get us home then."

Priestess Dieran tightened her robe as she followed the page through the darkened halls of the Lorien. It was far too late for any decent visitor, but the page had been insistent she come. Trimera at the point of ruin, four priestesses mired in the middle of it, not to mention the high priestess, and here she was being bothered with late night riffraff. It was enough to set her hackles in a rise and she prepared a ripe lecture for whomever had rattled the night guards so to rouse her.

To her surprise the page didn't lead her to the city gates or even the holding cells or receiving rooms. The boy seemed to be directing her toward the ward. That didn't make any sense!

"I say…" Drat! What was the boy's name? They all looked alike. "I say there, where are you leading me?"

The young man turned with his all-too-common features and general-issue page haircut. "Forgive me Priestess, but the petitioners requested to be taken to the ward."

The boy continued on his way. She was in no mood to rein in her anger. With each fist knotted in the skirts of her robe, she plowed on toward the unfortunate soul who had raised her ire.

The wards at the Lorien were separated into multiple wings. Each patient began in the Common Ward for sorting. A priestess would assign them to a specific wing after that. But the page didn't stop at the Common Ward. He turned, instead, right, toward the Hazard Ward.

The page pushed through the door and she stopped, startled to see the hallway packed full of farmers and children. As a group they looked exhausted and defeated but their eyes lit up as they caught sight of her.

The page approached two men, though one could hardly be termed so. "Priestess Dieran, these men have traveled all the way from Trimera to petition the priestesses for aid."

Dieran measured the young men before her. They could be Trimeran—she wasn't known for her eye for nationalities—but why travel all the way to the Lorien when High Priestess Pria was stationed in Trimera?

The older man stepped forward and lowered himself to one knee with visible difficulty. "Priestess, I beg you, please help my wife and son."

Dieran pulled her anger back, but not without regret. A priestess was honor-bound to help those in need. "What is wrong with your wife and son?"

The younger man stepped forward at this. "We don't know, Priestess."

The older man dropped his gaze. "It is…hard to describe."

"They went mad!" a voice from the crowd shouted.

"Tried to kill us!" said another.

"Scream their heads off unless we gag them!"

Dieran lifted a halting hand before addressing the man still on his knee. "I will see what I can do; what are their names?"

"Undano is my boy, Xiana his mother."

They pointed her to a barred door. The cells in the Hazard Ward were designed to prevent escape. Patients were only sent here when they were a danger to themselves or others. When she had been a student here she had spent a week in one of these cells until an accidental spell wore off. She had been attempting the Ludas Touch but had missed one of the minor steps and instead created a touch of death. Thankfully, it had been discovered before any casualties—well, any human casualties. She had killed three trees, her teacher's favorite fern, and an unfortunate mouse that had chosen that exact moment to scamper across her toe.

She pushed her own memories away; they would be of no use to these people. The doors of the Hazard Ward were set to lock when shut and only the hand of a priestess could open them. She flattened her palm against the wood and incanted, "*Halina.*" The lock snapped open and the door swung inward.

"Stay close, boy."

The page was at her shoulder, as he should be, but you could never be sure. Some took to the flimsiest excuses to take off just when you needed them. The cell beyond was dark and she flicked her wrist to send light to the solar stones secured in the ceiling and walls. They needed a recharge but they would suffice for an examination. The light revealed two occupants pressed back against the far wall, the boy cradled against his mother's side. They were bound hand and foot, gagged and blindfolded. Strange treatment for patients.

The cells were cut into the ground itself so they held a chill that was irregular in the Lorien. The temperature was meant to calm patients who were overexcited. The cold seeped up into her feet through her slippers. Careful to keep her robes off the floor, she crouched beside the woman and child.

She couldn't discern any immediate symptoms of disease upon a cursory visual examination. The restraints bothered her. They were in a locked cell, why the restraints? She inched closer, intent on removing the gag from the boy, but froze as a spark jolted along her arm and up into her chest.

She leapt back.

Something very strange was going on here. She made sure not to come into contact with either. She could see it now, the residue of magic on both. It was subtle but strong. What could have happened?

She moved back to the edge of the cell. She had no idea what contact with the spell would cause but she wasn't about to risk it. How to proceed? She had to know what the spell was doing to them.

"*Nitoro*," she whispered with a gesture.

The room filled with acrid smoke as a spark raced around the blindfolds and gags of mother and son. Each blinked to adjust to the light of the crystals in the room. Wide eyes rolled toward her, glistening.

Her body was hit with a jolt as they both opened their throats and screamed. Dieran threw her hands over her ears. "*Sila*!" she screamed and the sound was sucked from the room. Her eyes narrowed. She had removed the sound from the room, but not the fear from the two patients' faces. A child would be harder to calm when hysterical, so she turned to the woman.

She pulled back the silencing spell and the room burst into screams again. Dieran girded herself and took a step toward the patients. Inched forward as close as she dared, she pulled in a lungful of air. "Xiana!"

The woman's scream petered out but Dieran was positive it had nothing to do with her name. Xiana had curled her face toward the boy cradled to her chest.

"Xiana," she repeated, a little more insistent.

The woman flinched but gave no other indication that she had heard. Dieran watched in amazement as the woman placed her mouth near the boy's ear. "I'm here, Undano, Mother's here."

"You recognized each other, but not your family." She glanced behind to see the page obedient in the doorway. "Bring me the father."

The page ghosted away and she returned her attention to the two patients on the floor. The woman Xiana continued to whisper to the boy and she saw his face slack as he ceased his scream. Dieran pulled the silencing spell from him as the father stepped into the cell behind her.

"They do not recognize you?" she asked.

The man kept his head down. "No, Priestess."

"Tell me everything."

He risked a glance at his wife and son as they trembled at his voice. He swallowed. "My older son and I had just finished working the south field and were returning for the evening. There was nothing out of the ordinary. We got to our door and it was jammed closed. We went around back but that door was blocked as well. I called for Xiana but there was no response. We kicked the back door in but still couldn't see her. So we searched the house. When I stepped into the sitting room a weight crashed into me from behind. It was Xiana with my butcher knife. She was trying to kill me. She wouldn't respond to anything I said. We struggled with her but it was like she didn't understand us. Then we found Undano. He was the same way."

Dieran gestured to the page. She was impressed to hear him remove a journal from his jacket with no further prompt. Her estimation of him went up. "Patients appear to be suffering from delusion. There is a residue of a spell on both mother and child."

Dieran glided toward the patients on the floor. "I would like to separate them and attempt to remove the spell from the mother."

The farmer looked to her and she nodded. The woman struggled as he lifted her from the floor but her restraints kept her from doing much. Dieran kept her distance; she wasn't going to take any chances. She unlocked the adjacent cell and stood back for the farmer to carry his wife through the door.

The page followed behind her and she secured the door. She tapped the journal as the farmer lowered the woman to the floor. "I am going to attempt to drain the magic from the spell. If everyone would please stand to the side."

The page and farmer moved toward the cell walls, the farmer looking particularly uncomfortable. Dieran centered herself, drawing deep, even breaths to calm herself. Draining a spell was the safest course of action for defusing most spells and standard practice at the Lorien. So, why was she so nervous?

Eyes closed, she stretched out with her mind, concentrating on a simple spell that would burn magic and, in theory, remove the spell on the woman.

The air changed around her as she released something deep in her stomach and set the spell free. To the other three people in the room it would appear that nothing was happening. To her mind, the room lightened and sparks arced off the woman on the floor. She felt a wash of release as the spell dissipated.

The anxiety easing, she turned to the page. "The spell has reacted positively to the drain and I anticipate a full reversal—"

Her voice failed as she felt a flare of magic from behind her. Pressure seized her throat and her knees gave way and dropped her to the floor. Fog clouded her vision as the room spun around them. When her vision cleared, the page and the farmer knelt over her.

"Anders?" The voice was soft as it brushed against them.

The farmer's eyes fell wide as his face turned toward the woman behind them. "Xiana? You…recognize me?"

They turned to face the woman. Dieran allowed the page to assist her to sit. The farmer rushed to his wife to comfort her. Dieran allowed herself a moment of recovery. Backlash from a dissipated spell was not uncommon. When her head stopped buzzing, she turned her attention to the now untied woman. To her relief, the magical residue was gone.

She struggled to her feet, though she tried to hide how much effort it took. She steadied herself before turning to Xiana. Wrapped in her husband's arms, the woman appeared to be recovered from whatever the spell had done to her.

Dieran pulled herself from the page's support. "Excellent. Make a note that the effects of the spell have been reversed. Also note that a backlash was experienced, enough to knock me to the ground, but the effects were fleeting. Let us take care of the son."

The inside lock was more complex. She stood with one hand at eye level and the other near hip height. The interior was rough against her palms; not all patients remained in the Hazard Ward voluntarily despite what might be best for them. She formed a triangle of magical energy between her hands and the center of her chest. The spell fluttered before setting, but she was still off from the backlash so it didn't worry her overmuch. After a heartbeat, Dieran let the spell slip from her lips: "*Dolo.*"

The door gave and swung open.

The hallway beyond was packed, wall to wall, with grinlo.

Dieran's hand jerked away, pulling the opening spell from the door and slamming it back shut. Grinlo. In the Lorien. Her chest seized.

That was what the backlash had been—it had opened a portal to transport grinlo into the Lorien.

EPILOGUE

Asenog dropped the mewling child on a stump beside the stream. The nurses had argued when he came to take the infant, but Asenog was strong, powerful. After he had shown them Master's ceremonial dagger, they had silenced their cries. This was the largest of the infants, strongest, just like Master had said.

Asenog removed his armor and laid it aside along the bank. He was proud of his armor, collected over years from his conquests. Without the armor he stood naked to the morning sky. He turned back to the stump and used a claw to fling the swaddling aside. Careful not to hurt the infant, he lifted it naked into his arms. The child squalled as Asenog sank into the stream.

He took great care as he bathed himself and the infant. They must be clean for what was to come. The water swirled in eddies of dirt and grease as it rinsed from his body. Bathing was nothing he was used to and he hoped to never do it again but he did the best he could with the child cradled in his arms.

When he and the child were clean, he carried it back to the stump and laid it down among the swaddling.

Though the air held a touch of warmth, the cold water had left the child blue with cold. Its wail was constant now, piercing the forest with a trilling cry. His keen ears picked up a casting cry from a pack of wolves circling in on the distressed child. Its cry would draw predators from miles around, but Asenog wasn't worried. He was strong enough for any threat and it would be over soon anyway.

He removed the ceremonial dagger from his armor. The filtered light caught along the blade as he held it between them. The next part was crucial—he had to time it just right. Master had told him he could use a partner for this, but Asenog was not weak. He would accomplish his task alone and all the glory would be his.

He stared up at the dagger and trusted his Master knew what he was doing.

With a growling snarl he stabbed the blade into his chest—through the muscle and straight into his heart. His body convulsed as the handle jumped with the pounding of his heart. Light flashed across the glen and he fell to his knees as the light arced from the hilt of the blade to the chest of the squalling infant.

Instinct screamed at him to remove the knife, to call for help, but Master had been quite explicit.

His body convulsed as his heart began to fail but still the arc of light connected his chest to the infant—only it wasn't an infant anymore. Where the squalling child had lain now sat a lanky youth, naked and worried, but with a knowledge in his wide blue eyes. His Master's eyes.

A tremor rocketed up his body as a pulse of white shot through the arc and into the child. The form blurred and when his vision cleared a young man sat on the stump, devoid of fear but gaze filled with hunger. Its hand stretched toward the handle in Asenog's chest.

Master was going to save him, just as he said he would!

Another flash and the young man became Master, his hand closed around the hilt of the dagger.

Asenog smiled as Master leaned over him, his face next to Asenog's. He could feel the power flowing from Master. A hand cupped Asenog's cheek.

"You did well, Asenog," said Master and a warmth spread through him like molten rock.

The blade was jerked from his chest and Asenog crumbled to the ground in a heap.

Enjoy the Battle for Trimera? Please leave a review. Reviews help potential readers find new books they might enjoy and is the easiest and best way to help out an author.

Continue the Battle with High Priestess Pria:

The Rogue is defeated but the battle is far from over. How will Trimera ever recover…

High Priestess Pria has a lot going on. A Kingdom full of monsters, priestesses working against her, a budding relationship with Mian, oh, and escaping the trap she and Mian are currently trapped in. Probably should be first on the list.

Little does she know that the man she saw die, the man she and Mian killed together, managed to survive. That even now he plots against her and Trimera. Hidden in the Frontier, he builds his strength.

Wounds of betrayal run deep, but nothing will prepare them for what the Rogue has planned next…

High Priestess Pria is the breathtaking second book in the Priestess of Reia Chronicles coming-of-age fantasy adventures. If you like female warriors, medieval settings, and action-packed quests, then you'll love Tanya SM Kennedy's captivating epic.

Buy *High Priestess Pria* to continue the fight today!

Also by Tanya SM Kennedy:

Since she was an infant, Eylsa has been trained, beaten, and deprived. Such is the life of an assassin. Now a teenager, Eylsa is owned by King Mavrin and his son, Ashlan, to whom she is forcefully betrothed. In an attempt to stage a coup, Mavrin orders her to kill Darius, a powerful member of the Tribunal and the next target in a string of murders. But when Eylsa installs herself among Darius and his men, she finds herself swayed by their strange way of life—and attracted to the freedoms that the Tribunal offers.

For Brendan, Darius' right-hand man, allowing Eylsa into the folds of the Tribunal is madness. He can't understand why Darius would have pity for an assassin trained to kill him—it's like sleeping with a wolf at your throat. As he gets to know Eylsa, though, he sees her walls come down and her cold heart thaw, shedding the only existence she has known.

Together, Eylsa, Brendan, and the others must defeat the very ones who are out to destroy the Tribunal—and the peace of their society. If they fail, Eylsa's—and everyone else's—life hangs in the balance.

Tanya S.M. Kennedy is a feral forest witch haunting the beautiful hills of West Virginia. She stirs up mischief while recruiting her tribe of loud unapologetic women and animals.

At times she ventures out to spread confidence and weirdness through her writing. She can be lured from her cave with shiny objects, books, and cheese but is not responsible for what happens when left to her own devices.

Her books are a guide to feed all the misbehaving women in the hopes that they find a tribe where they feel comfortable to be who they are.

Step into Fantasy and find your Strength.

www.ingramcontent.com/pod-product-compliance
Lightning Source LLC
Chambersburg PA
CBHW030739030726
47497CB00001B/56